Park Avenue Purgatory

Park Avenue Purgatory

MICAH ENLOE

THOUGHT
CATALOG
Books

BROOKLYN, NY

THOUGHT
CATALOG
Books

Published by Thought Catalog Books, a division of The Thought & Expression Co., Williamsburg, Brooklyn. Founded in 2010, Thought Catalog is a website and imprint dedicated to your ideas and stories. We publish fiction and non-fiction from emerging and established writers across all genres. For general information and submissions: manuscripts@thoughtcatalog.com.

First edition, 2017

ISBN: 978-1945796388

Printed and bound in the United States.

10 9 8 7 6 5 4 3 2 1

For all the forgotten casualties of greed.

CONTENTS

Disclaimer — ix
1. This Little Bear Light of Mine — 1
2. Car Before the Horse — 5
3. Do You Pray? — 13
4. The French Finally Did It — 17
5. Rudolfo — 25
6. Miss Allison — 31
7. The Sign — 35
8. Scorpions — 41
9. Daily Bread — 47
10. The Transfiguration — 55
11. The Abyss — 61
12. This Is It — 67
13. Sandy — 73
14. The Barrette — 81
15. Pale Peach Silk Satin and Faille — 87
16. Brooklyn Baby — 91
17. Is That a Clip-On? — 95
18. Jealousy — 103
19. The Twinkytect — 111
20. I'm a Little Teapot — 123
21. Selena and The Revival — 137
22. The Sword in The Apple — 149
23. Sharp Objects — 157
24. The Inscription — 165
25. Cir·cum·lo·cu·tion — 169
26. As I Lay Bloody — 175
27. Southern Foam — 183
28. From His Tubes — 191
29. Another Tower — 197
30. From The Keys — 203
31. I Miss The Space Shuttle — 215
32. La Priere Du Seignear — 227
33. Philantropical — 233
34. Dawn — 245

35. Company Powerball   251
36. Whiteout   261
37. Absence   271
38. Watches   279
39. A New Tower   289
40. Humming   297
41. Proceed With Caution   309
42. Fart   315
43. Touch   333
44. Pit   341
45. Cockflutes in Fairyland   349
About the Author   359

Disclaimer

This book is a work of fiction and any resemblance to real people and events is purely coincidental.

This Little Bear Light of Mine

What is it that only I can write? What is it that only I can say? I, I, I, I. I even thought that this is how I would be begin, typing down I, I, I, for it's an act of ego, this, so they say.

And who are they?

I see their wisdom in chalk-white on my wall of black, reminding me to simply come here, show up, show up to the table and type. *Have the courage to write badly.*

Well, here it is, that badly written stuff.

Another, a woman's voice in chalk, reminds me to *set 1,000 words as a minimum output*, and I really want to slap her in the face, her lip quivering. Shouldn't I say something like, "She's a real bitter cunt to say that, to say there's a minimum, that, that, that dirty little *cunt*," something oh-no so offensive, to grab your attention?

The first draft of everything is shit, so says Hemingway. So perhaps he's right; this will all be gone.

My cursor will click right next to the "l" of "will" and sweep to the left and up, all the way up, to the left of the "w" of that beginning "what," right up there, below the bear. From *will* to *what*? And all that will be left will then be: "all be gone." Can I will this what into existence by simply repeating what the white gods in chalk on the blackboard say? *Start telling the stories only you can tell.*

Start telling the stories only you can tell. What's a you and what's a tell?

Start.

Start, start, start. I, I, I. What, will, I, start, with to figure out what my tell is to tell you my you?

Lou lou skip to my lou, who the hell is lou? And who are you, my darling?

My darling, Jack London, reminds me to never *wait for inspiration*, that I have to *beat it with a club.* I don't have a club, though. What I do have is a chalk wall to my right, a space heater behind me, an old picture of a naked man to my left somehow taken with a red filter—some sort of classic red lens that has turned the beautiful bearded man clay-like—or maybe just Photoshopped afterwards or Instafucked or VSCOcam-fucked-with—and I, I, I, I'm in front a window, a window, a second-story window, through which my bear lamp—vintage, Astoria Flea Market—casts a dull street-lamp glow out onto the street that has none.

I'm quite certain that this bear lamp holds a mystery yet to be released, some magic, perhaps chalk-white too, perhaps a board-black hue, and as dark as blood. It's Russian and old. It's still got the liquor stickers on it, now peeling. Someone from somewhere else stabbed an electric cord into his anus and stabbed a lampshade with a bulb right through his head, chunks of liquor-brain flying all over your face, fucked from both ends. And when I bought it, I do admit I was drawn to it, these ends, knowing, I must have them and it, this beautiful, lampy, rapey murder of something.

One of the problems with writing with coffee is the sudden onset of a coffee-induced shit. A moment ago, right after a "murder," I had to get up, take my fingers off the keyboard, walk to the bathroom, and put my fingers on a toilet seat. And when I walked I began thinking about what I'll write next. My mind even wandered into how this—this shit, and maybe even the electrical cord shit coming out of my bare bear anus—would somehow tie into my grand, grand story that only I can tell, rumbling in my soon-to-be-raped brain.

One day maybe this will be like those books turned into 3D movies and musicals! Maybe a comic book like *Maus*! Maybe even a shitty series that everyone loves but also secretly hates! Because no one ever really likes feeling culty and cunty to outsiders; it's something we learn, except of course if you're just naturally culty-cunty. Maybe I was born this way.

Or like when the writer is in a mysterious dark room, obviously rattled by something but intensely sure of himself to recount every, last, detail, of what unfolded the previous year or years that he fell in love, or saw this evil or that evil, and how when he finishes telling it, it all makes sense that he's sitting there, sitting here, in this mysterious room next to his own version of a bear lamp, perhaps a cigarette, perhaps a straitjacket—oh my gawwwd he was crazy this, whole, TIME.

Maybe *he* did the killing.

Maybe he saw it.

Maybe he was the one that fell in love, but he, another he, was the one that died, in *To the Brave Great Moulin Gatsby Rouge Kill a Godzilla Mockingbird Lighthouse World* now in IMAX, and on Broadway, and on Kindle, and inside your mom.

The other problem with writing with coffee is its unfaithfulness to you, how selfish it is, that even though I could have sworn the coffee would wake me up more, now everything is so dreadfully goddamned serious.

Who the fuck do I think I am?

Now Ray Bradbury, or maybe it was Oscar Wilde, it doesn't really matter, is making me feel guilty again and telling me that life is too serious to be taken seriously.

Okay, okaaaaaay, guys.

I really thought I accomplished that above, some necessary hilarity, with the mention of me getting up to shit—*wasn't that funny?* The fact that I took a dump in the first chapter? No? My anus opened up just like each of your ugly eyes right now? Two anuses gazing upon a toilet bowl of words? An exchange of the stuff of light and some dark shit?

Or the imagery of the bear bottle getting raped and then getting that lobotomy so he could light my way here, at my desk, in my mysterious room, and those on the street walking their dogs pooping on the snow still here in spring. I thought that would make this beginning a little lighter.

See, "lighter" isn't the right word there, or maybe you'll think this story is an actual "little lighter," and you're holding it there, alone, wherever you are, looking at its pitiful flaming flame butt-fucking your eyes on a flat screen.

I want this first chapter to go out with a bang, a hook, something that will get everyone reading, but nothing too important that I could delete later since this must obviously be shit anyway.

Shit.

2

Car Before the Horse

I seem to get texts at the worst times.

One from my friend Selena this morning, for instance, woke me up, distracting me from my sleep, 7:00 a.m., very fitting for my chalkboard wall of blood and words:

Creation is in part merely the business of forgoing the great and small distractions.

When I opened the door of my bedroom, I opened up the door to my surprise party, and when I looked away from the harsh camera light of the morning, I realized it was just me there in attendance, shocked that I was still alive. This is your birthday.

You're still here.

You are.

Still.

Here.

I woke up here, an apartment in Astoria with mostly white walls covered in red, black, silver, and wood frames of old maps, nude painted men, and much younger versions of myself looking pensive in other places that seem perpetually better than here, permanently flat in their framed doorways, affixed, connected.

Alaska.

Montana.

India.

There's a weather vane outside above the garage, and it spins as my coffee steams from the water burning oils out of the beans that were roasted somewhere after they were grown by some stranger whose name is now just a brand. Her name is Café Bustelo, her skin is yellow foil, her lips are red letters, and she picked these beans just for me.

Although, I always seem to picture anyone hidden from me—orange-pickers, coffee-growers, family, friends—in full burqas or colorful saris, all of them around the world, all of them are Indian ladies with baskets on their heads. Mezcal distillers in Mexico, all Indian ladies with baskets. Brazilian yerba mate harvesters, all Indian ladies with baskets. You; you're an Indian lady with a basket on your head.

On a roachy poo-poo train heading to the sex temples of Kajuraho embarking from the dirty dal lentils of Mumbai, I saw many of these ladies across the landscape, slowly walking next to the tracks selling fly-filled channah masalah, handfulling it to us through the window on ripped-newspaper plates whenever the train stopped.

They stuck with me, their nauseating e-coli veggies, their callused feet, their weather-scorched faces, the beautiful fabric draped over them, the golden piercings.

They were all so beautifully dying from life, yet oh-so-quiet and removed from it, even perplexed by it, as they floated next to the train with what seemed to them an uncountable number of people going somewhere else.

The more you stare in one direction, present, unmoving, as with stars in the sky on a cool night in Montana, as with faces in the palm fronds on a 'shroom night in Thailand, the more layers you see, all that's there when you're not looking.

From this vantage point sitting at my Astorian table, I see the steam from my coffee maker on the stove, then the rope of the laundry pulleys no one uses anymore because we always forget our clothes in the spring sleet, and then the weather vanes. There are two on top of the garage and two more on top of the roof of the old Hi Ho Silver building between the kitchen window and the trees next to the red and white candy-cane steam towers of the Long Island City power plant burning some kind of other bean picked by some other Indian lady—and the coffee is electric.

I'm baffled by that tacky silver brick on the building between the pulleys and the trees and candy canes. It's sparkling in the morning, yet fading and peeling off in spots, especially the chimney, perhaps from the heat. The more I stare, the more layers of curiosity peel, too. How many layers of paint were used, and when and where did she buy the paint?

Did she keep the paint in a basket above her head, and did it slosh around on her long trek home?

Did it seep through the dirty reeds of her handmade basket and the shameless dirty deeds of her ugly timeworn hands?

Did the paint then soak her clay-covered hair, with streams of living silver dripping down her golden, pierced face, with drops falling into the soil like boiled foil?

My brother texted me too as I sipped my coffee and subsequently spit it out after choking from his: "OMG I just watched a car in front of me hit a cardinal and it literally exploded into a bloody poof of feathers and I drove off the road."

Normally he'll send me pictures of my nephew cooking something, or wearing a new outfit, or going roller-skating, and my nephew is always smiling or roaring like Godzilla—a new generation knows about Godzilla and chocolate chip cookies and the youthful joys of roller-skating. I wonder if he'll drink Coke poured over that perfect slushy ice and then over-dose on Nacho cheese dip like we did on all our birthdays, nau-seously skating faster and faster and faster in circles, until it was time to open up all the new Legos and vomit on them.

That's childhood. Legos and fake cheese and skating through vomit.

Sometimes my brother and I will exchange gym songs, as we seem to be on a never-ending hunt for better and better and better songs that make us feel like killing and killing and killing and dancing at the same time, searching for that moment of violently happy: spinning around, beneath the stars, above the fire, the fire that's level with the hairy bison breathing there and watching us, as we hold our weights like arrows in the Montana of our wildest muscle-man dreams.

This time, though, he saw a cardinal get run over by a car, and we both did our LOLs and Hehehehes, because we knew how awfully symbolic it was, as our mother always told us that God speaks to us in a way only we, alone, can possibly under-stand. Each of us has a secret, a divine gesture that pops into our life, right, when we need to be reminded that we're alive, that we're supposed to be here, that we're not alone here, right here.

Mine might be the song "Clair de Lune," not too sure. When other people hear the song, they obligatorily admit it's "ummmm, pwwitttty, I guess" yet an "overplayed classical song," but I seem to hear it oh so rarely, beginning with that first time on a Yellowstone piano on my way back from Alaska when I realized I needn't be so angry anymore, at anyone, as the notes of the song pierced right through the mysterious palm fronds of my skin, leaving behind calm, slick, glowing silver wounds, healing from the moonlight of forgiveness.

My mother's is the cardinal. Every time she sees one she starts crying, and with tears in her eyes, she'll say "THANK YOU!" to the skies of blue and the steams of white and all that deep space house music above them. The cardinal's head will fidget around for a moment. Its blood-orange beak will spin north, south, east, west, and then it will fly away.

I think my brother's gesture is everyone else's gesture getting hilariously destroyed by something, a car, a fire burning all those notes of music, reminding us to just laugh at God's sick, slick sense of humor. This is true: One of Mom's cardinals from God got murdered by the windshield of a car, an explosion of red and feathers, floating in a sphere of tiny-tiny particles, points of blood for every possible direction.

Next to the table, the sunlight has now reached our bookshelf of shoes, some new, some old, all stinky. On top of that rests my rubber snow spikes that will no longer be used, for months at least, until the next horrible winter decides to spring and fling cold cum all over the face of another summer, and next to those spikes rests a pile of mail for my friend Thomas and his girlfriend, both of whom used to live here.

They lived here for eight years, and even though they're in Texas now, there are people who, for a very brief moment of their day, thought about finding them. And even if these letters were automatically generated from computers, perhaps the postman still looked at those letters and thought: *Does Thomas still live here? Is Thomas happy where he is? Will Thomas wake up again today?*

And then he puts the letter through the latch in the door and it drops to the cold tile, and he pushes his mail cart down the gum-lined sidewalk to the next house, and the next house, a Santa Claus with paper presents no one wants anymore because electric is faster. And so it's piled next to snow spikes warmed by the sun, above stinky shoes, beneath the ceiling, and level with me, a hairy beast breathing there, looking at it sleep there with all the others piled weakly and weekly on top of it.

The weather vanes are spinning again.

I sip my coffee.

My boyfriend is still in bed.

Will this be the day one of us is found dead?

Morbid, I always hear. That's just, well that's just morbid, Colin. You went too far. You went away to a place called TOO-MUCH. How could you think like that, waking up with such morbid thoughts on a beautiful sunny day like today when you have your whole life ahead of you—aren't you putting the car before the horse?

And I'd correct them in my thoughts and hopes and dreams, uhhhhh, the correct word would be, carT. But to answer your question, no, I'm not, because I, or you, could be covered in blood today. And it would be in the kind of way that's way before our time—or even tonight, as the moonlight reflects the bloody silver running down your nose as you take your last breath, with your companion, your partner whom God has given you, a basket of all your efforts balanced on your dead head, now used as a casket for your ashes after your bones are burned in a pile as papers forgotten.

Perhaps "car before the horse" could actually work, as a new expression used by those of us, we the blasé Luddites who feel more at home at a place that quietly and awkwardly floats and darts and farts outside of time, who are shocked by its truculent arrival every morning, how there's no difference really between cars and horses or which comes first in the proper progression and creation of things, one metallic, one with a mane, both a vain vane, how both cars and horses take us to yet another place or person or thing north, south, east, west, where life is better and flatter and framed with all the heat of people and birds and songs and blood we see oh so rarely.

3

Do You Pray?

In my writing room, I see a woman on the street in a slutty green top put something in the slutty green trashcan. And then she's off, off to her day. I'm jealous of the birds on the tree hopping from branch to branch collecting twigs and sprigs; I'm even jealous of that woman, my neighbor with the herpes lips, who every morning leaves the building across the street, puts something in the trashcan and turns left, my right, and sometimes she'll cross the street to my side. Her outfit doesn't always match the trash, but her life does, carefree and rotting, cracking.

Sometimes I crave my boyfriend Rudolfo's penis, his pubic hair, I sniff it. I lick it. The smell of urine—just a little bit—from the dribble of his day's pisses. The smell of sweat from thigh rubbing balls rubbing a thigh, from everywhere he went intently, clearly, and sometimes foggily.

Last night was really the first time, on all fours, I *rocked back*—that motion, me in control—into his erect, bulbous penis covered in lube. I had mostly focused on relaxing, on allowing him to enter me. Could I take it? Could I take it longer? Or would I have to tell him to stop and put on more lube? I'd sniff poppers or take a shot of whiskey to calm down, to tweak the chemicals in my brain that tell me to be cautious and careful, that thought that thinks it negative for one to enter another, the thought that avoids being smothered, drowned, falling under the weight of the water, the deep ocean abyss of water, letting yourself be crushed by it little by little, thrust by thrust into the earth's crust, and let love remain for the fish that can see in the dark.

Last night I pushed back, rocked back. I told him to slap my ass, and he told me to perk that ass up more and shut the fuck up, you little fucking bitch. With my head against the wall and my arms hugging myself and my hands clasped and reverent in a way, I acquiesced to him. His bare bearish beard scratched my neck and his twist twisty tongue, my ear. His body was stiff, and I pushed my body back as a piece of wood into his wood using my forehead against the paint of the wall, my head covered in white dust like ashes of burning Ganga bodies.

Holy Spirit who art in heaven and in my body and even in my dick, hallowed be thy name, thy kingdom come, I prayed.

How easy it is to be bitter toward those who so obviously deserve it, and then we see one glimmer of kindness, and our world is turned upside down. I still haven't made up my mind on how to be, how to pray, and what that even means.

Do I curse those who curse you?

Do I act calm when I see them ruining others, abusing them for decades for their own benefit, fucking their brains with cords and fetters and feathers and fur, whatever they can find, their souls, turning them into quivering slaves? Am I, as I simply sit on a cock and breathe, hurting someone else somewhere else?

As I push my body back and willingly, hungrily, envelop his

cock with my soul—come into me, cum in me and on me, praying, clasping my hands, eyes closed—each thrust reminding myself how silly it is not to let the waters take us down, down, down into the dark peace of being smothered by something other than ourselves, of being taken, possessed by another—even then, when something seems so divine and in a vacuum for voyeurs on rooftops watching us and gods living in the Astorian stained drop ceiling above us, even then I know I'm hurting someone, dripping on them, piercing right through them. Even if they're far away, all those nameless people, our comfort, our lovely pain, is destroying theirs.

Park Avenue beckons me daily and has since I began there a few years ago, but I fear something is coming, or something has changed, or grown, or shown, but I'm blind. I wake up early before all bitterness and abuse begins to find the clear and the calm and the chirping, in hopes that the former will simply fly away.

Rudolfo told me to "just breathe" when I began there, knowing that it was not for me. It's not me. It will never be me. "For now, just breathe while you're there," he said. "You've had years of pain, too many, and now you can just breathe," he said.

"Breathe there for a while. Stop, sit still for a while," he said.

Let things fall away from you. Let things grow. Find your peace again. Save money. Enjoy your new Astorian apartment instead of sleeping on couches. Work. Eat. Drink. Pray.

And ignore the thing that will grow in you as you wait.

All will be well. All will be gone.

4

The French Finally Did It

Besides coffee, the occasional Adderall—just a little nugget of it, a piece of a piece of a piece—the occasional pre-work masturbation, which only happens on days when the apartment is warm, because that usually means my balls are most full of blood and hangiest and in the mirror and then I feel the manliest, easily getting it up when I get up, I usually tell myself a Bible verse on my way to the N train and that's what keeps me going, getting up and getting it up and going to work on Park Avenue, where I think evil may have been a firstborn in the universe.

It's the one that helps you tell yourself that absolutely nothing in the universe can change anything about you and how much you're loved. That's the gist of it at least. And when I repeat it to myself every morning, I wonder if it matters if I leave out a part, and what about other languages, and what about *other* gods? What if I say Vishnu but I picture Jesus who acts like Buddha with a monkey heart exploding like Hanuman? Or what if I don't even say my name, say my name, ain't callin' me baby?

Sometimes I'll forget to repeat it on the way to work, listening to Abel Korzeniowski or Miriam Gauci or Tibetan chants—dings and gongs and high-pitched garglings, and deep-voiced men with deep hangy balls full of vibrating cum who seem so at peace just garbling about a bell, are they really on their way to hell? But I'll quickly say it before I open the mahogany door of the office. I won't ever enter the office before saying it, this verse. I've never forgotten:

Neither height nor depth, neither life nor death, things present nor things to come, angels or demons, or anything else in all creation can separate me from your love.

So in other words, if I'm finally killed today by a helicopter blade or a rabid squirrel as I'm eating a Sprinkles red velvet cupcake in Central Park alone, wishing for spring to hurry up and finish the fuck getting here with its warm flowery cock, if I find myself in the deepest part of the ocean in a yellow submarine, since we all really do live in a yellow submarine, a yellow submarine, or if I time-travel after kissing a frog who came back in time to take me with him even further back to some place I've never wanted to go, spending seasons hiding from it—the pain of the early 2000s—piece by peace with my prince of peace, while the future becomes *The Planet of the Frogs* with Charlton Heston making love to frogs next to the Statue of Liberty on the sand, or if when we finally figure out fusion in France after we evolve from supply and demand, and they rename France as "Fusion" (*Viva la Fusion!*) and Paris is now called "Thermonuclear" (phonetically "Therm-eee"), and the universe merges with its parallel and its parallel and its parallel and all light splits and everything is a rainbow—Band-Aids as rainbows, trees as rainbows, cellphones as rainbows—even then, even after all those ifs, if then, if then, I will then still be loved the same, or so I tell myself before I open that life-sucking hole of a mahogany door.

And in the brassy mirrored elevator on the way to the mahogany door, I'll get to thinking, is being loved the same no matter what the same as never being loved at all? How can we comprehend it, this thing without wavelength or speed or spice?

And then that thought will be sunken into a black hole, slinking and stretching past the event horizon of my understanding, and replaced with a sparkling dust cloud of something far more important, another nagging question—how many desks were thrown out today by trashy men around the world?

Not fruit, not milk jugs, but desks—exactly how many cubicle desks, and how does it differ from other days? What is the exact number of cubicle desks disassembled and slain, useless, and lain onto the sidewalk as mutilated imps for cherry blossoms to shit their wilting chalky white onto, for neutrinos to pierce into uninterrupted, a boy interrupted, through and through, unstoppable, before the 10,000,000-year-old sunlight finally burns and buckles the scratched wood-plastic-mix originally mixed and stamped in Beijing and originally dreamed up in a lab in Sweden that smells like horse meatballs—later experimented with, scratched, killed, and mutilated in America?

I can smell the gloves of the trash man; I know those gloves. I feel those gloves. I've been those gloves. They smell like bolts and $1 lunchtime pizza slices and Coke and old eggs and joy and oil. His hand reaches out for the desk parts on the sidewalk of so many places; he loves when people throw out desks. His hand quivers as it flies through the molecules of the air for that wood.

They crunch the most in the trash truck, desks. It's like celery between your teeth or bubble wrap between your teeth or a Kix ball between your butt cheeks. Every snap is an orgasmic accomplishment. You, my friend, caused sound waves to fly through the air.

The life of a neutrino makes me jealous, too, sometimes on my way to the mahogany door, how truly free they are. I tell myself I am completely free because I'm—squinting—always, always, always, always loved—and it really does work for me most of the time. I feel calm, unshaken, even when family dies, or as I get older when everyone wants to be younger. Ships get sunk or I almost choke on a paleo cookie dunked in almond milk—but always being loved makes me affixed to something, though, and I worry about that until I just squint again—always, always, always...

Right now neutrinos travel through my eyes, through my hangy balls, through desks, my mind and how I daily dupe it into thinking death-by-trash won't matter, right through that, through planets, through entire galaxies that are hidden inside that Kix ball tickling my asshole hair.

Whereas I am still forever afraid to be alone and released, they, The Society Of The Neutrinos, are forever freely traveling through our pitiful dictionary of 1,000,000 words to describe the entire universe, our imagination, our getting up in the morning, our Adderall, our coffee, our electricity, our desks, our trash, our breath, our lungs.

And before I open that mahogany office door to meet the demons of Park Avenue, I whisper to myself, *jealousy*, and then, *nor anything else in all the universe*, even jealousy, *not even neutrinos* traveling faster than light wearing stinky gloves pushing the skin of my chest all the way through whenever they want like that voodoo man in Indian Jones—*callleeee maaaaaaah suck-deee-dayyyy, calllleeeeeeemaaaaaahhhh,* they each say—not even the voodoo of neutrinos can take love away from me, like a fat Southern belle that still looks classy in makeup, "*I deeeee-clare!*" by the door of the daily cubicle pit, not even my curiosity of what it would be like to be unloved for a day, free for a day, or to be a child in a purple hat with string tied to my wrist, attached to a grandma like the orbit of planets around stars, and how I, what if I, cut the string with my teeth and each end is covered in blood and saliva as it snaps, that orgasmic snap, or all that we're willing to do or accept so that our résumé looks good for our next job somewhere else in a land full of angels who also can't hurt us, bosses, neutrinos, angels, bosses, neutrinos, angels, demons, jealousy, nothing, nothing, sticks and stones, or 1,000,000 words or none.

Even when I am walking the same sidewalk path to work like I did for years, a dolly being pushed by a mover, Dolly with a dick in *9 to 5*, Parton my French, fracking Monday through Friday for years, even when I leave my Astorian apartment on this day in the morning at the exact time as I always did, my biorhythms set in stone, on this day I thee wed my fate, I am crushed, my bones are crushed on this date.

I am crushed from a desk someone threw out the window when that neighbor girl with the bulbous herpes lips was standing there in the garage of her boyfriend whining, "Tim, throw me his goddamn shirt, Dusty needs his goddamn gym shirt for school goddamnit, today, damn it, just throw me his gym shirt so he can get to school," when Tim decided to throw a desk instead of a gym shirt, and instead of hitting her head like he had hoped, he hits me, in my knees, and from what I can tell, a story only I can tell, mostly severing them.

Nothing can hurt me. Nothing can hurt me. Nothing can hurt me, I declare on the sidewalk.

Nothing can hurt me.

That's what keeps me going, this calm, even when I'm flat on the sidewalk thinking how I'd normally be late for work for Lucifer, how very upsettingly boring and cyclical that is—oh yes, yet another big boss in the big-big city, yet another power-hungry Lucifer, wondering for years if the moment I walked away from him would be more *Devil's Advocate*, with flames, or *Devil Wears Prada*, with a smirk, or something else entirely, maybe more Sinclair Lewis's fat *Babbitt*, which I read in high school, but far less middle-class this time, and far more "poor door," as I listen to herpes-girl screaming for her "Tim" to "call 911 you fucking halfwit, look at this man's legs! OH dear Gawwwwwwwd help us," she cried, how when she surprisingly said "halfwit" I felt momentarily transported into something very oddly British, waiting for her to start rambling about eating with forks tines-down and complaining about her half-life as a Parisienne for a summer.

Tines down, I deeeeee-claare!

And as I thought, as I think, and listen to Tim, and to herpes-busted-face-slut-lip-girl, another neighbor Oracula, our neighbor who lives in the basement below our apartment building—the Greek lady who verbally and physically abuses her invalid brother on a daily basis—approached the morning scene and let her pit bull, Sunshine, actually lick my bloody knees, leaving a particularly beautiful slobber sheen on the bones sticking out, the swirls and bubbles of which gelatinously oozing such a Grand Prismatic Spring of color, such that I have never seen—yellows, reds, blues, purples, even greens—and in this moment I realize, perhaps it has now finally happened, perhaps the French finally did it, because I feel a parallelogram of my life coming, or perhaps it's already here, or gone, as the square of sidewalk shifts and bends beneath me.

All I see are rainbows.

And cheers erupt on the streets of Therm-eeeeee!

Oui, oui, oui!

5

Rudolfo

I don't blame you if you're annoyed already, bitching there with your Kindle, flicking your finger around like a conductor's wand, because I didn't take the time to plan—I loathe it actually, planning.

Weddings are planned and Save-the-Dated.

My friend Serena Save-the-Dates everything, and I'll tell her every time that the date has been "born again," and she'll understand that because she recently was, and I usually go to her dates, even though they're already ruined by all her planning, and I'll try to make the best of it, dancing when no one else is, to music that's subpar like the event itself planned for months, years, in advance, when it could have been up-to-par, but that damn Save-the-Date subbed it down deep into the waters below a golden spontaneous fiery cruise ship split in half and the helicopering bodies of all that it could have been.

So if you don't like tangents, if you want everything to fit together as a baby fist inside a man's butt, and every person I mention to somehow fit snugly into my *artistic vision*, which is something people say that just means a buttery lubeness, perfectly palatable and slippery for *you*, all tasty and slick and crisp and boxed up by illegals, get the fuck out now of wherever and whenever you think this is. Close the book, if this ever becomes one. Turn off the Kindle if they're still around by then. Dunk your dank shit-phone in your morning toilet of bear lamp shit, because that shit lasts forever.

When I got rejected for my first fiction manuscript, and the second, and the third, and the fourth, and the fifth, and the sixth, every agent and publisher told me that "there's no ARC—where's the arc?!"

They kept using that word, arc—is it even a word? I know of the arc in a calculus problem, or the ArK of the Covenant or *Ark*ansas, but I never understood how I could make my manuscripts turn more ARC-y for them, ARSEY? And I've realized that the more I tried to give them what they wanted, the more *arc*ane my stories became.

So now I'll tell you the truth, however it cums, wherever I am. That's my ARC now.

People die.

That's an arc, I guess.

The spring sleet and then rain comes, and then goes; that's an arc, I guess. We want so many clear resolutions, rising actions, oh yes, oh yes, that, right there, is the climax, and then, that, right there, is the clear resolution, or a very clear lack of resolution so we can then talk about how irresolute it is over a slice of pizza, as grease soaks up so many napkins that are thrown out, later licked by roaches and goblins beneath the East River.

My boyfriend and I met on a train; I could see the shape of his dick through his jeans. It had been raining, a previous spring rain, sleet finally gone—not unlike the one that's beginning to dump on Oracula the Greek, my bloody knees, Sunshine the pit bull, and herpes-lips girl, not too long after I managed to ask Oracula the Greek to pull Sunshine away—"Please tell Sunshine to please stop licking my blood" and call 911, the same number of blood sprays from that splintering desk splintering my bones and skin.

A matter of 911 splinters.

An antimatter of 911 blood sprays.

I could see the mushroomy head; he looked sweaty, like he'd gotten off a shift of something, or a workout, whatever it was, was obviously grueling, and the movement of the time there doing whatever he was doing had stretched his pants so elegantly over that penis of his and he saw me staring at it. This was back when I had been a mover for the rich and the famous and the cunty of New York, and I had finished my day as well with the black, Hispanic, and Hisblapanick convicts, at Ecclesiastes the Mover with a sandpapery glove in each of my pockets. They were always so kind, the convicts, and were obsessed with $1 pizza and Coke, but I guess *who isn't* except Indians in saris and other faraway dirty cheese-makers and fudge-packers?

I never planned to have met this man; I never planned to be so obsessed with penises, either; their shape, their proud throbbing heads—warriors they are—and how I saw it, his head, through the Kindles of a full train. So many Kindles on the edge of arms, clasping to them tightly but just loose enough that if you tugged you'd get it with a little snap of a thumb and an index finger, all of them glowing electric leaflets and branches at rush hour. One day we won't need fingers. One day our hands will be fully webbed and accessible to the Internet at all times.

Besides his penis on which I was so focused before the people crowded in the train as a forest growing in fast-forward, it was his eyes that I could see, that green through all the glowing gray leaves of Kindles and tired paper skin.

Save-the-Date, for today you'll meet a man you'll move in with.

Save-the-Date, for today you'll fuck a stranger over and over and the warmth of their anus will hug your genitals like a beer cozy left out in the sun that you're fisting for no good reason and it melts like buttah.

The blood of my legs is creeping over the sidewalk, engulfing all the oak-seed spinners that spring has sprung off the flowering trees above. Imagine being one of those seeds, resting there, thinking that even though this ground beneath you seems well too hard to ever penetrate with your roots dormant and soon growing within you, there's still hope; perhaps the wind will catch your seed sail and you'll helicopter far from Astoria to Brooklyn, or maybe further yet to Liberty Island where you'll grow—*you'll grow so tall!*

I want to be taller than Lady Liberty.

I want to be the beacon of a new country, not brass eroded into a tealy, grimy-looking lichen-mess of a woman, but a tree, a beautiful, beautiful tree, the symbol of earth and a column resting on the arc of the curvature of the universe.

I proudly rise above it with my leaves and proudly penetrate it with my roots equidistant from the horizon line.

My blood, however, was a Phuketan tsunami of redness, a wall of red to them, those seeds, suffocating who slept and hoped so calmly, just waiting there for the wind to take them to their future, having to settle for blood-waves instead.

They never could have known about that wave of color coming and how they'd drown and how some wouldn't because I stopped the acceleration of the onslaught of blood with my shirt from American Apparel, the one in my gym bag—the one with the rips, the one I was wearing when I met Rudolfo.

I know, that is his name, despite my efforts and requests for him to change it to something a little less syllabic. Such a task it is to say it, that layered word, a work shift, a lifting of a piano and then another one, a desk lifted and thrown, cotton stretched thinner and thinner over time to outline your throbbing man-rod, all to say his name, his name is RU, and then DOL, and then FO, fee-fi-fo-fum, and I met him in a train gang.

6

Miss Allison

I thought she may have been abused, or raped, beaten by her father, or still beaten the moment I met her, that very first day of joining Heller, Heller, and Hah on Park Avenue. HH&H as it's known, and as it will probably continue to be known, gaining in popularity, or so they have always told themselves.

I know that certainly Miss Allison told herself that, probably every morning, probably as she's walking down to Nottingham Grill to grab a banana, as she's on her way home in her new Mercedes—or in the car service, which she calls "carriage service" for some reason, when it has rained even just a sprinkle of a cupcake of water from above.

She won't go into Sprinkles Cupcakes because she swears there are peanuts in the batter, and even when we've told her we're pretty sure there aren't, she still has a panic attack, hyperventilating with white frosting on her lips to match the frosted white on her long black hair, straight and crispy, and only washed with Softsoap antibacterial hand soap—she nonchalantly mentioned, "I find it works best. I find keeping things simple is best. I use Softsoap for everything."

I could tell you her story, every little thing she had said that first day, her backstory, but I don't know how it could ever make you feel the way I felt in her presence; that feeling is better. Maybe you should try to imagine it, that feeling, regardless of my efforts.

Take everyone you know that has been wronged in life, everyone you know that has been taken advantage of, stripped, ripped, squeezed like a halved lemon in your hand dripping as you make a fist, as the pulp pops and those fucking annoying seeds that always fall—no matter how much you've dug out the dark spots you thought were seeds with a knife or your finger or your tongue—into whatever you're spraying the juice into, a salad maybe, or cauliflower simmering in olive oil during a sunset with the clouds pink and the Long Island City steam towers white just beginning to light up through the window. And through the trees that have filled in with thick green leaves; they all look like green plastic grocery bags squeezed through a shredder and thrown onto dead branches—still out of place in this cool realm.

Why are you here, life? How do you grow when you know how cold you once were?

It's as if their presence, the filling trees, is an insult, someone who forgot what you JUST said, even though they were standing right here with you the whole time, yet there they are, thinking they deserve to be noticed now. I just said it, yet you look at me now with that fresh face, that fresh green face, so lush, as if I didn't just tell you there's a cold, cold cancer in my cold bones that greets me year after year despite all the seasons' greetings of radiation.

Now take that disintegrating lemon, look at your grimace as you impress yourself with your bicep pumping, with your veins pumping, look at those veins, those bulbous veins and pierce them with the pinprick-black needle of the points of your eyes and suck the blood of power from them, your strong strong strong arms, and feel the lemon drip its last drop onto your cauliflower and pepper and paprika and leftover mushrooms—all in all a dish you know is just going to suck on this fine dumb Tuesday—and bring that lemon close to your face. Look at how mutilated it is, and sniff. Sniff that peppiness that seems so out of place in this murder scene in front of you.

That's Miss Allison every day, every waking moment that she breathes for Heller, Heller, & Hah, which, if I'm correct, has been every breath of her entire life that she deems worth something.

And still, that's not it, because lemons are beautiful, and Miss Allison is not. Even though you've just squeezed the bitter contents of that lemon into your shitty food, they're not hollow. Lemons still have pulp.

Miss Allison is completely hollow inside, and because, as I quickly learned, she would never be absent from the office when any were present, even those that vacuumed at night, she was a phantom lurking, an *understood letter* there in the midst of the mist of dust particles from the carpet that never flattens and always fluffs up the crust of dust.

There she is, always lurking there, Heller, Heller, & Hah & *Hollow*. She is that ever-present, sneaky sneak, that far-from-sleepy far-from-hallowed hollow.

After a time I realized that when she looked at the brass plate of the entryway covered in mahogany wood, she must have seen that *Hollow* there, and because she knew it's always there for her—or it will be some day if she just keeps working, never stop working—always there for Mr. Hah—then she'll fill her life with the juice she's been desperately missing.

Or better yet, she'll finally be rid of that last drop of blood left in her veins, becoming one with the walls, the numbers, the musty dusty misty carpets that will take her for a ride back to her family's home, the one she wouldn't dare give up I'm told, where all her friends are old.

Her best friend is 97.

And they laugh and laugh nervously about death, and how it's always around the corner—like peanuts in the Sprinkles cupcakes, for instance. And how they always make her lips tingle.

That's how she's always known something is wrong when her lips tingle. She would do anything as long as her lips didn't tingle.

If they didn't, all must be okay.

7

The Sign

It's many things, not only clouds, that provide hardly any blockade to our bodies being thrust into space toward the moon, where—after being frozen so solid so quickly from all those miles, our eyelids crystallized—we'll thud, and a poof of gray will rise, a kind of dust from all the space-hay thrown into the air for alien cows who hunger and thirst for righteousness.

I remember being on the roof of our apartment with Rudolfo, and we were talking about how the one end dips down too far, collecting water for birds who play in it like shrunken elephants on Adderall, washing their bodies with their beaks so diligently, beaks that seem to bend like trunks from the speed at which they're washing their feathers in the muck.

"I don't want to get too close," Rudolfo said, fearing the exposed wires that went this way and that like Christ's thorny exercise headband left there—someone just left it there for someone else to get zapped by its power. And as we backed away from the wires and the puddles and the elephants to the higher end of the roof near the tree, we laid down together with our coffee mugs—his with less coffee in it, as it often was, since the day he got sick and the doctors told him to stay away from anything exciting.

I remember looking up and being afraid: Is it getting worse as I get older?

Will it get worse?

When I'm 80, am I going to not even leave the house because I don't want to—after that first step after slowly locking the door—miss the step and begin floating up to the moon like a balloony buffoon?

That's the other one, fuckin' balloons; I'd gotten more afraid of them too. I had dreams about them. One of them, recurring, is about bunnies, a pack of white bunnies. They're nibbling on baguettes and eventually lazily make their way to the basket of the balloon, climb in, tug on the rope, hear that hiss, and fly up. As bunnies aren't the best hot-air-balloon pilots, which is what I imagine to be the reason that the balloon catches on fire, and the entire basket holding the bunnies, once a happy little place of breadcrumbs, quickly and hotly transforms its members into embers, the bottom of the basket especially, which, from the weight of each rabbit gives way to that basket giving birth to charred rabbit carcass bombs.

The sky is always full of black hot bunny comets and it's beautiful, especially as it's daytime, which causes a variety of white puffy trails jettisoning toward the earth, eventually making a thud on that very same roof. All of those dead bunnies land on our roof, and in that dream, I have this feeling that awakens me every time—the fuckers deserved it, eating baguettes like that, meandering about without any respect for anything.

Or air conditioners; every time I looked upon one—no matter where I was in the city—on a lunch break, walking home from the gym, the grocery store—I began chewing pumpkin seeds, handfuls of them in my mouth, packed in there. I'd try to swallow them but they wouldn't go down, that mass of crunchy buttery nutty salty organic wetness. I kept chewing on the seeds that were never there, and I saw air conditioners falling on so many people, each saliva bubble and cracked seed a box of Freon and cool. I'd look up at all of them and they'd all be tilting down at me as if I were magnetic, and they began falling one by one, on pit bull puppies that weren't even old enough to lick anyone yet, bloody like me or otherwise, or for their owners to set out to prove that they weren't beasts—especially Sunshine, Sunshine the pit bull, she, she's not a toddler-eater, no, not this one, they get such a bad rap, they all deserve a chance at a long life.

And now she'll never have that chance because an air conditioner has just fallen on Sunshine the pit bull's head and crushed it because she never thought for once to sniff and lick upward, choosing instead to look down, licking my knees, or what's left of them instead. First a man's legs, then a dog's skull. It's just a little crush.

Buildings too sometimes, not always; some of them are more ominous than others, tilting, too. Besides the bunnies accidentally setting themselves on fire, I'd also have dreams about ruining fashion shows. I'm always flailing my arms about right in the middle of it, and some production assistant is telling me to leave and then the designer leaves because this was her first show and she just, really, REALLY, needed it to be impressive for all of the impressive people who make a living off deciding who will be officially impressive next, and because of me just dancing around, flailing around, *haaaaaaaaaaaaaaaaaay*, everything was ruined for her. I'd walk up to the designer who had found a rock nearby somehow on a mysterious grassy knoll; she's there alone.

I always walk up to her wearing a see-through trench coat while I eat bacon-wrapped-bacon and then say, "You know, dying might just be a subway train getting stuck between two stations and the doors accidentally open, and there you are, an idiot, you just get off thinking it was your stop because you never looked and licked forward, and as you're leaning and licking in the wrong direction—that little air-conditioner tilt too far, tilting on the sill, tilting, teetering there before the murderous dark fall—you think, how confusing this is, that this *is* my stop, yet it *isn't.*"

And then the designer on the rock on the grassy knoll asks me how that helps her get impressive again, and angrily she declares, "I *deeee-clare*, you know what you are; you're an old dog. You ever seen the ones? The ones that are so in love with their owners that they don't even need a goddamn leash, but it isn't cute anymore because you've gotten so old and that's why they left you there on the sidewalk. You're an old dog without an owner, and you're all wet and happy and breathing heavy because you think someone's coming for you, to talk to you, to take care of you, but they aren't—like some dork at a party looking all around for god knows what or whom."

And that's when I'd usually wake up and look up at the drop ceiling with fresh new brown stain circles all over it from the roof leaking elephant piss from Rudolfo and I walking up there too much, especially when the sun would set and we'd obligatorily dance to Ace of Base, "and it opened up my mind and I am happy now," humming it in the rooftop wind, flailing about like space-hay, on days like that, that never seemed to end.

8

Scorpions

My bolo tie, hanging on the window, the one with the real scorpion encased in a clear plastic arrowhead, lights up every morning in my writing room with such a green-yellow glow from the reflection of so many leaves.

On the subway to HH&H, I usually look at hair on arms, the curvature of each hair on the folds of skin encasing the folds of muscle, each bulge a scorpion trying to get up and light up, a man's readiness to face the day—gripping his backpack, chewing his mint gum, a bulge of muscle on the jaw, a tinge of muscle in the forearm, sipping his coffee, so many things wiggling, his cock, his tongue, his cock's tongue.

Jackhammers pecking, birds pecking, men chewing and sipping, muscle tinge, muscle mint and coffee, all of this for food, for sex, for doing something in the reflection of light off green leaves, muscles encased in skin, skin encased in clothes, all that we won't do out of fear of jealousy, and of disease, and of babies, and of what would happen if we'd only listened to ourselves more.

Sometimes I'd see this one man with muscular-scorpion arms, with such healthy virile hair, and as he'd chew his gum and hold his backpack, you could smell the morning breath on him, the oils that have caked on his every crevice in the muggy night before, and next to him will be a woman. She's visiting her sister in the city and her hair is wrapped in folds of fabric. Even though he could only see her eyes, the New Yorker with his New York Rangers hat and his tattooed douche armbands fading green-yellow and getting lighter each day, with his city-tough and rough neck and his drywall-sprinkled boots that were there for him—just there—not meant to state anything to anyone, noticed how lost she was, this woman in the niqab, her eyes moving about in the slit clit of fabric, distracted by the ads, not able to find the stops so clearly lit up by the '90s-era screens. And even when she did find the stops, they meant nothing to her, because she needed someone to comfort her more than finding her way, those eyes, and get underneath all that fabric with her and tell her, whisper to her underneath all the black, that all was going to be okay.

He could tell she needed help, but he continued listening to his music, clutching his bag, shifting his sprinkle boots, surfing with the movements of the train. Nervously, she unfolded her fist of long red nails—disgruntled Macy's employee long—and readied one of them to pierce through the bad-breath air and particles of lint and toothpaste steam and coffee clouds and runaway beard hair and arm hair from the scorpions of everyone's muscles fidgeting in anticipation for their stop—letting loose a leaf of hair or two into the air and breathed in by someone you will never see again and someone you will see again and their hair tickles your nose hair as your nose hair catches their hair—"You're not going in there to my lungs Mr. Arm Hair," says your nose hair—and ignites a sneeze, as if parakeets and seagulls were laying eggs directly into your nostrils, cracking, yolks spraying out of your nose as spilled coffee from a train jolt—their wings flapping all over your face—and every moment they're bringing bright neon twigs to ready their arrival.

Her nail poked his sharp warrior chest and she mumbled through the cloth, a lady of the cloth, and he said, "What's that?"

Her red nail broke; her voice broke.

Her voice was garbled and muffled and frustrated and crackled, like all she imbibed and breathed for twenty years before was just Red Stripe in those Jamaican breasty bottles and Lucky Strike in those lovely white ballsac packs, until she found her life underneath the black curtains, a star. I don't know what was said, really, but I could tell from the cadence that she thought she deserved pity from us for her lack of preparation, her lack of planning, and from this man next to her.

She didn't humbly ask him; she wasn't sweet. She was perturbed, as if this very subway was constructed around her while she was taking a dump in a field, constructed simply to bother her, encasing her, and everyone inside it came today to enjoy her stinky purple perturbation, all of us voyeuristically masturbating to the situation there on her throne of ignorance, and we could tell she was never more thankful for how covered she was than she was that day, shielding her body from our eyes, except for her eyes, which began to tear in fear she would miss her sister again, rolling around the city, a tumbleweed in a terrorist's cape.

And when her bold red cracked nail scraped the sweaty heather gray of his shirt, I wanted him to fuck her. At 8 a.m., I wanted more than anything for her to like it, even though she said no. It had nothing to do with men or women and the things we do, but with how trapped, yet displayed we all are on a daily basis, regardless of what we think we drape and speckle on ourselves for spectacle, or without our even knowing what we do. I wanted someone to be stung, and perhaps for her thinking that the entire city should somehow now sleep just so that she could get to where she thought she needed to go, for food, for raiment, for life, for fellowship, I wanted her stung, I wanted her fucked hard, we give thee thanks, O Lord, Amen.

I wanted him to do it, the New Yorker. I wanted her to gaze upon the zip of his fly, the rustling of his hand so easily finding his hardened thick shaft, the stickiness of his sweating balls to peel away from his thighs as he lifted that shaft. I wanted to feel the wind of particles and hair and toothpaste and coffee and oils and muggy lint to wave my way from him waving and elevating his thick, bulbous New York dick at this woman—look what's comin' to ya lady, *THIS*.

I wanted to hear the rips of her cloth as he didn't even bother lifting it, the cloth—somehow his dick went straight through like a sharp red nail through Saran Wrap covering weeks-old potato salad and we even heard a slight delightful pop.

His deep voice, his douchey gum smacking as he stood there, is what did it for me probably. I think I sneezed and they both looked at me, the New Yorker unfazed, the niqabi woman as though it wasn't my turn to sneeze and I needed to first receive permission from her, squinting at me under her clit-slit.

Almost every day I wear my scorpion bolo tie on the subway, and when my stop comes for Park Avenue, I'll take it off and quickly put it in my gym bag for safekeeping. And when I get home I display it again on the window, proudly hanging it on the latch that sticks out because it never locks because it's so old as most things are, or as most things think they won't be, until morning comes again, and again, until it doesn't.

The layers baffle me, sicken me, and turn me on. I know there are details to trees, to birds and jackhammers and scorpions, and people who are perpetually encased in plastic arrowheads lit up by the sun from time to time and all need to be displayed at times, glowing in the morning at times, ready to strike and speckle.

Every person I see, I imagine them either getting fucked or killed—or lit up somehow, I feel powerful this way, all that I see is my creation—maybe by the sun, finally revealing all that they are, all that's hidden, all they wished they could show but for now cannot, waiting, waiting, hung, so wonderfully hung in the night, under clothing, before the morning, later looking at me with those eyes, those eyes like scorpion tails ready to strike all we like sheep have gone gay and astray on a train.

9

Daily Bread

I can't say exactly when I knew the place was cursed, HH&H, or maybe in turmoil with the gods, caught in a whirlwind of bad energy, karma, or maybe it's not connected like that, and there's no why or rhyme or reason or treason. Maybe some places, people, things, are simply tossed about for the entirety of their existence much more chaotically than others, and we want someone, something, some god to be responsible for it, for how sticky this feels. We'll tell ourselves over and over again the purple words on a Yogi tea bag, "I am beautiful, I am bountiful, I am blissful," while we're tossed and unstuck and stuck again.

We'll even tape it to our computer monitors at the office, that tea bag; clear tape will cover the DELL, and below will be that teabag with that doleful message in purple.

I've waited too long to explain it, too long, too much; I can enduringly taste the dust of the Oriental carpets and it's morbid, the tattered books about the Kennedys, the half-naked iron statues of Achilles, Zeus, and a variety of Roman emperors—or the massive picture of Napoleon.

Brass letters of the logo, Heller, Heller, and Hah on the front door.

Besides emperors and homoerotic gods, there are pictures of unfinished architecture sketches and really, really bad paintings of stock exchanges around the world. Plants of ivy adorn the entryway. All of it fizzes in my mouth when I mention the place, when I think about it, wherever I am, when I imagine the faces of the souls that enter there and slowly burn there, our mouths taped shut.

Everywhere where there's a window, there's an executive's office; everywhere there's not—the center of the room, the egg yolk of the place, "the pit," we called it, is where the cubicles of the less important folks like me sit. There are thumbtacks tacked into lists of phone extensions, paperclip cups, binders upon binders upon binders all in white, trays of work yet to be done, no pictures of family, no color, just beige cubicle walls covered in indoor-outdoor carpet and the sharp light of fluorescent tubes. Guests rarely enter the nucleus, the pit, the dungeon; most stick to the outer edges, where the executives are, all of them well-fed, all of them morbidly obese, losing their hair, thick wide ties and lint-free suit jackets, all freshly ironed by tired Koreans.

Those of us in the pit are skinny, wear the same outfits day after day, and are generally good-looking, especially in comparison to those in power, those with gout and other ailments, like diabetes that could have been prevented by never starting here.

Yet another story of complaining about corporate distaste, another employee unsatisfied with their life but happy with the pay: booo-hooo, Park Avenue is the center of all evil, booo-hoooo, my boss is the Devil and every one of us is an angel, us vs. them, as if the unified existence of HH&H is to provide the perfect antagonist in a story about an innocent protagonist, me, me, me, some kind of melted Prada-Kennedy-Bad-Brooks-Brother-gooey-pee over all the good brother named Mel, with a sister named Nell, as if every person in every tower erected here serves to destroy all things, tay-taying in the wind, sucking within it all light and warping it as it flies past us underlings so close to the Event Horizon, *and we have to decide!!*

We have to decide to stand up and fight!

Or just let it continue to suck, either/or.

I don't know if it's that simple, as much as we want it to be. Either or, either or, or maybe it is. Though, I'm quite sure the subway wasn't built just to annoy us, no matter how perturbed we may be by its inhabitants or the direction it's going so very slowly. I really wish it were.

As I work in a tower, I think about towers, towers now, towers that were, towers that will be, and why.

Soon HH&H will move into the tallest building in the Western Hemisphere; it's not quite Burj material, but it's close, as close as America will get these days, and it's right down the street. The majority of the building, though, isn't office space; it's condos. Most new towers seem to be condos now; perhaps the thought is, if an office space is "threatening"—a symbol of a way of life, spending, working, spending, working, live to work to spend—then what could be less threatening than someone's home, yet still allow the great beast to thrive as healthy and bitter as endive and a side of organic parsnips? Instead of building office buildings that make statements, we in America will build homes that reach the cosmos. That's where we are in history; we worship condos.

Before that it was offices, higher and higher office space. Before that, maybe castles with higher and higher columns to remind all who gaze upon the alligators and the moats and the rock who is in power over this field. Before that, churches, steeples, and ornate glass to call upon all to worship in that empty space—if we sing and pray here, then they'll hear us, god will and all his many forms like water. And before that, tombs, great and awesome tombs to declare in brick what they hope will happen—that we'll live forever. What will be next in the great history of what we collectively hold dear and most powerful—trees, back to gardens? Museums of art, of farts? Petting zoos? Skyscrapers full of pugs?

My therapist told me I was "hyper-sexual" and "hyper-morbid," which just made me think "extra-sexual," which then made me think "extraterrestrial." At the time I had mentioned my obsession with death and sex, how almost every man and woman I see leads me to thinking of them fucking or killing babies or puppies or Muslims or just anyone who takes themselves too seriously. And I asked him what I should do with that prognosis.

I don't even think he was listening, but eventually he said, "Explore the hypersexuality."

"Don't be afraid of it. Explore it. SEE WHERE IT TAKES YOU, Colin."

And then he patty-caked his quads, motioning me to sit on his lap.

And then I sucked on his cock and killed him with a statue of Muhammad who had the face of Betty White and the wings of a bald eagle as ears.

I'm not sure if it's because I was the last new homo to watch the *Queer as Folk* series and I was jealous that I'd never had a "Babylon" to call home, but where that led me was to never return to that therapist. I think I went once, because he told me do what I was already doing, and to continually return to a place called Bonne Vie, which is basically Babylon, without glitter, much darker, in New York, definitely not Pittsburgh filmed in Canada, but the same amount of drugs.

I avoided those, the drugs, but I've never avoided the men. They're drugs enough for me. And that annoys me, too, how typical that is, how cyclical, how expected—a man who likes men, a homo who craves to be in a room full of men the same way, raw, and here I go on my ecclesiastical search for more pleasure, more poppers, and more tongue. Boo-hoo I'm horny, and I want to murder, if even just the tails and tales of cum in my nuts.

The night will usually start with Rudolfo pouring us Bulleit bourbon Manhattans before we head into Manhattan. We'd put on 8Tracks.com and listen to some collections of deep house, or tech house, or some other manner of hybrid-upon-hybrid genre, and when we're good and tipsy we'd walk through Astoria and catch the N train into the city, which usually sobers us up when we see all the fat, shirtless immigrant 13-year-olds eating McDonald's, when we got to thinking they probably have much better food in whatever country their parents came from, but now they're proudly American, meaning they don't really care what happens to themselves or others as long as it tastes and feels good to them.

That's America. Feeling good.

Eventually every level of the club will be packed; it will be dark, and one level will be bluish, the other reddish, the other blackish, and every so often they'll flash the lights bright for a moment, *juuuuuuust* so you can see a little better who you were thinking about fingering on the dance floor.

There's a massive disco ball, and sometimes—when the moment is particularly exciting—they'll lower it like an alien spaceship finally enlightening us to the truth, all of our hands in the air, "light, so many lights, and, and, and rainbows!!!!"

Eventually it will get so packed that you have to rub your dick on someone as you walk by them. Rudolfo and I will sometimes purposefully get separated for an hour or so, so we can find someone to make out with, or touch dicks with, covered in spit, dick heads out, saliva line from our lips to our dicks, or to just dance with—another body, live porn, there's something about skin.

And that usually amounts to us converging some point later in the night, mentioning "Some Asian guy with a butter face wanted to tug on my dick a little" or "The guy in the pink hat followed me around until we kissed in the bathroom, at the pee trough," holding each other's dicks and kissing and pissing while some cheered in the long line of dicks along the trough and some groaned to hurry up so they could have their turn to look and tug and lick and piss.

We'll converge, share our stories only we can share, and then approach two more, together—usually taller and more muscular than us—to play around with until the disco ball would fall again or the DJ with the horns and long eyelashes would change the tune that usually sounds like chains whipping cedar wood.

One time we found a black man with a tiny dick, who made up for his not being the stereotype we wanted by kissing so wonderfully, otherworldly those lips, taking us some place better than stereos or types—the two of us—one in each of his lovely arms, as if to say *this little calf is mine* and *this one, too* and we felt loved together and the smell of sweat dripping on cedar on rust sprayed into our bodies like glass in an accident that wasn't even our fault.

I think it was three, okay maybe five, hours we remained in one place, encased in sweat, underneath the massive disco ball hall, three tongues as one, squeezing pecs, pinching nipples, hand-to-cocks, to the right, to the right, to the right, like some kind of non-profit logo of oneness and partnership, or just a sluttier Oppenheimer Funds, I the cock-asian, Rudolfo the spicy spicky, nameless the black mixy-trysty, all of us silly rabbits, and Trix are for homos.

Our eyes were closed and all we saw was darkness spontaneously destroyed by the ammunition and collision of light arrows and bullets and bombs. We heard our breath increasing more, grain stored, until the silos of our being stuffed-up and about burst for the mob. We tickled each other's beards, hairs of different genetic consistencies, the whole range of fine to rough and tough.

We were going to take him home, our beautiful mixy-trixy, but he said he had done too many drugs to get fully hard tonight—or morning—and plus we were about to throw up on each other anyway from too much Bulleit and Maker's, and so Rudolfo and I took a cab home—to the diner first, on 21st Street—where we ordered eggs and chicken fingers and noodle soup, shirtless, in a booth.

And when we walked up the stairs to our floor we groaned about how we "really needed that" and it wasn't insulting because we both knew that man cannot live on one cock alone, and we didn't talk about how we said "I love you" in the back of the cab earlier as it cluck-cluck-cluck'ed and tic-toc-tic'ed over the Queensboro Bridge into the vast, vast frontier of the valley of the shadow of Queens, and how in-between the steel rafters we saw the whole city before us gray and getting yolkier, the egglight drawing us closer and silkier—even as we cheated on each other, *with* each other, relieved of our gilded guilt—the egglight drawing us home again with the sound of the cluck-cluck-goose and dick-toc-dick and for once we didn't think about our bank accounts.

10

The Transfiguration

What was it, what is this, aliens, spaceships, a warp through the pit to another world, a closet, a magic lamp, paper, was it paper that took me there or here?

Or was it fame—I saw that singer, his yellow teeth, his coiffed and gelled hair that looked so elegant on the screen but in person I saw all that effort to preen, and the surrounding scene it caused—all of us trying to get one glimpse of that yellow hair—or was it the blood, all this fucking blood?

Maybe it was the pain of feeling so helpless in front of such power I had no control over, the power of life and death—my legs no different than those damn desk stilts, both broken—and how everything was so loud, especially after Sunshine's brain burst from the fallen air conditioner on top of the blood from my legs that split from the neighbor's desk. Desks and stones can break my bones.

Poor Sunshine.

Although I'm on a simple sidewalk with power lines and leaves and dog tongues and the caustic Greek tongue above, it still shouldn't have been that loud.

Upon seeing blood, the bone splinters, my ripped skin that

moment, I was taken, ushered forth, ushered-in, fucked-in, snowed-in, I think, to an even louder place that I can only describe as a coffee shop, not unlike Coffeed in Long Island City, the one with the rooftop garden every rooftop should have, not too far from the candy canes—we should be legally bound to have one, every person on the planet, if you build a roof, it better come with a beautiful garden.

We must all hereby grow our own vegetables and ferment our own hot sauce on our green roof or you, Mr. Hah, you wasteful, bloated, angry, greedy, abusive prick, you will surely be hung as the future's new "nigger," or so I thought I had to think.

It felt that way because I felt everything at once and heard everything at once, yet simultaneously I felt certain feelings coming to the surface, stars being born, galaxies coagulating—the site of a famous singer, yellow teeth, yellow hair, sitting at a table there drinking orange juice and coffee and chewing on a crusty panini, and he's over there in a chair with his ugly friend, so ugly in her Newsies hat and hoops and makeup fit for a geisha addicted to meth, because she'll always feel the freedom to tell him when he's "just dreadful" when everyone else refrains, and he'll always feel the freedom to tell her she's "special and pretty and kind" when everyone else refrains, her wishing he'll write about her, finally his muse, a song, he wishing he could find someone like her, but prettier.

Babies are screaming.

There are too many lights, and music from the 1960s is blasting—"Son of a Preacher Man"—and there's a girl who stands up to dance to it and I'm disgusted. I'm disgusted by her, but really it's the auto mall behind her through the glass that reflects on her Vaseliney face, swirly auto-mall cheeks, and the other auto mall next to that auto mall, and still another auto mall next to those, all swirling on her cheeks as she dances. It's sick. It's colorful.

I feel the bitterness of a man behind a counter, what it's like to slave away with a smile.

A life spent behind a counter underneath fluorescent lights wrapped in rainbow clasps to make them more digestible to passersby—he sees right through that shit, through your politeness, all those witty quips you spoke simply to get him to hurry up and bake those paleo cookies and make that goddamn cold brew. I feel that poke.

I am in a place where someone, something, is rubbing my face with a green liquid with a pungent sharp stink, like the vinegar and bubbles of hot kimchi. I am a jar, and my odor is released. A cloth dabs my face, and I can't see except a sea of green and the faint shapes of towers in motion all sucked to a center, the spokes of a wheel within.

My skin is brass, and there are workers in scaffolding nearby, some near my shins, some near my dick, some near my eyes, all with cloths, the men of the cloth, and they all have that green stinky liquid with them that makes the brass bright, and they scrub, and scrub, and buff until my skin becomes shiny again. I do not know why I went, but I—simply—have become a building for a moment, a structure.

Was it shock that took me here?

Is this a new power unleashed on the world, a mutation of how we experience the world, becoming the very places we loathe when the structure of our own bodies is compromised? Perhaps I will never know, but simply go.

Free latte, cappuccino, espresso, coffee, et cetera with a purchase of a bag of beans.

A sack of beans. It feels like that, too—burlap, brass, and bought beans.

—

Although the structures of Park Avenue seem so solid on a daily basis, coming up from the subway every day and grabbing a juice from the Mexican ladies, "carrots, ginger, all greens, and beets, no celery, I hate celery," and then walking along the brass and the men cleaning brass every day to keep that shine, it's a mirage of sorts, something that seems solid, but takes work to appear so. It takes work to forget the buildings of a city will collapse; they will darken if we do not shine them and buff them every single day with our fingers and toes.

They are no different than burlap, dirty burlap full of packed roasted beans ready to be boiled under the light.

Perhaps we are all but residences of warm bricks of star explosions and fusions and bitter beet-red iron juice flushing within, fusing memories and forgetfulness, picking and choosing what we'll form, what we'll leave behind as a hazy gas, keep this, leave that.

—

As I watch the city beneath me, as the workers rub my skin to buff it up, look at my muscles, as the taxis smear by in yellow as long-stretched gummy bananas of stretched light, as pigeons shit and humans spit and pray before entering this building and that building, I know or want to know that nothing can harm me here.

My thoughts and feelings are the people inside me. No matter their evil or their good, the abused or the kind, they are people nonetheless. The elevators are moving, the numbers of the floors glow red, the brass is bright, and people, the people are yelling and shitting and crying and breathing and dying inside me now, unhappy inside me, plotting their next move inside me, to somewhere else, and I am happy to have them there.

I am not empty, but full.

I am not cold, but hot with a slowing heartbeat of heat.

There is no silence, but the smacking of lips, that gnashing of teeth, swords unsheathed, tampons plopped into buckets of water, warm balls dropped below the seat, and the heat of computers warming dusty carpets always in need of stretching, with their subsequent poofs of dust.

I am living, I am dying, a structure of things outside, a structure of things inside, threatened by both, enlivened by both, fused and separated by both, and this is it, and altogether I hear a distant piano and the light of it all is a kind of a moon and the smell is a field of beets and the blood and the tongues of dogs and the perpetual bitter sweetness of orange juice in a mason jar at a coffee shop of babies, fat girls, and ugly, efficient, glowing things that are covered by colorful, tight things in an attempt to make them pretty again, and again, and again...

As I lay dying on the sidewalk, as I lay living on the sidewalk of pit bulls, desks, and herpes, I'm beginning to see that architecture is anatomy is cloth is brass is dirty is weak, and orange juice is blood is beets is people is shit is breath is feeling is better than nothing because even nothing has a companion, things that matter and antimatter.

Most everything seems to be a residence made warmer by the fusion of thoughts, some happily trapped, most angrily wanting to flee, and the ability to villainize is becoming much harder now, when I see how similar I am to the people, and even the places, the souls of which I had previously grown to hate.

11

The Abyss

My first day, I would quickly learn, was a day that Mr. Hah graced the office with his presence; they were particular days, unmistakable. I would quickly learn of a scintillating aura, a palpable aura, a foreboding flora, present only when he roamed over the Oriental carpet, each foot an imperial ship slinking across the water looking for gold, for plankton, for some new culture to rape.

Miss Allison wore her rouge on these days, but I'm quite sure she simply took a lipstick from her nightstand, the same lipstick that had been there when her mother the model, the librarian, the cellist—well-rounded that one—had lived there with her husband, the man who killed Miss Allison's real father, the only way he could become king of the largest dry-cleaning chain in the Northeast.

Times were different then; women shamelessly floated over the seas of uncertainty to men who could most certainly kill the most, make money the most, provide, no matter what the cost, even love, the most.

Miss Allison's mother chose one of these alphas, and on the day she did she sat down in front of her vanity and drew a red line on the bulb of her left cheek, the bulb of her right, the boob of her right, the boob of her left, and one from her hairline, all the way to her nose, dividing her life as she knew it in two. Sitting there, Miss Allison saw through the brass keyhole, not a mother anymore who would giggle in inappropriate settings about Peter Pan and talk loudly of his green tights and sipping on bubbly things, but a ruthless scepter, a floating needle who would pierce any fabric she wished to weave together a selfish quilt of opportunity and power. She saw this thing, this tilting needle in front of a mirror rub its face violently, smearing the red—shocking—like finding an Easter egg in the summer, now rotten, and dying that putrid egg in blood.

Continuing this family tradition, Miss Allison's face was a lobster claw that first day, a Red Delicious peel, the nose of a lewd Eskimo always rubbing into things she shouldn't be rubbing into, and it became obvious that this was her position, to rub her nose into your shit for rubbing's sake, growing redder and redder, and then rubbing some more.

My first day in the pit I was creating an ad using InDesign, something I had taught myself in about an hour, the hour after I told them I knew exactly how to use it, and as I would quickly learn would always be the case, I wasn't updating the ad as quickly as Mr. Hah wanted, my speed not allowing him to save his face, a face which was stuck in, "yesterday. I wanted this yesterday. Where's the update?!" he screamed at me.

I wasn't working here yesterday, I reminded him. This is my first day.

"Why are you wasting my time?!"

He began gritting his teeth there in his office, his best friend, a painted Napoleon, looking at us, and at Miss Allison outside of the office hovering as she did, looking through the peephole of every single interaction and reaction, poking, rubbing, shivering, twitching in fear.

"MADELINE!!" he screamed and threw a binder at me; the logo on it blurred as it twirled through the air, missed my face, and knocked over a black-and-white picture of the Pope next to another picture of John F. Kennedy. The glass shards of the frame kept together like the windshield of a car after hitting a cat thrown out the window overlooking a freeway.

—

All cats should be living in houses overlooking freeways, and all cats should be thrown out windows by kids with Down syndrome in a temper tantrum—I think those kids have a gift, they can see the truth faster than the rest of us—which is why I know that all cats should die, because of that one time a Downsy threw a cat out the window back in 1989, when our family was on the way to the beach. The cat hit the car in front of us, a Volkswagen Beetle, which didn't stand a chance against that fur bomb, flipping it in front of us, killing the family inside, and killing our trip to the beach that year, as we saw the family of four pulled from the wreckage, cracked, it seemed, cracked and red and spicy like Old Bay seasoning sprinkled into the eyes of summer. I didn't blame that kid though, the Downsy; I understood then that all cats are evil, and Downsy kids should be revered and respected as gods, or at least given the same privileges.

—

Oddly enough, so did Mr. Hah, which is why he, I later found out, donated millions to charity for them. As the binder swirled through the air, I made out the logo, The International Down Syndrome Foundation. Its blue letters combined together, the blue of them spinning so fast into a sphere; he had the power to create racquetballs out of words, from "Board Notes" binders for charity, to racquetballs, to killing the Pope like cats kill families on the roads to what was supposed to be a great summer with my brother, but we turned around.

"MADELINE!!"—Madeline Majenta Allison was her full name, a title she let only Mr. Hah utter, a title that seemed to make her shudder in both fear and orgasmic elation, her Kix ball popping, "MADELINE MAJENTA ALLISON!!! GET IN HERE NOW!!"

She bowed before him like a Korean department-store worker, eyes closed, gentle, her back arched like a lobster's, her hands tight and wrapped with invisible rubber bands, "Yeeeeessssssssssssssssss, Jung?" (his first name).

"What the fuck do you think? I NEED THIS GLASS CLEANED UP—"

She interrupted him, "Oh my, I'm so sorry—"

Confused, I interrupted her, Miss Allison, it's not your fault.

Napoleon observed, JFK observed, and the Pope slept covered in glass.

Just then a window washer hung on the building glass right outside the office where we were standing; the window washer interrupted with his squeegee sucks and sweeps and sudsy smears, and he watched us like a water bug watches fish below him, delicately resting and bending the glassiness supporting him.

The gravity of this audience combined and fused another racquetball into a fireball, all directed at Miss Allison, in a highly organized eruption, "One. CLEAN UP THE GLASS," teeth grinding.

"Two. WHERE IS MY AD? Three. WHO IS THIS," pointing at me, "AND WHY WASN'T HE BROUGHT IN YESTERDAY

WHEN I NEEDED MY AD?," his face now rhubarb-pie-mooshy-red.

"Four. I NEED A NEW FOLDER THAT ISN'T COVERED IN GLASS," squinting, "with tabs this time like I asked the first time. And five. CLEAN UP THE GLASS. Six. OUT OF THE OFFICE!!!!"

The rubber bands snapped and Miss Allison's fingers were released and she began flailing them about, "Right, yes, yes, yes, right, and yes to 1, 2, 3, 4, 5, and 6, I got it, yes, YES."

We both awkwardly backed up and slinked toward the pit of the office, when he screamed again, "SEVEN!!!!!"

We ran back and stood at attention.

He began banging on the window where the glass cleaner was listening to his headphones of something that seemed to match the coolness of the partly sunny day outside, something calm, something NPR-crisp. From the liberal bangs, the man almost fell off the window-cleaner ledge.

"WHY, IS, THERE, A, WINDOW, CLEANER, MAN, HERE, NOW, WHILE, I'M, WORKING?" he asked, grinding his teeth. He really liked to grind his teeth.

"Right, yes, number 7, got it." She began writing this—#7—on a Post-it that magically appeared into her hand, as if the mixture of her fear and admiration had somehow willed it there.

"EIGHT. Clean, up, the, glass."

Dumbfounded, I slothed over to my desk and continued the update to the ad; I heard Miss Allison picking up the glass with her fingers, then sweeping glass with her fingers, collecting the shards into a bloody glass pile within the Down syndrome binder. The window washer cautiously squeegeed now, headphones off so he could listen to us, far more interesting than *This American Life.*

And somehow Mr. Hah had teleported behind me in the pit, and our particles exchanged energy, touching me but not touching me, a very, very, very thin layer of magnetism separated us, but he might as well have been licking the hair on the back of my head when he whispered, grinding his teeth once more, calmly, creepily, crawlingly whispering, "Do I make you nervous standing, right, here, behind you?"

Uhhh, a little sir, yes, I said. But it's more like *uncomfortable* maybe?

Grinding, "Be. Decisive.

Learn.

From.

Me.

Beeeeeeeeeeeeeeeeee DECISIVE."

Oh okay, not *maybe* then, just *definitely very uncomfortable,* yes. 0% nervous. 100% uncomfortable.

"Good," still whispering.

Then he held onto the back of my chair and leaned over my head, looking at me in the eyes, our noses almost touching, "And nine, number 9, get me that goddamn ad," teeth popping, "yeeeessssss—teeeeeer—daaay."

Sure thing. Coming riiiiiiiiight up. 100%.

It was then that I tasted his breath in my mouth, the taste of moldy mint leaves and old-gold gilded fillings filled with kimchi, and then his long, stretched neck slunk away and went back to the glass, and everything was wet with something, yet dusty and quite nasty.

12

This Is It

This is it.

How many, billions of us, have roamed this earth? One foot on some glossy tile list of "to-dos" and the other on some dirty tile list of "completed," all those wisdoms that you keep forgetting anyway, with your ballsac dangling above that water in the swirling mysterious toilet of the present.

Sometimes you look down and you can see a reflection, your balls, your cock, your tainted love list of all those things you believe you're destined to love—because how comfortable, really, is destiny?

That thought, that although we're all sitting on this swirling shit-tornado of digestion, repression, expression, you're seated somewhere, that exact place you're supposed to be sitting—what a comforting thought, which helps you ignore the crack in the stall walls and all those eyes and all that stink engulfing you and Gulf War-ing you.

How many, billions of us, have thought that art is more important than this, than your breath right now, than that glossy reflection of your balls, water bugs delicately floating on the water?

This book—has it actually become a "book"?—are you actually reading this? Has someone actually found me?

And that book, this look and that, as if mimicry were better than the original, as if parrots spoke more clearly than their captors giggling outside their cages, as if anywhere could be better than right here, as if all those *over theres* are more worthy than all these *right heres*, when right here is what actually readies you for another there, yet you still think you have some to spare.

How many of us have said *that* again and again, in a trillion different ways? This is just one more added to the pile of water bugs, whose legs have lost their life and rigidity, whose frail bodies have sunk below to somewhere else, as if any of us really know where that is, as if we ever will, from the left of our will, to the right of this.

Maybe Jesus will come back and show us. Maybe we'll be visited by death and all her friends and our friends. Maybe these walls will talk. Maybe Manhattan will be a project again, but this time to finally figure out how to build the biggest bomb of all, how to make sure every single human that roams this earth knows that this, right here, is it, and that this, right now, right here, can get burned, cut, flushed, sucked, and swirled when we least expect it, no matter how polished your toenails are, and what tile or mile you think you're on, how to once and for all—never forget —that your culture is so fucking stupid (partly because you so adamantly think it isn't), that your flag won't let you last forever, nor will your dick, or your super-super-super-clean pussy, or your art, that art you're supposedly destined to share, or your family you hug, or your li'l Dandelion, your pug, and your empty grocery cart, or your benefit card you use to slice that number pad like an ever-trembling fault line, yours alone, to buy something sweet and something tart, how vegetables would have been better in your cart, or how much you don't fart in front of your fuck-buddy, the apparent nucleus of your self-worth, because that wouldn't be right, until a new millennium comes, and another, and another, until we will finally see no difference between burning bread and our body, so that we can finally, with things so clearly projected outward as fast as light, be here, our life, this.

This is it, a Manhattan of a project like that would be wonderful. Even so, life seems to be a toilet of surprises, especially now, sprinkled with some kind of glitter, flushing, sinking, exploding, again and again.

—

Miss Allison would often close the door of the "break room," if you can call it that. Break room implies some level of comfort. This, though, is basically a Zephyrhills water jug, a Keurig coffee maker—the worst coffee machine ever made, with the three choices (small, medium, large) that all amount to the same result: *depressing*. And a plastic table with plastic chairs, which look stolen from a church gathering for the purposes of taking communion after baptizing a homeless man—tasteless unleavened bread on stilts—resulting in the same.

Miss Allison's door is closest to this break room, partly so she could spy on all those that would come in late (and subsequently report it to Mr. Hah), and partly so she could "manage" the roaches.

In her mind, roaches, the size of hamsters, live in spider webs and they all have spider webs, indestructible permanent spider webs; they're loyal, too. Once they find where they want to nest, they'll never leave, not unlike her choice to stay at HH&H all these years, thinking she's some kind of hybrid creature that needs little blood or pulp to survive, yet waits, waits, waits, observes, spies, and pisses in her nest of cedar chips, Fritos, accounting papers, tuna sandwiches, and a matrix of line after line of unused bubble paper, just in case he needs to send something.

"Could you keep the door shut to the break room?" she said to me, on another day. Because she asked so nervously, I asked if there was any particular reason.

She began shaking. Her breath picked up and whooshed like a Dyson hand dryer and it stayed that way for a good thirty minutes, blowing all the moisture off my face. I just watched the wind as it flung water droplets off my hands, too. She proceeded to repetitively whoosh at me, "Sanchez is back. Dirty, dirty Sanchez. He's back. He's so dirty and he'll always be dirty, such a dirty dirty little Sanchez. He's back. He's so back. He's come back. Dirty Sanchez is back. I know I see a dirty Sanchez..."

After her speech, I asked, "Excuse me? Did you just...I think you just said *dirty Sanchez*, errrrrrr?"

"Yes, yes, yes, he's so dirty, Sanchez the Roach. He's back for the summer."

"Oh, is he now? Would you like me to kill Mr. Dirty Sanchez the Roach?"

Her Dyson breath, if you can believe it, hissed even louder, less Dyson, more Boeing Dreamliner jet engine now,

"WWwwwwwwwwwwwAIIIIIIIIIIIIIIIIIIIIIIT!!!!!!!"

Her legs whisked so quickly back to her office that if one could hold her by the hair and dip her into a cauldron of eggs, an omelet would have been beaten and ready to cook for a giant. I browsed around and saw nothing. No sign of Sanchez.

After knocking on her door, opening it, and finding her

hiding behind her desk crouched down like a hidden dragon fearful of a tiger-spider holding her eight paws over the big red buttons for emergency nukes, I told her, comforted her rather: Miss Allison, I think he's gone. He was probably just a quick night-crawler, curious, and now he's back into some pipe somewhere exploring the city like all the other roaches, far from here.

"Ahhhhhhhhhhhhhhhhhhhhhhhhhhhhhhhh!!!!! Don't say that. HE'S HERE FOR THE SUMMER. PLEASE, PLEASE, PLEASE, don't open that door until we find dirty dirty Sanchez and murder him. I WANT HIM DEAD THIS YEAR. I want death to come. This is it, no more, I want him dead. I don't want to see another dirty Sanchez again."

13

Sandy

I go and become *elsewhere*, yet here, over there, yet right now, and right here without fear, I think, and not just buildings; each time it has been peculiar, sometimes colorful, sometimes dreary, sometimes a drifting, others a warping, a tunnel, a rabbit, hole, an eyehole, dreamy.

Don't you worry your pretty little hole now; I will tell you about another.

—

As the deafening and deadening slobber drops of Sunshine spray across my face, as the screams of Greek and Polish—I'll tell you about that later, too—become muffled, as the wind picks up a bloody seed or two, as I see the desk fall and splinter, fall and splinter, fall and splinter, spring and winter, my bones cracked and healed on repeat, all of it moving in slow-mo, in time-lapse, in video rewind, and combined to a pinwheel of bourbon dripping on rusty chain-linked fences, of sidewalk squares shifting upward, downward, as piano keys, yet with a cold calm, of a tickling lip balm, an alleyway after a snow of hot chili peppers and mica crumbles and bison horns, I am now, what I am now, I am now convinced there is something to all this sucking from one world and time to the next. Something like *Alice in the Quantum Lola-Leap Malkovich Inception-Lighthouse*—yes, that's it—but whoever or whatever was, is, will be in charge—me? THE GOT DAYM TERRORISTS!?—of my gurney-journey must have had schizophrenia or an erratic sense of humor because wherever I was sucked in, warped out, whisked away was hardly ever the same.

It really must suck to be you.

Something is picking up the sand particles of myself, squeezing them in their hand as some crumble between their fingers and balance on a mysteriously bending floor, and the bulk of them are thrown wherever that something deems my porpoise-purpose—or lack thereof—yet some of them are left, yet some of them almost grow forward and progress, these crumbs, a return for you, for me, a Little Red Cockinghood.

The sight or thought of blood would do it perhaps, the memory of the grinding and gnashing of teeth, the smell of coffee and beans, the look of an Australian model with a mustache roaming the cobblestones of the Meatpacking District for the entrance to the High Line, his perfect hair, his perfect, magazine-paper skin—the feeling of being in the presence of perfection—and of course the feeling, the echoes, of being in the presence of the seemingly cursed.

—

Sandy worked in the cubicles immediately outside the pit of the office, around the yolk, around the abyss. She was a pitter too like me, although not technically. As she sat at a desk somewhat between the two worlds, she seemed to get dumped on the most, by us, by them, or so it seemed she wanted to feel that way.

While Miss Allison was the slave of Mr. Hah, Sandy was the

martyr, reluctantly solving problems that weren't hers to solve, yet also remaining hyper-aware of the sacrifice she was making, while making hyper-damn-sure we all knew it every single long sigh of the day, a sigh for refilling the stapler, a sigh for reminding someone they still had broccoli in the fridge, a sigh for her husband, the shit-less invalid, and a sigh for her daughter, the genius.

Each month she scheduled new highlights. Her teeth were veneers, after the dentists had given up trying to fix all that genetic crookedness.

She'd talk of dieting, "I'm on the SOUP DIET. This week is barley and chicken." Her drawers were full of extra shoes and bottles of maple syrup and Band-Aids. She's one of these office women who walk up to you and quietly tells you stories about their family as if they were secrets, as if you wanted to hear, as if I needed to know that—leaning in, "My husband had most of his intestines removed and now he has to shit in a bag."

Or, as I'm typing, slowly hovering her Samsung Galaxy two inches from my eyes, and flipping the pictures to the right with her short fake nails, each with a fake diamond and a harsh white line she'd call "Fwench style," hearing that tap of the plastic nail on the Galaxy, "Here's my daughter when she graduated pre-school. Here's Lilly at her new school; it's a school for the gifted. Do you know what her score was?"

No. I don't. What was it? What kind of score are we talking about here?

"It was ____ (insert some number that means absolutely fucking nothing to me)."

And then she'd wait for my reaction, which was an obligatory, Oh, well, that seems pretty high right? That's really graaaaaaaayt, Sandy.

"It was the highest in the country."

Holy shit. Really happy for you.

Then she'd laugh the highest pitched laugh possible, a laugh that kept going like the incessant bark of a neighborhood dog tied in an alleyway three blocks over and you call 311 for a noise complaint and you feel proud of yourself for complaining without confrontation but saddened that these dumb fucks won't get a letter from the city until 10 days later, and that bark, that laugh, would continue to penetrate through brick. It was a laugh that was not only faker than her Fwench bejeweled nails; it was layered with pain, rumbles of it from deep within below the fur and bad canned-food-dog-breath, to thoughts of missing intestines, to thoughts of Lilly's ambiguous future—one she hoped would not include also working at an insurance company for 15 years, doing everyone else's work, happily droning and drooling, "Yaaaaaaaaaaaaas, I'll do it, Yaaaaaaaas, Hah-Hah, Yaaaas," for 15 years, for 80 hours a week, to support her sleeping, regularly seizing husband despite the medication, and all the testing for her daughter despite it being so clearly unnecessary, confirming over and over again that she was, in fact, analogous with anomalous.

In the break room, a dirty Sanchez nowhere in sight, we'd unfortunately sip on some Keurig coffee poop-pods together, with flavors like Blueberry Hazelnut Breakfast Delight, and in between the conversations about herself and all her sacrifices, she'd make sure to let me know it was *she* who bought the almond milk, it was *she* who bought the honey—she alone. She'd also make sure to walk around the office—or send an All Staff email—reminding everyone to "clean up the fridge if you have anything stinky left behind," and that it was *she* who cleaned out the microwave, even though it wasn't in her "job description," and every time I'd hear another hyphen in her long list of duties and *she*-acrifices, I'd want more than anything to tell her to *she-she-she*-ut the fuck up.

She'd walk up to you—leaning in—as if she was telling you another family secret, smiling, eyes rolling back in her head past her veneers and under her bright awkward-blonde highlights, "Juuuuuuust letting you know, I'll be cleaning out the fridge today after work, so if you've got anything in there, it'll uhhhhh, it'll all be gone," and then she'd laugh, mumbling something else about her daughter or her useless husband, and most would just silently stare at her.

In the break room, sipping blueberry poo, she'd tell me stories of when Lilly was born, and how *that* was difficult for her, too; but she continued to hold her family together, just barely.

"A few days after Lilly was born, Timothy went out from Bellevue hospital to get us some food for us, because we were supposed to head home that day. Supposed to, at least. I could hardly walk—you know—just giving birth an' all. He was gone for twenty minutes, forty minutes, an hour went by, I mean, what was I gonna do, I was reaaaally worried. And so, in a wheelchair I, I, I, I, alone, me—with Lilly as an infant in my arms—strolled myself outside, in the cold, and it was then that I got a call from the paramedics. Timothy had begun seizing in front of a diner, and he cracked open his skull from the fall."

Oh.

My.

"Yeah, it hasn't been easy. My life has been on *hoad* really," *hold* she meant to say, but she never pronounced the L in the word, and just that one, that, one, word, perhaps from saying "my life has been on hold" so much over the years that the L had been withered down to a tiny little "a"-corn, wave after wave of self-pity, slosh after slosh of chewing on her own left titty, with her mouth open of course, smacking her lips like that tit was a canned noodle, until a *hold* became a *hoad*, a little sad fat toad tossed about in the bitter, tumultuous, foggy-bottom salt waters of Park Avenue.

"And he's had them often since then, the seizures, after the intestine surgery too. So basically I've had to take care of two infants. That also put my life on hoad, ya know."

One infant was a deteriorating man, genetically fucked, and the other was a growing infant, genetically gifted. And there she was, Sandy, in the center of the two, feeding both of them with her arms typing like long, wiggly, skinny-fingered breasts. Undoubtedly she viewed Heller, Heller, and Hah as another one of her babies, and with her third arm and breast and eye, she was insistent on mothering us, scolding us, yet always being there for us, even if we didn't appreciate all her sacrifices, not even in the very least.

—

One day I met Sandy's daughter Lilly and I met her husband Timothy, too, a grown man with exorbitant amounts of Sun-In highlights in his hair during winter. It was near Christmas, and they were going to go to the tree. Tim, with his faux-lights, was perhaps attempting to match his wife's more expensive streaks and panty stains, or maybe it was just Sandy's instruction, and at home people actually listened to her.

The little girl was colorful, sporting hundreds of stickers and pipe cleaners and barrettes, but arranged in beautiful geometric shapes and patterns she had created herself. Most things she did and said were mysterious, and Sandy and Timothy let her express herself without restraint in the name of being progressive, many thought, which in reality was just apathy and complete confusion in the name of being dirty Bronx poor—thusly, the exact kind of people who shouldn't be breeding a fused copy of themselves, I mean, who would want to copy not being able to afford a kid and then giving up on most everything extraordinary about life in order to have that kid, but then, they well, they just did, and look what happened. She looked like a Care Bear with shoulder length Sia-blonde hair, and everyone knew she had powers, yet everyone kept their mouths shut. That's what you do if you want to keep anything, away from you too.

It was near 5 p.m., and Sandy and Timothy were talking to Miss Allison about going to Rockefeller Center. Miss Allison moaned, "Oh geeeee-whiiiiizzzzz I haven't been there in ages; I just can't stand the crowds, you know. BE CAREFUL, especially of anyone with bags or boxes. As they say, IF YOU SEE SOMETHING, SAY SOMETHING, I always say, they say," which during Christmas would be a little difficult, they said.

Lilly ran away and ran around the office, and there was a moment when I realized she was standing right behind me. I could feel her there, an orb of energy.

"What's YOUR name?" she asked.

She held up a wand, a kind of Christmas wand with red lights flashing, and she waved it around and I saw fire as my eyes burned. I saw fire, sparklers on a beach on the Fourth of July, and paths of smoke from all the sparks and swirls then reflected on flopping fish scales on the flopping beached fish from a Floridian hurricane.

—

I see the smoke of factories, the smoke of China, of slaves and martyrs being burned alive; I smell India and it's flooded with the toxic waters of the Ganga, with feces and the crumbs of dead bodies. Maybe it will take some time before I make it or break it to her barrette in her hair, and from there, I know I will go home with them to see what haunts them, maybe what haunts everyone, and how they continue to ignore it.

But first, I think shall roam the spicy streets of Varanasi, amongst the snakes, sitars, and so many babies without real mothers.

14

The Barrette

In India, a sage of sorts strokes my palm and tells me who I am.

The man has buckteeth, skin the color of Reese's peanut butter, and a turban the color of Sunkist—that glossy orange aluminum, sweat condensation drenched and dripping down the sides of his face to the cans of his hands. He was sleeping on a cow next to the roaring Ganga and he tripped me with his foot as I roamed by. He begins massaging my back, my shoulder, my bicep, my elbow, my wrist, and then my hand. Smiling, he keeps on looking at me right in the eyes and massages my hand with the oils of his Sunkisty forehead. I let him, because he makes the little hairs on the back of my neck tingle. I let him massage my hand, look into my eyes, as beads of sweat drip off his black mustache that looks like the chocolate above the globs of peanut butter, next to all that warm chai Ganga water.

"I know who you are," he says.

Oh yeah? And what is that?

As skeptical as I am, knowing he must encounter many of us who are out of place and out of time, lurking like tree branches floating down rivers, mistaken for crocodiles, he lures us in with his bright orange swaddling hat, his lazy cow, his lazy eyes, and the fact that most of us think we aren't touched enough.

"You are a bottle of glass, and you are rolling, from one thing to the next. You are not grounded, but you are many things to many people. You roll and then touch. You roll and then you're kicked. You'll roll and then you'll be shattered."

Okay, I say.

—

I remember the many times I'd be sitting on the subway on the way home from work; my favorite thing would be to watch all the trash, human and otherwise. One day there was a Snapple bottle, empty. And from one end of the car to where I was at the other end, it slowly rolled through the fashion show of covered toes. As the subway picked up speed the bottle slowed down and slowly touched my shoe. The subway changed speeds again and it slowly crept away, and then back again it softly touched my shoe. I remember that bottle making me smile; I looked around to see if anyone had seen the bottle flirting with me and tickling me as it was. No one saw, which made me enjoy the moment even more, because it was all mine, the day a bottle came to say hello.

Speeds changed again, and it jolted this time like someone had thrown it in anger at someone else's shoe; the bottle popped a guy in the ankle, and his ankle began bleeding. He was angry the day some trash rolled quickly down the car and split his ankle open. He angrily kicked it away as he held onto his ankle in pain.

On another mission, the bottle found the doorway, and as if stuck in a whirlpool of the East River, the Snapple bottle couldn't leave from the area, slamming against the doorway, a fly knowing an escape is near but not quite understanding what lay opaquely before it, even though it's so clear to everyone else, slamming its head against the doorway again and again.

Within those few minutes, I realized how difficult it was to explain anything really, as one thing—this bottle, an empty glass Snapple bottle, slightly sticky—could mean so many things, could affect so many things, within minutes. All at once it was my lover, teasing me, taunting me, with its surprise and comfort, as if saying with its heart-shaped candy rolls, "Would you be mine?" and next became an attacker, ruthless, shamelessly bloodying the enemy as fast as it could, to a complete moronic fly with no alibi, unable to simply escape a silly subway car, beating its dumb head against the wall.

If a Snapple bottle could be so many things at once, an abandoned piece of trash, what about me, a much more complex organism on perhaps an infinite amount of missions becoming an infinite number of things to so many other things, yet I still remain that bottle of glass?

—

I am crying by the Ganga, the toxic, toxic Ganga, the smell and color of chai, filled with silt spices from the roof of the world, feces from the bottoms of our curry butts, particles of burnt bodies and incense and flowers and monkey brains and stains.

—

As Lilly's barrette I can see a tea party.

Sandy and Timothy are going to have some friends over. I see a tuft of blonde hair. Sandy had bought some scones from Whole Foods, but she doesn't quite get the idea of allowing a tea party to be dainty. A stick of butter and cold cuts are piled in the center, a wreath of meats and cheeses and breads. And the tea isn't looseleaf; it's just Lipton, in packets. Lilly is playing with her own neon-pink tea set, so she and her friends could feel a part of the adult party, the more refined adult tea party in a shambled Bronx apartment.

Timothy is screaming. Sandy is screaming. And Lilly has remained calm, asking, "Are they back; are the Heffalumps and Woozles back?"

That was how Sandy explained the poltergeist to Lilly, that sometimes in real life, just like in Winnie the Pooh, angry things, attackers, will suddenly befall your home when all was calm before. They'll just pop, roll, or float into your life, and you'll have to "just keep adding honey to your tea and be quiet," sipping your tea, as a "mommy's good, good, good girl!!" because one day the ghosts will be gone and everyone will forget they were even here, but "they'll never forget when you were a bad, bad, bad girl."

Like in that moment, the Heffalumps only show up when Timothy is on the toilet. He's scratched by them—his back—and Sandy is running to his rescue as she always does, holding the lit sage, the crucifix, the statue of Hanuman—the monkey god—and the confetti, Lilly's addition and addiction.

She insists, "Mommy, I bet you the Heffalumps and Woozles don't like confetti; it's too colorful for them. It's blinding since they're already so colorful, it's too-much-ly and so morbidly satisfying for them! Daddy's scratches are always deep and wide and black, so dark. You have to show them color to shoe them away again. It's like Pooh's honey, but if Pooh were honey-boarded by Piglet, see? You and daddy are the pigs. Once they see enough they'll go away again. Be a little piggy, Mommy! You're a pig, Mommy!"

Sandy, too confused to be hurt, too apathetic to be nervous, seems willing to try anything really, especially since the other guests will be here any minute.

15

Pale Peach Silk Satin and Faille

Pale peach silk satin and faille.

Pale peach silk satin and faille.

Pale peach silk satin and faille. I hear these words over and over again.

I once heard them at the Met museum, at a show for Charles James, and all his dresses. Rudolfo and I walked into the room, all black, with quotes of this man in gold on mirrors. Many of his best dresses were displayed, with dim lights on them, and next to the dresses were robots and accompanying screens, which together helped all who passed by dissect each dress so that we could see into the mind of this man, all the layers, all the stitching, all the thought that went into a dress that would strike, as one thought, when complete—stunning.

This display at the Met reminded all who passed through the robots and fabric of the intricacies involved in gowns such as these. Within the description of one dress were those words, *pale peach silk satin and faille.*

They stuck with me at the time, the way they rolled off my tongue, yet how complete the phrase sounded. It was a sunset inside my mouth and it burned sweet, yet I felt a rough fuzz of some kind of sadness, with a smoothness, an ocean salty smoothness—the stuff of shells worn down, fish worn down to dead to alive to dead again, the crashes of waves, the ruffles of silk. When I said those words I felt as though I knew him, this designer now dust, sandy bones; I felt as though I knew everyone with those words, that the black room was surrounded by all words and that all words were made of melting gold, impressionable with brittle teeth, ephemeral, malleable, yet strong and bright.

All words are a display really, gold etched onto a mirror of something else, a reflection of work, of intricacy, of robots, and explanations, of so many people, lungs and intestines, or lack thereof, lips moving, or lipless listless sunsets breathing, and gone again, for more to come through again, a hole in the sky, a home.

One of the golden quotes on the mirrored wall:

A great designer does not seek acceptance. He challenges popularity, and by the force of his convictions renders popular in the end what the public hates at first sight.

Whatever substance, whatever fruity flesh of those words were, I thought, is the essence of those other words, *pale peach satin and faille*, that when I utter them it means *that*, that we are fickle, that the gold of words is rearranged and displayed differently, sometimes insidiously, that more gold is found and poured each year, that some of it is lost somewhere in the process, that pale peach satin and faille could have meant nothing to this man, or what it means to me now, to look at the sun until your eyes burn, and tears drip down your face from the flesh cooking, that you can be the only one on the beach, but you won't be alone, for you're no different than sand, organisms cover you and flow through you, that a million blocks of golden words are within you and you bite them every day, changing them, making them yours, giving them new meanings with more of your teeth marks.

Rudolfo and I spent most days at the Met roaming through the Greek god wings. Thankfully enough, we've been forever honest about our mutually inclusive problem—our exponentially increasing carnivorous lust that would draw us to fuck statues if we could, standing there underneath the lights, carved by uglier men out of jealousy and love and hate and worship.

We usually drink prosecco and make fun of all the rich Asian ladies who always seem to roam that particular wing too, how we are not too different from them, those Asian ladies, craving bigger and bigger men, sitting down on the benches to gaze in a sex haze, wishing the bench was a horse to take herself to where this man slept in her dreams, and how she'd never forget this wing, the wing of men, on her trip to America and how later that night she'd find one under the Queensboro Bridge and how he'd give her stone crabs for her trip back to Tokyo, and how she didn't get it all taken care of for quite some time because she wanted to remember that itch as long as possible, before she'd have to forget it again as she sadly nuked her noodles and took a shit with the door open so she could watch her kinky game show, with sushi rotting on the kitchen counter, and a robot puppy barking softer and softer, no batteries for the dead puppy because they all went to her dildo, alive, and the coffee is electric.

This is what we hope would happen at least. We'd roam like that, let our minds wander, and let the bubbles wonder where they were in our mouths. I fear what would have been if we hadn't been honest like that. Rudolfo was my first boyfriend, and as often happens when men are awakened to their lust for other men, it's usually best to go on a rampage. I chose otherwise, to stick with him, yet stick with words to stick and state just how often I wanted to fuck and rape, and murder the air with the contents of my nut sac, and who, and how, which, as expected, was endlessly, even Greek statues, and in front of everything. I wanted them all.

Pale peach silk satin and faille.

Say it.

Say it again.

Do you love it the way I love it?

I love that "faille" is actually a word, that there's a word that sounds like fail, but could be the ingredient for such a dainty, glorious, yet successful thing one could use to adorn their body. It's as if genocide were spelled jhenocyd and it's what makes ice cream taste so good.

Yes, I'll take the vanilla dipped in jhenocyd.

And no, I don't care that it's dripping into my sushi-stuffed pussy.

16

Brooklyn Baby

It was a morning like your morning when I woke up and looked to my right and Rudolfo wasn't there.

His earplugs were sleazily left in the bed, which was anomalous too, because he always places them so snugly in his porcelain cup with the lid—the one we got in Williamsburg, Brooklyn at the antique store for three dollars and fifty cents when everything else there was fifty dollars and three cents—right next to the little statue of Jesus with the broken arm and the broken legs, broken with time, glue disintegrated.

Outside in the empty lot, rare in New York, empty lots, there's a larger Jesus with a hole in his head, encased in glass and filled with fake flowers. There's a lock to the glass door, perhaps the encasement occurred after someone shot Jesus in the head with a BB gun, *ya just poked Jesus's eye out with that*—well, and half his brain.

Pale peach silk satin and faille.

Pale peach silk satin and fail.

On top of the glass box is another statue of Mary, much smaller in scale, and she's leaning to one side so she kinda looks like Jesus's creepy Kentucky Derby hat. And surrounding them aren't horse tracks but rat and cat tracks in a small square lot that *could be* a great garden, but is overrun with the wilds and weeds and whimsy of neglect. At times we'll look out the window and Oracula the Greek's retarded-or-something brother will be standing there in the thicket, looking at Jesus, placing his bets on who will win and who will fail, and when you open the window everything smells like honeysuckles.

His earplugs were there on the pillow though resting there like sluts. I walked into the bathroom—our pink bathroom—pink tile, pink ceiling, pink toilet, pink faucets, which we left pink except for the fern we hung from the skylight to give it a little pop even though it always reminded me of a hairy green chia-head lynched and surrounded by cotton candy, chuh, chuh, chuh, chia, DEAD head.

Thomas, the previous tenant, now a Texan and getting straighter, must have thought it soothing, all this pink in the stink.

That morning though, Rudolfo's body was wrapped around the toilet like a sticker-label, his face stuck to the glassy-glossy toilet rim, his chest stuck, his knees stuck, and he was shaking, eyes rolled back into his head, eyes white like adhesive on the label, and his face said abysmal.

I feared there were two dead-heads there and the coffee he'd been brewing screamed as loud as I did, hissing and steaming, rattling and bubbling on a hot burner.

I twiddle-toed everywhere as if the floor tiles were burning too, and my hot and heavy lungs puffed my breath into clouds, slowly floating to the skylight, forming condensation droplets that fell down to the fern, caught some fern seeds, fell more, and intertwined with my tears that dripped onto his blank face. He convulsed there, and I held him there.

He was cold; I was hot, until the ambulance came, drove us past Jesus with that bullet in his head, past the steam towers, over the Queensboro Bridge where we would later float over so lewdly, gray, and relieved at dawn drunk, but this time the city just looked sharp and the water all wrong, slippery and loose and dirty and skimpy, a man-thong wrapped around the city hardly keeping anything or anyone contained.

Sometime later he was diagnosed with a brain tumor that they first thought was a benign cyst from birds.

The last time he visited his family in Brazil, he went to his father's farm full of birds and other creatures; so they thought that that could have been it, which was a relief at first if you can call it that, a bulbous alien bird egg growing in your brain. But no, after further testing, as if to confirm again and again that he was a genius too and as a silly mother I couldn't believe it, it was just a tumor, a plain bad brain tumor, nothing special. They drilled into his brain, and gave him scars in his hair, and we couldn't help but feel Jesus in the yard perpetually observing the weeds was perhaps previously jealous of our lively chia heads high above him. And so, he, Jesus, had to make things even, to cut one of us open so he wouldn't be so lonely in his glass box with Mary above him obnoxiously drunk on mint juleps and white power.

Since then Rudolfo couldn't drink coffee or do much of anything, or he wasn't supposed to, but we partied anyway, and had sex, and found strangers' tongues in the night, and drank in the light of the night, and sometimes I'd catch him from falling onto the subway tracks when he'd get dizzy from so much fizzy Italian cocktail bubbles, and sometimes he'd sleep all day and I'd do his laundry, or I'd wake up every morning after that morning and look over to make sure he was there, sleeping with his earplugs in as usual, breathing, hoping he didn't die in the night, or seize in the night for seizing the day, so they say, which is always something people say when they don't care about their bodies anymore, which is maybe what we were doing, not caring anymore. Yet I'd still be hoping he wasn't in the bathroom again, stuck to the toilet, printed on it as a fresh flesh-label of something far worse than indigestion.

And I'd get up and go to work and the pigeons that flew so fast that they sometimes looked like eagles would watch me strut along the sidewalk, and I'd put on Lana del Gay in the morning and burrow into myself to hide myself from the H-cubed attacks that were guaranteed to come again as an abusive messiah, "Come again?!" everything I said attacked with this gritty-toothed attitude of "COME AGAIN?!" listening to *Brooklyn Baby* in Astoria, Queens, imagining I was just, one, borough, down so I could *really* sing the song, confident of the lack of divine geographic isolation, that brain tumors and shots in the head have a purpose in the entire population of humanity, that evil bosses and evil emperors and kings and the plague—they're all related, you know—weren't there to simply ruin your life so specifically ubiquitously, little by little, until everything's a brittle by brittle vapor of sorts.

And on my walks to work I'd realize I was jealous of Rudolfo in a way, that he was granted a way out of needing a mahogany doorway in a way, unhinged, that we couldn't have seized it together, what this exact way meant, gotten drilled by it together, that now we were on different paths, in different boroughs, yet in the same city, getting even closer somehow by growing further and further away, me toward brass and cubicles and paying his medical bills, him toward chemotherapy and more holes in his head.

17

Is That a Clip-On?

When I'd come home from work, one of the only things that would give me comfort, I must now admit, wasn't anything I told myself or prayed or believed, but the sight of Rudolfo looking over old pictures, shirtless with the window open, finding a share drive amongst his things that he thought he had thrown out in a dizzy fit of rage and confusion, his sickened brain acting up again like a stray cat throwing up and then licking its paw, or just wanting to break something, sick of having to throw up again.

The scar on his head grew endearing to me, a line of bulbous comfort, a reminder, that we are fruity vessels, fragile, which can indeed be sliced open, drilled into, things taken out, things put in, things forgotten, things remembered, things like scars as horse-race hats placed or clubbed on our head.

From his surgery, I feared the worst: that they'd take out that small chunk of time of when we first met. I feared he'd become a vegetable or a drooling fruit, withering and withering into a raisin.

In his fragile state I grew attracted to his strength, to his particular brand of masculinity, resilience, fortitude, that he was determined to hold onto memories, and to me, that he squeezed tighter now to things and to my body, lemon juice on cauliflower. He looked at me now as if I were always about to run away on some mysterious Swampass Express, as though he were about to catch me and keep me after a long day of letting go and forgetting I was alive. He held on tight and we seemed to float together through a new Amazon forming and the sloths swam near us riding their alligator friends as harnessed racehorses.

I'd unzip his pants, and slowly caress his thick, mushroomy dick head with my tongue; it became a teat of sorts for me every day, coming home to it, dehydrated from torture on Park Avenue, longing for some kind of virile milk. I'd gag myself on that dick head.

Then I'd put both of his balls in my mouth and massage his ball skin with my tongue and taste him.

He'd say, "Do you wanna sit on it now?"

And I'd hold onto the arms of the computer chair and let him enter me, painfully at first, and then valiantly, a scorpion winning over his prey, cracking the plastic exoskeleton, and it was only *then* that I'd truly pray, or wish, upon the roof-stain-stars twinkling above us, *Let us grow in our love, let this grow, let us remember to forget everything but this,* and then everything would blur, our wood floor, the great pain of each thrust, his hands holding on tight to my sides, and my head eventually rubbing on a magazine on the dining table when he'd flip me over, and then I'd come on the floor without even knowing I had, and as his cum came into me and dripped down my legs, mine dripped onto the carpet, too, covering the red rooster pattern beneath the table, drops all over the beak, the tail, the feet, a cum-covered cock.

And then I'd go for a walk, and the sun would be setting, and the breeze would give me honeysuckle, but with jasmine too, and daffodil. I'd walk slowly and I'd think to myself, "Is *this* an epiphany?"

I wouldn't reach any conclusion, anything expressible with words, but I'd know that something was good, the smell of pollen, the sweat of it, something was revealed. I was so in it, too much so, within its midst to really observe perhaps what one would normally observe on the outside looking into their lives, and so my epiphany of my having an epiphany would just let me float to the grocery store, elated, as the sun floated down, deflated, and I wouldn't think at all about going back to work the next day.

—

"Is that a clip-on?" Mr. Hah said to me on another day, first thing in the morning. He then began saying it often first thing in the morning every morning thereafter. He'd find something he thought was funny but just passive-aggressive enough, a dig with an implied call to action, and he'd repeat it until the windshield wiper blade of it was completely the fuck gone, and then he'd repeat it again so that it sounded like rusty metal scratching glass in Siberia.

No, it's not.

"Oh okay. Well I really like the tie and your shirt that you're wearing."

Surprised, could this really be an actual compliment, coming from this dark-souled man? I don't think I'd ever heard him complimenting anything, instead, beating it down, abusing it, wishing everything to be an ant, his ant, crushable, scraped away.

Thank you, I said.

"Never wear them together again."

There it is.

He continued, "You look like a goddamn clown. Didn't your dad teach you how to tie a tie? Throw a football? Ride a bike? Didn't he teach you how to like girls? Or did he just teach you how to be a homo-cock-lipped-clown with a clip-on?"

So I said, my dad's dead. He died in Vietnam, and I was a rape baby actually. To be clear, my father raped my mom, then went back to Vietnam and got shot in the head about seven times. Is that the same as being a clown?

"What did you say to me?!" His usual teeth grinding began, the red face, the veins pulsing.

Oh, nothing.

"How dare you say something like that to me!" At this point he ran into his executive suite bathroom—I heard rustling—I heard him take a piss that seemed mostly outside the toilet bowl—then he came back out, and his face was back to normal. He was calm and smiling, and he sat down on his swivel chair and turned his back to the office and started typing an email. I walked into his office.

Softly he said, "Soooooo, is there something I can do for yooooou?"

Yes, I said. I know you're going on vacation for the next couple weeks, and so I wanted to run a couple documents by you to make sure they're worded precisely the way—

"What did you say to me?!" The red, the grinding, the veins returned yet again.

"That's the most insulting thing, ANYONE, has ever said to me. ANYONE!" He straightened both of his arms, lifted them up like a zombie and then squatted down to the height of his desk, and in one quick motion he washed the windshield of his desk with the blades of his arms. The picture frames, the business cards, the pens, the Kennedys, the picture of his blonde wife and blonde-Asian, blasian child, and the old tattered picture of his Korean parents, all squeegeed to the floor, "Ship pal nam, ship pal nam, ship pal nam!!" He began speaking in tongues and babbling in Korean, which I later found out means, "Fuck you man, fuck you man, fuck you man…"

To the entire office, "MADELINE ALLISON!!!"

Calmer and to me and softly hyperventilating, "I've, never, taken, a, god, damn, vacation, day, in my, entire, LIFE. You *do* know that we have multiple offices, right? Did you think maybe I was heading to one of those, ya dumb fuck? What kind of luxuries do you think I have? WHAT KIND OF LUUUUUUUUUUUUUXURIES"—he really spread that one out—"do yooooooooooooooooooou"—that one, too—"think I haaaaaaaaave?!"

I thought about his Park Avenue apartment across the street from the office, where he sometimes goes to take a nap, and where his wife and child sometimes come up to stay when they want to go shopping or to a musical, on their private Learjet, after riding in their private limo, after doing nothing at their private mansion in Palm Beach. I didn't mention any of those, though.

Sir, I do not know what luxuries you have. Just wanted to run the exact wording of these documents by you before you physically left the office to wherever you might be going, to wherever that somewhere else may be, not right here, but over there.

"Again, with the insults!! Do you think I just whimsically flutter-fuck to anywhere I please?! TELL ME!!" He picked up another binder, but this time it hit me in my cheek.

I brought my hands to my face to cover up the blood slice.

Miss Allison and Phil—who was the obvious brains of the firm and the only with the ability to calm Mr. Hah down—came to attention.

"Jung," Phil began, "How, about we go for a coffee and talk about the Directors and Officers' liability policy for Amnet Corporation? Colin, please go with Miss Allison. Miss Allison, get the first aid kit and help Colin with his face. We're deeply sorry, Colin, aren't we, Jung? It'll never happen again, right, Jung?"

"I do NOT take vacations, for anyone. My Dad, *MY* Dad, taught me that at least."

Selena and my brother would always ask me why I stayed, why I didn't tell someone, why I didn't sue for a multitude of reasons. And I gave the answer many give; I needed the money. I didn't have the time. For food, for bills, for raiment, for friendship, for fellowship, for Rudolfo, for Rudolfo's family, and for mine, to pay for the pain, for silly choices, for ignorance, we give thee thanks, O Lord, Amen.

—

From Lilly's barrette I can hear her thoughts, how layered they are, that she communicates on many levels, masking her image and her place. Her hair tickles the plastic, and I see, in the past, where that plastic comes from, how many Chinese hands and Chinese robots, temperatures, all it took to make that barrette on its long journey to America, to then be attached to a little girl with special powers, a seer, a psychic, a sage, one that no one ever listens to, but if they did, they'd be safer, better off perhaps, a piece of peace at least.

She tells me there are others like her, but not many, not too little, not too much, somewhere in the middle of what's necessary and what's not and whatnot.

I can see how every morning she cries and tells Sandy not to go to work, how no one should go there, how she starts seizing too sometimes before she has her eggs.

She was the Indian man with the cow next to the Ganga and she took me there to talk to me; she knew I was observing her. She knew I, some spirit, some orb, was within her silly Chinese-factory-made pink barrette. She wants to help me. She wanted to tell me she knows who I am; in exchange, she thought I could get rid of the demons haunting her family, but I don't know how.

One of the offices of HH&H used to be in the Twin Towers and on the morning before September 11, Lilly screamed at Sandy, "I see fire, I see fire, I see bodies on fire!" She didn't stop screaming this for 24 hours, and so Sandy stayed home and avoided being burned alive from jet fuel and conspiracy theories and "sand niggers" and the Bushes.

Of course when Sandy told me that story thirteen separate times, she spun it in such a way so as to avoid implying that her daughter had superpowers, because that would be silly, to imagine other worlds within our world hidden in between all the color. She attempted to express that the real story was how she had "to stay home from work and use up a whole, entire, PTO day, geeeeeesh, and try and get Lilly to stop screaming. It was so much screaming. I really just didn't know how to stop it. It was really hard on me, to *hoad* her down, you know?"

Yeah, all the screaming is the story here.

I snap the barrette and I thank Lilly for showing me that I am, according to her, that same bottle being kicked around in my thoughts, and everyone else's thoughts, at home at home, and at home as other places, and that someday I would shatter into something or somewhere else, and she can't tell me why or when. That I am stuck for now, in the net-present-value of all thoughts, all places, and all times, in one, rolling and empty, yet sticky, shaky investment, trash repurposed.

She was perturbed by my lack of insight for her and her cursed family, and she unclipped her barrette, and then threw it out the window toward the clouds, and all I remember is being dizzy and twirling and being fucked again by Rudolfo, starting on Park Avenue and ending at the same time, and the sun was setting and I really need to get some eggs afterwards, and maybe some greens, and possibly some lube from Duane Reade because spit is getting a bit painful, but I like it, thinking about pain, to forget about pain.

It's the most beautiful distraction, to be needed by someone so desperately that it hurts.

18

Jealousy

I get jealous in other ways.

When I'm sick, I want everyone to be sick or sicker, deathly ill, until they suffocate. I want time to stop acting like it actually stops so that I won't have to hear its fraudulent jingle of keys and change in suit pants' pockets. I'm jealous of silence interrupted by cellos, sufficing with phone calls instead, and jarring intercoms and the strings of encased wiring that slither into glory holes where rats suck on copper cocks.

While sitting in my cubicle, sometimes out loud, afraid of writing about the despair of my cubicle, I'd read article after article about how *sitting kills* instead; I was a sort of a cutter, with each article just a little bloody slice of a speech of controlled pain, how even if you exercise, even if you have been for years, you'll still be killed from the stubs of your atrophying thighs 90-degrees to your Tums-filled Yum-Yum tummy, a cesspool for cancer, a *NeverEnding Story* quagmire where thousands of white Atreyus sink into the mud of your gut, absent all the shirtless little boys in leather to grieve all the little horsies entering into the ether.

It's a breeding ground for the frothing inbred squirrels turning good cells into bad cells cracking open their nutty shells, those that have fallen on the rotting heads of all those horse carcasses within you. The shells and cells will be ensconced within the horsey-eyeball-sockets now empty except for a kind of a goo, and the squirrels will reach their creepy little fingers in there and grab them, stuff their cheeks as much as possible, digest, and then shit them back out into the muck of the swamp of all kinds of shit mixing and doing horrible things as you sit.

"Treadmill desks" will save us from all this, if we could only walk a little while typing, or do squats while holding a laptop, sweaty conference calls, or hitting a racquetball against a cubicle while flitting through a clitting little PowerPoint. I got jealous of treadmill desks the longer I sat at work, the more I felt it growing, a bone spur of sorts, things growing where they're not meant to be, me weakening me, I weakening I, eye for an eye, angering me, as my ankles would surely and soon turn to cankles and my feet would get stinkier, massaged only by the hum of my hot computer tower.

I'd browse other jobs on Glassdoor in search of a better "culture," refusing to look at anything with less than 4 stars, or something with *unlimited vacation*, sickened by statistics—*40% of Americans didn't take any vacation days at fucking all*—or of course, a place with treadmill desks.

Some days I'd secretly apply to 10 jobs, sometimes 15, and I'd get jealous of noise. How free it is. Sound waves bouncing off walls. Out windows. I'd stare at my empty inbox except for the junk mail of Groupon after Groupon for $60 steak dinners—*what a catch!*—with meat so devoid of flavor and nutrients or a succulent Native American séance—all of it stripped away at the mechanized cow Auschwitzes and fields of dreams of the heartland of America, today's Chevrolet—that I'd begin choking on a tasteless chewy pointless colorless Starburst of disgust in my throat.

On these valley days of quiet, opposite the peak days of hurled bombs whenever he, Hah, hee-haw the jackass was around all day, Miss Allison would run to the window after Mr. Hah left the office—even for five minutes to get a coffee, the rare times he didn't ask someone else to get it for him—and she pat her nose on the glass of the conference room and looked straight down to the sidewalk below, bustling with fresh flowers for dusty empty apartments, except for the occasional bustling of rich kids pushed around by Black and Tan ladies, and puppies who eat better than most everyone else on the globe.

Miss Allison always looked down, deciphering the sidewalk movements to ascertain whether or not he was here or approaching. She talked to herself as if the entire office cared for her mental notes and play-by-play updates—providing a Google Maps monotone voice of his every move throughout the office, throughout the city, throughout the country, throughout every cavern of her heart.

If Mr. Hah exited the building, his Brooks Brothers tie teasing the wind, she paced around the office exclaiming, "He's walking, heeeeee's walking, Hah, is, walking, he should be downstairs in about two minutes, well three minutes if he gets to talking, he's making a left now," and at the window, she looked through the glass down, she always looked down, a perched bird staring at a crumb, the executive limo, which was driven only by Mr. Sherry, because we all knew that Mr. Hah doesn't get along with anyone other than Mr. Sherry, because Mr. Sherry doesn't mind if Mr. Hah yells, addicted to the nectar of his name—"SHERRY GOD DAMN IT!—all sherry sherry quite contrary and swigging it at every stoplight, blaming Mr. Sherry for the color above, as if by the power of his name he could stain the green to red.

And once Miss Allison saw the gray of Mr. Hah's head and the door opening for him and the head ducking into the black, she screamed in delight and looked behind her, as if the rest of us were right there with her, an audience previously waiting for her announcement, that the act of a particular play had been completed, when really we were just sitting, typing, browsing articles about how it's bad to just sit and type, how everyone in America is somehow okay with this, and to just sit and think about sitting too much.

She never saw that, though; she saw curtains. She saw thousands of faces with her. She screamed and giggled, "He's made it, HE'S IN, HE'S IN!!! Okay evvvvvvvveryone, three minutes, just like I thought, he's IN. HE. Has. Made. It. To. The. car. Everyone. WE ARE GOOD. We're clear." And then she asked the airy audience if she should call him, now that he was "on the road" to see "if he needs anything" on his way "back to Palm Beach?"

Someone always shouted, "Go back to your fucking office!" and usually that was Phil.

Out of everyone there, whereas Mr. Hah held the halo of darkness and eggshells and all-around-AWFUL to the place, Phil held everyone and everything else all together, and it showed in his waistline. Whereas Mr. Hah was the greedy, ill Korean dictator of the place, in need of attention, while threatening acts of war and terror over the slightest offense no one could have ever anticipated to be an issue—like one day one of our fellow pitters ran to the bathroom in tears because she printed out a meeting agenda on the "wrong" paper, really because the right paper (one of five types we have) shifted with his moods—Phil was the father, the one who bore the brunt of all the real, relevant worries of the business, the marketing strategy, the first line of offense for getting good insurance deals for clients, the expert in absolutely every aspect, chockfull of everything, the biggest as well as the kindest, a wild bore who'd silence his own anxieties with whiskey and steak for quite possibly every meal, forgoing any Groupon and just paying full price until the gout set in.

I was often confused by Phil, the liaison between the Devil and the rest of us and the demons, the big fat buffer, the butter on an otherwise moldy, crusty piece of bread of a place.

Why did he do it, why did he put up with all this, when he could have simply run his own business, elegantly so, progressively so—perhaps even with treadmill desks for the rest us?

One time when Mr. Hah was in a meeting with some fluffy executives with fluffy hair, the kind of people who are only thirsty for seltzer water, or coffee with very particular sugar amounts—really, 1.5 packets?—who the fuck are you?—and Phil rolled over to me and whispered, giggling from the deepest parts of all the sugar-buttery parts of his heart, "I'll give you 1,000 dollars if you walk into that fucking meeting and just eat your bi-bim-bap and kimchi but in that conference room," as Korean food was the only food we were allowed to eat at our desk according to Hah, the Bath Haus of Hah, "Just in silence though, using your chopsticks. And turn a game on, on the flat screen. But smack your lips and grunt like Hah does."

I just about went, as I am normally one to say hell yes to all dares, but I sincerely feared murder, which is why I'm sure Phil felt confident enough to ask, because he knew I knew I would most certainly be murdered for interrupting that meeting, that fluffy, fluffy, sugary, nonsensical meeting about commercial liability insurance policies, and Miss Allison would most certainly chop up my body in front of everyone for him if he asked, or perhaps punch-hole my skin and wrap my body in a binder and file it with the rest of her things.

We'd always hear Phil roaming the office, but not in allegiance to Mr. Hah, just spouting off things like, "It's fucking comedy, this place, fuck-in-com-ed-y," and then he'd playfully make fun of me drinking kale juice, "What the fuck is that that you're drinking, fuck-in-algae? FUCK-IN COMEDY, THIS PLACE. IN-SAN-I-TY."

And to his bursts of statements like these, Miss Allison always uncomfortably followed him around and obligatorily laughed—or so she thought was her obligation—which made everyone even more irritated by her, even Phil, reacting with, "My dear Miss Madeline Allison, what the fuck-ing-HELL are you doing following me around cackling like that all around the office; you sound like you're gonna have a heart attack. Go back to your fucking office and call Mr. Hah. You know you want to."

Not understanding it was a joke, she'd run as fast as she could, sometimes knocking over a statue or a painting or two, ignoring their crashes on the floor, slamming her door, and you'd hear her dial his number on speaker, "Jung!? JUNG!? Hiiiiiiiiiiiiiiiiiiiiiiiiiiiiiiiiiiiiiiiiiiiiii, is everything all right? Do you need anything?"

"Madeline," and you'd hear the teeth grit through the phone, and you could see bite marks on the plastic, and molars crumbling into keyboards, "I just left the building. What could I possibly need! WHY ARE YOU CALLING ME?"

Then she'd apologize.

Then of course we'd hear on speaker, "While I have you though," Mr. Hah would say, "could you go ahead and set up a meeting for..." and she'd have 13 more things to do for him, unnecessary meetings, chartered jets to the Hamptons, a research project on what exactly a "Bitcoin" is because he was embarrassed when he heard it in a meeting and had no idea what it was and why on earth she didn't warn him about this new Bitcoin thing. You know, usual duties for the accountant.

Sometimes Phil would be absent because his gout would act up, or because the trains from Long Island were delayed or because he was on a business trip with Mr. Hah to Beverly Hills, before which he always had to go the hair stylist in Koreatown next to a Noraebang and above a kim bap joint with Mr. Hah, so that their styles would look the same—corporate, business, fluffy 1980s sides, sharp part—*plus-size-circuit-riding-American-salesman-North-Korean-dictator chic*, that aesthetic with the golden rule: <u>you must always wear your suit jacket when you're outside, even when it's 95 degrees, because this means you mean business and you're really strong, strong enough to endure nipple-and-poop-sweat in the heat.</u>

Phil would roll his eyes and go with it, mumbling, "It's comedy, it's insanity, muthah-fuckin—(and the Long Island would come out)—caaaaaaaaaah-me-dy, it's fawwwking cawwwh-med-dy, what is that fuckin' algae, what the fuck are you drinkin', yah kale, yah got yah kale cunt-cock-shun again ovah heeeyah?"

He'd walk out the door to meet Mr. Hah at the car, and Miss Allison would run again to the window as she'd always run to the window, not for Phil though, for Hah, always for Hah, to make sure he found Phil on the sidewalk, as if anyone could miss him with that jubilant wobble, "caaahhh-me-dy, fahhh-kin cahhh-me-dy."

Sometimes I'd get jealous of Phil, because somehow he seemed immune to the wiles of the drudgery of the prince of the power of the office, the sitting, the tears from all the girls and sometimes the men, the dust of an old-school mentality struggling to survive in a new era of sneaker-and-jeans CEOs and the tech startups of Silicon Alley across Manhattan, the recyclers, the Obama voters, the living-wage-lovers, the parasites, and the "Koch-hating Euro-loving faggots," as Mr. Hah put it.

Phil seemed to embrace, happily even, the blobbity and ugly fluffity that inevitably grows when you're prostrate, drooling on your keyboard till the prostate blobs grow, and your soul is awakened only to be burned by the whimsical fluffery and cacophony of a phony CEO in desperate need of therapy and a punching bag and a good buttfuck from an actual jackhammer and a Xanax, among other things—a lobotomy from the Virgin Mary?

Perhaps it was the steak and wine; perhaps he had another secret yet to be revealed, a long-term plan, some date saved, the day he'd finally do something different. I was jealous that he had this, this possible way out, when I was there sitting, typing, and here I am rolling, rolling, spinning from a puzzling power, perhaps within the butt of a cigarette or the butt of that goddamn bear lamp here in my little red writing room, once vodka, now antique, once dark, now a little light of mine, this little light of mine, wondering just how do I let it shine?

19

The Twinkytect

There's always the hum of something, a squeaking, something peaking in the orb that you are, wherever you are, wherever I am, what I am, that squeaking, the wheels of a vacuum cleaner, the hiss of a coffee tower steamer, walking on moss in a forest in Alaska that moment you thought you, just heard, silence, the moss sucking in everything, so you thought, but then that trickle, the fickle stream.

It was the Fourth of July and we heard the boom, boom, boom-chick-a-boom in Astoria Park, and we knew the soldiers back from the handmade-Afghan-let's-just kill-all-the-sand-people desert were all waking up in unison like vampires, stiffly, plankly, blankly in one line, and the only thing that moves is the axle of their ankle as their head rises up, echoes of that axle blowing up, and their friend's—their brother's, their father's, their lover's—leg they saw flying through the air with the rocks, the blood, the sand, droplets shining in the desert sun in every direction, a firework on the Fourth of July.

Rudolfo and I ran to the roof of the apartment, up the ladder, and through the cubbyhole to the sky, and through the leaves we saw the sparkly blood droplets of the bombs not too far away in the night in Astoria Park, but Socrates Sculpture Park (below Astoria Park above the Costco parking lot that could and should have been a park, so, that along the water there could have been one large park instead of hot dog buns and macadam) looked dark and cryptic in comparison. We slept there, on the black of the roof beneath us, with the black of the roof above us, and we held each other sweetly and sweatily in the summer night, with its summer night mist, and we felt like floating in the midst of the mist, and we levitated there in balance with each other, one see-saw between the dark earth and the dark sky, and it was then that we completely forgot about the previous winter, its quiet, and we embraced the loveliness of the beat of bombs and blood and heat.

We stayed there the entire next day, and as the sun woke us, we took turns going down the ladder. Each time I went I feared I'd fall down the steps and my bones would split, ironically enough, and Rudolfo would have to find me, but, I would muse, he'd be okay with everything because we had such a beautiful night and such a beautiful day that it would suffice, his memory, and his memory would last him a lifetime, that one night, this one day, and he'd never want for anything or anyone else because he had that. He could wear a nightgown and push a Costco cart around the city, never showering and letting his beard go gray and let it all shrivel and listen to nothing anymore, quoth the maven of doing nothing more for years, until he met me on the wing of a butterfly maybe.

There on the roof we had blankets and coffee, books and beer, and we rested in the summer sun, covered only by the overarching leaves of the massive tree in front of our apartment that shielded us from the light of the freedom bombs that woke up all the soldiers in the city across New York the night before.

We rubbed coconut oil on our skin, and where we had scars, we rubbed Vaseline Men's care sunproof lotion 30.

My scars were from bars, fighting with dickheads about the need for lots of parks instead of too many parking lots built by the companies they worked for. Rudolfo's line across his head, the one that went from ear-to-ear on the back of his head, as if he were hiding a zipper within his hair, I covered in sunscreen gently. I squirt the white blob onto my finger and it splattered and sploofed and queefed like Heinz ketchup does—the new bottles, how it flops and sprays out of the plastic bottles instead of clumps like gays out from the glass ones, following your fucking them with a knife.

With a dab'll-do-ya on my finger, I said, "look away," and he faced the flags in the distance, the tattered ones above the grocery store that look like a World Cup was held on the roof 10,000 years ago, all the countries faded, tattered, split, and ripped, yet still flapping just a bit. He looked that way as we both sweat in the sun and shade, naked, our clothes from the night before in a pile to be burned as piles of paper forgotten.

As if my fingers had E.T./Elliott power, I slowly followed the zipper on the back of his head and covered it with white light. It looked like cream cheese, that power, and I said so, and he said, "Thanks, fuckface."

Anytime.

—

The night before we had contemplated double-penetration at a club. We met a little tart-fart at Barracuda, a little hairy twink with glasses.

"I'm an architect," he said.

We didn't care.

This was after two bottles of prosecco and fried pork chops

113

and arugula at Malaparte in the West Village, after one-buck oysters at Fish with cheap beer, after a picnic in Chelsea on a pier various blocks above the pier where all the gays are supposed to go, which we named Queer pier, or just Queir, and we were baffled no one came up with that name already. We brought a gray blanket stained green from many other days in many other parks. I think we were at Hudson River Park, right on the water, and our blanket was on a hill and all we saw was gushing water, and shirtless men, and the freedom-fuck tower, and a Brussels doggy that liked Blue Moon and orange slices and licking strangers like us.

He was with a French crowd, our Blue Moon lover, and they of course had a cornucopia of cheeses and grapes and other grapes and other cheeses and crackers that they all dared not eat because it was more for the idea, for the display that they were indeed having a picnic in the park in New York, for *this* was living, and they wanted all the city to see, and they wanted themselves to see, so much that they didn't even bother watching their children play about and their little doggy.

At first I thought the little girl was alone and she was trying to kill her puppy, holding it over the railing into the water and giggling. I ran off our blanket and asked her what she was doing, and she decided against the murder and handed the little Brussels-fuck to me, with her parents and her parents' friends still bathing in all their hot cheese and the hot cheese of each Fwanch word lazily dripping out of their mouths in a conversation about having a conversation and I kinda loved them for it.

Goddamnit, did we want to steal that dog and push that little girl into the water and shoot her parents, the oysters watching her drown, the oysters watching us fuck their dead bodies, and applauding with spit, later to be picked, split, and tickled with the tip of our tongues as little champagne-bubble clits, until we realized that wouldn't make us any happier, murder, or having something—or someone to take care of—as we both knew too well, it doesn't really change much. If you weren't in love before, you won't be after your Brussels or your little girl. Maybe it'll help, or maybe you'll even die thinking that you were, but you weren't.

I think the world would be a better place if it were filled with more puppies than children, at least 50/50, or maybe 80/20.

I attempted to read *To the Lighthouse* there in the park that day, and I attempted to read it on the roof the next, and shamelessly succeeded with a maximum input of 9 pages in 48 hours, digesting each, and every, word, and they wouldn't fully disintegrate in my body; I wanted them to linger there in my acid, rumbling, and rumbling, and twirling in a way that only the bubbly pink sunset could remedy.

At dinner we talked about living really, really tiny on a hill, how someday soon we needed to leave all this and find land and build a house on top of a trailer bed with a mini-heater and one mini loft bed, something off the grid powered by solar panels and lubricated by rainwater that drips down into a cauldron collector of sorts, how we really didn't need a roof as much as we loved it, or even a city, because cities were like children and puppies, a distraction that often feels like love, and sometimes is, but more often than not isn't.

In unison in a trance we said, "I want bison near me, and my own vegetables growing, not on the roof like our peas and basil here in Astoria, but next to a vast landscape that is self-sufficient with its own energy and death and life. I don't need anything. I don't need space, except the space that the wild provides. I want the forest to be my living room, the ocean, the sky our companions, the sand, the dirt, every tiny particle of my soul."

The more and more and more prosecco we drank, the less and less and less manufactured things we wanted in our lives, and our great commitment to less grew and grew to smaller and smaller.

Eventually we met the little architect, drunk on this idea of little, with our big cocks as hard as the twin towers, each of us with a full Manhattan in our hand. I kissed the architect first, while Rudolfo rubbed his dick between his ass cheeks while all the other gays were jealous of the two very-beary-beardies about to double-fuck the wittle-beary-beardy on the dance floor. He sucked at kissing; he actually sucked, Dyson-vacuuming my face. Rudolfo didn't care; he wanted to rape him, his dick intertwined with my dick, penetrating the little twinky-tect, a thick braided double-Twizzler shoved in a baby's ass.

Through the crowd of witnesses and beards, our breath grew more whiskey sour and impatient. It was getting late, and we felt bad getting more free drinks from one of our friends behind the counter. Someone spilled a drink on a cock on purpose and began licking the liquid off it like a ravenous kid who only liked the butter on the corn but not the corn and we knew we were through because why wouldn't you like both?

—

Whenever I'm alone, walking down the street, wearing particularly tight pants and a fire hydrant is spraying water for children and there's a rainbow there only at one angle but no one notices but me, I find myself thinking everyone notices me. As I observe couples and groups that wish they were couples dripping barbecue juices down their chins they wish were the saliva of the other and beer bubbles they wish were the laughter of the other—*if only I could always make her laugh, if only he thought I were bubbly, I bet he wants a bubbly girl*—they glance at me, and I glance at them.

I assume in that moment, with water droplets not but one foot away from me in an *arc*—oh look father-fuckers, an arc—of drippy-droppy praise, that all has stopped for them, even the water, even the rainbow hidden behind my skimpy cut-off jeans. They're looking at me, they wish they were me, they like my body, they wish I were with them, but they know I can't. I have a place to go away from them, and their place is right there dripping pig fat down their Adam's apple, through the flabby once-were-pecs and dissipating in multiple directions once hitting the bulbous country of the sitting-kills gut, oily ski paths down the cancer mountain that ends in a sadly hidden micro-dick.

And those eyes, and those, and those, I'll make contact with all of them, and something will zing and ping within us, just for a moment, a droplet hitting the hot macadam and dripping onto leaves still not ripped from the sun's crackling, leftover from winter, and still not vacuumed from the street cleaners in the misty mornings, misty from pit bull drool.

Perhaps this is how I secretly went on, and go on, right on, man, finding myself just a pinch, a drop, a spray, thinking I'm a hidden rainbow more valuable than everyone I walk by and they all know it, too. By golly, they must be less, and I, I, I must be more; they're not thinking what I'm thinking. If they don't know what I know then they're clearly missing out and they wished they knew, every single person.

Yet now I'm beginning to think my power over others that

I thought I had is dissipating; there's a tightening to the fire hydrant; the children don't even notice it anymore. No one ever really did.

We're eyes connecting to eyes, mystery and hidden things pinged and dropped to other equal mysteries and hidden things and because you see the rainbow and you think it's beautiful and you're going somewhere doesn't mean all who are watching you walk by are doomed to fail at everything like you hope. They're sitting; you're walking. Soon you'll sit, and they'll walk. Coffee will slide down throats. We'll all get naked on a roof somewhere someday and die on a sidewalk the next.

—

Rudolfo and I hardly moved on the roof that day, and hardly heard anything but pigeons. And there was a faint classical moodiness softly pulsing from one of our iPhones on Spotify. We stood up to find them, the pigeons, in the sunset wind. Our dicks pushed to the right from the sunset wind, our hot tanned balls slunk to the sandy sparkles and specs of the roof, and we saw a sculpture from the Socrates Sculpture Park in the distance from the roof, bright and metallic, silvery, lines and lines of thin metal stretched on poles, useless and bright.

People were walking underneath the stretched metal and were captivated even more than we were, how the metal flowed with the wind so violently, appearing speedier from all the flashes of sunlight bending and sparking. We could see this all from the roof; we could hear it all from the roof, and the flutter of the metal and the wind sounded like pigeons cooing and yodeling like they do when they're hiding under the subway tracks in Astoria when it rains. The cooing softens your wet steps as you walk up to the train, as if under each step were a nest anew, and another, and another anew, feathers and twigs forming beneath your feet.

It sounded like that, like the air was filled with the sound of pigeons. And the other way the dead ancient flags atop the grocery store were whipping and tearing like knees popping from strain, like popcorn popping from a corn cob thrown into a microwave, and the cooing was the butter to it all, softening and salting any harshness of the day like cum.

We laid back down and rested on pillows we had brought up from the apartment and looked at the black of the roof with the sandy sparkles glinting like little camera flashes from plankton in a famous dark sea. We breathed, we breathed, we breathed, we breathed, we breathed, we breathed, we heard, we heard the popping of old flags, and the Chromeo pigeons in the park, and we thought of how the many lines of metal stretched across the park looked like jump ropes, the way one flung up and the other next to it flung down, flung up, flung down, and between it a kite of rainbow wind from the blur of an actual kite caught there and twisting in circles, caught on the metal, nowhere to go but in circles, hopping and playing between the jump ropes, alone except for our eyes, art in an airy artless arc-less gallery.

Underneath the sandy sparkles of the roof was the dark sea tar clumped and shiny; like almond butter mixed with cracked black Sharpies it was moist, and bright, sticky, and oh so black. A little parakeet sort would step in it, confused, and then fly away, black and sticky, covering her nest gloomier, wherever it may be.

"I'm glad we didn't double-fuck that twinky-tect," Rudolfo moaned, "I don't think I could deal with him today. He wouldn't fit into *this*; we both probably wouldn't have been able to fit into *him* anyway…"

And I thought about how I needed to see God, how I felt like black tar, sticky, and bright, but stuck without any flashes it seemed, being spread all over nests of other people who don't even know I'm really there as they slosh their pulled pork and cheese and jizz and grapes in their mouth and let it all plop out in clumps of apathy and loneliness and I get stuck to that clump sometimes, thinking I had to be a part of them, of everything, all its life, all its color, all its death and darkness all mashed up in a half-digested hairball of a stranger's glance, or a vacuum kiss, or a rainbow kite stuck in a park sculpture, twirling and swirling in the pigeon wind, and it's okay because you'll just get another kite won't you, and all will be well and you'll forget the snares you left behind because they mean nothing to you once you forget them.

Where are your fiery pillars?

Did all your prophets know the words they etched on letters to churches were breathed by the very Holy Spirit of everything—did they know in that moment it was upon them, an epiphany, and that one day this letter of mine, this list, this ramble, this, very, book would be holy, revered and mumbled, hands clasped, below trees and steeples and subway tracks, billions and billions of mouths cooing these very words, to *you*, for millennia?

Or was it just a day like today, feeling in between, forever in between, weeping and whipping and gnashing and ripping on the one side from countries and flags forgotten like spleens cut out, and the sounds of pigeons in the park on the other softening the sun above, and your boyfriend's dick in between your thighs, covered in coconut oil, organic, from Costco, birds covered in tar searching for food for their babies recently hatched out of frail eggs, and nothing lies between these exact words, each a naked body before you on a thin, paper, blank-black roof, with nothing above but space, the blue, the white, the black, and all those stars, and planets hidden, and notes of explosions and burning, a jump-roping of time and place, merging as a pale blue-gray sunset moon, that very sound, a pale-blue gray moonlight in the middle of the day, these very piano notes, "Clair de Lune" jump-roping from my dumb phone?

I wonder if the prophets thought they were prophets, and if, when they heard a silly song, they knew God was suddenly there with them, as if he hadn't been before, or if they felt like birds with black talons, fluttering around confused, or if they just wrote whatever the fuck they wanted, using their hands to use their heart, to write, the story only they could write, daily failing at some kind of minimum output, thinking whatever was dripping onto and into the page was just a first draft, and the first draft is shit anyway, and they'll clean it up later, but they never did and look what happened.

20

I'm a Little Teapot

I'm a little teapot short and stout; I'm a little teapot short and stout.

I told you bitches that I went and that I will go other places; you probably thought I was done traveling, droning on and on about my life with a man, brain tumors, bad bosses, memories, bourbon, and the obvious pain of unmentioned losses.

I'm uhhhhhhhhhh, one of those camping coffee pots, oh yes, and all that bubbles within it, the blue ones with the white speckles, with the edges rusty, the cracked periwinkle revealing a more meteoric hue that adds to the aura of a cabin.

It's Wayne's cabin, a man with land grandfathered into Lake Clark National Park in Alaska surrounded by volcanoes, bears, and teal glacial water. I feel warm but sturdy, disturbed yet purposeful, and my eyes are everywhere, each droplet of steam from the teapot and emanating throughout the cabin, soaking into the slats of wood cracked and creaked and creeped with time and the pressure of a winter's snow after snow, and the wolves that dare to jump on the roof, sometimes later shot by Wayne when he hears the steps and growls, later worn by

Wayne when he rips the flesh apart and hangs it and dries it and wears it as a fur coat.

I've been here for what may be years, observing him, listening to him, grasped by him, new water filtered from the stream and poured into me, coffee grinds stuck inside myself, some not seen for months when he washes me clean in the stream, baptizing me again and again and scrubbing my cavities away, brushing the plaque of every morning's use with a Brillo-pad-of-sorts that he made himself out of an intertwined nest of colored, racist pipe cleaners.

Those days at the stream when I am baptized in the waters of the mountains, where melted teal sways through the rocks and through the eager fins and sharp snouts of King Salmon, where the sediment slinks with the waves, hailing from higher places, colder places where fragments of dinosaurs still roam, encased in cold, cold glass, where life, through the icy dead, is truly respected, preserved, the bones that prove how long, how so very long, how so many zeros, zeros, zeros, zeros of days, it takes for that water to decide to become water for me, for Wayne, for the world to flow, and clean, a simple coffee pot—those days are the days I feel the most.

It's then, when Wayne holds me in his hands, the whole world in his hands, and scratches the metals of my heart, and cleanses me with the waters of so much time—salmon eggs lost, or pieces of purple wild flowers, the bones of placoderms and mammoths, and so much piss from so many creatures drained from the sky, from the valley of the shadow of the bears, from the rain clouds that travel there from faraway places—I feel closest to him again, to who he really was, and perhaps the reason I have been here, that I am here, just a page to you, but years for me, observing him on that wood stove, from the stream, occasionally tipped over and left alone.

He becomes every man to me, how alone we all feel and how we often desire *that* more than anything else, to push everything away, to have a few simple, functional things, to eat and observe the cosmos and all that thrives and dies within it, with such an ever-constant raucous that all becomes quiet, something first disharmonic, to a collective murmur, to nothing.

—

Earlier in my life I spent time here on Lake Clark, as a teenager, bustling with the clear symphony and song and dance of discovery, yoga in the sunlight on the beach, spending hours listening to the eagle shrieks over the mountains in the afternoon, steak in a shotgun-guarded tent at night, always weary of the bears, always worshipping the bears that simply played in the water, or shat, or fucked, or looked—just looked at us—just looked like us looking at them.

I obviously never forgot the first time I saw him then, Wayne, the wildest of men, the quietest of men, the strongest and weirdest of men. Animals followed him like a god—geese, goats, dogs, cats, even eagles—and maybe he was God, and I saw him two ways.

At times at night he, with a candle, mostly unnecessary in the Alaskan summer night, would approach us along the beach where we had our tents and guns, and he, with his ax dragging along the rocks, as the head clanked every pebble, with his face lit up by the candlelight accompanied by that dusk light, accompanied by that ax-dragging sound, would always look so shriveled, worn, neglected, somehow beaten by clocks in socks.

He not only seemed alone, he seemed lonely in these times, perhaps because it seemed that he was completely autonomous, needing only nature and fur and his goat and ax or goose, but he was making an effort with us with this approach, vulnerable and un-Campbell's-cannily needy, to walk a mile walk from his self-built cabin in the cove of rocks nearby. I saw him first like this, his beard unkempt and dry, full of leaves, his buttoned-down shirt ripped and stinky, his pants tattered, and his ax, pathetic and sharpened only by a harsh beach. He talked about himself very little, while I seemed to crack at the sight of the reflection of candle or firelight in the green grassy glossiness of his eyes, a tender, frail green that made me feel comfortable and serene.

I told him that I came here to find myself, that everyone in my family had died at once, except for my father in the war, how they were all burned alive—my twin sister, my mother who was raped, my baby brother, my grandfather, my grand-mother—when some bad wiring in an antique lamp had sparked and burned the Christmas presents, *and the blizzard, all that snow, you know*, trapped them in with a soft, calm, wall of white that still didn't melt with the coals of their bones while I waited, stuck in the airport, *eating a bagel.*

I told him that I ran away because I didn't want to be a part of an adopted family not knowing myself first, that I didn't even know what that meant, or where I was from or what America meant, that no doubt they were looking for me, my brand-new brother, my brand-new mother, and no doubt look-ing for their gold I had cashed in at the pawn shop to get here, the bush pilot I paid, the first beers I drank with him, how he told me he saw a lot of my "types" up here, babbling types and liars and those who seek without wanting to find, how most just wanted to grow pot, smoke it, and then go back to school "somewhere fancy in the lower 48."

I didn't cry as I let the wind of my emotions flow over the grass of his fragile eyes, but I'm sure he saw a kind of mist coming from my mouth in the cool night, and condensation steaming from my eyes, from pain and the strain it took to stretch it all out of me, these lies, my insides bubbling and boiling over, yearning for release, and I didn't know why I couldn't say what I needed to say, and I told him so.

"Up," is all he said.

And then many minutes later, "You won't find yourself just looking around here, some of it maybe, but you'll find more answers up. Look at all of them."

He blew out his friend, the candle, and poured glacial water on the fire. We sat in the perpetual blue dusk light together, neither day nor night, neither height nor depth, and the only light on his full beard—and my sprigs of one slowly forming—was the dull light from the stars and moon aching to shine, the pitiful sparks they made on the teal-milky water that turned to metal, and the sky was a periwinkle bruise to match my life, a perpetual ruse, and the stars were un-glinting, permanent white spots of old, old paint, falling to the earth.

Our friendship began that night, that summer. Sometimes we'd hike together in the day, me aimlessly so, he always with a purpose, to find some track or trap, to collect some specific piece of wood, and no matter what, it was always long and far away and we'd always be back late, those same pale-paint stars fixed upon us again jealously, confidently, and oldly.

The Alaskan summer sun would cut everything crisply, as if everything below in my previous life was crafted with dull scissors, but this, this was something newer, such precision—I saw the speckles on rocks and the touches of gold clearly. I'd see the amber fur of a bear behind the bent-over spruces stunted from cold foundations below, and here, silence was satisfying, palpable, even spicy with life and echoes, as if each staunch mountain were a pillar in a great hall and we had the great privilege of walking in their great gala they prepared all for us, for us just to scream, or walk, or simply hold onto a piece of driftwood. That was reason for celebration. That's Alaska.

Wayne would always midday break out some lunch he had packed for us; I of course didn't bring anything—I was always a bit of a silly fish latched onto the shark that he was, and I knew all would be well roaming with him, the ecosystem that he was.

Others in my camp chided me to "stay away from that Wayne," that he was "a little coo-coo," that all the time up here alone made him snap and sometimes he saw other people simply, as simply the curious animals that we are, encroaching on and threatening his cabin, rumors of axings and shootings and bones beneath his cabin, but I didn't believe any of it.

Plus, piled around our camp there always seemed to be copious stacks of *pregnant porn*, clearly someone's thing: pregnant girls with big bushes pissing into beer cans, pregnant girls shitting onto teddy bears, pregnant girls drinking their own titty milk and fucking themselves with dildos that looked like babies.

That, or stacks of aimless talk about rolling cigarettes, both of which didn't so much fit into my yoga regime—and Wayne always seemed eager to go somewhere and take me with him.

And so I went.

Whereas at night he looked shriveled, pitiful, faded, and tender, when the sun was brightest and most precise, every move he made, every breath he took, every little rare word uttered, every bite of smoked salmon, every button unbuttoned, every sweat-covered hair on his beastly chest cooling in the breeze and lifting boldly like eagle feathers swooping for snakes would tingle the back of my neck with a kind of power, a mesmerizing magnetic force, which forced me to memorize every line of his face, his bulging hands.

Within those hands lay entire landscapes under skin with a history that seemed longer and deeper and more virile than the very mountains upon which we often tread together that summer, the swirling gushing streams through which we waded, the rocks over which we lay, shirtless in the summer heat, that knew more humans, and hominids, and apes, and creatures than we could ever comprehend. His hands were museums, and my eyes roamed their halls every day. His chest was a volcano erupting, billowing, and symmetrical with lava paths that lined the crevices of his muscles, formed from roughly ripping wolf skin, lifting dirt, hacking up wood, lifting giggly goats and the silent flesh of wolves and bears and fish, and all of it seemed to drip to the sharp, rocky valley of his stomach and under his belt. I'm not sure how old he was, possibly 40, but in that half-life, he seemed to connect to every year he ever lived and every year he might live still, standing there, a seesaw of himself, a lone wood plank of himself, balanced and needing no one to go for a ride.

Now I know, but at the time I didn't know why, how stunned I was when he slowly unbuttoned that flannel, peeled it away in the sunlight, the sweat dripping off his moist rocky pecs to the dry sunny rocks below us, dripping along every vein of his thick, thick arms, the particles of dirt and dust always glittered on his golden skin.

"What are you waiting for?" he'd ask me.

I'd slowly take my shirt off, too, a little embarrassed, hardly filled-out and gym-less at that point, but with him I felt his manliness, as if it was warming me, and because of him, I could be manly too, and proud to be whatever I was in that moment, my own wood plank, seesawing in the present, needing nothing but simply this place to stand up and teeter and balance before him.

I could hardly speak, with both of our jeans somewhat slinking off our waists from the sweat, and we'd simply keep walking, hiking toward the ice peaks.

"You're strong," he'd often say, even though I never believed him at the time. I didn't doubt his sincerity; I just found it difficult to believe, for myself, what he said about me. Instead, my throat would fill with grass and sediment and fur, and so when he'd say, "Your arms are strong" or "You know, you walk like a man should. You walk strong," I'd just nod, asphyxiated from wolf fur, bear fur, his skin.

We'd walk, forging our own path through the thicket and the terrain would rise and rise and throb as we'd head toward the steaming mountain. Walking together, he'd touch my sweaty neck, already mysteriously tingling simply from his sunlit, glossy-gruff presence, and he'd simply keep it there, his hand, for what seemed like ages, resting, calmly, until it slid down my back, there too for even more ages, guiding me through the thicket, "through *here*," stepping on the moss that felt like pillows beneath our boots.

The spiders in the moss would flee, hearing us approach, and we sometimes rested on the moss whenever there'd be a wizardly collection of it, covering the entire forest floor with a living jade comforter. Sometimes he'd stand up slowly while I still rested, looking up to the blue of the sky, the leaves of green in the trees above, the green of his eyes that just looked like two more leaves twinkling and fluttering there among the trillion, and the geography of muscles and dirt covering his body provided such a sturdy place for the fur of his chest, which seemed to perfectly match the dark brown sticks of the wood behind him, tree trunks as thicker chest hairs, all coming and growing from the same place, and, looking at me, unblinking, he'd slowly unbutton his jeans, and pull them down.

As he slowly lowered them, he'd smile a little, looking at me. He grabbed onto his hearty dick like he grabbed onto his earthy ax in the day, sturdily, focused, and released himself with a gush and a whoosh and subsequent sigh like a river finding a path it once knew in a valley of the now un-dammed.

Still looking at me, only looking away to look up to the clouds, he noticed I remained fixated on his penis, the first on another man I'd really seen up that close, "You gotta piss, too?"

Again, choking on dirt and rock and moss and eagle bones in my throat, I nodded.

"Well then, my fellow man," he said, "come piss with me. Come here. Stand with me, right next to me."

I stood up. Holding my neck once more as he often would, Wayne still looked at me, grinning, and said, "You're a man, you know." He massaged my neck a little, still looking at me, breathing. His breath smelled of warm cinnamon tea and sweet tobacco, which combined smelled like burning sandalwood.

He seemed to know at the time I was unsure of what that meant, "…a man…" as if he knew there was always an ellipsis fore and aft of it for me, dots and vast emptiness and blank pages between those dots.

And so he repeated himself.

"You are a man. Piss with another man. Don't be afraid. You are strong. Let me see your penis."

I remember holding onto mine delicately. And Wayne

scoffed encouragingly, "What are you holding onto, a cup-cake!? Hold your damn dick like you mean it, with a purpose, like a man. See? Like *THIS*."

He waved his up and down sharply, as if his dick head weighed pounds of iron ore, and then down slowly, and then up, still pissing, with the thick stream impaling bright yellow frequencies into the moss. Between the bones of my constricting rib cage, I managed to rustle out a "gotcha" and followed his lead and attempted to get my stream as thick and far as his, coming close, moistening the moss all around us, watching the spiders run with the bears.

Then we'd button our jeans again and leave our shirts off and continue walking through the woods to find a trap he'd set with a rabbit or a wolf still wiggling.

He'd unsheath his knife dangling on his belt, and his back muscles would twinge and sharpen and bulge and relax as he'd swiftly and jerkily slice the neck of the creature and bleed it out; laughing, he'd rub blood on his chest—and then mine.

Serious, "Hold still. I'm going to teach you something." He'd rub blood under my eyes, and on my forehead, and then he'd say, "Close your eyes and open up."

He got a new batch of blood on his hands and dripped it on my tongue, and then his fingers would be in my mouth and he'd say, "Close your mouth. Suck it slowly off my fingers. Think about everything around you and above you. Think about your family, and fire. Think about volcanoes and ash and blood."

From quick movements and murder, to jubilation over blood and giggly over his kill, to ceremony and respect for the particles of everything, he'd make me stand there for quite a while and make me suck more blood off his fingers, dripping it on my lips, and making me suck it off his hairy fingers again that smelled like moose jerky mixed with India.

Other times he'd tell me to strip completely naked, "Pull down your pants. Take off your shoes, and close your eyes."

He'd slowly, gently, and ceremonially cover my entire body with blood in the sun, my hair caked with blood, my balls covered in blood. He'd massage my balls, my taint, my thighs, with blood. He'd drip it down my back and it flowed between my butt cheeks, down my legs, and onto my ankles and into the moss. He'd drip the warm blood on my dick head and let it drip down my shaft.

"Don't be ashamed. Let your manhood get hard, harder than rocks." He'd rub my entire body, massaging it as he spread the blood everywhere. "Think about the blood drops of all things. Let it seep into your skin, into your dick, your balls, your chest, your heart."

And I did. My throat would clear. And I really did. I thought of a kind of a rape, my father raping my mother, raping all of us of our innocence, in a kind of a barn after a long dance with puzzling moves.

I thought of my grandfather holding onto my grandmother as their clothes burned, and then as their eyelids burned.

I thought of lava and sweat making its way down Wayne's chest. I thought of his beautiful dick and his glacial river of piss. I thought of bears and eagles, goats and geese, goats and cheese, cities and moss and comforters at the mall, and how spider-like we are, always hiding in the moss, running with the web of moss together, afraid of what's to come when it's just blood and piss and fire, nothing really dire.

And in those moments I grew antlers and horns; in those moments, covered in blood, washed completely with Wayne's ax-wielding, rock-splitting hands, perhaps I felt present and still for the very first time, and it felt honest for the first time in my life, like I wasn't running away anymore or seeking anything, teetering there naked in the wind.

—

Perhaps this time I shifted, rolled, and have become a glorious coffee pot to remember those times and what it was like to be washed, eyes-closed, baptized in the blood of everything by a man almost divine, a man like Wayne. How easily we forget, again and again.

It feels the same, like steel wool on my insides, and hot, burning and cleansing me with many streams and liquids at once. Years have obviously passed and he looks different now. I've been watching from every water droplet of coffee steam, much more the face I saw at night when I was young than the full body of a man I saw by day, those days I got older and bolder from his presence.

His jeans are tattered more often and he walks around the cabin a little more aimlessly, loosely, and forgetfully. Tobacco remains litter wood planks, and holes go un-patched, where mice find warmth in the winter. The furs are old, hardly any new—much smaller animals now too. Books take long naps all about. He's hardly left the cabin, watching the bush planes buzz about with the eagles, and they drop cans of beans for him, which he eats one by one, occasionally humming something. Or sometimes all he'll have all day is a bit of coffee from me.

I can't help but think that I took something from him all those years ago, that he bequeathed something to me then, and I feel guilty now, watching him slowly die alone, most of the goats gone—killed by the bears—most of the geese gone—killed by the wolves.

Sometimes he'll write a letter with the pages of a novel he rips out; he just writes over the printed words in cursive, and when he's done he burns the letter in the stove. I can never quite tell what he tries to write, always hunching over, and maybe he can't either, starting over. I wish he longed to write me, that he even remembers me, and that he misses me so much that he isn't sure what to say because that would be so beautifully tragic.

Or I hope he's writing poetry for generations and generations after him, when they'll find him and his cabin and his ax and bones all covered in ice, later a river, even just one poem in a cube.

Somehow I know I will come back again. From the teapot, with as many eyes as there are white spots on the aging metal as there are stars, I'll watch him die from the wolves finally trotting through the cabin door wide open.

He'll be naked, and as his limbs are ripped to shreds by the growlers, I'll see him the way he used to look, bright and strong in the sunlight. I'll hear him tell me once more, "You are strong. You are a man," and we'll piss together one last time.

I'll see his face turn toward me the way he used to look at me, his face merging with the canopy of leaves above and the sticks and the stones, until all that's left are bones, and the tongues of happy dogs shining his brow with his own precious blood, precious to me at least, and a wolf tail will knock me over and I'll tumble again and spill to the creaky floor and the old cold coffee will seep through the cracks and I'll go down, somewhere else through the dirt, completely poured out.

21

Selena and The Revival

Around the time of Rudolfo and I almost-double-penetrating the Twinky-tect, I believe, my friend Selena invited me to a revival of sorts in the city; she said it wasn't about snakes or human slave sacrifices or anything.

These were "real people who had real gifts from God, intermediaries between people and their truest divine nature within," she said.

I had certainly seen a change in her. While I was mired in the duck-muck-butt-fuck-life of HH&H and the evil sorcerer that hovered above it, tired with the realities of rubbing SPF lotion on brain-surgery scars in the sun, or rubbing SPF lotion on school loans and hospital loans and credit card systs, mired and tired with confusion and the silence of brass and glass, I tried to believe everything would one day pass, finally picked to be kicked away, finally blown by some mysterious breath, and I wouldn't have to take responsibility for any of it.

I, I, I, a candlewick, had been burning, getting drier and blacker and more lifeless. Something was smothering, and the oxygen was lessening, as the smoke rose less and less from me every day I spent on Park Avenue.

Selena used to be fat and stuffed with drugs every weekend, and now she seemed skinny, happy, and always doing yoga in the oddest of places, and involved in what seemed to be the oddest of Christianese cults, a cult that made her happy, though—that was clear.

She had gone to these city revivals multiple times, and each time she came back from them with a glow on her face, as if she had spent months at a Jim Jil Bang, where little naked Korean women scrubbed her entire body with rough rags, over and over, with pubey soap, and she rinsed all of it off, the stresses of Kentucky Fried Chicken in the Bronx, walking by there every day to her job of helping the inner city children to not make the same mistake their parents made, such as living in the Bronx, or getting into fights about chicken and trash or who gave you that rash, until shots were fired and one killed the other quickly, leaving behind single mothers and fathers with children, mothers and fathers who barely finished single-digit grades, and the spokes of the bicycle wheel kept flapping over that player card, the Joker, and it sounded like a bus tire flat and flapping on pavement. That's the Bronx.

She'd just "float by Kentucky Fried numbly on days after a revival," she said, and as if her senses were heightened, "all smells, all tastes, all oils and blood, would be one sound" and smell to her, an ominous but shockingly serene incense taking over all that she was.

"I can face anything, I CAN go to this silly school and talk to these silly parents, and I'm going to help my father build his gun shop in Miami because I know he needs this, it's the least I can do, and God has prophesied that I help him."

She told me this at a coffee shop in Astoria, the Queens Kickshaw, with the overtly antique and New-York-in-the-'20s dim lights flickering on her tan skin so it made her look like weathered and warm-hued wood, yet flexible as if perpetually ready to be bent into a new boat. I sat with my ice-cold brew, and she had her cappuccino on the ground, talking to me through her legs, face, and butt facing me, doing a forward bend, and her hair gave the cappuccino behind it a Broadway curtain, and the show was really just that, sitting there, foaming quietly behind hair.

"You should come tonight! I'm telling you, you'll be changed forever. You'll be addicted…juuuust like you're addicted to Rudolfo's pretty, Brazilian, capoeira, MEAT STICK DICK."

Some of her hair grazed the foam, and I spit my coffee out a little at her surprise raunchiness—I think I bring it out in people, the raunch—and as the cold brew made its way through my beard like a slow tsunami through the village of Le Hairs-on-End, nervously, I contemplated. I dabbed the sweet black destruction on my face. I questioned, what if they start telling me, "Jesus is speaking now" through a projector with a bad song displayed and he somehow says to "stop fucking and getting fucked by men and stop wanting it, too"?

Selena ignored my question with a giggle.

Years ago I wouldn't have dared venture into a tent revival again, having been to plenty in my youth, always sitting there awkwardly, moved, yet knowing the contents of my heart would always be uncouth to the spiritual realms, unfit to walk on hallowed ground near burning bushes, as I thought about the sweat running down Moses's arms and holding that hard staff of his. I always thought about what was going to happen if we all didn't stop loving all that gold and cheating on our wives whenever we'd one day get them, and that Chevy truck, and our two children who'd make us proud when they went to Liberty University in a town famous for lynching "darkies," and both our children became preacher/commentators on Fox News every Sunday after they ate their taters, talking about how Jesus is speaking to us, and how he wants us to buy more for our children and never adopt, except our unconditional love of capitalism and the golden bull, which are some of the American fruits of the Spirit.

She was doing the downward dog in the middle of the coffee shop, and the barista didn't really give a fuck. He even nonchalantly walked to his phone and changed the music to Aruna Sairam, and the mood changed from Americana-coffee to Indian spice and all of us felt like sweaty, amber-eyed reverent monkeys on stools before her as she danced on the coffee wood as a goddess of something but we weren't sure what—some higher consciousness, some freedom, some ominous intoxication from a netherworld, drawn we were, but afraid—and we let her stretch and dance and twist before us as we sipped our brews and as her cappuccino sat still like a lotus on a lily pad in Times Square flooded.

Her hands were sharp like pistols, and her skin was blurred gold, multi-layered with a thousand arms as the Carnatic twings and twangs tilted her and set her aflame with something hidden yet unmistakable.

"They know me here; it's okay," she said, "I was tweeting constantly about these fuckers right when they opened, before all their rave reviews and gourmet macaroni and microbrew beers…"

Okay, I'll go with you.

"Oh good!"

She unraveled and we talked about the World Cup and how Rudolfo didn't care that Brazil lost so badly, and how he wanted his country to explode—a civil war within it—so that something would change there, so some direction of the country would be evident.

When we arrived that night in Harlem we were handed numbered stickers like stars in Auschwitz, and the building was an old garage recently painted, remarkably clean, white, and the lights were modern and Ikea-cheap-and-sassy. About four hundred people crammed into this garage and somehow we were all able to sit down on burlappy blankets.

The air smelled like body odor, motor oil, old Bibles, summer trash, jasmine, and the old candy of old women. There was a crackle in the air, an unraveling of that candy, anticipation, annoying as it clicked and twisted, but endearing and comfortable, the breath of a grandma. It didn't feel like New York; it felt like a bit of everywhere only *I* had been to and no one else. I wondered if everyone felt that way, if every memory, every step previous to the one right before they sat down here seemed present there like it did for me.

Selena was in a very contemplative, prayerful state, eyes closed, even with everyone chatting around her. She was taking this very, VERY seriously, even if many others around her weren't, including me. I was aware of the energy of the room, but other than that I didn't have high hopes for the night, second-guessing the numbers they gave us—they gonna do some kinda card trick with this and then ask for money? They gonna tell me everything vague after I ask something vague and then we'll all leave feeling an even vaguer purpose to our lives, clouding over the suffocating clouds already within us?

An old, old woman slowly hobbled to the stage; her hair was gray, braided, and long, and she wore a homemade dress with a fabric covered in little purple flowers with little leaves, but from far away it looked like polka dot, a long, weird, polka dot dress. Her tits were saggy, and she might not have been wearing a bra, but it didn't matter, for those tits merged with her hips into a Silly Putty stretch of skin.

"How many of you are here to hear God!?"

The crowd rumbled awkwardly as we all stood from our blankets and clapped; some had their hands already in the air.

She screamed again with such intensity, a war cry she hoped would break through the ceiling and echo elsewhere, through years of exhaust and layers of white, white paint, "WRONG. YOU AREN'T HERE TO HEAR GOD; YOU'RE HERE TO HEAR JESUS!"

And the crowd went wild, as if Moses just picked up the basket of his former self, covered in tar, and threw himself, that little baby in a basket, crying, into the pit of split earth and boiling lava and gold before him. The crowd jumped in, fully immersed in the spiritual heat that this old lady seemed to conjure with the rumbles of her boisterous, stretchy-titted chest and a Bible in her hand that she flung about as though she were attempting to form opalescent bubbles in the air after dipping the pages in water and Dawn dish soap. I felt slapped with it, all those hot sloppy soap bubbles and screams being hurled at us. I think we all did.

Selena still seemed to be levitating by herself with a little calm smile on her face, and her head tilted ever so slightly as though someone were slowly swaddling her with warm basmati rice and silk, whereas I seemed to be choking on sour milk as kimchi slid down my neck.

Oddly, the old witch-doctor-Bible-lady asked, "Has anyone ever heard of Jack London!?"

I automatically raised my hand; about four other people did, too.

She pointed at me. "YOU!" With wide, sweaty, wizardly red eyes she asked me, "WHO was Jack London?"

He was a writer, a naturalist, a—

"ENOUGH!!!!" she said, cutting me off.

"YOU ARE RIGHT AND DO YOU KNOW WHAT JACK LONDON SAID!?"

I slowly raised my hand again, but the old lady swung her Bible around again as if to say, "I'm done with you; you already had your turn."

"You can't wait for inspiration. You have to go after it with a club!!"

The crowd went crazy with this for some reason, chanting, "JESUS, JESUS, JESUS!!" after that Jack London quote about creativity and how one should approach writing.

I didn't see the connection. I wondered if they, too, had this quote written on the walls of their writing room at home like I did.

And she continued, "That's right, everyone, well, Jesus doesn't want us sitting around, for he spits on apathy, he loathes it, we are his CHILDREN and we have all the power in the universe and we are seated with him and we can come to him with freedom and confidence. We have to go after Jesus with the club of our hearts!!"

Well, this was what they wanted to hear, apparently.

The crowd, once lifeless puppets comparatively to this point, were now animated and tugged and jiggled and wiggled by strings all over their bodies, violently pulled and yanked every which way; they were one mass, an anemone of puppet limbs wiggling in violent waters, and I stood stiff, a cold, curious sea-horse.

Even Selena was writhing about in her yoga-fied creepy-Indian way, and I was petrified, rock-hard in a park covered with animals fighting each other for bread.

My eyes, in unison, both turned slowly to my right like one of those cat clocks, and I whispered to her, Selena, Selena, am I hearing this right? Did that old lady just tell me I should "beat Jesus with a bloody club"—or that my heart has a club within it—errrr?

She smiled and danced, and I felt quite left out.

I closed my eyes and I pictured somewhere far away from there, away from the stink and energy of desperation, searching, seeking, clubbing. Although I was perpetually stuck and angry and lusty—and perhaps I was the only one—I still didn't want to club God to get him to answer me. I don't think I'll ever know enough or care enough to really club anyone, let alone God. I didn't want to go that far, and perhaps that made me a lonely fool.

Then I saw the green bench I go to in Central Park on some lunch days (when Mr. Hah isn't on Park Avenue and the office has some kind of piece of peace about it, except for Miss Allison fumbling about and tripping over the carpet due to her withdrawals from her drug, her man, her overlord, her abuser).

I was always able to walk for a full hour on those days and bring a salad and just watch the ducks fight the rats in the shade, and I'd sit on the green bench with my legs folded and eat my kale, beets, and such from the deli. I'd sip my apple juice and sometimes glance at the retard in the wheelchair one bench down, groaning at the ducks and rats, rooting for his team. And on my right a man would practice on his electric

piano and the auto-beat he'd set would never match the classical song he tried to play over it, yet somehow it didn't bother
me, all his repeats, how hard he hit the hollow plastic keys, how
they reminded me of the teeth of middle-aged women chewing
on ice, comfortable, yet wondering where their husbands were.

—

I went there, and I am there now. I watch the water and I
wonder what pollution, what tires, what trash lie beneath the
waters drained into this deep beautiful puddle of the city, and I
hear Sarun again, the sitar and the drums, the twangs and the
hums, and I feel like a hot bison resting there, covered in fur
and heaving with breath, waiting on the long wooden lily pad
of a great plain and on my shoulders are falling the shriveled
seeds and crackled leaves from the wind un-clinging things
above and within me.

I pick one up; it's gray and pitiful. I start laughing hysterically, just at how shriveled and sad that leaf and seed cluster
look, how it just plopped on my shoulder and onto the bench
so bored-ly.

As I hold that pitiful seed, I feel a tugging and a pinching and
a buzzing; my hair is being shaved for war, and I, the mighty
bison beast breathing there, am sleek and droopy like a Sphynx
cat, ugly and raw, yet smartly subversive and powerful, ready to
butt heads with my prey in the park of my apathetic, club-less,
tired and mired-up heart full of secrets and lies, secrets foaming with mold.

—

"*HE* has received prophecy!"

I opened my eyes.

I was the only one standing up. Everyone else had sat down
by now, and for I don't know how the fuck long. I looked

around. I looked at Selena and she was on the ground too, but crying, looking at me. They all knew.

The old tatter-tittied woman with her Bible hands was seriously about one inch from my face, breathing on me with her Pizza-Hut-peppermint breath, "HE HAS RECEIVED THE WORD OF OUR LORD….Please be quiet, all of you, and…*let us pray.*"

And I softly mumbled, SSShhhhhhiiiiiiiiiiiiiii…

A couple people heard me and snickered at my profanity on "such hallowed ground."

Still standing, just the two of us, she—peppermint-Bible-lips—and me, with everyone around us worshipping or snickering, she said something so that only I could hear it: "My son, don't be afraid. I know the Lord has spoken to you. We all have gifts. This is mine. You have one, too."

Oh, okay, I said. I mean, honestly ma'am—and I leaned in to her—I think I was just daydreaming or something.

She smiled and then reached her hand out to me very slowly, confidently, and then placed it on my neck.

I felt tingles again the way only Wayne would give them to me. "God speaks in ways only *you* know, in divine gestures only to *you.*" And then she touched my back the exact way Wayne would let his hand slink down, too, as if we were hiking up a volcano again, hidden behind the garage of the night.

She had my attention, but I was still doubtful I was experiencing anything other than reverberations of past feelings, memories, some form of lusty déjà-Bible-Poo-vu.

She then closed her eyes, and for a moment I stared at her eyes closed standing right in front of me, and I just felt a little awkward staring at this old lady with her eyes closed. So I closed mine, too.

She spoke, a little bit softer now, just a little bit softer now, coldly and sweetly, from the mouth of a baby who had walked for hundreds of miles naked in snow after slurping on creamed corn and snowflakes from milk from a pig teat, "You are between worlds, between time and even here, you think this is a line, you think everything is another line. With borders within which you must hide. Although it seems murky, you have a clear purpose on your travels. You are a chosen one, a traveler, one of the wanderers, on a capricious journey ignited by blood, by sex, by injustice and cruelty, by the beauty of men, BY THE BEAUTY OF MEN, by the sickness of men, BY THE SICKNESS OF MEN, and as a spirit stuck between, you will flow where you think you shouldn't flow but flow you will and you will flow where you think you should flow but flow you will not. You are as a shriveled seed, cracked and weary, floating and falling, yet soon you will sprout and when you do, you won't know when or why, and you will feel dead, but somehow you will reach new heights and you will tell us all something—something very simple in the end of all this, and you will change something, but we will probably never hear it, or even see it, but it will be there right there, in front of us in mid-afternoon, the light of it burning through our eyes and we don't feel a thing."

I opened my eyes.

—

Lilly is looking at me, covered in blood, both her hands covering my ears, and her hair is braided with candy and she is crying and her hair is on fire but it doesn't burn, and I foam at my mouth, watching quietly, and the rainbow-foam creeps down my lips as a tome, and into my beard, and down to all that I once knew of my legs.

22

The Sword in The Apple

The room was bleak; the clouds above Park Avenue were those clouds that suffocate, reciprocate your feelings of dread with more dread, a murky mirror of distaste for everything around you, each sound a chapter in the book of the dead.

As I sat at my desk that day, yet another day, I looked at the windows of the office and watched the condensation form more and more as the clouds rolled in from Lady Clit-erty, her stale brass breath, green from spoil, thick from toil, deadly, stiffly, lips unmoving, but dreaming and driveling about something about plenty, and the feathers of popped plush pillows ripped from the trillions of rusty knives and bayonets and nails that made this country fluttered and fucked as one through the streets at a steady pace and cooled the walls of all our lovely, empty condos.

There I was sitting in my chair from China, staring at my organic apple from Maine, recently cut with a weak butter knife made in India, plastic and molded and boxed—I broke two in the process of cutting my morning apple. I washed it with Dawn kitchen soap, fearing the illegal alien hands that had touched it and just knowing they, for damn sure, y'all, I declare, never washed the shit off their fingers.

And when I was taking a piss, Mr. Hah had taken my scissors and stabbed all my apple slices, leaving one unmutilated, a stone compared to the others, which had been turned into a pulpy field of dirt, manure in a field of awkward angst covered in the morning dew to the detriment of many, to the benefit of a few, and the scissors stuck out of the apple slice like a sword and I didn't dare touch it. I didn't want to be the one to pull.

As I sat and looked at what was left of my big apple, the thick harbor clouds of spoiled milk toiling through the avenues smoother than silk, rippling, crippling the sight of cab drivers looking for hands in the air waving like they just don't care, I read the note on the Post-it below the apple again.

IF YOU TELL ANYONE, I WILL KILL YOU. THIS ISN'T A JOKE. I WILL STAB YOU WITH THESE SCISSORS IN YOUR NECK.

At which point, Sandy, of course, began her usual dreadfully boring diatribe, thinking I, the human blob behind the gray cubicle wall, would care.

"My mother keeps calling me, well really it's my husband that calls the most complaining about my mother, see she'll get really bossy with him, but he doesn't know how to handle it, so he'll then call me and tell me that my mother…"

I wanted a salvation from her lips, drooling with the pangs of entire herds of people in boomerangs of bad decisions, bad genes, worthless existences, except to serve and complain, whine and abstain from ever thinking they could rise above what others expected of them, all for an electronic pay transfer and the worthless paycheck "copy" sent through the mail—"for your records."

As she drooled and typed and droned, I thought of escaping to young men in the morning, thick arms, thick thighs, covered in sweaty black hair, the spicy glory between the pits, the balls rubbing against thighs, basketball shorts and the lovely dickheads flopping two and fro like a clearly built tower of brownies covered in Saran Wrap and jiggling in an earthquake.

"...and her rotator cuff is shot, just completely shot, which doesn't help her hip replacement, which is why we now go to the Jersey Shore hotel now, instead of going to the beach, because the pool is much easier for her, you know, that way she can kinda float—and you know she has to *hoad* her hand up in the air because of her rotator cuff..."

I looked at the apple flesh. The blades. The note. I thought of my throat. Rudolfo's head. Our bed.

Would this be the day one of us is found dead?

"I mean I've told her they have, I think it's called, arthritis-scop-eh-dick, surgery now, really, really, REALLY advanced nowadays, but she won't do it, and so we have to go to the pool now instead of the beach now, but baby Lilly doesn't mind really, she loves the pool anyway just as much. I mean I would take more than three days' vacation this year, buuuuuuut there's just SO much to do around here and I'm needed so I guess I'll..."

I overheard Mr. Hah yelling, shaking the droplets off the windows to the gum on the sidewalk below, "Why the fuck is the Internet down, Madeline!? YOU SHOULD BE PREPARED FOR THIS..."

He'd hang up, and take another call, "...well I don't see why we don't change the conference room into another office, just a really big office."

Sandy still going, "...and then I'd tell her, baby, you can't do that, you CANNOT waste food, people are starving, and you know her, you've met her, you know how smart she is, yet she wouldn't finish her food!"

Uh-huh.

"And my husband, you know him, he's so passive, and so, then, when I get home, I'M THE ONE who has to tell her to finish her food, that she can't be eating all these snacks instead of the meal we prepared, I mean, think about India, there are people starving there, think about all those damn Muslim countries trying to hoad their terrorist families together starving, too, in Paki-ghanistan and stuff..."

Mr. Hah picked up another call, "...no it isn't. NO. NO. NO, NO IT ISN'T. IT ISN'T HERE. You don't know jack shit. You're a dumb bitch. Next time set up the document right for me, with the binder that matches the fucking thickness of the document. So, SO, LISTEN, THE FUCK, UP, leeeeeeeeeeeeeet's recap, the RIGHT document with the right information, and THEN the right thickness of the binder, got it? SAY YOU HAVE IT YOU DUMB DENSE BITCH."

Sandy, "One time she fell in the ocean, and that was the year we knew we had to go to the pool, it was time you know, I remember we looked over and saw my mother getting tumbled by the waves and she looked like a hippo or a beached seal or something and there were people screaming and Lilly just pointed at her."

I laughed a little bit. Does Lilly not like your mother either?

"No it's NOT FUNNY, she could have drowned."

Oh. Yep. Not funny, uh-huh.

"So theeeeeeen, the next year of course we decided to go to the Jersey Shore where we go now, but stay at a place with a pool. It's been really great every year. We've gone there for eight years; it's kind of a family tradition. We're all about family. We all love the pool…"

As she droned, I thought of calves on my way there, in the subway, the pack of us flowing off the N train like identical cranberries packed to the rocky shores in a river, and we flowed up the stairs. Men's bare legs, women's too, they look like table legs when they're on their tippy-toes, all that weight of their entire body to such a sharp point. Piercing into the cement.

I heard Miss Allison running around the office, actually running as per usual, and the way she pounded her feet sounded like a desk being dropped from a crane, each step an explosion of wood on cement, thin legs cracked, blood splattered, cranberries flying through the air and hitting the walls, blood drops in our eyes, splinters in our lungs from every step. Her gray hair followed behind her horizontally from her speed and pieces of her hair floated to the carpet—you could always tell Miss Allison had been there, because she shed like a dying Golden Retriever every time Mr. Hah was in the office, and because she was everywhere, all the time. On those days, when we left the office we had to pat off the fur covering our pants, our faces, our bags—sometimes we used tape sticky-side out and wrapped it around our hands as a makeshift Miss-Allison-hairball removal device.

"Slooooooooooow, the heller, heller, and hah hell dooooooowwwwwwwn," Phil screamed from his office; he screamed this across the office every time he heard her run. "SLOW. DOWN. You're gonna hurt yuh-self."

And sure enough, she did. She usually did, knocking over a painting, knocking over a plant, a tacky bust of some warrior known for being a dick.

"I'm terrified of being fat," Sandy continued, a little bit somber now.

I mumbled, so are you already terrified now?

"What's that?"

Uh-huh.

—

Later on that day, as per usual, there were numerous fiascos, one involving Roman numerals, for example.

Apparently we had run out of Roman numeral tabs, and the ones we had ordered weren't exactly the same shade of black, even though Avery assured us that they were the exact same numeral tabs that we always ordered, which of course set off Hindenburg explosions throughout the office, every blimpy office member catching fire from the stress of avoiding getting yelled at, apples stabbed, Post-it death threats, binders thrown, busts busted and hurled through windows.

—

Later on that day I was actually able to sneak away to the park even though Hah was in town. In the park I had coffee with someone who got fired from H3 a few months earlier, one of Hah's many "concu-taries" over the years, and in the park we talked about why she decided to leave.

I'm surprised you stayed that long, I told her.

She said she was too, especially since, "Mr. Hah used to get drunk and forced himself on me multiple occasions in front of everyone," and how sometimes she let him because she liked the way it felt to get almost-fucked by the boss, and how she hardly ever said no and so she never felt the need to tell anyone and especially not about the three abortions, one for each letter, one for each of those three times she did say no and how that turned him on too much and how those no's turned to yesses the more he pushed, but she was happy now to be moving on from HH&H, because she always felt wrong there, abused, but "it was partly my fault for staying, by sitting there day after day, by not standing up. By my staying I knew I was passively saying 'everything's juuuuuust fine.'" They gave her one-month severance, just one, to thank her for her eight years of service.

She asked when *I* would leave, and I told her that I didn't know. I needed the money, school debt, Rudolfo's sister's surgery, Rudolfo's surgeries, and even though Mr. Hah's threatened me—even today—he's technically threatened everyone else too and they all seem to be alive and un-murdered so far, well, at least not by Hah's hand or his scissors, and I wanted to tell her what I knew, but I decided to wait. I did tell her about the apple-stabbing incident, but not about the note, or what that note implied, or who actually died.

She said she wasn't surprised. "Jung used to pour hot coffee in my purse when I supposedly 'ruined' his schedule for the day, or that this luncheon or that meeting was scheduled, no joke, two minutes late, or because Mr. Sherry didn't pull up to the curb close enough and he had to 'look dumber than a Jap-Chink' reaching out like that," but then he'd buy her a nicer purse, which was supposed to make up for ruining the contents of her previous purse, like pictures of her nieces, nieces who, "I do admit loved getting those hand-me-down Louis Vuittons that smelled like coffee, old paper, and ink running."

In the park, as we slowly ate our salads like sloths happily eating flowers, we overheard a girl excited about her boyfriend, "He's a Muay Thai fighter, but like, when I come out of the shower, he's like, like, he's like READING. It's sooooooooooooo great, I really like him, he surprises me. I mean, a fighter, AND a reader, you know…" And we watched her friends around her suck in her every word like little fish sucking on shark skin, quiet, wiggling, and hungry, as the shark yapped and went wherever it pleased, incessantly biting everyone's air with every critical word.

When I got back to the office Miss Allison was running again to Mr. Hah's office, but this time with every desk-splitting-pound of her step she barked out a guttural, manly "FUCK," and then "FUCK," so that for most of the afternoon I was at least thankful I couldn't hear Sandy continuing to talk about her dumb fat mother flailing around in a Jersey pool, rather "FUCK-FUCK-FUCK-FUCK-FUCK" this way, then "FUCK-FUCK-FUCK-FUCK-FUCK" that way, and then "Sloooooow dowwwwwwwwn" and then "FUCK-FUCK-FUCK-FUCK," and then from Mr. Hah, "Remember, confidential. You know the meaning of that, right? Is it clear now?"

Oh yes, the clouds have parted for me; I understand completely, I said. And the bunnies continued to burn.

23

Sharp Objects

What is this, that space between the tape-plastic adhesive and that which we want so badly, to understand and stick to the darkness destined for us or maybe the light, the great unknown, clinging to the nibs and nodules of moments, paths wanted, lovers wanted—sometimes just for an instant—that wall of transparent calm that keeps you steady there, looking steadily at the tracks, looking at a man on the subway platform about to jump, the hairs under his nose as straight as a brush, the dust particle floating right in front of his pupil but then swirling away from his breath when he huffs and decides to puff away.

Stickiness and still hesitation, fixated on the color of neck hair, fair, unfair, we think and muse about both standing there. Why are we not perpetually ripped and flung toward all that enraptures us, sucked in, blown, hugged by every stranger ugly, depleted, tortured, *beautiful, bountiful, blissful*, all of it a teabag label taped over the Dell logo of our computer, the tape opaque over the black, the letters of the logo bubbled up slightly, and so often life feels like you're petrified there at the 90 degrees of one of those DELL L's, sitting in your chair in your corner of the pit, taped there, and it's hard to continue breathing sometimes, suffocating under all that plastic and goo.

At 36th Avenue in Astoria on my way to Park Avenue in Manhattan, a woman, obviously pregnant stepped onto the train with her hot pink tights. I saw her vagina clearly formed around the seam, and her belly was taut and it teased the air first before her face like the bow of a ship, that BULBOUS BOW, it's called, underneath, where the dolphins like to swim, and she held onto the pole, looking around. Robotically I looked around too thinking it was my duty to tell the other men to get up, let the woman sit. My curiosity held me back. Is it really best for her to sit? Does it make her stronger to sit, or weaker?

By our offering our seats are we actually atrophying her muscles so that she becomes less stable everywhere she walks?

My stop came; I left her there on the pole, not unlike my father leaving my mother in a barn that day long ago, ya know, after the rape. Geee gollly, that gosh darn rape.

—

I hear her there now, my mother, covered in hay and blood and it was if she saw the wheat separated from the chaff for the very first time, the corn husk husked from the yellow teeth of the corn cob before the yellow teeth of her family bites for a sample of the corn's sweet. Her toes are grimy with the grease of sliding around on tobacco leaves. The red tractor stands up behind her, still, unmoving, and no one sat in its chair. The stray kittens clamor around her, curious of her salty tears. She shakes, and she shakes the ground with each thud of her heavy heartbeat. It was a construction site, her heart a massive drill pounded and pounded into the bedrock, deeper and deeper down below sea level. The cats are construction workers, shaking with the thud, but unsurprised by its faithfulness. This was work. This was expected. Heartbeats are normal, even loud ones like hers that are now about to break in new foundations. She eventually stands up to meet the tractor, gets another metal pale, closes and locks the barn door, and then begins washing her flowery homemade dress after filling water into the bucket and grabbing a chunk of lard resting on a two-by-four.

She continues singing, this time scrubbing blood instead of milking, and I see leftover milk drops drop from the teat, my view whitened each time and then cleared again.

I am a teat, and everyone sucks.

—

When I got off on Park Avenue and came out from underground I looked at the Chrysler Building that shimmers more some days, less others, depending on how bright the sun is, and it seems like everyone looks to it to determine their choices that day. Will they sit quietly, un-bright and still, or will they blind you with movement, warmth, stabbing the sky with a needle and commanding it to stop and go?

They'll look to it and ask themselves, will I get a haircut today? Will I buzz away the white hairs? Today will I do laundry instead of sit in the steam room at the gym and wait to look for the flash of a dickhead or the droop of a ballsac? Will I wait for the fat men to watch me de-towel and hold my hand out seeking alms from the water warming slowly for my poor skin?

And they gaze upon the bruise above my butt where my bone has rubbed so often against the mat, sit-up, after sit-up, the result of all my efforts to look nothing like them. They must know this, and yet they keep looking.

Behind the Chrysler in the morning I had a vision of the tower, Bill Cunningham tower—maybe it's actually there, maybe a vision, maybe a warning, and it was being built high above the needle and even brighter than the Chrysler!

Helicopters buzzed about it, and floating cranes lifted and zapped and capped. It was a sculpture of a bear and on top rested a great beacon brighter than anything mounted on the skyline. All the surrounding buildings of Brooklyn pointed their rooftop solar panels toward the tip of the building so that it sparkled during the day and rivaled the brightness of the sun and brightened Chrysler even brighter.

Beneath it was the face of a bear that matched exactly the face of this little bear lamp of mine, in my dark little writing room of mine, here, surrounded by the quotes of writers now long-dead and red and still read, the Russian vodka bottle and the tan shade, the chalk on the walls it softly highlights, keep going, *write 1,000 words.*

Just 1000 words each day, *minimum output.*

I felt proud, yet underwhelmed, productive, yet used. It was mine, yet I couldn't claim it as my own. And there it will be! A 4,000-foot-tall gaudy-bear-shaped super-tower, where only those that appreciate the contradiction of life, of the start, of art, will be allowed to live freely and thrive—as long as they contribute monthly to the e-zine and the art walk, where all people of New York will be called, with a mighty roar, to come, walk through the studios, and see what these creators are working on. There's no free Target Tuesdays, every day is Tuesday there, and every street connected to it, and all the avenues as you now know them will be dug up and replaced with a garden, a High Line, but a level line, for all, and the traffic intersecting will flow underneath it with the moles, and all who come to the tower will roam as dirty beasts through the thicket, the birds, the bees, the sculptures, the paint, the trees, the creepy projections that mean absolutely nothing, and the entire city will be filled with avenues of green and towers of creation. Gone are the days of planting one tree per million parts of people. Things finally flipped, and park was connected to park to park, and sidewalks were more foreign than the sound of French, and sidewalks were uglier than the sound of Russian, and nothing was ever cut in half again, legless like papers and words forgotten.

What is answered prayer?

Is it something you get, or something you'll never get, or both at once? I have often gotten exactly what I asked for, only to be disappointed again, the memory of things answered faded, its stickiness lost, a request to the sky to be sealed again by something else, petrified and ripped again, only to be taped down again after that again.

Is this the song of life on repeat?

My mother called me this morning and told me that I should "command" and "will" things to happen "in the name of Jesus." God is inside us, she said. And we are inside God, but we aren't God. That's God. Inside but not inside. Answered but unanswered. Taped down yet ripped off.

Somehow, as the interwoven fluffy and hard mold of an old lampshade affixed atop an electrically raped vodka-bear, we are one with God, the presenters of a light hidden within, yet separated by the dust of thick skin.

In the shower I tried, and cried, and looked through the dirty skylight above our pink tub. And as the fern branches wiggled, I commanded—someone, some thing, the lines of time, the record grooves of sound—that something, to jiggle and bend and play something new. Build a tower right now, not the future. Delete this dead-end job from my life. For clarity.

For stability. Rip me away from this job, to let me see everything. Destroy my father wherever he is for what he did, for Mr. Hah for what he did, but forgive only me for what I did, yes, that's right, only me.

How often do we do that?

Every moment really isn't too different than prayer for one side to win at a college football game. *Dear God, please let FSU win, and let their team lose, regardless of the fact that they have an equal amount of crying fans on their side, praying for the same damn thing, beer and the balls of sweaty men.* Because this prayer is within ME, surely God will answer me more than them, forgive me more than them, give me more power than them, and let FSU win again because at least our mascot isn't as racist as the Redskins. We actually give money to the Indians, and that makeup on the logo is the same Chinese-factory-made makeup discovered in a Florida fountain of youth, right around St. Augustine.

God must laugh at us; there must be so many mumbles in the ears of heaven as we reach for the sky with all our efforts, generation after generation, towers of royalty, pride, money, oil, condos, and next perhaps towers of art. It must all sound like one collective stinky fart, our cities as shit particles and little dust particles in front of a pupil in the eye of a suicidal homeless idiot, compared to stars forming at least.

Yet perhaps our hearts beating sound like great thuds, earthquakes breaking the walls of the clouds, and what a lovely dance it must all be, all children, all still bloody and something close to thankful for another beat, thankful without knowing they're thankful, another beat, another beat, another beat, beat, beat, heat everywhere all over the world, a needle in the sky, a needle in the hay, a needle in the street, lard bubbles on flowers, a baby in a belly next to a pole, every day we decide to keep going instead of jumping onto the subway tracks, or on pitchforks, or off buildings, off tobacco barn rafters into a bucket, when we do nothing but sit across every land. There's gotta be something to this.

I'm finally finding it so astounding how many of us are choosing every moment not to die, not to kill, not to kill ourselves, despite our pain. What a gesture to heaven we make with this, to stay alive, even now, today, while we're so clearly surrounded by so many sharp objects waiting to be used.

24

The Inscription

I, I, I hear. I see Phil has gone away.

On this day, we dedicate this tower, Bill Cunningham Tower, with these words of Phil Cumberbundles, the man who not so long ago held it together for everyone, absolutely everyone, the buffer to the world's madness, but then finally gave in to what he once believed to never be an inevitability for him, wailing this, The Rant—THE NORM, THE EMBODIMENT OF COR-PORATE MUCH-ADO-ABOUT-REALLY-NEEDING-TO-GET-FUCKED-IN-THE-ASS, ABUSE-SPEAK, HAH-SPEAK—across an office, cracking, red-faced and gaudy and gaut-y and fat from all the pressure of hell close by:

"Goddamn it do I have to babysit every fucking person in this godforsaken shithole? Do I? You tell me, do I!? Now I've gotta dial this fuck-tard pussy-tinkling shit-for-brains momma's-boy in the middle of the fucking day, to say, oh, OH, let's see here, HOW ABOUT YOU CALL YOUR OWN GODDAMN CLIENTS? And so, here I go, dial dial dial, PHIL, let's dial Mr. fuck-nips... 'Yeah, YEAH HI, hoooooow are you ya little assbag assmonkey? Oh you didn't hear me? You think I'm just humping myself, just kidding around for the hump of your hump-a-dump-shits-and-giggles!?

I asked you a thundercunting quesssssssssss-chun, thundercat pussylick!…Graaaaaaayt, SO glad to hear lunch went so well with you and the boys downstairs. Here's a thought, go ahead and grab your twatlips. Go ahead. Grab 'em. I'll wait for you to grab them. Grab your twatlips and then go ahead and squeeze, HARD, so you remember this one. The next time you and the rest of the fucktart fuckup fuckbutter fuckheads downstairs decide to go boozing around for two hours at lunch, how about you go ahead and dickslap yourself with your dick-long clits—oh you didn't understand me? I said, GO AHEAD AND DICKSLAP YOURSELF before you leave the office, and check your cuntass email before you leave, you goddamn cumdumpster! Ohhhhhhhh, poor li'l baby, so you diiiiid check it, awwwwwwwe, WHAT WAS THAT, JUST ONCE? Here's another thought, instead of acting like a two-year-old, sorry to burst your cumbubble, but check your cunthole email on your cunthole phone! And you wanna know why? Because when the suckasses from the land of fruits, flakes, fuckups, and faggots, i.e., your client in Californ-porn-eye-yippy-eye-yay-gay, emails you three times when you're boozing and splooging all over each other's dickheads, and then the shitbag fucking calls you three times, who's the real shitbag then? Hmm? BECAUSE IT AIN'T ME, FUCKTWAT!! It's you!! But you know what? Who has to deal with this bag of flaming shit? ME, dipshit. ME. I get this fucking fagfuck calling ME three times while I'm trying to run a GOD DAMN BUSINESS WHILE YOU TWO COCKFLUTES ARE SWIGGIN' TEQUILA SHOTS WITH THE OTHER SLUTBAG-SPICS OF PARK AVENUE!! Yeah, yeah, I don't hear anything, I bet you two are rubbing each other's chesticles and clitfaces in be-goddamn-bewilderment. Wait, what was that? Was that you attempting to QUEEF a response out your shit-spittin' queerhole? But bawwws, but bawwwwwwws, blahh waaah waah—SUCK MY COCK, bitch-tits. Pulllllllllllllllll the dildo out your honkey-homo McFagget mouth, and lick the salt off your last rimjob, and the one before that, lick your lips covered in fagshit and salt, squeeeeeeeze that lime allllllllllllll in that tight little hole, one last time. Go ahead. I'll wait for you to squeeze that lime in that hole. Now, stick your tongue in that twat-waffling hole, and LICK—lick it good, feel that tarty fartyness, and then…GOOD, you're actually asking questions!!!! I tell ya what, I'll tell ya. THEN, ya kike jackass-junglebunny wop-dyke choadlicker, you're gonna march your whorebag dickstick back over to your office—you're NOT going to come talk to me—but who are you gonna talk to? No, NOT fucking Batman. YES, riiiiiiiiiight, not fucking Superman either ya pantystain, although I bet you want both of their big thick cocks up your ass right now ya fuckin' tranny-stain. Who then!? Riiiight, THE COCKFLUTES IN FAIRYLAND ACROSS THIS LAND IS YOUR LAND THIS LAND IS MY LAND FROM CALIFORNIA TO WHEREVER THE FUCK OUR CLIENTS ARE, DO YOU UNDERSTAND ME!!!? Am I making myself clear, shitbreath? Great, and before you come back to HH&H kill yourself because you're fucking fired and I hope your little girl chokes on a goddamn peanut.'"

25

Cir·cum·lo·cu·tion

[sərkəm lə kyoo SH(ə)n]

Stories only I, I, I can write. I, I, captain.

What does that even mean? What has that ever meant? Isn't everything we write a lie, a replacement for what actually is? I read one word within Proust's *Swann's Way* on the subway the other day on my Kindle, and about half of Gertrude Stein's *Paris France*; well, it might have been two words, I can never really tell how far I've gone on my Kindle. If only Kindles deflated as you read them. There are page numbers to be sure, but somehow I know they're all lying to me.

I mean war and thought of war, the French say if you can remember three generations of war it is enough.

The truth is, I've been avoiding something, for years now, and that is, the truth. And within this—this very fiction—embellishment of what is, what has been, what will be, words upon words on a black chalk wall of pain, can I really find the story that only I can write, drenched in blood without oxygen, a naked body without rain dripped upon it on a sidewalk, my father, whose life was severed slowly by the civil war within his own body?

The truth is, it's so much easier to imagine people to be fully evil with no good—that he raped my mother and then was shot in the head like Jesus because he deserved it—because then everything is so clear, siphoned, and finished within me. The truth is, everything feels so utterly—I can hardly think of a word, let alone two—pitiful?

Is it the magic of the lamp, the vodkan electricity within us all that shines far beyond the realm of the ever-so-yellowish globe within every black room of our hearts, glowing far beyond papers forgotten and onto that sidewalk chalk, the words of the dead, reminding us to never forget them, the words and the dead? Write, keep writing, lie, and lie again, if at first you don't succeed, lie, lie again, keep lying until you can tell the truth, until you can admit how confused you really are by all of it, until you're lying down yourself. How attempting to tell it *exactly* how it went won't do, how circumlocutions into worlds would be and could be and should be, my fantasy, won't completely do either, but are necessary all the same for everything to keep going.

And so I seem to continue rolling over all of it, attempting to forget the pain of losing someone. And does it really matter whether you understand my position or not? Won't it all still remain so far beyond pitiful? Written on tablets? Hidden in arks of arcs in parks and nearby avenues?

How many words are the right amount of words?

What if I, I, I the author of my own life story, were to come right out and say it like it is, all boo-hoo like it is, oh boo-hoo: *My father's lungs were scarred from chemical poisons after painting A-10 bombers for years in a factory called Fairchild so that our country could have nicely painted tank-buster planes to fight far-off sandy wars against far-off sandy people, and when*

workers started dying, they conveniently tank-busted their com-
pany name to something somewhere else so they wouldn't feel the
shame of white crosses on fire in military cemeteries.

Does it really make you, or me, feel anything now?

Are we within his lungs? Did we see the chemical mist seer
the vesicles daily? Did you witness a stomatal stigmata? Did
you hear him cough every morning and every evening for
hours for every year that you knew him so that the phlegm, so
gloriously rainbow colored and bright, could simply drip down
a drain and make its way to the sea in a story called *The Young*
Man and the Sea? Did *you*, did I, I, I have anything to do with
it, too legit to quit?

I wonder if we followed that phlegm to the sewer and the
sea, could we, immersed in every detail and every possible
word as symbols, just shifting symbols of those details, then
truly grasp what it's like to suffocate in front of your own family.

And then after years of attempting to understand just what
the fuck was happening to you, you still—after boxes of
research in a moldy Floridian shed—came up with absolutely
nothing.

And then you die.

Were I to write trillions upon trillions upon trillions of
words and novels, one for every molecule of rainbow phlegm
excreted from my father's lungs, and were I to write just one
word—pitiful—both would feel the same to me.

Were I to imagine him to have raped my mother and gotten
shot, our family's simple enemy, an unmistakable evil, oh look,
Hah, Hah, Hah, our own family-friendly Muslim terrorist who
blew up the pillars of our family—or were I to see him as some
kind of martyr for a hot place that needed him to do some-

thing, anything to survive, a simple worker bee in the wrong place and time and country, and splat, wings and stingers scattered on a salt flat, both would be, the same, to me.

For neither accurate description, nor fiction, nor truth, nor words upon words, chalk on walls, seeds on sidewalks, glasses rolling on subways shattering, can do anything to bring him or any father back. It's all somewhat useless, yet for some tugging, a pull, a pool of blood, I feel called to share it now so pitifully nonetheless.

What does it mean when you don't get a sign but you get signs from other people getting signs? Old friends reaching out to you tell you something after years of nothing, because they've had "psychic visions," they said, shaking over the phone, of you, that "You must tell the story of your father, *somehow…*"

You must.

And so, somehow, I want *you* to feel confused, annoyed, bored of the unplanned litany of a slow choking, even if just for a moment as much as I have been, by the reality of dying, bleeding out, right in front of your face. Because that's what it feels like, death. There is no beginning, middle, and end, no clear arc or happy park, yet the story progresses forward with arcane echoes, a light from somewhere that stays within you—is that memory? Energy? God within? All this fuckin' vodka within? That's dying.

I don't believe in being serious about anything. *Life's too important to be taken seriously.* Well, Ray & Oscar, fuckin' homos, neither do I, you, he, she, it, we, they.

I want you to taste the fruit of the fatherless. I want every word of mine that you chew, every unnecessary word of this *story that only I can write,* to be tasteless, yet a cake, gratuitous, yet deliberate, rubbing it all over your lips until you finger-fuck your face.

I declare, I want you to feel my power!

Wherever I go, feel the power between fiction and mostly fiction, because it's all felt the same to me, time, words verbatim, the way we organize all our countless books into these clear-cut piles, this goes here, and this goes there, this is wrong, this is right, this is dead, this is alive, see, look what happened, because it makes us feel better to think we have that kind of control over life, over all information, details, and the way we express those details, when the truth is, it's all quite a tossup, especially since this is the first draft anyway, and the first draft of everything is shit.

And, motherfucker, this is only 800-something words. So, I guess I failed getting that 1,000 like a real writer is supposed to get it, got it, good.

Keep it simple, stupid!

Kiss kiss, bang bang.

I have them here with me, the words, however powerful and few, or weak and pitiful they might be, glowing at me across the pond in the Land of the Free.

And, fatherfucker, if you don't like it you can go fuck yourself with your quill, and run around and shake your 1,000 tail feathers, because I am alive and you're dead to me and I can do what I want.

26

As I Lay Bloody

As I lay bloody on the sidewalk, looking at the bones sticking out of my legs, blood squirting onto the seeds, I could have sworn I had been here before. I could have sworn I would have already gone, at least to the hospital where the doctors wouldn't flinch when I tell them to fuck themselves and give me more morphine or whatever it is that you give someone when they come this close to death in a battle zone, stitches, oranges in baskets, pillows made of cotton candy, and dog food—things like that.

There are no pillows, except for bags of recycling. There is no music, except for final breathing, hissing, the cackling of the pit bull, the cackling of Sunshine, the breathing of that neighbor girl with herpes, the gunshot from the boyfriend who had decided to kill himself instead of calling 911 because he heard the Dreamers were being deported now if they got in trouble. Better to gain control of your death than lose control of your dreams.

This, the sight of me, for him, had been the last hiss, the lass crackle and cackle, wounding me, a fellow Astorian-American on a street lined with trees and so many wires. I was hooked into them, those wires.

I had even written to my Congresswoman—Mahoney? Bellini? Baloney?—and I told her to get control of all these wires, hide them, so everything felt like the West Village, cozy, red velvet cupcakes always around the corner, instead of McDonald's around the corner and so many barbed wires and neighbors with herpes all over their lips that you somehow see more clearly at night when they walk with a hoodie on, and the glow of their phone shines so whitely on the sores. The light is thick and fluorescent. The sores look like trash cans covered in snow, moonlit and silvery and slithery.

This must be the present; isn't that what matters most? Presents? Presence? It's been 10 years I think since my father had suffocated, and here I lay on the sidewalk, bleeding out.

Perhaps he felt the same.

With a slow turn, I was able to look behind me and see Good Oracula.

You see, there was Good Oracula, and Bad Oracula.

Good Oracula, the Polish lady with the Shih Tzus, she lived right beneath Rudolfo and me. Isn't it funny how good people are never timid? The day we met her she and her puppies ran up our steps and we could hear her long hair braid dragging behind her, longer than any hair I have ever seen.

For Christmas she would decorate it with baubles; for summers she would wrap it on her head and wear one of those Jamaican head wraps, which was always so odd to see on a Pole. One day I asked her why she had let her hair grow so long—was it religious? And she told me it was what an angel had told her to do the day after she got electrocuted by lighting by a pond in Poland. Apparently the angel had told her to move to America and clean the Empire State Building for decades and to never cut her hair until a day she'd know what to do with it, until then, dragging her hair on every step of the tower the very same way she dragged her hair to say hello that first day in the apartment.

She handed us donuts she had made herself. "I'm so happy you move in because Thomas so dirty and other Oracula below me so dirty. I tired of dirty sandwich. Here, here, take donut. But eat all so no roaches."

We knew we'd like her from that first day; we knew she was Good Oracula. What's not to like about someone who greets you with donuts and broken English? The fact that she was so shameless about it, her broken English, reminded us, we listeners, that it really didn't matter how well one spoke or communicated really, where they were from, how they wore their hair or what they covered it with, just as long as you were clean and you weren't timid about liking donuts.

Anyone who's dirty and who also doesn't like donuts is always reason for concern. Her presence was always a reminder that life sometimes is like that—so much simpler than we thought it just had to be. Donuts are next to godliness.

Bad Oracula the Greek, who lives in the basement below Good Oracula the Pole, on the other hand, that very first day we moved in, told us "Don't let spics in home. So many spics steal things. You know there too many spics now in Astoria. They kick out our people." I think she assumed we were Greek or something. Rudolfo responded in Spanish, and has never pet her pit bulls, convinced they are the animalistic toddler-eating expressions of her bad, bad soul.

We found out later that she has sex with her brother, the invalid who grunts and groans when you wave at him while he stares blankly at Jesus in the glass box. He seems sweet actually, but his lips are too paralytic to expel anything really understandable, except drool. He smiles at least though, which is much more than Bad Oracula, who's usually covered in a grimace or dog hair or a disheveled wig or hamster-piss-chips or the legs of roaches. See, Bad Oracula is dirty, and she doesn't like donuts. Her brother probably likes donuts, but he's dirty, too. And he drools.

Of course she makes her invalid brother-lover attempt to walk the exceedingly muscular pit bulls. When he does, he usually falls on the ground and breaks yet another bone and then the police come and Bad Oracula will insist it was *their* fault he fell, the government, the government doesn't care about how expensive her medicine is, and how slippery the sidewalks are. She says she's handicapped, but she has plenty enough energy to call someone a "fucking nigger" or "sand nigger" or a "spic" or my favorites, a "spigger" and a "chigger," at least once every other day on the sidewalk with Sunshine, and the accompanying full onslaught of movement that usually happens after that is more exciting than Carnival in Rio, sloppy slaps instead of sloppy kisses. We usually watch from the window munching on happy paleo brownies or magical donuts from Poland.

I'm not sure where we fit in, good or bad, in their minds, perhaps somewhere in between, but in this moment, all I must be to them is bloody.

Good Oracula's hair is sopping up my blood.

She's telling me, "Isss okay, issss okay, Colliee, Collieeee (she always calls me Collie), I make a turn-ta-kit out of my hair. I make turn-ta-kit out of hair. I cut for you. I must cut my hair, for you. I make turn-ta-kit. Angel tell me."

Of course Bad Oracula is slapping herpes girl after calling

her a "dumb spic who hurt neighbor people and make boyfriend commit killacide," and herpes girl is crying—partially out of fear, and partially due to the sound of the gunshot stamping with sound just how very screwed up even more her life is going to get after this moment.

She made a list in her mind to feel powerful against the moment around her:

- Slap fight with old Greek lady who sleeps with her drooling brother.
- Pit bulls trying to bite my leg, but not the one that's dying.
- My boyfriend, just, shot himself.
- After my boyfriend accidentally throws desk at neighbor, aiming for me.
- Neighbor is covered in blood, pretty much legless now, blood squirting everywhere.
- Nice Polish lady is attempting to stop neighbor's blood with hair she's been growing for 40 years.

Herpes girl just got the hedge trimmer and helped Good Oracula cut her braid. Everyone is crying now, for very different reasons, except for me. When Herps and Oracula pull on the hair to create a tight knot—I finally hear Bad Oracula calling the police, albeit after an argument with the operator, insisting she had nothing to do with *this* incident either and that Herps had slapped her first—I don't know if I closed my eyes, but it was then that I was, I am, I am what I am, my father's oxygen tubes in a living room in Florida sometime in the Year of our Lord 2002.

—

Isn't that just so completely miraculous?

Perhaps it was from the power of that Polish angel that told Good Oracula to go clean the tall towers of America. Perhaps it was Sandy's creepy genius clairvoyant daughter who did it. Perhaps it was the fucking French.

I see myself, a former self more than 10 years ago, readying a notepad. I feel my father's worn nostril hairs, his red nose from a lack of oxygen and too much Franzia box wine to numb his body even more, as all the meds seem to do jack shit.

I think it was prednisone, codeine, all manner of drugs and steroids, quite the cocktail that still proved to be wimpy. I hear the hiss of the oxygen tank, and when he breathes in, the air is cool and sterile. I'm making juice in the kitchen for my father, as was custom for over a year, his last year. It was comprised of carrots, apples, zucchini, cucumber, tomato, and celery. I ask him if he wants an omelet. He says something like, "No, but you can make me some tea with honey in it. Just for a minute in the microwave. Then put a tea bag in it."

While I juice, I ask him, so when would be a good time to write down your story?

He coughs, and I feel the vibrations of his failing lungs. Everything cackles and cracks from the ever-present rainbow of phlegm. The warm Florida living-room air combines with the cold oxygen tube air and it feels a lot like good and bad living together, breathing together in his body. My father is nervous. And I am apparently nervous, too.

I felt as though I had to perpetually make a list of things, hyphenated points of his life, my life too. I had to do something to write down who and what he was so that some day I could read it again to faintly remember him again, to hold onto something, anything to keep him from training away to a distant land completely, some part/dot/bullet/blade of a moment, the bloody skeleton of what is, even though we both knew these lists, these stories, are just that, lists of details of stories of parts of our lives, yet somehow, for brief moments, we know it's important, the stabbing motion and emotion of the thing.

"What story?" he asks.

Of your life, your story, and a timeline, you know?

"Well, not right now."

Some more hissing ensues and nothing imbues. A hawk outside flies by one of the large windows from the towering oaks. A spider makes its home in some Spanish moss above. A snake slithers in the yard. And the Snapper mower sits still, in the dark, in the garage.

When's the best time for you, do you think?

"Afternoon, or early evening," he says with a sigh.

"You know, after my morning coughing, and before my evening coughing."

Not that he didn't cough during the afternoon or early evening; it just wasn't as incessant. The house didn't rattle with his lungs as much, with leaves and seeds falling out of the downspouts onto the ground as wet, chunky propellers and rotting dirt.

27

Southern Foam

By golly what is this gloom, what is this confusion?

It has come upon me like a hood, drooped over my forehead, and although it's light, I can see it just a little, the way you see eyelashes when you squint while straining to look at something clearly for the first time.

I used to love Spanish moss after a warm rain, the way it droops and attempts to reach the sandy roads, where salty rusty bikes rest in the grass and fallen leaves, fallen not from Fall, but from a year of being so tired they simply snap. No one hears except a hawk or squirrel or spider, and they watch it fall as many have, and it tickles a bike spoke and balances there until someone picks up the bike the way they used to go to the beach. Used-to. Everything feels so beautifully used-to. That's Florida.

When Rudolfo and I went to the Hammock, Florida, it had been some time since I saw my mother, and she so desperately wanted us to meet her new boyfriend, whom she'd been living with for quite some time, about as much time as Rudolfo and me. I dreaded this, as this, this place, had always been a place of such sunlight and happiness, bright sunlight working its way through the moss hanging from the many towering oaks—the last, it seems, in Florida, "old Florida," they call it—so much light that it twinkles sometimes during orange and lemon and grapefruit peel sunsets, until it rains, and they all look like animals lynched, squirrels suffocated with gray tails, lynched and dangling there for you wet. You worry, they'll fall on your face when you look up. Broken air conditioners. Dead bunnies on fire.

—

I brought back an old clock, supposedly my grandfather's. It says Made in U.S.A. I brought it back from Florida because it looks like something Tom Ford would like. But when I got back to my dark Astorian writing room of trinkets on my left, pipes and books and pictures, and black chalk on my right, words of dead lynched authors, the dust of which falling daily to the wood floor and the iron heater that steams when it shouldn't and cools when it shouldn't, I noticed the clock was covered in a green goo on the electrical cord. Perhaps it was someone's old toothpaste from the year of our American Lord 19 roaring 20.

Perhaps it was the innards of old electric things, grease and melted wires and such, melted from time. Whatever it was, I had to clean it before I plugged it in my writing room as my bear lamp watched, perpetually aroused from the light fucked through his anus, calmly looking at us, me and my grandfather's Tom Ford clock, peaceful. It didn't explode from the new millennium electricity as I had suspected; it just hummed loudly, but not in that tick-tock charming grandfather clock way, but the hum of a hummingbird trapped, stuck in a place and time it shouldn't be.

—

My mother's boyfriend was a tall, lanky sort of thing, stunning, yet lanky like a stick; he carried a mini-Bible in one pocket, the size of a few quarters, the kind with the red letters, everywhere Jesus supposedly *spake* words of holy rare steak. And in the other pocket was a pistol. He'd say things like, "Yeah...sure...I'd come to New York, if y'all just got rid of all the people there."

When we got to the Hammock, something came back, perhaps it was this same gloom, this same confusion, I don't know quite yet, but it was there, palpable like old recently expired meat, on sale, edible because it was frozen quickly and saved on that final date.

Their house was built by him, and it was a collection of surfboards, surfboard, surfboard, driftwood, driftwood, glass bottles, sliding glass doors, and old cars. Synonymous with the hammock, the oaks and palms surrounded the place and brooded over, always threatening to fall, thus far choosing against it for a hundred years or two, and the only spaces in the canopy were the places that the home had carved out on the ground and where the trees hadn't covered the sky above it just yet, with little patches of light then that would pierce through the skylights and twinkle with the mossy sunlight and mossy moonlight and mossy lynch-light.

In the front was a garden of broccoli, beets, carrots, and loofah, or "loaf-ah" as my quirky mother would pronounce it, despite my many corrections. "The loafah really takes off; you plant it someplace, like right here, and look—it just makes a vine and goes."

"Bourby loves using the loafah to clean the boats and the cars."

Her boyfriend's name was Bourby, short for bourbon, which he no longer drank. Like the stray cats popping up when you least expect them, bourbon bottles were scattered here and there, within the garden, above the stove, next to the hot tub. Within them sunflowers were drinking rainwater that had replaced the alcohol that had been within them years ago during apparently darker times within *him*, before he met my mother on a double blind date (and the other two of each pair were actually blind, so they decided to musically switch chairs because who wants to deal with all that metronome-tapping on sidewalks their whole life unless you're already used to it), who "lights up my life," who "saved me from the poison," Bourby would say about her, and even if I tried to be even happier for the two of them, it would be impossible. I am convinced all my efforts would fail in vain, a weather vane spinning aimlessly, pointing everywhere and anywhere away from this place of being perfectly thankful, perfectly thankful she had someone with her again—though, physically healthy this time around.

In the back was the fire pit, the fish pond, and the hot tub, and above them all was a makeshift yet beautiful thatched roof of old surfboards, sliding glass doors, and palm fronds. The fish pond was empty, but the actual pet cats, Bulleit and Daniels, searched for gold anyway. A skilled craftsman and retired builder, Bourby had somehow created a beautiful home out of the oddest of materials. The bed headboards were all driftwood, painted, and arranged in geometric patterns, accompanied by my mother's quilts. The TV was a projector they had found and a roll of paper, under which was a corkboard wall that sometimes would be used as an idea board for another project. It was wonderfully littered with scraps of paper and scribbles and thoughts and diagrams—how they were going to build a hovercraft out of lawnmowers, how they were going to create yet another story on the house despite the voice of Florida telling them they needed an architect's seal on the matter, how that anti-mattered to them, how between the hot tub and the fish pond they were now going to grow worms, which they'd shit on, and then use the worm shit, from the worms eating their shit, as fertilizer for their garden—along with the fish guts from their many fishing trips on the inter-coastal waterway right next to the house, the one that "goes all the way to Maine" and the one that "sometimes you can see dolphins and manatees and stingrays and occasionally alliga-tors," all the things Floridians always say to impress northern-ers visiting.

When Rudolfo and I walked into their Floridian Pee-wee Man-house, solar-paneled and exceedingly comfortable with unneeded blankets and cats and more trinkets and collectibles and decorations than the way Ruby Tuesday's used to be, chock full of old and new Americana and especially Floridicana, like fish nets with pictures and shells, my mother began screaming.

She always did this when she saw me or my brother, and she'd jump up and down so much it seemed like she was one of those early airplane experiments that shook and shimmied and sort of levitated but never flew, mesmerizing and endearing all the same for her unabashed effort to make you feel loved and flying high—you couldn't help but reach your arms out, smile out, and allow her to finish pure love emanating and ricketing and humming within her.

"I...am...so...honored you guys came down...to...see us!" And she truly was. She did her motherly shimmy-shake with Rudolfo, too, attempting to take off again as the cats ran away terrified.

"Welcome...welcome," said Bourby, reaching out his hand as a good Southern gentleman. I've never enjoyed those Southern man-shakes, opting for something between a man-shake and one of my mom-shakes instead, something like a man-hug-shimmy, which makes most men feel uncomfortable, as I purposefully hold onto them and squeeze for that onnnnnne second or two longer than most enjoy, far beyond a simple Southern man-pat on the back.

And to welcome us completely, "Rudolfo, so you'll be in here," Bourby said and pointed to the room on the left. "And you'll be over *here*," pointing to what would be my separate room on the right.

Oh. Okay, I said.

My mother, attempting to conceal her embarrassment as I attempted to conceal my anger, attempted to politely explain the homophobic burlap-sack separation that just occurred, and we could see that she knew it was ridiculous and humming and sewing quietly there, in need of some kind of quick stitch, "It's because you're not married yet is all…that's all."

Ahhhhhh, I said, ignoring the fabricated alligator in the room, a room created, by hand, by two unmarried people, a widow and a widower, who also clearly loved each other.

And in that moment I remember accepting the fact that Bourby could probably be a murderer and I'd still be fine with it, because my mother was the happiest I've ever seen her.

And that's the way it was there, impressively self-made, natural, and relaxing, a bike ride to the ocean, a walk to the river full of animals that could swim to Maine if they wanted, beneath the hundred-year-old oaks, yet a gloom, an ever-so-slight gloom and dark room would overtake me every time I came to—or even thought about—the place.

Visiting for a long weekend with my boyfriend, although a first for me, and after years of being an expat to the north from the backward jungles of the south, I thought that the gloom would have gone away, a children's game no longer played. And it bothered me at the time, because I knew it was something far deeper, far more complex than Fox News perpetually in the background as a poisonous cacophonous incense, or the incessant *Prayer of Jabez* for *prosperity*, accompanied by swigs of moonshine for *health*—because "I don't drink bourbon anymore; those days are OVER," said Bourby with every moon-swig, or the fact that many of my old friends had made decisions I could never agree with if it were me—for instance, coming back here to raise their children instead of raising their consciousness by seeing the world—but something far deeper and churning than all that.

It was as though my soul were the sea I refused again and again to see, and because of the previous night after night of twisting, the morning had brought such a foam to the beach more persistent than mother turtles, and it was inevitable that some would stick to the sand in large, nebulous blobs, which little puppies would run through, or the occasional human foot. And its blurry saltiness would stick in between your toes and your puppy's paws, and it was beautiful, but stunk of rotting fish.

28

From His Tubes

From his tubes I hear the forgotten words.

I hear the hissing.

I hear the breath like stars collapsing daily. I hear the moss swaying in the sun outside. The snakes in the yard slithering. My mother in the kitchen talking about how we should take our church clothes off and get comfortable. I hear my dog, my one-eyed dog Lucy, snorting and farting over the joy of all her new bones that we gave her. I smell the mold, that Florida mold that never seems to go away, the same mold that came back with me to New York when Rudolfo and I eventually came back here, happy for fires with friends, happy we don't live in my hometown where green beans are pickled above the fridge, slightly out of the way but present like the subtle bigotry there and Obama digs, that he and the dirty-Injuns and the sand niggers are ruining America one baby at a time, how anything but white must be black, just look at what they all did on 9/11, Usama and the darkies, Usama was an Indian woman in a sari covered in a nijab covered in a headdress with a basket on her head, and how it just slightly seems like there's a dim halo of, if they could, then they would: gather up everyone who challenged them and their beliefs and pickle them too in jars as beans later to be eaten and shit out for worms to shit out and pour over all their garden vegetables and loafahs and repurposed sofas under the oaks and nightly frog croaks.

That mold, that Florida mold, covered my backpack that I took back to New York, and it covered the photos of my mother and father that I took back with me too, my mother as a cute little farmer girl in Lancaster, my father as a handsome Navy man in paint, because that's how I always want and maybe should remember them, my mother before she had to work in the field, my mother breaking her own back without me even lying on a crack, callusing her feet with tobacco tar, my father before his years of beleaguered asphyxiation, which no book of lies of mine or yours or a whore's diatribe could ever describe. It would get into blankets, that mold, old clothes, old pictures and trinkets, and it would stay within them and on them unless they were boiled.

Because that moldy-stinky foamy-Florida gloom would threaten return, I hesitated to bring anything back with me to my new life in New York at all, because I feared it would somehow grow again, the mold of our garage that would always remind me of lungs failing, coughing, hacking, and watching another human deteriorate like an oak leaf wilting, like moss finally letting go of the tree, hovering to the ground as a repeatedly shot paratrooper, helpless against the gravity pulling him to a rusty bike wheel.

From the tubes I see, on the couch I say, okay, how about just a *timeline* of your life then? Just a few little clicks of time then? Just a hyphen or bullet or two will do.

And right now I am scared of what I've always been scared of, that what I say now won't be right, that it won't be wrong enough either, that I'll ruin all of them, his words. I'm scared I won't remember them correctly even as I listen to and see them brightly now.

They were piles of papers forgotten in a garage, his words, and now they litter my desk and they smell like mold, that mold, as I unravel it, his tale untold, except to me.

Papers and papers of my sad rambles in the hotel where I worked at night, papers and papers *about* his last rambles or lack thereof, papers and papers about driving across America in pain and how America smells like incense made of books and rotting bones and oxygen and sweaty balls. Those precious few papers, his actual last rambles, are all scattered and scatter-brained together under the foot of a silent bear.

Under the foot of the droplets of a boiling Yellowstone geyser.

Under the foot of factory particles in the smog in another city of demons beyond other wooden doors.

How can you recreate/repeat/reduce/reuse/recycle your father's last words without fucking everything up?

Do I simply retype what I typed *then*? I read them again, my thoughts in shambles, and I'm quite convinced that they were even shittier thoughts than these shitty thoughts right now.

There aren't many of them, his last words, and they've been gathering garage mold for over a decade and sitting in the dark bins of photos in my brain. Roaches crawled over these pages, tickling them every so often, flicking them, flicking me, asking me, mumbling, humbling, is it time yet?

And the answer was always no. I've been cautious to proceed.

All that's left of him is a tiny, tiny stone reminder with his name and some dates etched there, with an American flag next to it and a large tree next to that. I visited it once. And other than that, it's just pictures in bins, pictures in my mind, feelings that echo from time to time, but as time goes on they fade too as the mold grows more in the dark, as the foam flutters on an empty crab shell, as wet moss slips to the ground like a suffocated slug, and these last words that I have kept in the blackness, waiting for just, the right, time, to share them.

I think I've been frustrated, because, besides faceless stone, the only thing permanently left is something so impermanent, fleeting, and futile—letters on a white page.

Like the ashes of a body burned and scattered in the ocean, so are last words on a page, Save-As'ed and stored on hard drives, printed and hidden in dark bins, each letter a mold spore spreading and eventually melting away into the movement around you.

Each letter is read and red, so holy, so rare, and each red letter is so pitifully the most important thing out of everything else, all this fucking fluff, because it's what he actually fucking said, and not how we all remember him, our interpretations, our circumlocutory distractions and fictions and attempts like, "And ye shall know the truth, and the truth shall make you free," versus, "They answered him, We be Abraham's seed..."

I mean really, We be?

And so, he says, there on the couch, nostril hairs violently one way with an inhale, violently the other way with an exhale, seaweed in a hurricane,

"You can start out by saying, in the beginning God created Dennis."

"I started working when I was two years old. I learned the value of the almighty dollar. Nobody gave me a car or a college education. I was grown up by the time I was four. I killed my first man when I was five."

194

We laugh, he coughs, mom talks about a beef pot roast, Lucy farts and grunts, and then I say, so what about your father?

"My dad fought the Indians in the Dakotas. He hopped on trains and traveled the whole of America as a bum basically, stealing food, sometimes from pigs. He witnessed Pearl Harbor. He fought in every major battle in the Pacific, and then he saw the A-bomb dropped on Japan. That's where that sword's from [he points to the sword]. Got it off a dead Jap officer who was nuked."

What did he look like, my grandfather?

"My dad had biceps like coconuts; he had tattoos up his arms too. He was like Popeye, kinda short like our neighbor Joe, but really stocky. He used to box on the battleships, and swim, boy could he swim. Your brother looks like him a lot in the face. Bluish-black hair, brown eyes. You have his arms, and my eyes. He dropped out in the 8th grade and left home when he was 12. Did you know, he built our house, too? He went to the damn Home Depot and bought a manual for building homes. And he built one."

What about you? Your schooling?

I left when I was 17, in the 11th grade. During that time, I used to skip school, ride horses with ice and beer in our saddlebags to a bar 20 minutes away, get drunk, and then ride drunk back 20 miles. One of the worst memories I have is when my dad and I got drunk together one time, and we got into a fistfight. I hit him, and because I hit him, my father, he cried. I felt about this big.

[He pinches his fingers like he's holding a potato chip. Tears form and begin to drip down his cheeks. He wipes them away.]

I worked construction for a while though until I got my draft notice. I mainly worked with prisoners and ex-prisoners all over southern Missouri. I used to drive this oil truck rig up the hills of Missouri and about killed myself. It was full of oil that sprayed the ground after we first laid the seed down, and then used [some machine] to shoot hay over the seed. Then the oil would make the hay flat and make it stick. And that's how we made grass on the medians all throughout Missouri. But when we got to our hotels, we'd get ready and we'd go out and raise hell, drinking, and eatin' catfish."

29

Another Tower

Holy father take me there.

Take me there. Holy father take me there.

I have complained about many things, about the jolt of the office printer behind me, the screams of corporate banality in front of me, get thee behind me Satan, when all I desired was silence, and then about the jolt of silence when all I desired was music, how we're never happy with where we are and now you've seemed to answer my prayer by taking me everywhere. So do what you must.

I want to see the future. Take me there. Holy blood, take me there. There's so much blood.

Take me there through the calls of insurance clients yawning and pawning about exclusions and endorsements or how much they think money will let them live forever—or at least—how they act like they care if their children will be taken care of, when deep inside, within all the terms and conditions of the papers of their soul, they simply wish they could hole-punch everything and put it in a binder and hold onto it, libraries, pope catacombs they think they're building now beneath the salty cathedral streets of Park Avenue and all the bitter dead angels above.

There is a flood looming and it's not from above, but from within, and we'll all get off the train to find it raining from cracked pipes and crack pipes and the workers, spitting and smoking, will brush the collected water down the steps and it will fall as a dirty waterfall and we'll still complain on our way to work. We have things we need to accomplish. Nothing is right. And we've never been surprised or had an impression about anything.

I want to see the future.

What will be the next thing that we regret?

What will be the next thing we forget, create, hate, and think we love more than breath, more than water droplets laced with grease and rat hair trickling into our eyeballs as rewetting drops for the contacts we hate because we want the laser, and the laser before the drone's ball sac is implanted in our eyes if you can afford it because it makes everything better but, oh, is it risky. What will be the next thing we know we shouldn't have lynched, we know we shouldn't have burned, the jhenocyd we shouldn't have ignored?

I see a tower, another one, for now the sky is filled with them, but this one is the most important, we think. It shimmers in the night, and during the day the façade changes with the weather. It bubbles when the sea foam gushes in from a nearby hurricane; it cracks when the sun is particularly scorching. We seem to have figured out by now that instead of fighting nature, we could simply mimic it, flow with it, become one with it. When snow falls, the tower becomes a slippery crystal, and in the summer when life is sweaty and lush, it's a foreboding grassy glassy spear that reaches the clouds, at 1,776 times as tall as the towers, dumb and still, dead and arrogant, of when I worked at Heller, Heller, & Hah, 1,776 years ago, when condo developers thought it was right to respect dull heights more than creativity.

I am a white eagle, one of the thousands that nest in the towers with coves and perches for them, and from faraway it looks like a skinny island in England (INSERT NAME later, that damn village in that documentary on Netflix that I watched with Rudolfo, the one that once had villagers on it who used to live off eating so many birds that they eventually got sick and threw up bird bones and then bile, I guess the name doesn't really matter), little white dots covering the brown and green. And as a lawnmower forms inevitable geometric shapes and diagonals as the grass is cut, so the name of the tower can be seen clearly, but intermixed with other fine lines: The Soup Tower.

There was a time, a revolution, *after* the one that finally empowered artists and writers and made them the most powerful people on the planet, for quite some time, that is, until they too began to wage wars against one another from barbaric jealousy in the name of freedom, instead of barbaric greed in the name of the same as we did before.

Millions of towers were erected for them, too, beginning with that first one, the Bill Cunnilingus Tower with the inscription from Phil Cuntybundles, and there was a time of peace when we truly expressed ourselves and found that helpful and found that more important than money for a while until we began using creativity as the new currency, belittling those who didn't have it, until new Pollock-like fishy-painter-Hitlers and wishy-washy-writer-Nazis came and went and the world regrouped yet again, learned its lesson yet again—never trust an artist, never trust a writer especially, completely at least, for he lives to spy on you, his life is an ulterior motive, to write a flurry of words about you, to make fun of how important you think you are, and if you let him he'll keep going until he rips out your heart and drinks your blood in the moonlight, silver liquid dripping down his sari-covered nijab and all over his hairy chest, and it's the most beautiful thing you've ever seen.

This time, this revolution though, it was about food, and the billionaires that survived the previous revolution left their fortunes in whatever artistic currency it was (like walking into a coffee shop and throwing paint on someone's face—the more colorful paint gotten in the eyes meant the more elaborate the cappuccino art produced by the baristas, who were of course at that time named "artists," until we realized it was just milk and they always did the same damn Christmas tree), and families left their trusts, and entire countries disbanded their paintbrushes and their claims on who-said-this and who-made-that and left it all for one thing, this one place, The Soup Tower.

All religions, all cultures, all peoples of the world, eventually with time, whittled down their hearts to their simplest forms—what is at the center of the Tootsie Pop of survival? What can we all do? What can we all lick and lick and lick together cross-eyed?

And a white eagle fell at that congress of the moment from running into another black bird and everyone thought it was dead and said bye-bye, black bird, but it really just got knocked out for a while, and then a man began cooking it on a fire made of glitter and clocks and feathers and foam and the world ate bird meat together.

The highest calling of this time isn't to succeed, not to create, not to destroy, not to retain, not to cover our belongings with insurances, umbrella coverage upon umbrella coverage upon umbrella coverage, excess liability in excess of in excess of in excess of in excess of, or to remember your dead dad and his dumb life and how you pretended he was a rapist for a while (I mean you weren't even really that close, which many times I thought is the reason why you like dick, intimacy only at the very end, until I realized that kinda thinking is just milk and Christmas trees, too), but all of it left for the rain, so that things can grow, to simply eat together, all people.

And no one takes their first bite until all have at least something—some form of soup or bread or bone or bile—in their hand ready to lick or slurp or suck.

Something seems to have clicked for us, and looking back we all seem to know that *hunger* was worse than burning Jews in ovens or lynching niggers or saying the word nigger because it's wrong to bring up a bad past by using words that were eviliciously-lynchy-famous then and then later *not* saying the word nigger for freedom of expression, for freedom from all bad feelings, until we stabbed each other with keyboards and paintbrushes in its name, attempting to only feel good all the time, or letting only the douchebags who were the meanest and richest run the world dictating our breath and our life's calling, bawling, and what we do with our fingers and lips and the contents of our character and the contents of our shit on a daily basis.

We realized that hunger is worse than all harm because it's the complete absence of love and the result of forgetting we're not much different than white eagles here, flowing with the wind, flying with the seasons, thankful for the sun's bite and the foam of the stinky sea and how it carries sand or a seed to something somewhere even if we can hardly see it.

Somehow the air feels different, maybe indifferent; there's a humor in it, the beginnings of a resounding giggle, from remembering how silly, how painfully silly we had been, and still will continue to be, how we know as we chew and chew how we will regret how we are once again at some point in the far beyond, how our lives and the things we do seem to be closer to the curves and the repetitions of rotini, the pastan crevices of which can both comfort and shame again and again until we come out from the other side renewed, forgetful again of where we once were, yet evolved ever-so-slightly from coming out of a spiral, from forgetting and then remembering again how to sit still and love.

30

From The Keys

From his tubes I hear the words.

From his tubes I hear the hissing nearby.

From the keys I feel my fingers pound each key, and I remember those dark days, every letter on every finger, those days where only lists of words comforted me as my father slipped away from me in the night, those days in the day where cucumber, carrot, ginger, and apple juice weren't saving him, and I attempted to extract every word from him the same way his lungs attempted to extract every particle of oxygen out of the air, out of the tubes, out of anything he could, sucking on leaves and screaming at the stomata within their skin, with both of us doing very pitiful and shameful jobs, but the first draft of everything is shift anyway.

I know I like to make lists in the way my fingers touch my face, 26 faces, each key; there's such a mission to every letter, as if by my making lists, I would create the new structure of something, a new skeleton, new organs, a Frankenstein of needs met, vegetables gotten, chicken gotten, and all would be well the next morning forgotten, if I just made a list in the night.

From the tubes of my father's bitter nostrils, from the keys punched, beating my face to a plastic pulp, to the electricity of the computer hum of a seaside night job blowjob hotel, that electric whiteness, fizzing blankness, warmed me then, and I can feel it right now.

I can read it now, bubbling as the seeds drenched in blood begin to grow and cut the cement and soil and rock and magma flowing beneath me.

In the beginning was the Word:

—*My wart is getting bigger on my thumb.*

—*I'm at work as a night shift front desk receptionist here at Hammock Resort, Florida's Newest Premiere Untouched Resort, listening to some jazzy-Koooool ambiance cha-cha music that makes me want to dance for some parts, but then during others, it's ruined as if the DJ jazzy mixer guy decided to mix in the elevator jazz with the kool stuff. Or maybe he just threw up on the record.*

—*I live in a spaceship next to the ocean. It's exactly one minute from my job. Some would call it a glorified cinderblock trailer with one lousy octagon dining/kitchen/piano/TV/breakfast-nook-room with a bedroom wing on either side, but I like to call it our family spaceship. There are daunting oak trees all around it, which make it seem more like a pimple on the earth's skin, underneath its burly beard. I hate beard pimples—the worst. Garlic works. Sometimes it doesn't. The wart on my finger is getting larger. Garlic didn't work for that. Sometimes it will throb; I'll look at it and be disgusted with myself, realizing I'm a person who gets warts.*

—*Before I type out these lists, and others, I'll often first use a red Sharpie on a folded piece of computer paper and I'll write down whatever comes to mind, but mostly, simply, what I'm going to do each day, or what I'm doing right now, which in effect, verifies each act's existence, this moment and I'll smell the stench of the Sharpie each time.*

—"Chester the skin doctor" with a little hyphen next to it, knowing that "wart" is supposed to go next, but, in case someone finds my list, I don't put it down.

—I've already had the wart burned off once by Doctor Chester, who usually just gives people Botox injections. He's one of the kindest men I've ever met, probably never needing or wanting Botox for himself. He seemed kind until he burned me with liquid nitrogen with a subtle smile, almost apathetically. It was quite creepy actually, even when he told me "it's okay," when he only charged me for the visit, because I told him my dad is handicapped and I am poor and I don't have insurance of any kind, for myself and especially not for anyone else.

—The juice I made the last morning consisted of cucumber, green grapes, and kiwi. I also made carrot-pear-apple-pineapple juice. And I chopped up a couple cloves of garlic and ate them raw to kill whatever plague seems to be eating me up right now.

—It feels as though my brain is eating itself; maybe it's not a cold, but a parasite that I got from Lucy licking her asshole/ vagina area and then on to my lips, my arms, the hair on my legs.

—This evening when I got up, laying in my pink swirly sheets my mother freshly put down this morning on the Murphy bed, I first imagined myself at the Belle Terre Swim and Racquet Club, where shriveled retirees usually stare at me and say things to me like, "I'm not like YOU anymore," when I get red-faced lifting a dumbbell, or after swimming when I get out of the shower naked to grab my towel in my locker, letting my warm nuts slink to the ground like moss.

—In my dream I was working out alone and just one other, a sweaty girl in an orange bikini. Mirrors all around. 70s music

playing as usual. My shirt was off doing the bench press; she was struggling with her 3-lb. weights. She was pushing them up in the air after squatting down, down, tightening her thong around her butt cheeks. She asked for my help. Somehow it was nonchalant and casual for me to pull off her top and bottom and fuck her from behind while massaging her tits. There were various positions on the bench, treadmill, and presses. We lay on the grey gym carpet, sweating, panting; she tickled my chest hair with one hand, the other rested on my warm dick and long balls. Breathing heavily there on my bed, I wiped off my jizz mixed with baby oil. Then I read some Psalms to her, and then some of Jesus's red letters to help myself feel just fine for one day, free, forgiven, righteously angry, just for one day, released, red-faced, red-lettered and released.

—Lucy, by the way, is getting bitchier by the day the older she gets. She's turned into quite a bitch. She's like an old bitchy woman. Just like the 10-pack-a-cigarettes-a-day squirrel-lady that used to live caddy-corner to us in the green trailer who'd throw hot water on the neighbor kids while feeding and talking sweetly to the squirrels...until the Hammock Wrecking Crew (the crew that nowadays slowly goes around picking trailers at random to destroy, making way for the New York yuppies) apparently came and knocked her green-goblin trailer down. I remember driving by there one day; the lot was empty. Perhaps she took her squirrels and left with the wind.

—Perhaps she died and her bitchy spirit entered Lucy, and with each bark and growl, Lucy's really just become more and more frustrated because she can't boil the cold water she's given each day to eventually throw at us to scar our faces with all the letters of the law. Bitch. I actually never met the green trailer woman, but I bet she did throw water on the kids. Or maybe

Twizzlers because she just wanted a few little friends and had to settle for squirrels.

—My mother's father was apparently an asshole; he gave us a desk, though, on which I first write my lists in red before I get to work for the night shift, where I type them out in black now, needlessly so, thinking someday I'll look at this shit again. There's a key ring, like for jail cells, one for every drawer. One day I opened all of them up, red Sharpie fragrantly asphyxiating the room, and there was jack shit in them, and the key ring isn't medal; it's a shoestring.

—He died from a ruptured aorta at work.

—Whenever I'm on a Nazi cleaning binge in my room comprised of my fold-up Murphy bed, my grandma's old lamp—she's sweet, my grandma, a step-one though, because my real grandma hung herself in my mother's childhood family tobacco barn because she was depressed and being depressed was apparently shameful and Satanic for Mennonites—my grandpa's desk, some pictures of my brother and I on the beach, taken for our mother and father, and then there's a Walmart glamour shot of my mother wearing sequins and a poofy scarf, of course clothes strewn about, storage, Baby Oil for whacking off, and a rocking chair.

—I'll have to call Dr. Chester and ask him to burn it off again I guess, the wart, and with the same insurance-less discount. It keeps coming back, and it looks like little particles of dark mold beneath my skin.

—Dad and I sat on the couch today, and we tried to talk, but he couldn't, so we watched Cinderella Man instead. My whole life I think we've watched more movies together, sitting there together, eating popcorn, farting, laughing, watching fake stories of other people's lives together, than we've actually talked *together. During the rough fights, when Cinderella Man was getting whooped, Dad would yell out, very seriously, "Come on, Cinderella Man!" even though he'd already seen it multiple times. And then we'd pause it because the juice I make him every day gives him the runs. So he picked up his tubes, which are connected to his oxygen machine, which constantly hisses and clacks and purrs.*

—Twenty-four hours a day.

—The kind, fit, sweaty, muscular oxygen man comes each week in his blue oxygen truck that should have a jingle really, as if it were delivering ice cream. He quickly fills the liquid oxygen tank that sits outside our door on the patio; it's shiny and it wobbles now and then with weird noises, a dying R2D2 out back. It's basically a container for "oxygen in bulk," which can be hissed out into a smaller carrying case used for "day trips," which are rarely taken. Through the dirty sliding glass door, sitting there outside, collecting leaves, R2D2 seeps out white steam like a constant geyser, eventually lowering its contents, eventually requiring another fill-up from the Oxygen Man.

—The permanent MACHINE, though, the even hissier-and-pissier one that sits next to the fridge, only requires water, the air inside our stuffy spaceship, and some plastic supplies that are also brought to us by the happily-diddly-do Oxygen Man.

—Dad picked up his tubes, his antibacterial Chubb Wipes, grunted a few times, and walked to the bathroom. He went about seven times during the course of the movie. I just farted garlic clouds.

—I played soccer earlier tonight and got sicker. I wasn't going to go, but I looked back in my dark bedroom covered in clean white clothes that still look perpetually dirty, hearing more of the hissing, clacking, and my dad's coughing, and realized it was

either THAT or running around a bit with a ball. I chose running because it felt like I was going somewhere, with anyone, but
death.

—Lists help me get things done.

—Most of all, though, they help me avoid things I don't want
to think about. It makes me feel better to write down "type stories," then HYPHEN, "Father," even though when I come home
from work, I'll immediately have to go to sleep, or Dad is too
"out of breath," or I'll go to the gym, or we'd rather watch a
movie again than talk about what's happening, or I'll have to
take Lucy for a walk, or eat, or clean my car, or clean my room,
or make a list.

—So I'll just make a list.

—Yesterday at dinner, after having some more fresh juice,
Mom toasted joyously, "To Health!"—and Dad was still, with his
head in his hands wearing his liquid oxygen tubes, hissing on the
glass table and his juice unmoved.

—And after Mom's glass and my glass clinked there in our tiny
spaceship living room and we all said, "Mmmmmmmmmmmm-
mmm," loudly, in an effort to get my Dad to lift his head up to
take a sip, then he did. And then we waited about twenty more
minutes for him to say the only prayer he ever says, the one he
learned when he became an Eagle Scout long ago, partly at my
mother's insistence that he say it, and that we wait for him to say
it, the man, "the spiritual leader of the home," and surprisingly,
partly at his own insistence that he say it too, finally said, "For
food, for raiment, for opportunity, for friendship, for fellowship, we give the thanks, O Lord, Amen."

—And each comma was about a minute or two of us waiting,
and my mother and I sat there with our glasses held high, waiting, and almost in tears waiting, for how brittle his body is

becoming, peanut brittle you get on St. George street in St. Augustine, the oldest city in America, but we held them back, the tears, and we all drank Franzia box wine and ate cow meat together. And to lighten the mood as he always does when things got too serious, my father somehow found the air in his lungs to scream out a,"HOOOOO-WAAAAAAH!!!" like blind Al Pacino in Scent of a Woman.

—Then I went on a run with an old high school friend, Timothy, in the dark on the sand and under the oaks, talked about how "unhappy" I am here, how "depressing" it's getting to be around someone who's depressed and sick, how I want to just go anywhere...even though I know deep within that it won't solve anything, or be wise, to run, even though I knew deep within, that those words I just said didn't at all describe, well, THIS.

—How I'm purposefully holding back, yet searching for some way to leave.

—And when we ran and talked, I could have cried. I felt the same way inside when I've cried in the past, what one normally feels before they cry, and even as they're crying, but I, I, I for some reason, held the tears back yet again because I didn't want to stop running just to cry; I just kept going and kept it all in without making sense of any of it. Timothy listened well, but of course didn't understand. How could anybody if even I couldn't?

—He eventually talked about how he has to get so many "pastor internship ministry credits" in order to graduate. Then we played dominos with about 20 random people at his house. Then I went to work, and here I am. I stole milk from the fridge here. I am what you call a BADASS.

—"Tomorrow night I play soccer. I want to do that more than anything," I just said out loud, and now I punch the keys. I've been playing amazingly well. Everybody wants me on their team.

Perhaps it's because I go after that ball like it's a tiger with rabies and it's clawing at my family and trying to rape each one of us, one by one, and it feels good, to murder a rapist. It's what real men do. They go to war and they kill rapists.

—I'm so fucking hungry right now.

—And with that, flashes of Jack Nicholson's Shining face come before me throughout the night, here in this abandoned hotel. It reminds me of California. When I think of that state, I think of hunger, of free Quaker food, of no pride, and of being past hunger, into some sort of monk-like desire-less state of levitation above all others, or cynicism against all others, either one, because there's not much difference.

—Out there I remember contemplating stealing. My college roomie Darius, who drove out there with me, told me not to do it. I was like, "come on, it would be so easy."

—Instead, I used half of certain items, returned them to Safeway, got the money, and bought lattes to remind myself of how easy and foamy and sweet FSU was, how Spanish moss swayed there too and how it looked like the long hair of mystical Southern queens.

—I remember walking around all of Berkeley one day with Darius after having only free coffee samples from every single coffee shop we passed. That was breakfast. I remember looking at these pink-purple flowers that were too bright. My eyes hurt from looking at them. Every time I passed them, they were always too bright.

—Tons of them, like some sort of pulsating color blob from another world. Nuclear-Fusion Pink. I could only say, well, nothing, or something like, "look at those flowers."

—One time we passed them and, magically, their pollen poofed some destiny for us, right after we found Darius a brand

"new" (to us) shining mattress on the side of the road. Spankin'
new it seemed, especially since he'd been sleeping on a "futon,"
(we called it), which was really just broken boards, splinters, and
a sheet with holes and stains.

—After inevitably becoming the weird Florida poor kids who
came to California thinking they'd find fame as writers or even
something better, dragging the result of our search, our prize,
our stained mattress up the stairs of the fraternity house full of
stares and dirty rich horny Asian boys, Darius decided he liked
the more uncomfortable futon instead—'cause that's what he was
used to. We saved it, the mattress, for guests who never came.

—I just had tomato soup and an English muffin and Benadryl
and Zicam and even more garlic.

—Now the music is all suck. Well, fuck. I'll turn it off.

—This whole Air Force idea my dad has implanted into my
head has got me daydreaming again, trying to find positives. For
example, what if I became a General? Or a Colonel? Perhaps
I'll get laser surgery and I'll become a pilot, even though at this
moment I can't picture myself doing that in the slightest. But I
could. I could do many things. (In the military you sign up to get
laser surgery, and after a while they just give it to you. At least
that's what the recruiter said.) Or what if I got a medal of some
sort? Then, I also picture myself blowing something up accidentally, like with a missile. Maybe even a city full of French people.
Or half of Haiti.

—One of my biggest reservations about the whole thing is having to shave my beard off. I feel like it's my power. And I'll probably get even more man-pimples without it. Or having to pee in
a barrack trough in a line, all of us soldiers acting as if we can't
see each other's dicks. Actin' all cool, shootin' some B-ball outside
o' the school, when a couple a…and what if I get erections again

in the shower when I look at the other boys, like I always did at camp in the Boy Scouts?

—It would be amazing though if I moved up in the ranks at least once. That would be one more than I got in Boy Scouts—"Tenderfoot," I was. My brother was all Mr. MacGyver-perfect-son-Eagle-Scout, whereas I cleaned the kitchen, dressed up in mom's clothing, watched dirty movies at friends' houses, burned things in the woods, and fake-masturbated with stuffed animals and my hand until I found out about a thing called jizz and all the lubricants to be found in a beautiful thing called the refrigerator.

—Then later on down the road, my brother got one too many tattoos during his Lynchburg-Christian-Crazy-Liberty-Town rebellion. I stopped purposefully hanging out with, as my father says, "the fags of California," and recently got me a girlfriend who was all right with fucking for the first time as well at 23. Then she moved to London, and my penis has never been so sad. And everything is starting to switch, and lately every midnight I've been putting my thumb up my ass with lotion supposedly from London. Brown's I think. How appropriate. Yesterday I tried two fingers. Tonight I'll try three, my dying father, a son, and the Holy Spirit.

—Tomorrow I'll wake up at night and realize I have to wait for something else.

—Dad said something interesting to me today in one of our brief bonding talks sitting across each other at our glass table that wobbles, and when he told me, right then, I realized that it was the one truth I was never told. Or if I was told, I never understood it until now, but even now I don't want to believe it, because it's so hard to digest.

—He also said this to me:

—*"One of my biggest regrets was not accepting his offer to work at his nursing home as a nurse. He paid for mom's education. He was going to pay for mine; he said to us, 'I wish I had you two.'*

—*We said, 'well what do you mean?' He says, 'If you work for me for two years at the nursing home, I'll pay for you to become a nurse. Dennis, I think you'd also be a great nurse.'*

—*And I immediately shut it out and said, 'Male nurses are queers, I ain't doing that.'*

—*And in turn, I ruined my health and my lungs because after that I started working at Fairchild in the factory, making A-10s, using Beryllium. Even MY Dad told me, 'Son, Never work in a factory and stay in the military.'*

—*Both of which I didn't do. I got out of the military because your mom didn't like it; she'd been up there in Mennonite country with all the conscientious objectors for so damn long separate from the rest of the world, thinking everyone and everything's EVIL if they aren't GOOD. So I got out, and I don't blame her. It just seems like I've been flailing and rolling around ever since; it's amazing, though, what I did with what I had.*

—*I wish my dad could have seen me, how far I did get, working as a contractor operating three entire Navy bases. He wouldn't have believed it."*

—*And then he seemed to feel tears brewing inside, too, but decided to hold them all inside, just like me, running and hiding, even when sitting on a couch, suffocating and stuck, in between life and death.*

—As I type, my wart starts to throb again. Chester doesn't care. He's fast asleep with that same creepy smile.

—Bitch.

31

I Miss The Space Shuttle

Phil got so upset that day—the day of the rant, the words of which later inscripted, of course, as I said, onto the tower for artists in the future, well before the revolution, naturally, for the tower of soup.

Phil got so upset that day because his three kids were run over by a black limo rushing down Park Avenue. And I overheard Mr. Hah talking about it, too, to his perfect blonde wife on the phone down in Palm Beach, the one who so famously puts together THE ILLUSTRIOUS OF THE PALM BEACHES, a who's-who of sorts, and far more important than its listing of accomplishments—what business was sold to whom, or how much they donated to what poor village outside N'Djamena, Chad, even though it was full of Muslims who spent most of their day praying to the "wrong god" and tending to "motherfucking camels, but we gotta show the world we are open-minded, that camel-fuckers deserve our hard-earned money, too"—it was all about the couples, a who's-who of perfect smiling couples, smiling with Orbtizy sparkle-teeth on their dyed-green lawns near the beach, with their respective palaces and cars and pools behind them. Houses and people and pools and smiles. She considered it her life's work really, and other people found it better than most things they had done or donated or created because at least *this* people loved putting on their coffee tables. And if you got featured in the Illustrious, your life had truly begun.

Naturally, I got looped into the design of this and that for the Illustrious, and certain English corrections, which were never listened to—like ending a thought in a preposition. It seems that rich people have a certain way of saying things grammatically incorrect that somehow sounds better to them; sometimes they'd even add a British accent to certain words randomly, like "toilet" would be all drawn out to "tooooooooooooooy-laaaaaay" which always sounded like "ole!" Then again, that's where British accents came from anyway, as we know, an entire class' need to sound more important than they really are. Basically they had watched too many Cary Grant movies thinking accents were the key to class, when we know it's really just having wonderful hair and letting people stare.

I had walked into Mr. Hah's office the morning of the apple-stabbing (which would happen later in the day, along with the accompanying subsequent note of warning—to not repeat what I had just overheard).

That morning he slammed the door when he truculently arrived to his office, but he thought it had latched. He thought he was alone. It swung back open, which I thought was an invitation to continue about the business of the day. I had been warned previously that—closed door or open—"never wait, DO YOU UNDERSTAND ME, Never, Wait, even if I'm on a call, everything is important, always. Nothing can ever stop!"

Standing there at his opened door, the Pope covered in glass watched me as I waited and simply watched Mr. Hah's head shake as if a cat were swatting at it and his head were a capricious ball of yarn. He was whispering to his wife, Helen, and I heard her screaming over his whispers, "Don't tell anyone, did anyone see you!? It was early anyway, no one saw you, but fuck, what about Mr. Sherry?!"

"I took care of it. But fuck, but fuck what about Phil, his children, I ran over all of them, ALL, of them; I was pulling Mr. Sherry's ear and telling him not to brake for anything because I was running late and when he kept going so goddamn slow...I pulled his ear really hard, and the ear ripped off a little and he turned his head and screamed and closed his eyes and went through a red light—I didn't even realize how close we were to St. Christopher's School. I saw their bodies rolling. I saw one of their heads roll down the street, decapitated, and plop into an open manhole. Another splattered into a wall. And another exploded under the tires. It was sooooo damn foggy this morning too and we were going so quick that no one saw anything."

I heard his wife giggle through the phone, "You've gotta be kidding me, one of their heads fell into the sewer?"

"Jesus, Helen. Yes. Into the goddamn sewer."

"Okay, well, but Mr. Sherry, we can trust him, we don't have to worry about anything?"

"Yes, anything...nothing. Nothing. Anything."

"Uh, are you sure?"

"Yes, I took care of it—but Helen, it's what *you* would have done, right? There's nothing I could have done. It was the fog, it was just one of those days we can't control, and it's best I came straight here, right, tell me I did good, tell me I did good...."

She giggled again and then boldly declared, "I declare, you are powerful. You are wise. You are in control. You will do what you need to do to make us more successful than our wildest dreams. It's what God wants for us. Your parents brought you to America for a reason. To make money. To become better than just white and powerful or even black and powerful, but better than both. To fight more than anyone has ever fought! We deserve this!!…And we're not gonna let some stupid kids stand in our way. We will, we WILL run over more if we have to…"

He nodded his head and then he turned around to see me, standing there, waiting for him to finish, in between the sides of the frame of the doorway.

This time he threw a paperweight, just missing my chest, that went through the drywall and into the conference room. "What the fuck are you doing in my office what the fuck did you hear TELL ME WHAT YOU HEARD NOW OR YOU'RE FIRED—or worse."

And so I told him, creepily calmly somehow, Okay Mr. Hah, you killed all of Phil's children on your way here this morning. Phil doesn't know yet. Mr. Sherry will be paid globs of money, and we'll probably see him in the Illustrious next year once he most likely moves in next to you and all the other murderers down there I guess.

—

And in that moment I knew I should tell the police at some point what I heard, but something within me held something back, something made me wait a little longer, just a little bit longer, somewhere in between right and wrong. Simple, sick curiosity perhaps—just *what would this creature do to keep his empire intact?*

And somehow deep within Phil's heart, he knew what had happened because he was in the foulest of moods when he

arrived that morning, as if all evil from that act—when a heart-
less machine brutally slices and dices up teenagers on the street
and dumps their brains in the sewers for the rats and the workers to eat—surfaced as bubbles of angry blood on his tongue.

Fiery words ensued. Things changed. The Rant ensued and
changed the world forever, when Phil, the kind buffer Phil,
finally became truly corrupted and accepted THE NORM,
THE EMBODIMENT OF CORPORATE MUCH-ADO-
ABOUT-REALLY-NEEDING-TO-GET-FUCKED-IN-THE-
ASS, ABUSE-SPEAK, HAH-SPEAK.

Somehow his body knew to react first, clandestine neutrinos
of warning flowing through him, along with the secret light of
a far-off explosion, speaking in angry tongues at all of us, The
Rant, which later would be justified when he got the call from
the police after my walk in the park that they had some bad
news, that he had three mostly unrecognizable bodies to iden-
tify, that they were really sorry that they don't know what happened, that there were no witnesses, that there was too much
fog, and as Phil's body had already reacted in mysterious anger,
completely unlike him, the calm plump buffer, upon *hearing*
the news, after feeling the news, that his children had been
slaughtered on the street by an unidentified black car in the
white fog of Park Avenue, he said nothing.

The Rant had already come and gone.

As such, there was simply silence after the call.

And then this.

Since he and his wife had not had sex for thirteen years, and
since he was planning on leaving her anyway, and since his
children were the only reason he came to work, each one jus-
tifying each brass "H" on the door with no letter of his own,
suddenly, yet calmly, he felt, with the anger darting through

him unknowingly at first, each lonely neutrino slicing freely through his organs, all that was left was a peace, the emptiness, the silence, the ephemeral tube, the secret leftover lube each neutrino left in its wake, and it surpassed all of his understanding, all traffic lights, every insurance liability he had spent his entire life crafting, past the daily construction sites of our minds, daily erecting new meanings for our lives, and the reasons we get up every day, new words, new breaths. And now within that peace he felt as though he were simply now left behind.

He let out a whimper. "Wait for me, my loves," and he reached in his desk, pulled out the very first two letter openers he had ever received, brass too, arranged one blade next to each pupil, stood up, and fell forward to follow his children when the brass finally and quickly cracked through his skull as two bright horns through the back of his head.

After the music and thud of Phil's body ushering forth, and after Miss Allison's, "What was that, is Mr. Hah okay, that sounded like a body, I've heard that sound before, that sounded like a body..." and after she ran by Phil's office, completely ignoring the puddle of blood spraying and soaking into the dusty Oriental rug, she ran straight into Mr. Hah's office but had to wait, because he was taking a piss in his personal toilet.

Sometimes it seemed as though he hooked up loudspeakers to his bathroom so we could hear him piss, as if the sound was the aroma of one thousand wolf cocks emanating throughout the office like the angel of death warning us that he indeed owned us and not to try anything except wait for our next command from the alpha dog and the omega piss on our face—but remember, never wait.

Sandy got up from her desk and ran to Phil's office and, of

course, began screaming as though *she* were the one who had just stabbed her own eyes with swords of brass, as she fell to the ground with Phil far from ranting and rubbed her face in his blood so that plenty would get on her hair, so that she could tell us later, many times, how she, "was the first one on the scene…out of all the shit I have to deal with…this too, *THIS*, and I don't think I'll ever be the same, I don't know if I can *hoad* it together, I mean, Phil was a really close friend," even though we knew she didn't have any.

Miss Allison, decades-numb and blank-faced, looked at Phil's body next to the desk, with Sandy crying there and rubbing blood on her face—with her blood-covered fists waving in the air and screaming "whyyyyyyyy, oh god no, whyyyyyyy," when really she was just thinking yet again about how she probably shouldn't take a full long weekend when she goes on vacation next in New Jersey, not with everything that needs to be done now—and Miss Allison looked at it all like it was a little bird pecking on something it shouldn't.

"Well what's *that* doing here," she said declaratively.

That, she said.

I dialed 911 without even saying anything, because I decided to get up and throw up in the bathroom. I came back and sat down as the operator was still speaking on speaker phone. I still didn't answer. I thought about silence. I thought about the note on my desk that morning, the apple, and the scissors that were stabbed through it.

Miss Allison ran to the break room, began brewing some Keurig shit-pods in case Mr. Hah needed some emergency coffee, and grabbed all the bubble-paper and paper towels that she could find and then pitter-pattered back to Phil's. She began sopping up Phil's blood with the paper towels and then wrapped the bloody mess in bubble paper like she was going to ship it somewhere far away from us.

"What are you doing, what, in God's Holy name are you doing, Madeline!?" screamed Sandy. "This is a CRIME SCENE. YOU CAN'T TOUCH AAAAAANNNYYYYYYYTHING," she cautioned, thinking about all the *CSI* she had watched in her life with her Sun-In husband, and she continued to warn everyone about the "gravity," she said, of the situation with her blood-smeared face and blood-soaked hair that she refused to clean off, with tears and snot torrentially spraying and dangling off her face.

Mr. Hah waited at the door for the police; the operator still kept questioning if anyone was there. I continued to sit the way I always sat there, stuck, with the cancerous realization that in a city of millions, I had no real friends. Maybe Selena. Whenever she wasn't in a trance with that grandma-witch-doctor, which was most of the time, anyway.

So, yeah, no.

We weren't let out early that day, even as the paramedics came, even as the place was covered in yellow tape, even as the sword in the apple hidden in the trash can unnoticed in the pit muck, even as Phil's wife came to the office, delirious, and saying things like, "Yesterday was my anniversary, 21 years we were together, 36 years actually of being with him, so lots and lots of roleplay, which eventually didn't work," and she laughed hysterically until she began punching Phil's face in its puddle of blood, until those officially with gloves helped pull her away—and Sandy helped too unofficially.

But I sure had a job. I was employed. I had a paycheck. I could pay my bills.

Miss Allison was nearby attempting to hand Phil's wife paper towels as the officers and paramedics kept telling her to leave. She kept handing paper towels to anyone that walked by her, and she roamed around babbling, "paper towel? How about you, paper towel? You? Bubble wrap?"

Or someone else in the office, still typing or speaking to a client that their insurance policy had just been placed and, "allllllllll is well," how all their belongings were now insured, especially their jewelry and their art collection, due to their new collections policy, would then say something like this after their call while drinking a Keurig shit-pod: "You know, life is a series of bombs and slowly melting butters. Today seems like a bomb. Most days just feel like butter."

Or another would say, "I miss the space shuttle. We *really* can't trust those damn Russians. Thank god for Elon Musk," attempting to cover up the sound of cameras flashing and the garbles of walkie-talkies and how we'd all need to be questioned eventually.

Someone else discussed how to get rid of skin tags, how Phil actually had a lot of them, and how he once told them how to get rid of them—"See, when you got all this extra weight, a few kids in the stomach, a few kids in the ass, a few kids on the face [pause for chuckle], you gotta improvise. Phil knew that, too, rest in peace, and he always told me the best way to get rid of skin tags was dental floss. You wrap it around the fat to cut off the circulation. Eventually they just fall off, rest in peace."

We were finally OK'ed to leave early for the day, by 30 minutes, after Mr. Hah sent out an All Staff email that said:

"Dear Staff:

Due to today's incident, we will be observing an early close.
Our thoughts and prayers are with Phil and his family.

Best,

H."

On my way out, in the lobby I walked past a woman with the largest hat I've ever seen. It was the exact same size as the five-gallon water jugs that we have in the "break room," but it was made out of fur, dyed red. The lady looked about 80, and she was hunched over from osteoporosis, which, from the sight of her hat, may have been caused by her hat collection over the years, because you can bet she had more of those fuckers at home, custom-made to be absolutely and ostentatiously ridiculous, as if to say she carried a goddamn piggy bank on her head.

She had two canes, too, which made her look like some kind of frail and flashy spider crawling away from a bigger beast behind her, slowly crawling across the glossy marble, and as I walked by I asked her, Yes, ma'am, do you keep a slave midget in that hat, errrr? Ma'am?

"Whaaaaaaaaaaaa did thisssss maaaan ssssaaaaay?" she said to no one, trying to turn her massive hat-head around.

I then leaned in the way that Mr. Hah would always lean in on me when I wasn't strong, and I whispered to her while also gritting my teeth, It looks like you're carrying a human slave inside of your hat, and honestly it wouldn't surprise me if you did, but I do admire you for your balls. You've got big balls lady, a big, sweaty, hairy, ball sac, and a lot of strength to be carrying that sac of shit on your head like that all around the city, and at least we know you're coming, and we can prepare for you, from about a mile away, ya dumb old pampered-princess-fuck.

"Whaaaaaaaaaaaa did thisssss maaaan ssssaaaaay?" she moaned again to no one, and I felt powerful for a moment, confusing her, and speaking what *felt* like the truth for a moment, because she seemed awestruck by it, nervous, and uncomfortable.

And as I left, the swivel door moved slowly, as if there were grains of wheat beneath the marble and shoe grease, and I realized every day we grind up all that wheat we don't see, and someone somewhere makes bread from it, and carries it somewhere else in a basket on their head, and someone somewhere else adds yet another page to THE ILLUSTRIOUS OF THE PALM BEACHES.

32

La Priere Du Seignear

I pray that the reality of your PRESENCE WITHIN ME—all around me, within the neighbor's snow plow, and its gears that warm as it flicks the snow into a pile, within the bulge of his sweatpants, how the folds of heather-gray stretch around the white underwear stretched around the cock, how he begins to smoke and the tuft of air he flicks out his lips cheerfully mocks the lighter dust on the trees that flick their clouds too, under the paws of Yorkies hesitant to walk on the salt scattered and melting, how we long to be so useful on days like these, and those days, and the days to come, in anticipation of impending disaster, such as, will the roof cave in from the accumulation, even though it never has since 1920, but the newscasters say it could be the worst ever, that we should prepare for the worst, and like upright citizens brigading down grocery aisles, goose-stepping their way to the Chobani, we hurry on this day, or that day, or the day to come, because we have been warned more particularly, be sure to stock up on water, be sure to get your snow plow ready, and shovel all night long so it doesn't feel as bad as it could be, within the power lines of my apathy, my empty Bulleit bourbon bottle soul, dark liquor long-poured out and replaced with dusty water sucked by shriveled sunflowers lying there calmly next to a bear lighting this dark room of all my efforts to breathe each moment well, within every letter written, and then later—decades later—dumped in a bucket and left for the rain under the Florida moss, the father in the snow teaching his child, now that the work is done, now that the sidewalks are cleared, how to walk on snow, how to throw a snowball in the air as the Yorkie shivers, let the wind catch it, and let it fall and shatter into pieces and combine with the rest of the white powder beneath their feet, how he steps slowly and tells him to "be careful," how the majority of his life will be spent attempting to find a balance between being careful and being extraordinary, how it seems the two battle each other daily, how sometimes simply surviving can be extraordinary, something your ancestors couldn't do for as long as you have, within that child's arm stretched toward the sky as his father grabs hold of his glove, how their hands don't touch and there always seems to be a distance between us and those, this, that that we love, layers of fabric, cold, squeezed, and then they let go, invisible force fields overlapping and repelling each other, divine particles interacting and saying hello, and for some reason it's time to begin working again, and I wonder what the hurry is all about, can't snow simply sit still and be snow, can't we simply sit still for a while, but the grocery aisles fill with armies holding grenades of ground chuck and chips, Coca-Cola and beans, water within jugs they'll never open for a decade until it's time to wear it on their head, within all these things, collectibles your father once wore hanging on the window, scorpions encased in plastic, beaded adornments from Native Americans, and crosses and dog tags worn by your grandfather in wars that begat wars that begat wars, we

be Abraham's seed, tranny heels on your shelf from Halloween
and sometimes on a Wednesday too, a tobacco pipe never used
for fear you'll suffocate as well, more a reminder of how men
once were than how *you* are, maps of National Parks in Alaska
and Wyoming, a mug that has my father's name on it followed
by our last name, our seed, how Rudolfo insisted I put it on
my shelf instead of use it, how I wanted to use it, so my lips
would touch where my father's lips touched, how I decided
against it, how it rests there next to a picture of my brother
and I together as children, with our wispy-'90s moppy-air and
color-blocked polo shirts, how we look so mischievous, as if we
knew then my father's mug would sleep next to them, our precious little former selves framed, and on it would be etched a
Navy eagle laying what at first looks like an Easter egg but up
close we know is an American bomb, and books I gathered in
India, like the *Wheel of Life*, which I hardly ever read because it
still scares me that life could be so revolving, rolling, swirling,
that we could have multiple points of entry instead of just one,
or the *Bhagavad-Gita*, which always comforted me because it
seemed to highlight the reality of shameless war without completely condoning it either, that it may be necessary at times
but you'll indeed be covered in blood for it, and then a picture
of Lucy taking a nap in a dog bowl as a baby, how I wonder
if her bones are in the same shape and if one day they will be
found by excavators in the future when we begin to worship
Boston Terriers as gods, within my bowels that rumble from
my second espresso, and how the shit comes soon to remind
me that we're all shit-slinging buffoons on repeat to think we've
got it all figured out, that we can actually fight the cold when
it comes, that we can build a fire and we won't have to eat our
dog—IS FINALLY LIT, I pray that the reality of your presence

within me is finally lit, or maybe just lit even more, and let the light be even clearer, so that life—and its death—won't be so damn confusing.

And here again I haven't reached 1,000, goddamn it, and I am a failure.

And to think, how many days, years, I didn't write a goddamn thing about it, and look what happened.

I think I've finally convinced myself, or maybe just convinced myself even more, that no one will ever read this, even after a new tower is erected, and a new one, and a new one, when, Humpty Dumpty, they figure out how to put my body and brain and soul back together again—what will be next?

How will we evolve, revolve?

Once we realize art is a useless, pitifully delicious imitation, wonderfully delicious the way McDonald's is delicious, and once we realize that to eat—and to let all of us eat, every human—is love, until we become so compassionate that we forget everything else we discovered and learned, we'll become quite stupid, and fat, all over again, but in a new way.

What tower will be erected then, what will spire even higher and brighter and more organically than wealth, or Russian-and-Chinese-backed super-condos, or art and expression, or love and compassion?

Even after the new tower to hungerlessness and thirstlessness for righteousness is erected, beautifully erect and veiny and squirting cum every 90 minutes into space, and the creatures that inhabit it, how they regularly ride on horses in the desert alone, content, and how they often dig up the bones of my MacBook skull resting there beneath the glitter of a thousand years, and they flick the switch of me with their electronic head-lit cocks longer than anacondas, and they read these very words, THESE VERY WORDS, I've almost convinced myself, convinced even more, that even then, in that moment, they will laugh a little bit, affecting them just for a moment. And then they'll simply leave it behind, of course, after they place it on a rock made of Play-Doh and titanium and glacial silt and fur and hamburgers and flags, and they'll beat it there into that squishy stone with a dance and a club.

There, you see, 1,065-ish, now you can Save the Date, and all is well, and the roads are clear, and the state of emergency is now over, because we planned so so so well, and look, we prayed so damn well, and we have all been spared the worst of the storm, and it's so good that we were all soooooo stocked up, but I do admit I really should have shoveled the roof because it really, really, really, really could have caved in, guys.

33

Philantropical

In the future, we'll all be monthly subscriptions for 15 minutes.

—

Do you need anything before I go out?
She answered, "Oh, so much…"

—

In the future when we walk on sidewalks, we'll all be asked if we're Jewish rabbis, not just those of us with beards.

In the future, corporations like H&M or Urban Outfitters or Zara will be the only places left that host parties because they are the only entities that can afford rent in the city, and we'll all be dancing with merchandise all around us wearing a 24-hour ticker-tape of advertisements per 15 minutes of useful information. We'll no longer have 3, or 14, or 147 different gadgets and appliances, but one unit per person that changes as we change, morphing when it rains, when it snows, a projector the size of the freedom-fucked-up tower, a watch the size of a mustard seed, whatever we need, whatever size or occasion, and the device, when it's turned off, will look exactly like one of our many cancerous moles that keep getting bigger as we sleep in slipshod tents in the Rockaways and take the bullet train to work that clicks and clacks at 15 miles per hour.

Full grown Boston Terriers will be geishas of the city, roaming around with stunted legs and slithering torsos since we've raised them in leather bags for millennia, pretty much a worm with a Boston Terrier head inside a Louis Vuitton that turns into a sleeping bag that turns into a tent that turns into an airplane—all the while the Boston never leaves, with its head sticking out of the purse-plane like a propeller that flaps slobbery lips and snorts instead of rumbles or propels or jets.

In the future, when we ask secretaries what they need before we leave the office to the outside world to grab an English tea made by Mexicans, to restore your sanity again with fresh dirty air as opposed to stale fresh air of mass carpets below mass air-conditioning vents, to pass by blurring taxi medallions, millions of dollars tacked onto yellow paint, medallions representing proof that they deserve to be there and no one else does, the secretaries will cease to say "Oh So Much" like they do nowadays, because outside will be inside and tea will be made by everyone, and all air will just be air as opposed to fresh v. stale v. dirty, and money and medallions will be gone and replaced with pigeons—your worth is determined by pigeons and eagles or really any bird, and since there are trillions per person we're all gonna be just so, so wealthy then.

And there will be dreams of new kinds of thinking while wanting to kill old ways of thinking just like now, and people will have to die to make way for the new, and there will be those of us who are called geniuses and those of us who are called antiquated when we once were called pioneers, and many of us will continue to fear we've been left behind in some way or not ready in another.

—

I don't know what day it was, but it was one of those beginning days of H^3, well before Phil's children were run over, well before Phil stabbed himself in the eyes the way he always dreamed he'd do it, the way everyone at H^3 dreams they'd do it, but it was one of those days that the secretary said, "Oh…SO…MUCH," with such intensity that I felt the sadness in her voice, deeper than usual—perhaps her surgery the day before had helped her become all the more particularly gloomy and snarky, perhaps it was the anti-inflammatory medicine for the stitches or the Irish whiskey on her breath—but we so often seem to pay closer attention to things when they are ever-so-slightly not *as per usual*, even if the usual is also mentally disturbed. We get used to that brand of disturbance, thus determining that that disturbance is no longer disturbed, rather still, normal, calm, expected, unconditional, and that's just the way "is" is. I noticed her particular consistent gloom that day was exaggerated. I could actually taste the dry chicken meat in the tasteless noodle soup of her heart.

I resigned myself to getting her tea and a cupcake, yes, that will make her feel better, and it will make me feel better by making her feel better; it'll be my good little deed for the day, not from Sprinkles this time, no, but from Magnolia Bakery at Bloomingdale's, yes, since they taste better anyway even if they don't have a cupcake ATM, someday maybe, maybe a cupcake drone that hovers in front of your face and shoves it in little by little, buzzing about and later self-destructing.

As I suspected though, well, fully frickin' knew, they were closed, as most of the city was, as the blizzard continued to blow and wail like a horny whale on a sidewalk outside.

It was to be "the storm of the century" the meteorologists

said, and even the mayor warned not to leave our home or do anything, even talk, don't even talk, don't even fucking talk, for you'll add to the wind sure to come, and it did, that wind, but it was gargantuanly more than the worst of predictions—four feet, or was it eight, eighteen? Something like 18 hundred feet.

Yet we few who lived near the office came into the office, me in Astoria, Miss Allison in Long Island—even though that island was supposed to get it even worse than Manhattwat island—Sandy the martyr in the Bronx, and the arcane secretary, incessantly ill with something we were all convinced was simply her way to get out early every Friday, coughing a little every Thursday.

Even though it was illegal for us to travel, we the close-to-the-office few were texted by Phil with a passive-aggressive "It would be helpful if…" kind of a text, one which was sure from Mr. Hah, down to Miss Allison, and then up to Phil, tasked to disseminate the madness to us while all of us were in our homes, cozy, swaddled with blankets and fresh jizz and space heaters and espresso particles poofed off our chapped and recently lubed lips and recently lubed dicks and fallen onto all the valleys and the warm light shadows of the jasmine leaves parched and heater-dried in our living rooms of such a life quickly turned to crippling death by a work text.

And when I got the text of work-death, die to work, work to die, Rudolfo gave his litany of "what-the-fucks" and said that I should "just say no," for it was something similar to a drug, this enabling of the madness (as if there wasn't something called an out-of-office reply, or phone-forwarding, or the World Wide Web created in the year of our lord, 19-way-too-long-ago-to-still-be-afraid-of-fucking-using-it), warning me not to give in, this time at least, that they could do without me, that that crazy

FUCK Miss Allison could answer the phones her damn self, as we all knew she was the reason we all had to go in, with Mr. Hah hardly ever giving All Staff emails or making executive decisions at all (really he did nothing except yell and hoot and Hah)—except maybe if someone killed themselves we'd later find out, thinking it's weakness to cancel things, as that's what his Korean father always told him after he was let out the Japanese Auschwitz-y camp, holding onto everything like it was the last grain of goddamn Korean rice or last secret chunk of rat meat in your goddamn pocket, later to be boiled in a hot stone pot.

Never cancel anything, son. Because you might be put in a concentration camp at any moment. Never stop working, or the Japs will murder you.

We knew that Miss Allison most likely rented a *Shining*-style Canadian snow tank that ran on maple syrup and Mountie blood to get to work, and that we were somehow expected to do the same, rent a *Shining* tank, find a Canadian cop, kill them, tie a rope around their legs, hang them from a tree, slit their neck, and let the red gas spray into the tank, and then squeeze a used pancake in there, too, because that's what good work ethic is—being present somewhere, VISUAL, like a watch, even if that somewhere is nowhere and everyone there is gone, even if that watch is broken and has been for quite some time, for being trapped yet displayed honorably, shining metal in a blizzard, a bit of chrome from a taxi bumper seen beneath a snow mound, is, why, we, live, and die, didn't you know?

And I knew everything was closed, but going through the motions of asking the secretary if she needed anything, and exiting the building to go find something, even a cupcake—even when glass was breaking in the 70-mile-per-hour winds, leaving no difference between the geometric shapes of snowflakes and the jagged edges of skyscraper glass—I felt comforted by leaving, as per usual.

And as I left, after hearing her long, drawn-out, guttural and druggy, "MUUUUCH" of "Oh So Much" I overheard Sandy the martyr crying on the phone to one of her relatives, secretly confiding in them—loud enough for all of us to hear, though—that her husband was accused of being a pedophile, even though he had *never looked at children that way*, she thought, but it didn't help that Lilly told everyone at school that someday he *would* be, which started the whole thing anyway, she thought, and got all the mothers talking at school, "you know how they are there."

And when he came to pick up Lilly from school—still at the same school, as the doctors still didn't know what to do with her—she smiled and said, "It's okay, Daddy, I told them all now, so that in the future, when you *do* become a pedophile, they won't be so surprised."

Shocked as much as he thought he should be, he slapped Lilly across her already rosy cheek, drawing blood and a crowd in the parking lot, and as he—truly sorry—began to console his daughter, caressing her cheek, blotting her blood and tears with the cotton ball he usually kept in his pocket that he rubbed and tickled when he was nervous, reminding him of a fuzzy young clit, the mothers wandered and pointed, "Sir, get your hands off Lilly. I think you're being inappropriate. What you just did is wrong, and what you're doing now is even worse. WE ALL KNOW, sir. Just back away. Lilly told us, WE *KNOW*."

Lilly smiled nonchalantly, knowing that this is exactly as she had foreseen.

And Sandy just couldn't "take it," she said, as if whoever the listener was should have agreed with her with an "I know you can't."

And I thought, really? You can't?

Are you *incapable* of taking it? The big hard dick of the truth? Is the pussy of your life too tight?

Oh, you can take it. You can take that big dick.

You all can.

When many before you have been tortured and stabbed and hung and electrocuted for reasons far worse than having a genius time-whisperer for a daughter, you somehow can't take the fact that your husband will someday become a pedophile and today was what really started to become proof of what you so desperately haven't wanted to believe for quite some time, that you picked the wrong man, and somehow his excessive use of Sun-In didn't give it away?

"It's just too much for me, why does this happen to me? Why does god hate me!? I can't, hoad, on..."

And the person on the other line gave their "oh no, he loves you, OH SO MUUUCH," how this is just a test, how you keep the family together, you do, you really do, how *you* need to send your daughter away, because *she* needs help—she's the problem, not you.

And after hearing her "I have so much work still to do I gotta go"—in a blizzard? really?—because, really, insurance broker-age firms are almost as important as hospitals, if not more so, for we essentially are the ones responsible, the mechanics, like heart surgeons are mechanics, for making sure the wealthy have all their Ferraris in order, for making sure the wealthy are keeping up with their imitation Jasper Johnses, and their jets and family trusts are all taken care of in case something evil happens, so that they can be reimbursed for what they knew was bound to happen, so that they can remain comfortable, how we are the mechanical surgeons of enabling a lifestyle we wished would die away but continues to grow somehow, refusing to admit we're a part of it, as we daily stitch up any loose ends that the wind and the rain and the sun and the moon rip apart so rudely and utterly classlessly—*I declare, how could they!? The brutes. Oh do leave me alone, I need the toil-laaaaaay ever so much, hand me a doil-laaaaay!! I saaay!*—I slowly shut the mahogany door in search of my cupcake in a blizzard.

And as I slowly shut the mahogany door, I forgot about that morning, even as I traversed through a New York covered in the feathers of a cold, expanding Chinese pillow, with the white feathers of each feather-flake falling quickly onto my tongue, each the flavor of a manufactured lo mein noodle of arcane instability so completely unsustainable, how I continued walking unceasingly, it seemed, until I got there, but this time, distracted, without my daily prayer.

I had forgotten it this time, perhaps when I needed it the most, and decided to listen to the howls of anger within me, blowing all around me too, with each howl, a dark step in an Alaskan whiteout on a glacial hike in New York, a blotting-out of previous words, and I knew I was hiding them, those cracked bloody sidewalks, well below all that snow, how they'd continue to rest here outside of time, the black cracks and curves of a hidden holy red letter, even when red-and-white candy-cane factory steam towers were turning the world into a giant Peppermint Patty of old white men still in charge of ruining our lives somehow—at least, as I shut the mahogany door, it seemed easier to think of the world that way, *conspiracies* instead of *personal responsibilities.*

As I left for my cupcake, well, *her* cupcake, I heard Miss Allison running desperately toward the door to get my attention, but I slammed the door and she knocked.

You can come "in," I said as I waited by the elevator.

I said, You don't need to knock, to *leave* the office by the way, Miss Allison. I hope you know that.

She didn't hear me, nor did she want to.

"Hiiiiiiiiiiiiiiiiiii Colin, so, sooooo Mr. Hah wanted me to ask you if you could drop this off; it's a package, verrrrrrrrrrrrrrrrrrrrrrrrrrrrrrrrrrrrrrrrrrrry important, and it needs to get there within this week, and so I think we need to take care of it as soon as possible, LIKE RIGHT NOW."

You do realize that everything is going to be closed now. Do you want me to leave it on the sidewalk, and whenever the rest of the city comes back to work—ohhhh, in about five to one hundred days most likely, probably when they find my body in the snow—they can see that it's resting by their own revolving door?

"OH GOD NO. Someone could steal it."

Or, yep, the blizzard could cov—

In a rare moment of clarity, she then asked me, "But, but, but, but buuuuuuuuuuuuut, where are YOU going right now, then? I was told you were going outside, but why would you go outside if everything is closed?"

It's a very good question, Miss Allison. I tell you what. I'll take the package and I'll see if they're open even though I already know they aren't.

And then back to her normal, "GOOD. Ohhhhhhh K, good. THAT MAKES SENSE. Mr. Hah will be soooooooooooooooooooo pleased, and I will email him to tell him—you know, gonna call, I'm gonna call him—so he knows how much you're problem-solving today! First my email issues, then this! You're on a roll, aren't you? Just rolling around solving problems, helping people, aaaaaaaaaaahhhh-maaaaaaay-ziiiiiiing!"

I sure am, Miss Allison.

"So, TO RECAP, you WILL take the package, and IF—if, if, if, if—they are open, then you will drop the package *off* with the door man with extreeeeeeeeeeeeeeeeeeemely explicit directions to where it should go. Otherwise, you will BRING. IT. BACK. Yes?"

You are more correct than the very definition of correct.

Giggling, sheepishly, she handed me a large Post-it and she said, "HERE are the directions."

In the elevator, I looked at them.

She had drawn a stick figure of a person with a smiley face. And this wasn't her being cute and flirty-old and weird; she was completely serious. In her mind, this smiley face represented *333 Park Avenue* (I called the secretary to find out), because if the package was delivered to that address, then that is the exact expression that would be on *her* face, a smiley face, even though Mr. Hah's face would still be unchanged and most likely a frownie face or a kissy-poopie emoji.

And then again, on my way out the door, I prayed the prayer I had never forgotten on my way in the door, every morning, until that morning, *Neither height nor depth, life nor death, can separate me from your love*—neither Post-its with stick-defigured humans drawn on them with a pencil, to be used, somehow, for directions, nor forgetting to say the prayer that I thought was the only thing keeping me sane, but I guess I was wrong again. Prayers or lack of prayers might not do anything to me either. Unchanged.

And in that moment I got a text, because, in addition to the worst, I seem to get texts at simply the best of times.

It was from my brother, as usual, and it said, "Have you ever thought about how Jesus could have had a small dick?"

It could have been massive too I guess, I replied, which would have looked really weird on the cross, dick head poking out like that.

"How's the blizzard? Speaking of Jesus's pensisesesessesses falling from the sky, have I ever told you how when I was going to my right-wing evangelical Baptist college, pre-cigarettes-and-depression, my roommate—who was also the worship leader at a speaking-in-tongues-without-an-interpreter black church—used to always try and snuggle with me 'for fun,' but I never thought anything of it? (By the way, is that what you and Rudolfo call it, snuggling?) Anyways, then he moved deep into the hills of Tennessee, where he became a meth addict and began leading gay orgies in a cabin instead of worship services in a church. Just recently found that one out, on Facebook."

And we did our LOLOLs and He-he-hes, and I told him that that was pretty much my goal in life, except a commune of tiny solar-paneled homes (with WiFi) arranged in a circle with a fire pit in the center for orgies and far more natural drugs and watching stars in the nude (while our adopted children and pets stayed inside crying until they starved to death watching us have so much fun off the grid), and that it was exactly what I needed to hear right now, in this exact moment, a reminder of that, and then I clarified, we don't ever *snuggle*, we butt-fuck for hours until one of us can't take it anymore because one of our assholes starts bleeding too much or we ram it in so deep that eventually one of our dicks gets covered in chunks of shit. Ultimately, one of us is incapable of allowing the other person's dick to enter our anus anymore. In other news, I think I need to get a douche. I'm actually going to go to Duane Reade in search OF DOUCHEBAGS. That way the only reason to stop fucking will be too much ass-bleeding, which can always be cured with a tampon.

"Oh, is that a thing for homos?"

Ass-bleeding and tampons?

"Douchebags."

Well, there are different camps of belief, I texted, but I think I should try it because every time I take it up the ass I usually end up shitting on Rudolfo's dick—whereas Brazilians, like the civilized French, have self-cleaning assholes.

"We Americans are so full of shit, I guess."

After my "Oh so muuuuuuuuch," I then ground the grain of our iced revolving door and entered the elements again in search for a cupcake I knew I couldn't find, holding a package with the address of basically an emoticon, which would have guided me fuck knows where.

☺ Park Avenue, New York, NY

And as I walked in the blizzard I thought of warmer places, what life would be like on islands without men, islands without women, with new words that were regularly uttered by slutty sloths instead, where codified good deeds laced in poison were no longer labeled "philanthropic," but rather as they should be, with a brand-new word like "philantropical."

34

Dawn

Hunger, blood, suffocation, your eyelids are slowly sliding across the branches of the veins within the barky flesh of your eyeball, sliding across your neighbor with the herpes lips, her barky sores cracking like popcorn whores popping their cherries slowly, as if all that you see lying, moving, before you were the oily sheen of the plastic of a microwave window, and your nose is touching the oils, adding to the oils that are already there, and all that you see baffles you, like when the poutine routine of a moving man in a moving van leaves for work in circles, and then the trash man in the trash van comes to get the by product, crushing it quickly before you. With undead dogs shaking their last booty shakes, there's a long line of fur before you, using the same pipeline of water from upstate New York, that same longest leaky tunnel in the entire world, all to get to the fire hydrant leaking too, fur for, and fervor for, the dogs and you, and you feel like someone really just called you a pickaninny.

One day words and dogs and men and veins and family branches will all split and fuse, cracked by air conditioners from heaven, suffocated and squished by all that lay living and popping behind the microwave that will continue to heat and pop and spin, and the beeping alarm isn't for what you see, but for yourself, to get out of the way.

Something will open the door, and it's you who will be eaten, by all you thought was food just for you, how you controlled it with your fingers, each letter punched, each number clubbed on a helipad, a maxi pad of hunger, blood, suffocation as you slip out of the world's ass-pussy.

Or was it a microwave? Does it really matter?

My god this is shit, too.

Uhuh.

Well, okay.

What's up, shut up.

Good Oracula and Bad Oracula are yelling at one another, Sunshine's dead, an illegal boyfriend lies above with a bullet through his head, and the herpes on li'l Miss Herps-lips are cracklin' and popping like popcorn rosies, and you?

Where are you?

You're on the sidewalk looking at your legs that look as though they'd been drafted for a millennial war that came and went, and you're somewhat saddened you won't receive a Purple Heart—someone cutting out yours and replacing it with metal, and that makes you a hero now, because a bullet or a bomb found you faster—yet you're relieved that, besides your arguing-immigrant-diseased-and-dead neighbors, there's not a lot of pomp. They are your only audience, and oddly enough that is okay.

Fuck the pomp.

As I lay dying on the sidewalk, waiting for the bright red lights and sirens of thick New York men to lift me up, pudgy angels with smoker-coffee-Orbitz-donut-kimchi breath, I am thankful as I squint. No, that's not the right word; I've always thought "thankful" made me feel guilty, as though most of the time you were in a state of bitterness and you had to make the conscious choice to *become* thankful.

What I feel is beyond feeling, the tingle of unconditional calm—a fine line blurred beyond nothingness and love in perpetuity. If there is any confusion in the moment, as I lie squinting at the microwave play before me, it's a kind of vertigo as I look up to find that metallic line, yet the more I look, the more everything blurs from the steam from the rainbow from the birds from the words from the carousel spinning on the train of life leaving.

—

Life, and its true glorious moments have little to do with where you think you'd rather be or when or how much, but finding a piece of blurry peace after being rejected by your efforts to even simply walk down the fucking street, a piece of a day just like today, or to send in a manuscript again that no one wants to read, again, to finally find a job that you think would perfectly fit within the record grooves of your soul to produce some kind of Hi-Fi symphony around and around in some kind of living room for guests who are soon to come, after being rejected by your efforts to forget all those painful moments of the past you thought best to fling up into an old, old oak tree of somewhere and just let it dangle there like a dingleberry full of scorpions and spiders teasing you when the wind blows every so often, dropping little bits of your nature to the ground, forming a gloomy moldy jungle within you, after being rejected the 99th time, 99 books and a bitch ain't one, and then accepted the 100th time, this, accepted perhaps only by yourself, and how that particular *this* feels like gently ceasing to breathe, because all your lungy efforts to get there or then, or when or here, do not actually dictate all that you see or what-you, what-you, what-you were, or who you'll ultimately be, which could very well be free.

Life is sitting on a couch with tea.

Life is feeling the butthole of your lover with your finger and getting an erection underneath your long johns given to you by an American soldier in Afghanistan who had a surplus of Polartec gear.

Life is having a cold, yet as you sniffle, you bite Rudolfo's neck, and you push him away a bit to look at the teeth marks on his neck. You push him further still to look at the swirl of the cowlick on his head, how one strand stands taller than the others, a spire of the present surrounded by so many towers of presents, how "present" is simply a word for all the many things more important than your own poof of a life as a poof, the bristles forming around his jaw from where he decided to shave and where the hair decided to reject those efforts too and how knowing it, or not, we let the fur come, grow, and sew what it will as it covers our face, where the midnight shadow connects to his sideburn.

Life is falling asleep from too much Mucinex and laughing about how I got rejected once more for a job I thought could take me away from the hell of Heller, Heller, & Hah, from anger, death, and limbo, from things and memories I did not want to face freely. Laughing about how this is what most of what life is, so many rejections that you're spammed and jammed close-to-unceasingly with it, praying unceasingly, rejected unceasingly, and you're on this couch, just waiting for it when you finally get it, still, sipping tea with cayenne pepper, chunks of ginger, lemon, and Bulleit bourbon—yet another empty bottle you place on your desk because it seems like your only accomplishments lately are emptying bottles, placing them next to your bear lamp, another bottle, vodka in the shape of a dark bear—100 ways, 1,000 ways, let me count the ways, everything has shut you down, cut your legs off, ripped out your throat, sewed out chunks of your brain, chunks of your bank account, chunks of a past you thought best to hide because, what could you possibly do with them, thinking you have to wait until everything's perfect, until you're inspired, until you're consistent, until you can start on the 1000th draft before you begin the first, just 1,000 words a day, so many chunks that when together seem more like pebbles, and ever more sand, and ever more neutrinos, that you're now, sitting here sipping your tea with your own Rudolfo, quite open, so HERE that you feel far away, so NOW that you feel you never were, so now that you feel you always will be, so wide open that all you can do is yawn and then suddenly it's dawn.

35

Company Powerball

"If I ever have a daughter, I'd name her Olive, because at least she'd remind me of the peace I wish I had. And martinis. It's always good to be reminded of martinis," said the secretary on another day, with an Earl Grey tea in her hand and a fresh new blonde streak in her hair, completely gay just thinking about this fake daughter. She'd get these streaks, and you could never really tell if it was a style she was going for, dyed, or if entire sections of her head had died from the stress of Mr. Hah, leaving them colorless.

Miss Allison chimed in as per usual from fixing the Oriental carpet nearby, sending plumes of dust, skin chunks, paper fibers, and minuscule bloody mist droplets—now long dried—of Phil's blood, no one thinking that a poof of it could have traveled on office air-conditioned zephyrs out of his office the moment upon which Phil descended to the ground to meet his children, the one with the funny walk, which didn't matter now, when most of his life there was such a fuss over it, now irrelevant, or the one who could draw so well. Phil's office was covered in her framed pictures, whereas Mr. Hah's was gruesomely littered with the faces he *wished* he knew well, and tried to impress upon all who entered his office that he in fact did.

Right, you, JFK and Napoleon were besties.

Miss Allison tugged a corner of the carpet on whatever day this was and wanted to be, many days after the office death—regularly referred to as "the series of unfortunate acts of God" so as to remove ourselves from having any responsibility for it whatsoever—and when she tugged, her eyes crossed a little, focusing on the often-trod leaflet of the carpet or a red swirl pattern, not even thinking Phil's remains could have been hurled there from the puff of the vent the moment Phil stabbed his eyeballs with the letter openers, sending blood geysers to the drop ceiling when the brass spears exited the skull from the fall.

I thought about it quite often, though. I thought about breathing in his blood every day after that day. Yet as a violinist anticipates and is quite cognizant of the next move of the conductor, I remained focused on the task and strings and notes before me—the right sound, continue to make sure it's perfection, however perfectly stale and twisted the sound may be.

I focused the bow of my efforts on the strings of the purpose of the office: I declare, the music of insuring the wealthy must go on, and will go on, regardless of who dies or when or who lied about how or why anything happens. Some days my purpose was to simply listen to the office camaraderie forming, a camaraderie that inevitably and mysteriously coagulates after an office death.

It's not as though everyone became bestie-bestest-better-friendsy-friends all of a sudden like the Pope and any Downsy with face boils in the crowd, but suddenly many around the office spoke in "we."

We could do this and that.

Powerball for instance, rose to 700 million, and instead of everyone leaving on their own to get tickets during lunch, hitting up the same chromey-crumby newsstand outside the Home Depot on 3rd Avenue, Miss Allison exclaimed to the secretary and to me across the cubicle wall, "How about, WE, ALL, go in on Powerball!? I think that would be fun to do together, wouldn't it!? WOULDN'T IT!? Right, guys!?"

She immediately sent an All Staff email, the first one of its kind to circulate since Mr. Hah signed the death note "Best" with a comma after it, one just like this, ",", which was quite, quite creepy and business-efficient for a note to all the staff explaining that the Vice President of the company had killed himself with letter openers.

Everyone pitched in 10 bucks, and we ended up with around 80 tickets or so. I only had six bucks on me, but Miss Allison was feeling extremely generous. "I gotcha, I GOTCHA, don't worrrrry, I'll spot you the rest."

She had her rouge on. Her eyes were sparkly because Mr. Hah was in town and at a business luncheon. She made sure to call him on his cell, though, to ask if he wanted in on the company pot.

"WE'RE allllllllllll going in on it…" I could hear her down the hall exclaiming to him on speaker, making it official, "IT'S THE H, H, & H COMPAAAAAAAAANY POWERBALL POT!!!"

Throughout the day the expected conversations ensued. "If WE won, what would you do with your share?"

Both the secretary and I would buy land, and maybe set up a trust, and probably hire a lawyer and an insurance company—not this one, though, Hell, to the Hell, & to the Hell no—to make sure no one could take it from us for some silly reason. She would adopt a daughter and name her Olive, since "all my eggs are cracked, the yolks dripped out, molded, rotted, down the drain already, so I think I'd like a North Korean refugee child. I just recently watched a documentary about the North, how incredibly malnourished they are, how they....Did you know that they basically worship the Dear Leader? It's absolutely sick, the great lengths people will go to in order to tell themselves that someone is good for them, and what they have is 'good,' all in the name of not wanting any 'evil' around them, which is just fear fermented and covered in red pepper flakes, fear of being put into a concentration camp, really, and coming out shriveled versions of what they once were. It's a great motivator to lie to yourself I guess, for years, until the lie fades away, blurs with the truth, until you don't remember what is what anymore, taste buds burned off, and all of a sudden you find yourself bowing down to the dictator of your country because you truly believe he is now a god, responsible for all and only the good, magical, divine, and not possibly responsible for any of your pain—because that's all fuckin' America's fault."

Since she knew Mr. Hah almost as long as Miss Allison, I asked her, since she brought it up, didn't Mr. Hah's parents go through a concentration camp?

"Ohhhhhhhhh we better not talk about that. Please don't. We're not really supposed to bring that up. Mr. Hah has explicitly told me to NEVER talk about it. Let's just talk about the lotto, so...so, what land would you buy, where?"

Oh. Okay.

Montana maybe. Well, I said, I like the idea of it probably more than my desire to actually want to live in Montana. I like

the idea of restoring the bison herds to their original numbers, which would require basically buying up most of the
West, many ranches, parking lots, fences, to simply disband
and move away, another Trail of Tears of sorts—but for the
sake of the buffalo, and instead of Injuns, it would mostly be
the white man crying, but for the best this time.

"That's real neat. Well I, I...I would buy land in Costa Rica.
I hear it's nice down there to retire. Not that I'm ever retiring.
I bet if we won I'd still be sitting here, dreaming about Olive;
I really don't know how to do anything else. Plus, Mr. Hah
would probably need me even more because he'd have even
more money then, to buy more people to hire."

Miss Allison barged in. "What, what, what'd I miss? Okay,
Okay, SO. So, I scanned allllllll the tickets and sent them to
everyone so they can see proof of all the tickets and in case anyone doesn't trust me."

At that she began giggling and kneeling all the way to the
ground laughing, tears running down her cheeks. This had
apparently struck a much deeper chord, trust, what she had to
give up for loyalty, more than we could possibly deduce.

"Wait, OH GAWWWWWD." She popped back up like an
alligator at a carnival ready to be bopped by a klutzy teenager.

I asked her if she was okay.

"Oh yes oh yes, I, I, I, IIIIIIIIIIII AM, BUT. But, oh
gawwwwwd, what about Sandy? She's been sick with the flu for
this entire week. Her entire family is, too, even Lilly, all got the
flu. IT'S SO TRAGIC."

The secretary interrupted, "What's your point? She isn't
here."

"BUT BUT BUT, should I call her? I should really call her to
see if she wants to join the company Powerball pot. Hmmm.

Should I call Mr. Hah? I should really get his advice on this, I DIIIID say we were aaaaalllll doing it, you know, *THE* H, H, & H company Powerball pot. Do you think if we don't include her that he'd get angry? By the way, when did you last talk with him? Was he finished with his luncheon, is he on his way back? Oh gawd maybe I should call. Tell you what, I'm gonna call him, get his advice, THEN, depending on what he says, I'll call Sandy and ask if *she*—heck, even her husband, maybe he wants to join in, too? Errrrrrrrrrr? Even Lilly, Lilly could get one, too, you know, for college and all. I'm gonna cawwl hhhhhhh—"

"Him?" the secretary rhetorically asked as Miss Allison darted down the hall and ran to her office, partly because she thought she heard her phone (sometimes she'd hear it when it wasn't ringing, phantom calls like phantom pain from legs blown off), and because she wanted to get on it right away, lest she get yelled at by Mr. Hah for dilly-dallying.

"Mr. Hah absolutely HATES dilly-dallying," she'd always mumble to herself, counting things on her fingers, tasks yet to be completed, that no one asked her to do.

And you'd always hear the secretary mumble somewhere in the office after Miss Allison's mumble somewhere else in the office, "He doesn't just hate dilly-dallying; he hates *everything*."

We continued our Powerball conversation, "You know, the last time, the person who won was a single mother who was living in a homeless shelter. Whenever I hear things like that, I can't help but feel there might be a little justice in the world....Did you hear about the falling ice last week?"

I told her I hadn't.

"There was a man who saw a woman standing on the sidewalk with her stroller, and a large shard of ice had fallen from one of the new towers—I guess they hadn't thought of all the different design elements that jut out could be perfect collectors for chunks of ice—and the man had to quickly decide who to save. He grabbed the mother, and the baby was…cut in half by the massive skyscraper icicle."

The secretary took a sip of her tea like it was full of vodka and her Olive, unamused.

Miss Allison ran back, "I think it's best that I call him *here*. *We* should all call him together, riiiiiiiiiiiiiiiight?"

Before we could even respond she was already dialing him on the secretary's phone.

"Hiiiiiiiiiiiiiiiiiiiiiiiiiiiiiiiiiiiiiiiiiiiiiiiiiiii Jung, Hiiiiiiiiiiii, so as discussed previously," and she was leaning down to the speaker of the phone as though her voice already didn't carry itself across the entire pit of the office and all the surrounding suites like Phil's now completely emptied out, most of the carpet ripped up except for that Oriental rug, family pictures and drawings thrown out, "We decided to call you because we weren't exactly sure if—"

"Who the fuck is WE!?"

"Hiiiiiiiiii, yes hi, soooooo here, sooo it's ME, your wonderful secretary, and Colin the problem solver!"

"What the fuck do you three fucks want, because I don't even give one fuck, let alone three fucks, definitely not six fucks, didn't I tell you that I had a meeting after lunch—oh, wait—I shouldn't have to because you're the one who scheduled it and put in on the mother fucking calendar. Are you dense? Did your mother make you eat lipstick *not* just for fucking breakfast, but for every fucking meal, too? Did your father keep you in a closet until lunch time, and sometimes dinner, and sometimes days on end, oh WAIT, oh wait, HE DID, which I forget sometimes, until it makes you do completely stupid things like this, like interrupting me in the middle of a multi-million-dollar deal. Do you have millions of dollars for me? DO YOU? If you do, then by all means continue." We could hear him gritting his teeth, molars occasionally popping from the pressure and crumbling off his lips like Tums.

"Ohhhhhhh, my, Jung, I'm soooooo sorry because seeeeeeeee that's the thing," she was shaking, and now her lips were touching the phone speaker, saliva dripping into the holes, "seee, it's about *the* HH&H Powerball pot and I wasn't sure if maybe—"

"What!? THERE. IS. A. REASON." He took a moment for belabored breathing and more grits and livid, vivid cheese. Now his gritting teeth sounded like two rocks scraping each other, or an anvil being beaten with a large hammer and a clumpy glowing piece of hot metal in the shape of a shit log, or the shriek a subway makes when it comes to a grinding halt when the wind chill is -8 degrees and it sounds like an eagle is being tortured in a cave. "THERE. IS. A. REASON. I AM. IN. THE. CORNER OFFICE. LOOK AT IT."

Miss Allison actually ran away from the phone to go look at the corner office.

"Hello!?"

We told him that she had run away, to go look at the corner office, as requested.

"GO. FUCKING. GET. HER."

"Hiiiiiiiiiiiiii, I'm back. Your office looks GREAT. ALL IN ORDER FOR YOUR RETURN."

"WHAT!? MADELINE FUCKING FOCUS YOU GOD-DAMN NUTJOB OR YOU'RE FIRED, OH, KAY!!?? DO YOU UNDERSTAND ME!?" Then things went to a whisper. "I am in the corner office. I am. Not you. You're in the back with all your hamster papers, which I've told you time and time again to clean up but you haven't, and so—how long have we been together—you know by now not to ever question me. I'm in the corner office. No one else. There's no one above me. No, not one."

She ran back to her office to go clean. Papers were flying everywhere. You could hear thuds of files being thrown into the wastebasket, quickly, each thud matching the thud of her beating heart about to explode from the horror of making another mistake.

He was still on speaker, "Hello!? HELLO!?"

I spoke up and said, I believe she went back to her office, Mr. Hah.

"Oh, you BELIEVE, do you? I tell you what. It's good to believe, isn't it? It's always good to believe. At least you beeeeeeeeelieeeeeeeeeve. That'll get things done that only I can get done. Idiots."

He hung up.

The secretary and I looked at each other. She took another extremely audible quadruple-"r" slurrrrp of tea.

"You know what my biggest fear is?" she asked.

She sighed.

She slurrrrped again and then said, "It's falling ill when I'm on the subway, when we're under the East River in the tunnel. I'd be on my way to meet friends on one of the rare occasions my friends acknowledge my existence in this lonely city. We'd want to go for drinks. We'd want to have—as you may have guessed by now—extremely dirty martinis, empty vodka bottles everywhere. But I'd never get there because I'd fall ill from the speed of the subway zipping low under the water, the pressure change maybe, or maybe just because sometimes—lately—I've felt more and more faint, from this place, and so I'd open the subway door between the cars to get some 'fresh' air in the dark, and the car would jolt as it often does and I'd flip over the springy railing. I'd get run over. I'd get run over for weeks on end, maybe months, again and again, and the rats and whatever else lives down there—the bubonic plague down there—would digest my body a little more each day as each train that passed by mutilated my remains more and more into a kind of ground chuck. And only after those many months would people start looking for me, but they'd never find what was left of me. I'd just been run over way too much for way too long."

36

Whiteout

They have come to me, more words, papers forgotten, now remembered.

I had been in the steam room spraying nasal spray down my left nostril—my head tilted back, my nostril a black cavernous ice cream cone—and the saline dripped down my throat like the chocolate at the bottom, slowly seeping out all over the hands inside my lungs.

My steammates and I looked at this beef of an Italian sitting there with us; we had been raving about the wonders of neti-potting in the cold, how we each of us had deviated septums, how we all still have issues with breathing. The beef had even had surgery, but apparently it didn't work. He was curious about my saline bottle, if somehow I were the genie next to it, and his wish was to know what exactly neti-potting was and how it could fix his life.

He was gorgeous, the beef. The other guy next to me and I had masturbated with each other at one point. I know that he knew we both knew we wanted the three of us to whip our dicks out, snort saline in the ice cream cones of our black breathing holes, and ignore all the buzzes of texts outside, ignore all dry air, all cards that people still sent in the mail—how now paper is only used for weddings or deaths—my mother sent me a card with a picture inside it of my father's grave with an American flag someone had stuck in the earth next to it—and just revel and tremble in the treble and bass of the triumvirate of steam and manly love, all of us sons of the other, all of us fathers of the other, all of us brothers of the other, arms latched on the other's cock, thumbing the curve of the mushroom.

But it never happened. The Italian beef left, mind opened, thankful and curious of this, this, this new remedy! The pot of netis one can purchase at the Reade of Duanes, how it's simply mimicking an ocean that your lungs long for, but you never give it. You just give it office air, cold air, and scarf breath, and the tongues of those you think you're supposed to love.

They have come to me, the words.

As I sat drying my balls and my beard on the bench, As I approach the night of my life, *As I approach the night of my life,* and at the time I did not know when I would need these words or what they meant, but they came to me then. And so I typed them in my phone, in one of my THOBSERVATIONS folders in my organizer app, because I could never really distinguish between random things I saw that I wanted to remember from the thoughts I had about them, the things I simply sucked in, the things I truly created on my own, and so I merged them altogether into one list.

I like to make lists.

They help me avoid things I don't want to think about.

And now here I am again in the dark night of a curious room alone, except for the sound of something outside of me that sounds like a snow blower, the man next door attempting to get ahead of the winter's night snowfall once more, because his family would be proud of how low their driveway was compared to the neighbor's when everyone thought they were guaranteed to wake up the next day. A scraping, a blowing, a spraying, and light sprays through the pellets and flakes and fluff of something outside myself, a mysterious light, a lamp, a bear, a care, a care bear.

I am squinting. I hear piano, I see the usual bottles of empty whiskey on my desk, papers and bills and invitations to weddings I still have yet to go through, broken chalk, and one-fourth of an apple, and here I hear a piano darkly in a night that was not forecast to snow—yet here it is again, that snow—and everyone prepares for it, or fights it, or ignores it.

There's a man brooming off the top of his car and he smells like dog saliva, and his face is proud disgust, proud for having been the one to find it, to dust it off, to be rid of it. He is a man, and he has disgust for the lice atop his car—that's what it is, he tells himself—lice from the sky, eggs, larvae from above, and it shouldn't be here. They are enemy combatants.

You are a man.

You are strong.

And now I hear a sudden Manhattan of the mind, and I realize that it's right now that I need those words I wrote down so long ago in the steamy future that my past's memory's daily breath called a phone.

As I approach the night of my life, as I look out the window of a dark room writing, I see the red on the Philippine flag, the red on the Cambodian flag, and how the reds drape next to all my trinkets I thought at one specific point in my life were worth keeping. A pipe I never use for fear of lung disease. A picture of my mother. Kurt Vonnegut, cut out, the Associated Press stylebook, a photo album in the shape of a cow, and the millions of rainbow Post-its from previous manuscripts no one wanted and possibly not even me, I now—wherever now may be, possibly all three, being then, here, and a future when—know that the lure of men, their nipples glossy with beads of steam, their mushroom cock heads wiggling in the air and batting each molecule surrounding them with such a friction that it hurts, it's a mirage, these men, all men, even those you love and loved and will.

Of course I know now that those three, love, loved, and your last will, form a thicker substance somehow, as if your hand is cooled by it completely, pressing it bare in the snow and you don't want to lift it away to see the imprint because the paint and pain of the unconditional cold is a pleasure beyond peace. Somehow these men, Rudolfo, my brother, my father, they're worth pressing into the white just a little more because although they, too, are a mirage as all-we-like sheep-men are and gone astray and gay-we-are, somehow one's a palm tree, one's the cool sand surrounding it with a coconut, and the other is a cool lake with friendly sloths and tigers pleasuring themselves.

They are shapes in your mind, outlines of letters, not simply the wiggles of heat and blood and steam playing with themselves next to you. Somehow they're worth more in the vast dead of things, trinkets you want to remember on the shelves of your writing room, scorpions encased and hung from the bolo leather and lit up from sunlight in the morning, as if that light were an ever-present reminder of the neck that once wore it often, your father's neck that was squeezed too tightly from so many armed forces it seemed, and you couldn't do anything but just sit here where you are and listen as the light within him, within you too, fades by a prism of seconds divided, and nutrients ingested—all that color, beets, greens, rainbows of freshness and life—they and you are nothing more than paint in a rusty bucket on a sidewalk:

What sticks out to me today, which I've thought about a lot, is how parents hope that their kids—the next generation, YOU—will do better than they do, than I do.

My father had an eighth-grade education. My mother—high school. Mom always wanted to become a teacher but never became one. She actually wrote poetry. She was first in her class. Her family went from Jefferson City, Missouri to Rupert, Idaho in a covered wagon in the 1900s, early 1900s. They farmed.

I have a whole side of my family that lives in California and Idaho that I've never met. Big farms.

She married my brother—half-brother really—Gordon's father, and then had him. He owned a whole city block in Kansas City and was a wealthy man. He died after mom and he got a divorce. She could have been a wealthy woman if she could have paid the taxes.

I have an idea that my mother had my sister Lorraine out of wedlock. She took a job in a nursing home. The nursing home allowed her to keep her kids there while she worked there—Gordon and Lorraine. She was a cook. To this day, Gordon will not eat oatmeal; that's all they had to eat.

Mom and the two kids lived in a slum, in the ghetto, on a street called Antelope Street in St. Louis. My dad's relatives lived in the same flat as my mother, brother, and sister did, and they introduced dad to mom. He just got out of the Navy. He got a job on the railroad, and they all moved to Cahokia, Illinois—where the Indian mounds are. By that time I was born.

So dad built the house, worked on the railroad. Then he lost his job and he lost the house.

Times were tough.

Is that because he had his black friend over and people didn't like it?

Well, that's another story, but it was part of that, yes.

During that time that we lived there, Dad had a black Navy buddy and his family come over a lot. And I had a black babysitter, too. The neighbors burned a cross on our front yard. Some neighbors come over and told my Dad that they "didn't like niggers." Dad didn't care what they liked or didn't.

We moved to a couple of different places, had apartments. Dad got a job at McDonnell Douglas aircraft in St. Louis.

I went to grade school and junior high in Illinois.

During the time we were there, Dad bought a new house. At a place called St. John's Gardens. We had a pretty nice house. We had four bedrooms, a couple baths, a double- car garage. A nice screened-in patio.

Wait, so when did you go to high school in Missouri?

Are you going to let me tell my own fucking story or fucking what? Only I [cough] I [cough]I can tell the damn thing.

Dad was born in Sullivan, Missouri—he got this idea he wanted to go back to where he was born.

He had a friend at work that actually bought a farm in Sullivan, Missouri. So we went to visit him for a week

[Arms in the air—to hold on a second]

[Cough syrup swig]

[Coughing fit for about 15 minutes]

[Another cough syrup swig]

[Another]

[Lucy's barking at our old neighbor outside on his walk with his cane.]

[Lucy's chasing yellow butterflies in the sunlight in the yard now.]

[Mom is beginning to sew her new quilt.]

[She lets Lucy in from outside. Lucy's thirsty now.]

[Mom is sewing patches of our old childhood T-shirts together into one sewed-up memory that can keep us warm.]

So, Dad looked up some relatives in Sullivan, and they told us of a farm where the guy needed somebody to live in the house and take care of his cattle. So we sold our house in Illinois and moved to Missouri.

Okay, so this was during the summer of sopho—

Probably.

Right around this time Dad was starting to get sick.

We never knew what was the matter with him.

Starting to get weak. So *we* took care of the cattle. Wood stoves and a fireplace and about froze our asses off. Gordon and Bev would come and cut wood for us, and that's how we kept warm. We took a bath in the kitchen in a galvanized tub.

Looked like something you feed the pigs out of.

So the family would go in another room while—

Yeah.

So they lived in that farmhouse for about two winters, I guess. Dad bought fourteen acres of ground next to it and bought a trailer, and we lived in a trailer. I learned to hate school, left all of my friends, and went from living in the city to living in a rural area and really didn't understand.

But I did some things I had some fun at, but I never adjusted. So I quit school. Started working construction.

I dropped in once in a while during my senior year.

I worked construction for about three years, got my draft notice for the Army, and I joined the Navy. My high-school principal kept my diploma ready even though I never finished and I told him—I wrote him a letter and told him—I wanted to go to college in the Navy. So you know what he did for me? He *whited out* the day I was supposed to graduate and put in the present date.

In other words, I was supposed to graduate in 69, so he put in 71.

Sooo…

He put in that present date, 71, not today's date, to make it official, are you fucking dense?

[Both of us laughing]

When I was going to Sullivan High School he'd beat my ass every other day. Dorcy Schaper. I thought he was the biggest prick. He was a West Point graduate. He actually treated me pretty good in the end, especially with that white-out.

He did make me take a bookkeeping course in correspondence. Got an A in it. And he gave me my diploma. University of Missouri sent me a book to read, I'd go to the library, take the test, seal it, send it back to University of Missouri, and they'd grade it.

Then I'd do the next chapter. You have to sit there under somebody so they could say you weren't cheating.

[Coughing]

[More coughing, Swig of codeine this time]

[Coughing]

[Phlegm on tissues that look like rainbow slugs]
That's all I got for today.

37

Absence

Our lives are glittered with the lack of it.

Until one day, one moment, we truly feel it, when our food is gone, your partner is gone, the birds neither hop nor hope nor chirp. Words don't cum, they struggle to leap from your cock. You're a bird on a roof and your talons are holding onto the ice above the cheap roof panels. The bubbles in your coffee wait for the air above them in your room to press them, to pop them, for the air within to strong-arm the thin mucosal layer of swirly shine that encases the air within from the air outside, a glass window, fragile, waiting for time to break it.

You'll get up in the morning, and where he once was in folds of skin, all you see is the cotton folds of socks, dryer-spun and shrunken jeans you forgot to take out along with the trash. You wake up and reach through the folds hoping to find breath, a heart you for many days previously neglected to realize existed faithfully, consistently, fluid, but what you find instead are the folds of underwear in clumps, wife-beaters in clumps with stains of cum the warm-water-only washer would not dare burn out hotly, and you're thankful it didn't clean as thoroughly, for at least now the off-white reminds you of all that you had.

I feel a heat coming from behind me and to the right. I love it because it's warm, but something isn't right. It's too much, it's off-angle, and I desire to turn it off, this heat, but I know it's all I have left of him.

They say absence makes the heart grow fonder.

Who are these people, they?

And when do phrases like this become oversaid to stone, framed in stone, ready to be thrown at you to death in moments like these, with each one ripping the flesh of your cheeks right off, cracking your skull, your blood spraying about the courtyard of somewhere with a crowd cheering to the geyser of your blood, hoping to soon bring your body to the Parthenon to burn, as your ashes float up through the hole in the roof, each little speckle of dust shining in the midday sun, and there you are, a kind of gray mist stretching from fire to the end of the sky. You're face-up, up, up.

Absence makes the heart content to have nothing, be nothing, love nothing, the exact opposite of growing fond of anything or anyone, even yourself. At first yes, this is true, this fondness, but then it dissipates to something else entirely.

When Rudolfo died, I was at work on Park Avenue at you-know-where, and I got a call from his best Brazilian friend, Jewish, too, and all lox-y and matter-of-fact-ly, yet sweet like coconut. As most calls about death go, you know they're coming, even before they go. Perhaps it's a sniffle in the air, the hesitation on the other end, or something far deeper, the absence you feel before it cums, as if the very fabric of the universe, its socks ripped, its underwear crumpled, its shirts stained, had been thrown on a dark bed nearby you and no one even bothered to fold it while it was still warm, and it's the pain of knowing you can't fold it because it's too late, and now there will be wrinkles.

When he told me that Rudolfo lay on the sidewalk in front of our apartment, something I too am quite familiar with now, face-first into the ground though, same amount of blood, but simply stiff, with white grocery bags ripped and flared out on either side of his hands like angel wings, how one of the Oraculas, the good, possibly the bad, the ugly, it didn't matter, had found him, with one of their dogs, Sunshine back when she was still pitting and bulling, or maybe the shaky Shih-Tzu, it didn't matter, sniffling, crying first among those of us creatures living, and how quickly whatever dog it was found the carrots for the juicer afterwards, how quickly the dog found the meat for the grill for later, how quickly the dog had found Rudolfo dead so unamusing, how quickly the dog had simply…moved on, how we, Rodolfo and me, were just beginning to realize what this truly meant—fondness for each other—that the life within Rudolfo had gone, yet his body remained in some form, stiff and angelic, flattened and ready to be hung up somewhere as a statue to be worshiped by fickle crowds in the future.

I felt the heat then, there at the office of Heller, Heller, and Hah, and first I said "hah haaaaah HAH" to him, knowing what I had known but still hoping somehow I was wrong, that I did not in fact feel the patchwork squares of the fabric quilt of my life crinkle and wrinkle, and he said, "Colin, he's gone," simply, like that, definitively, and to think just that morning, I had reached to my right, and he was also flat, but breathing, face-up, up, up, the white all around him, not the suffocating plastic of grocery bags and dirty carrots, but our crème sheets and white pillows, our crème skin and wide white eyes, both of us looking out the window to see the little bit of snow that was promised by none, but here nonetheless, surprised by its audacity, to show up like that like it had, each white puff a world separated from every other world falling to simply accumulate and then be still and then melt and then evaporate and then fall once more.

He was shot.

And the irony was a fruity pulp on my tongue. How I had ultimately chosen to avoid the wars of my father, and the wars of his father, and the result of playing with toxic boats and planes and guns, fearing at the time that they'd find me out, that I'd get boners in the showers of hordes of nude dirty hot men, and that I couldn't say "yes sir" without getting aroused, choosing other paths instead, yet, here in peace, war had still found me and taken from me whom I had come to see as my closest ally in life, two soldiers in a pit, cold but in love together, warming our guns with the lube of persistence, to never give in, to never give up on those things that we believed we were born to do.

It was a cop's son, seven years old, who had found his father's gun, and brought it across the street to show his friend, a Sikh, the son of an electrician—an old, old man with a long white beard and a turban who'd often walk down the street, never on the sidewalk, and we'd cross paths often during sunset on those days Rudolfo came inside me, and his face was always so stern yet peaceful, and I found him beautiful, cinematic. His presence seemed to validate my existence a bit more, his walking down the street calming my walk down the street. That something so connected to him, his own son, and another son wanting to impress that son, the essence of youth, a fleeting impression, was the reason Rudolfo was gone, that they held the gun up together at the next person that walked down the street, for fun, and how they just wanted to say "bang bang," how they never meant to pull the trigger at the man with the groceries, how the heat behind me wasn't heat at all but anger, rage, years of hidden bitterness, how I wanted right then to tumble both their little bodies in a dryer on HIGH until I couldn't hear any more screaming.

—

After my dreams of maggots eating the blood of paper cuts all over my body faded, I would take sick days and click through photos of him, of me, of both of us, until one day those went, too.

Apple said it was a computer glitch, some kind of update error, and because of this error, all of my photos were gone but one.

Somehow this felt more painful than that first day. My photos allowed me to believe that he was still alive in a way, because I could see multiple faces, in various places, and when I'd speed through them, we seemed to be moving.

—

Mr. Hah not only noticed my absences from work, but also my absence while at work, how I'd give half answers, how something would always be missing, misaligned, crooked, a word obviously misspelled, which he read as me purposefully attempting to sabotage his business because of what I knew about what he did.

Sandy went on and on about her thyroid problem she thought she had, her constant ear infections, and I'd mumble just out of earshot, the truth, that she didn't have any problems, except her insistence upon poisoning herself by only eating cans of nutrition-less soup and gummy bears, pounds of them, which were making her more obese by the seconds divided by a prism of ignorance. And she'd never hear me, and I'd smile. I'd wear my lovely pearls as the swine around me oinked and bound insurance policies bound for strangers.

When the flu was going around, Miss Allison kept saying "I don't do well with viruses," as if anyone does well with them.

Mr. Hah said to me often, "What planet are you on!?" And my responses were always lofty and pearly, like, Pain is so, so, so tiny, compared to the avenues of beauty I've seen, Mr. Hah... trying desperately to believe it.

"What did you say? What are you playing at? Get the fuck out of my office." And binders would fly and hit bugs on windows and Downsy kids would get funding from a madman-murderer/CEO.

And we continued to support him in all his efforts, simply by our presence, because we chose not to simply walk away, or to speak the truth loudly, and risk what life would be like afterwards.

One day I asked the secretary, How do people like him survive? How can someone be so evil, abusive, power-hungry, so obviously out of control, so obviously the worst kind of human being, yet still remain in power—what's more—gain more of it daily?

"All this is true," she said. And she prefaced every word with, "To be clear, I'm thankful for my paycheck."

And she'd say something like, "He's smart. He's very careful about who he cultivates and where and for what. People like him, they'll always be fine. If the world goes to shit, they'll just run to their gated communities while everyone else shoots each other."

—

When I got off the phone that day with Rudolfo's loxy-coconut-Jewy-bestie, with generations of children burning inside dryers, I simply said, *Okay* to the news and hung up.

I stood up.

I walked out of the office and took the subway home, and when I got home his body had already been taken away, but the yellow tape and the sirens and the cars were still there. I walked past them, put my key into the keyhole, and I stared at the names above our doorbell.

His last name and mine, right next to each other, with a "/" to separate yet equate. There was tape on either side, too, to hold both sides down, but the adhesive on my side had given way a long time ago, which made my name coil up so you couldn't see my name, yet his name was clear, taped, and firmly affixed.

I felt guilty for that, that by my side's lack of adhesive, by any previous lack of commitment to this man, or even any steamy nomadic eyes, another bullet, hot, pierced through his skin and left an ephemeral tube. I ran up our stairs, got some tape, ran back down, and taped down my side so both our names were clearly above the doorbell again. I stood there and rubbed each side until the skin of my fingers ripped off and bled.

People asked me questions, friends came over, flowers came and wilted, cards personal, cards sterile, began to fold and curl like the leaves and flowers around which they were littered. And I felt guilty then, too, because it all looked like a kind of celebratory confetti, all for me and nothing for him.

Absence does not make the heart grow fonder.

Absence feels like laundry.

You're at the Laundromat alone, but surrounded by people, by fluorescent lights above you and a drop ceiling stained by previous drips now dry, by telenovelas and soccer matches that excite many but mean absolutely nothing to you, and you wish they'd shut the fuck up with that Spanish but you don't hold it against them, and there are washing machines spinning with suds like cappuccinos and the laundry is Lavazza espresso burning for you. And you look up. You look up and all you see are dryers full of other people's laundry, other people's children, other people's lives one step ahead of yours, and you have to sit there and simply wait until they're finished. You have to wait your turn, and you can't do anything about it. There are people all around you waiting in anticipation for things to be finished, hurried along, folded, flattened and crisp, warm. Your laundry, though, is cold, clean but cold, clumped together in a wire basket as a pile of rainbow fruit pulp from carrots, apples, cucumbers, ginger, many healthy, splendid things.

You're the only one sitting there with your cold wet laundry, waiting for your turn, powerless, in line, in much more than what love or fondness is.

Absence makes the heart content to have absolutely nothing, no books, no jobs, no conditions, no power, no success, no failure, no demons within, no mother, no father, no lover, no angels shot before you by little children giggling like air conditioners with lucky bunny tails ready to crack your head open, which somehow feels a lot like love, which somehow feels a lot like nothing, because it also feels a lot like absolutely everything all at once, and within that hum of the dryers and the lights, the chattering and the warmth, the stains and the metal, there's that pickle-jarring peace that's only found when you gaze upon death once more.

And it says, Open up. Open up, and sniff, bitch.

38

Watches

Most of the hours of my life were spent convincing someone I deserve to exist. I deserve to be in their presence, at the company, worth this much, but not that much.

And here, look, I have this list of things I've done, a list I've done for others, all the points of which have been spun to make me look even better than I am so I look even better than someone else.

Oh, you shouldn't have that beard, because somewhere along the way we got to thinking what grows out of our faces naturally isn't fit for a land of carpet, stale air, and large men with little resolve to listen to whom they once were, a more hopeful ballsy version of themselves, large men who have now convinced themselves and others around them of their largeness with their repetitive conversations about gout flare-ups—Do you feel it in your fingers? How about your toes? A fear of smallness covered up by a thick outer layer of bigness.

Even as I type and die slowly here, even as I listened to gouty conversations from obese and angry men, angry at the less ballsy versions of themselves that they became, convincing themselves that the money made it all worth it, the large homes in New Jersey made it all worth it, perhaps it wasn't a choice. I wish it were a choice, because it is for me, and by seeing others make the wrong choice for even more years than me, I am comforted, validated by the ubiquitous fat of the land.

The truth is, I am plagued—and gifted—by objectivity. I can see the evil in the good and the good in the evil. These men, Phil now gone, Hah who seemed would never be gone, may have never had a choice the way I did, the way I do, the way I always will.

This may have been their one path, and there was no wood with a divergence, just one concrete simple sidewalk for them, and everything still smelled like honeysuckles somehow, whereas I joined them, coming from somewhere else, another wood in another world, and here I thought all along they, too, were lying to themselves, hiding something within themselves, words, bright letters, waiting for something, putting on my rouge and pearls—because it's easier that way, to think every-one has the same hot pain aching within their fingers, finger by finger, letter by letter. This way I could look at Miss Allison, at Sandy, at the secretary, at Phil, at Hah, as simply the sad crowd that we are, all of us encased in the same brass letters, displayed and trapped as words on a wall.

And the snow outside on Park Avenue would churn down and left in the foreground, down and right in the background, and together they would churn in the air, one scene with the other, where you think you should be, from where you are, but for some, it might all have just looked like snow, and the roads to New Jersey were getting covered, and we should really head out soon, guys, but since you live in Astoria, can you stay and help answer the phones? Clients might call.

It was always easier for me to think that this crowd was making the same decision I made every day, to bite my tongue, to taste its blood, to ignore the snow-slow churnings within me, and that this was all a temporary sickness, a "stepping stone," but the truth is, it could have been much plainer for them, less plagued, less in between, less gifted, simply what it was, and they could have been heavenly happy with it and who am I to take it from them now?

Miss Allison's mother may have force-fed her lipstick at her house daily and made her put on pearls while she cried and ironed her own leg hair; for her, HH&H could have been a respite from her life at home. And because her guilt, iron-burned in her heart, could most likely never dissipate with any forgiveness or any therapy, vacation, or any normal and healthy work environment, it made sense for her to be abused here daily, because for her it wasn't abuse. Screams sounded like singing because they didn't make her lips tingle. Plain bagels and gummy bears tasted like carrot cake and champagne because it lacked the consistency of makeup on the teeth.

Whereas to some it may have been a simple heaven, comfort, and they were absolutely true to themselves by staying here, and their definition of thriving here, for me my life on Park Avenue has been a purgatory upon a purgatory upon a purgatory, a multiverse of waiting upon a waiting next to a waiting. For within me, *want* and *don't want* fought each other like a play of snow as you watch it out the foggy window above Park Avenue, with the dirty skid marks on the white fluff beneath you.

Whereas Sandy may have been able to ignore the yells from the executives or the power of her otherworldly daughter, for her too perhaps she never chose ignorance or knowledge, there was no apple. For her she still roamed in a pure garden of corporate America and to her, her family was proud because she was running her family proud, a strong, powerful, white woman, addicted to canned soup. She was raising a daughter, which was for her the loftiest of a canned dream she first dreamed when she was the same age as Lilly—even though Lilly knew, and I know, that there are much higher dreams of sleet, and hail, and rain, a long list of so many choices! Here she was flying high at one height, always high. I'd told myself that I was surrounded by dishonesty, offices of men and women lying to themselves, when really, it may have just been me who thought I knew where and how I'd be better off somewhere else, yet I was the only pussy without a magnet.

I'd use the grid to figure out how to get off the grid. I yelled to the cold air on days where most in the office were gone and I remained, trapped with my own thoughts. This is what I don't want. This is what I want. Where is my divine gesture?

I don't want to wait years for more than two weeks' vacation. I don't want to wait for years for millions of dollars to buy plane tickets.

I don't want to become a beggar with a bad back.

I don't want to live so I can pay for a place to put my pictures. I want good food and exercise. Now.

I want to meet all kinds of people from all kinds of cultures. And I want to tell them they're both dumb and beautiful.

I don't want to care about my credit report or my 110 grand of school loans going on 120 grand.

I want to make videos and write and have sex and be with my Rudolfo and go wherever we want when we want.

I want to be healthy, but I don't want to lie to myself for hours and hours of my life simply for money, simply because I'd be making use of past decisions, a past list of moments of my résumé, as if all of it were ever a part of a big plan of mine to be someone specific, as if people were only lists were words were breathing.

I want to continue to surprise myself and get uncomfortable so I can live with myself.

I don't want to wake up years from now poor and hungry and relying on other people who've had the courage to stick to one thing.

I don't want to wake up years from now rich and bloated relying on my own pain for not having the courage to leave and try many things.

I don't want to give myself false choices, as if there were only left or right, want and don't want, death and life. I want to share what I see, make fun of it, be inspired from it, and never give up, and then shut up.

I want the snow of the city, the warmth of the sand, the breath of the mountains, the hum of the jungle. I want it all. I want to give up everything to have it. I want to know how. I don't want anything.

To gain your own voice you have to forget about having it heard. I want to hear my voice and then I want to forget it forever.

I want the drama of the city, the muscle, the useless beautiful flair for everything new and redone and undone and fun.

I want the dirt of animals, the viciousness of nature, the regrowth and regrowth and regrowth and the fangs.

I want it all at once, faster than a previously undiscovered particle flying through me before the light.

And whether I wanted it or not, and whether you want it or don't want it, I want to be elsewhere again, anywhere but dying, anywhere but living.

—

And so I roll some more. I have now become a recycled salad box; hey, whuddyaknow folks, it looks like Whole Foods.

Above me, blurry, I see a woman in glasses, tired hair, a striped shirt that looks neglected or overused, and she carries multiple bags. She's one of these girls who seem to scour entire grocery stores to find the smallest possible plastic container—maybe it was two stuffed grape leaves, maybe it was a chickpea salad with seven chickpeas, or a side of tabbouleh for a toddler—and she's purchased that, along with a bottle of water, all so it felt like she was "having lunch" like she said she would, but she and everyone else knew otherwise, or, again, perhaps it feels better for me to think that, to calm those many times I followed others, thinking others were also following others, but in their hearts they were leading, everyone was but me.

I see the napkin holder and the napkins fluffing out from it from whomever did the replacing, stuffing in twenty or thirty more than could fit so that the return trip wouldn't happen for longer. This way the worker could spend time in the break room fixing the back of her shirt, how her undershirt was too small and it would come up out of the belt, much like the napkins she avoided refilling, overflowing and flopping every-where. She'd have extra time to roam the produce section juu-uuuuuust a grape-in-the-mouth longer, sneaking one in as she passed by, startled by an "excuse me" from someone who didn't care about the grape—in fact, who quite admired her fuck-you with that grape to management, even if the management was most likely kinder than most.

We all want to rebel against something, even if it's a good thing, or better than most. Its comparison doesn't matter much, for we still have that same desire to reach out and touch faith, grab that forbidden grape, plop it in your mouth, and pop it, suck the juices quickly like your first time swallowing cum, afraid it will be too sweet, too bitter, gagging a little, but happy and satisfied more than anything, shaking. We want that shake, that itch.

I see a man next to her eating another box salad that matches the recycled cardboard skin of my own. I wonder who is sitting behind me, who is digging into me, smacking their lips on the contents of myself, jabbing my insides with a weak little fork. But most of all, I wonder about that man I see; he's wearing Sony headphones and they look brand-new. They're the kind with the detachable cord, in case you're cramped in a subway in the morning and the roof above you when you exit is raining down slosh that the maintenance workers have sloshed down the steps from a burst pipe, and has subsequently sloshed a couple more flights down to the N platform, where many run out quickly and many run in, out and in, and thanks to those detachable headphones, the cord did not get caught on a brisk woman shaking her head from anger—as if all these people banded together, conspiring to give her a bad day, the nerve! As if everyone around her was in on it, making the decision together. As if everyone above conspired to drip water only on *her* head.

It was her purse, a brass buckle, and the cord caught, but popped off the headphones, and slid right along. He passed right through and nothing was ripped off his head.

And that man has been thankful and sliding all day long because of it, thankful he chose these and not the Bose, because those didn't have a detachable cord option, and today would have been altogether different—a baby born and in the room no one had scissors. There would have been yanking and biting and stretching and eventually there would have been blood.

It seems as though the woman can sense this, that he was having a pleasant day, that today more than other days swirling in his mind against which he was comparing this very moment was the way events were *supposed* to go. It's as if they were made for him—only him. He was averting disaster this morning, and who knows how many other times he slid right by the brass buckle of death, Sony-lubricated, and fleeing easily once more.

Her appearance, on the other hand, seems to oppose him completely. She isn't angry with him. She holds no bitterness as she uses her fingers to slowly pick up the slimy grape leaf muck with rice and such, and when she bites it in half, it looks like there is a glimmer of power in her teeth, as though she were imagining her ex-boyfriend's dick, as if she was finally doing now what she now knows she could have done then, way back then, slowly biting his dick off when he face-fucked her hard in the middle of the night drunk and screaming how unthankful of a bitch that she was, that she'd never make it on her own, not with *your* salary, not with that brain of yours. You're meant to be pretty. You're meant to take my dick whenever I want, to gag on it when you least expect it, because I own you, you see, and I don't care if you're choking and you can't breathe, you worthless cunt, just remember that you like it like that first time when you didn't want it but realized you did after enough spit dripped off your chin in the alleyway.

She's biting into it like that, slowly and powerfully, locked like a pit bull jaw on a great blue heron in a Florida swamp, momentarily satisfied, taking control of her past like that. That stuffed grape leaf is a reminder, that although in some ways he was right, that it is difficult to survive on your own, it's not entirely impossible like she had previously thought, and thought, and thought, and thought, until one moment she finally didn't, and finally slid away.

She's looking at the man now, how he closes his eyes when he listens to his music, how his texting and browsing seem to come second-to-the-music truly soothing him more than any update or status or tweet or kissy-poopy emoji could. She wants to be a part of that song, an accompaniment. She wants to sing along with good things. More good things. She knows now there are good things and bad things, and everything in between, and it took her years to get here, this in between, this knowledge of all the many types of struggles there are, how she had to choose one struggle over another, that struggle would always be there, just a different color.

She puts the other half of the grape-leaf-dick down. She looks at him and gracefully lifts her hand up off the table and lets it float to his shoulder. She squeezes his poofy goosey jacket slightly harder than a stranger normally would. Startled, the man takes his headphones off and looks at her with a *yes*?

"Sorry, sorry," cowering but determined, "do you have the time?"

The time? The man is confused.

So enraptured in the timelessness of his music, he has to remember the word, and what it represents, or what it tries to at least, that land, that space, that smell, that breath that lies, exactly, at the center, of the tick-tock of things, of the life-death of things, the dumb-smart of things, and the right-wrong of things. The great hyphen of being stuck. Time.

Once he remembers what it represents, that they are here but wouldn't always be, he is then bewildered why the woman couldn't find out for herself. Doesn't she have a phone? I see it right there, he thinks, and he resigns all confusions with the fact that her phone *must* be dead, and thus, her touch, from grief. She wouldn't have reached out otherwise, unless she truly needed to.

In many ways she seems clearly sad, rattled, tired, and hungry—hungry to be a part of things again, anything, anyone, other than who and where she was before.

She also went elsewhere.

In that touch, that reach, she went elsewhere to an earlier place, a more innocent time, the time of cigarettes and watches, the time when strangers would ask for "the time" because they didn't always have it, the time when cigarettes so very inconveniently introduced you to new things and sometimes its poison felt great, worth it at least, that camaraderie of strangers that seems so different now.

Now, the cigarettes, now the time, now the coffee is electric, and everyone feels so very conveniently alone.

39

A New Tower

In the future, nothing will be sensationalized the way absolutely everything is now.

We'll have collectively realized by then, the way we know asbestos really isn't good all around the way we do now, the way we know now to protect our lungs from chemicals wherever possible, fiberglass, paint, Gulf-War-airplane-factory-beryllium now, do you think we're alone now, we'll have collectively realized that overreactions are simply the energy wasted which could have otherwise gone into researching and inventing a better solution. This isn't to say we'll be emotionless then, or without rage and malice, but somehow we'll all just know that sensationalizing is poison, unhealthy, and asphyxiating long term, and anyone who still uses it will be labeled a new kind of idiot or murderer.

I see another tower, and this one I cannot tell if it comes before or after which time, fore or aft, below or over anything else, but it was there, it's here, and it will be there, and by our standards it's impossibly constructed.

And behold, the base of the tower was as thin as a hair and it shimmered in the sunlight like one spider web string covered in dew. At the tip of that thin line another section began and V'ed at 45 degrees for miles, and the farthest away it was from that tip, the thicker it became, forming somewhat of a flattened reverse pyramid and tilted. And at the base of this pyramid—the tallest point of the structure—there was a great light shot into space and its glow rivaled the suns and it was difficult to tell if light was funneled in or if light was emitting outward.

Below the structure on the ground were miles upon miles of grassland with millions of buffalo and wild men, commingling, cohabitating, and it was difficult to tell who was ruler of whom.

It was clear a reverence was pervasive, a reverence for everything, yet intertwined with that was a whimsicality, things flipped, reminders here and there to not take too seriously the brief lives they live, and for them brief was 365 years, and all men and buffalo were 1,776 feet tall.

Some men and women were naked. Men admired men, women admired women, and men admired buffalo, and all would caress the hair of the other, the armpit of the other, the genital of the other, but not for a release, but to stretch out the moment to simply admire, an ever-present divinely edged orgasm, even worship what curled and sweated and engorged before them. Young calves rested with old men. Old women lay with feeble buffalo. Young men as well as old were continuously *laughing* while *studying* while *worshiping* while *fucking*, for at this time, all those words meant the same thing. There was no need to separate them anymore into separate thoughts, because they all accomplished the same and felt the same.

Money was everywhere, not for exchanges of goods. It was left over from our time, and all efforts were made to preserve the bills for papier-mâché for party hats and study hats and sex hats in the shape of upside down and tilted pyramids, and they never waited for the hats to dry. They let the glue drip down their foreheads and cheeks like blood like silver like words of many moons forgotten. Sweet grasses and teas were imbibed while discussions of which moon they'd explore next and in which galaxy, what geological feature they'd hope to find, and how their favorite colors of supernovae changed so regularly.

There were toasts like now there are toasts, but they were never to celebrate, always to inspire,

"Explore, explore, explore, the stars, Explore, explore, explore the skin, of everything, (moment of silence) *especially the pussy, especially the nutsac* (chimes chimed, gongs gonged) *thus sayeth the Lord* (then a few would fart, then they'd laugh)."

And they'd start scribbling formulas on tables, and they were proud to tag things that way, by what they discovered, by what they created, and anything built—whether the pyramid that harnessed and worshiped the power of the sky, a table, a hat made of money, or even their body—was covered in the color of formulas solved, new words created, where they hoped to go deeper and deeper into *space*, and deeper into them*selves*, because they saw no difference between the two, for these words meant the same thing, too.

They prayed unceasingly and danced and slept and caressed and dug deeper in the name of this, for this was God to them, discovery, reverence for discovery, reverence for laughter, the concurrent collective and individual recognition of how much they didn't know blurring as one.

Each moment of laughter was validation of this reality, that they were just one part of the whole, that this all was a holy playground of growth and destruction, that it was possible to explore it—even harness it—without taking away from it. They realized the cycle of things, that there was death, that many things would go away, including themselves, their planet, their star, their life, their towers to living together freely, but they also knew what poisons to avoid, what mutated and muti-lated the joy and essence of things, and with every toast they reminded themselves.

Explore, and grow, but laugh when things die away, because you know that all at once you put forth what your strongest effort is at the time to keep something going, and you also know that in the future of this future there will be a new way to make it last even longer, and again, and again, and again. You pray to all that you do not know, that unanswered formula, and you dance to all that you do, and because it's a confusing dance of paradoxes, tics fighting with tocs, you fucking fart right in the middle of it to remember where you're from and where you are when you're roaming amidst the chalk-white starlight and the black space between misting together as one.

Those who flew the fastest through time looked like witchy trash men, for their hair was long and never cut, braided with musical instruments from every time before them, drumsticks and chicken bones, sparkly broken CDs and violin strings, chopped up guitars and computers, feathers and fathers and everything fleeting and forlorn and eventually torn but remembered, replayed, replayed, echoes like radio signals spi-raling outward and never-ending from their original move-ments and notes. They flew through space naked and their balls hung lower with time as they stretched their efforts, deeper and deeper, past asteroids and rings, explosions and formations and the way the universe continually sings, and you can see the nutsac jiggle from a hidden wind, and the hair glows like a comet from a kind of glitter interwoven from an exponential curiosity and lavish velocity.

They are strong, and their skin has hardened from radiation, and their muscles have formed new layers upon layers, and dust has formed new paths on their bodies the way water leaves behind crevices and dry creek beds on dead planets now being restored thanks to them. And yet these nomads, those tasked to bring something to light which has never seen light, are tasked with something deeper, as many never return from the point at which they aim the bows of their arms—but with them they keep the camaraderie of solitude.

We might think they're "lonely," but by this time that word too had died out, and the definition of "love" was consolidated to encompass that, too, as when one aims toward what they love and what they must seek most, it is quite a deathly lonely affair, which, once beyond that initial emotion, can also be a beautifully sparkly thing, a friend's or brother's or lover's or father's sparkly silence, if you let them also go where they someday must.

Women's breasts, like the balls of men, flew behind them too, and these warrioresses gave birth to children who would follow the paths of their mothers, women and men, born from above, conceived by the holy semen a new hue yet to be found. They fly through the universe and these god particles would enter them and they'd feel rebirth growing within them, and after a time twins, quadruplets, sometimes thousands at once would expel from a mother and fly behind her, and from her speed the umbilical cord would rip and these children knew what to do—detach from everything and everyone to find something.

And when they did, sometimes they would return to a planet, and sometimes they wouldn't, because *return* didn't mean anything anymore, either—how can one return when every place and every time and every person and every particle is your home?

There's not one planet, not two, but all. When an "astronaut" (to us)—to them, "priests"—would return as we would understand it, there was never a celebration, nothing sensationalized as if they accomplished something, as if you had a feeling about it one way or another. Their task was never-ending. It seemed laughable to note any return with a thank you or a hyphen or a bullet or a cup, as if it were empty before and by their return had filled it, as if we had lost them, were scared for them, but not anymore.

This was nonsense.

When the priests returned they roamed the fields laughing and exploring like everyone else did, making love to everyone, with the ground, with the buffalo, and only when that priest felt the need to express all that they had found, another tower would be built, beginning first with the base, a thin line, between the hell of now and the heaven of now, shimmering like the others and strong, but above this base a new shape would form and a new light, and with these lights that shone through the far reaches of spiraling galaxies, new worlds were discovered, new ideas, new creatures, and even new features of our bodies.

We still could see though. We still had eyes.

And if you were to look at our planet where it spun within our muscly arm of the Milky Way, with lights shining in every direction stronger than lasers, and spinning, then, from that perspective, it seemed as though our world was truly celebrating something, a launch party of sorts with spotlights not on clouds but formations light years away.

And we were happy to do so.

We were doing our best. From the fields of buffalo there was a calm and respect, a little-ado-about-everything, but from the fields of stars there was a hilarity and a joy that surpasses all our understanding.

40

Humming

There's a humming above the snow, and it hums, *You know that I love you, but I don't care. You know that I see you, but I'm not over there.*

On some days at HH&H when I'd walk in the park during lunch, I'd find myself staring at a hunk of limestone with a hunk of white snow on it. I'd get close to it like a lover, and I'd pull my hand out of my pocket and place it on the rock. I tried to imagine what it felt like at the center of that rock, if the center was so different from the outside that the inside seemed silly to the outside and vice versa. I'd blow on the snow and each flake would fly away like chalk dust, each particle a freckle on some redhead ashamed at how many they accumulated around the nose, that rock-hard nose, that strong nose in the sun.

And like sweat from a redheaded go-go dancer on a pedestal in a dark club full of homos, all of us enraptured by each violin string of muscle beneath the skin, each freckle lit up from the spotlight, each suspender snapped and reddening his so-easily-reddened skin in harsh lines that somehow seemed far more endearing than raunchy like they were meant to be, like baby bum spanks, leaving hand marks for us, and that sweetness made us wanna taste him all the more, his innocence covered in the freckles of manhood that can, by a poof and a whiff and a sniff and lick of some nameless observer, blow it right off him and all that's left is the young boy he still feels like from time to time, but not on nights deep in the thump of the gay Heffalump and lustful Woozle, we the gawking and colorful elephants with our snouts in the air throwing our penises at him, eat mine!

OH GAWWWWD eat mine!

And he loves it, and it makes him redder and he smacks those suspenders and he dances faster with the DJ cloaked in darkness except for the white horns on his head, and he sweats, and like that sweat dripping through each wonderful hair on the bulbous power of his chest, and like sweat that makes its way over each bump and crevice of his stomach and through the furriest of furries and the blue veins of his cock to the tip, so did I roam through the park on fire in the cold, invigorated by it, its white, white deadness bringing me more to life again somehow.

—

I had left in a hurry from H^3 one day because I was feeling ill from the stories one of the underlings was gloating about. It was about Mr. Hah of course, and this underling seemed proud that he knew this information, that it was a privilege to have it, how we should respect him for his having it. He had been there longer, back when Mr. Hah was worse supposedly. He would date princesses and refuse to date anything less. He'd seek them out from around the world and invite them to stay in the highest condos with the best views and even though he didn't own these vistas he'd pretend like he did. He bought dogs for the weekend so that the princesses would find him friendly, rich,

but approachably American—what's more American than having a big fluffy dog that doesn't respond to anything you say
and pisses everywhere but it's okay, silly dog. I mean Mr. Ruffles.

That's cute, isn't it?

There was one princess he was dating for quite some time,
"something near Persia," and "we'd hear him fuck her in his
office and he'd say the oddest of things" apparently.

"You want me to fuck you with an apple!? Is that what you
want!?"

"And we'd hear her whimper a little bit but all seemed okay,"
and the underling said he'd continue with the same foodie-fuck
imagery, "You want me to put some fucking almond butter on
those fucking sliced apples and get them good and oiled up
with almond butter just fucking dripping all over them and
then you want me to shove each one up your goddamn ass you
fucking dirty little princess-whore-fuck!?"

They'd hear glass breaking, sinks breaking, and of course
Miss Allison would stand right outside his door and report:
"Everything's okay everyone. Mr. Hah is juuuuuust having
some alooooooooooooone time, kaaaay?"

Of course she'd scream this across the entire office then, just
as she does now.

"You want me to take my goddamn dead dad's kimchi from
his concentration camp, that shit he'd make in dirty pots he
found that people would use for shit-cans and piss-cans, and
you want me to pick up that fucking spicy kimchi and SHOVE
IT UP YOUR PUSSY DON'T YOU, YOU SPICY LITTLE
CUNT FART!?"

And when Miss Allison would hear these ingredients used
in the fuck-banter between the devil and the princess of Persia,

she'd pull out her clipboard or notepad and nod her head and then write down a list.

She liked to make lists. They helped her remember things. And through oversimplification, they helped her forget things between the bullets, things happening right in front of her behind a mahogany door.

- Kimchi.
- Apples.
- Almond butter.
- Shit-can pot.

And she'd listen intently for anything else he might ask for later that she would of course proactively spend the entire evening making sure to find. And the next morning she'd list all the things she found for him during one of their many meetings and oftentimes he'd be angry of course at first, but then he'd say, curious, "Well, I mean, since you already got all the things on your list, there's no sense in taking them back. You might as well just give it. GIVE IT HERE, DAMN IT," teeth gritting, molar-bowling-balls sliding across old sidewalks and black-pinned fences.

She'd continually be running back to the mini-fridge and pulling out all the ingredients that he might need for all his fantasies to come true, the usual duties for an accountant.

"During this time he did A LOT of coke," the underling continued.

When was this, back in the '80s? Was he like the frickin' Wolf of Park Avenue or something?

"This was about seven years ago."

Oh, interesting. Just discovered coke then, had he?

"No. He started doing coke when he got to this country and never stopped really until a few years ago, so we're told."

I asked, Wasn't he with his wife then? I mean, she's no princess. I'm sure of it. A Southern belle maybe, but no princess. A princess of *darkness*, maybe.

"CAREFUL...careful with that talk," he said. "Yes. Yes, this was while they were married, and oddly enough she apparently encouraged it. Because it would be 'good for the business.' And she was right. He used to go out to lunch every day and invite a select group of people along with him to these 'lunches' that would last all afternoon. Well, *I* was asked one day, especially after I had just closed a MAJOR deal. I was finally in the IN crowd around here, takes a while buddy, quite an accomplishment, and *I* knew this because *I* was just asked to 'lunch.' I went and it was one of the best days of my life. I'm telling you man, they were doing coke on the table. They were dancing on the table. Some of the guys were even circle-jerking each other under their napkins while they looked at girls across the restaurant. Not me, though, not me. I wasn't into that. I'm not gay."

You're not into circle-jerking your colleagues? You know, *I* would be into that.

"OH. Oh man, you're too much. Tooooo much," red-faced and laughing, squirming a bit. His dick was actually getting hard, too.

Uh-uh, I asked, staring directly at his bulging excitement, so what happened then?

"We got arrested. Well, Mr. Hah got arrested when he poured a bag of coke on some random lady's tits and he shoved his face in her cleavage and fingered—well, *fisted* really—her pussy with coke on his hand, really pushing and punching it in there. You ever hear him go around the office and say 'ya got yer white fist out don't ya!?' and then laugh oddly and hysterically?"

Yes, many times.

"He's talking about that day. He's proud of it. Well, the Persian princess found out about this of course. She was devastated. He had spent almost a year with her in that apartment overlooking Central Park, one of the tallest towers, not anywhere near the ones being built nowadays, like the one we're moving to, but it was impressive. He'd sold her quite well on his wholesome American doggie act—with the exception of all manner of that fruity-kimchi-kink, which she was reaaaaaaally into for some reason. She loved the dogs. She loved their lovely life together. She had been hinting rings. She'd make him watch *Breakfast at Tiffany's, An Affair to Remember*…all these old movies in New York girls cream their pussies over."

So how did she take it, finding out about the coke-fisting incident?

"She threw the dog off the balcony. When it hit the sidewalk, it exploded all over Mr. Hah as he was getting out of his black car. All over Mr. Sherry, too, because the window was down, and the guts splat all over their seats, all over their faces."

Whoa.

"Later on that night, after he attempted to apologize for what happened, *she* jumped off the balcony too, but," almost peeing his pants from laughter, and I could see his full hard-on, a big thick mushroom head on his cock too, a lovely portobello beast of a cock, "she hit a tree and then an awning, and then a car, and then a child. She's a paraplegic now, the princess. Haven't you seen that princess in pictures zooming around her palace blowing into that thing like Stephen Hawking? I think they're making a movie about her actually; she's done a lot for abandoned dogs and cats around the world. She's even picketed in South Korea, partly because they eat dog still, boh-shing-tang wong ching-wong or something I think it's called, and partly—*I* THINK—to somehow make a dig at Mr. Hah's heritage. Like she's protesting *him* whenever she protests the way they get their dog meat, what she wishes she could do to him, but can't now, since she's in that retard chair."

And what's that?

"Beat him with a club, until his flesh is tenderized and ready to boil in a hot stone dog soup pot."

Oh.

"Oh, and here's the kicker my man, that woman? In the restaurant, who 'threatened to sue'? At least that's what it said in the papers. *Weeeee* all know around here that that was actually a paid prostitute by Helen. We're quite sure this was all a plan of hers. The dog, the princess, the attempted suicide, everything."

Genius, I guess.

"Definitely," with a little dab of pre-cum seeping through his suit pants, "Because they didn't suffer one bit. They made sure to have the highest legal liability limits possible when this pussy juice hit the fan, and then they had all these press releases and events to counteract, you know how it works—and well really just further the fuel—all the bad press. What was obvious, though, through all this bad press, was that Mr. Hah was *untouchable*, due in part to his stellar, comprehensive insurance plan. Afterwards, all his friends he was trying to make, all those 'right' connections that were so far away before, all these Park-Avenue-Palm-Beach uber-wealthy gated-community types," whispering, "with questionable histories with the law, started knocking on our door."

Ah. Hah.

"Hey man, we got jobs, right? It's a good thing the judge ruled that it was in fact a suicide attempt, because there was a 50/50 chance that the Hahs were going to be charged with murder. A lot of people think Helen pushed her."

Do you?

"Whooo knows with that one. *Mr.* Hah though, naaah, naaah, he wouldn't. Mr. Hah, he's a great guy. I'm so thankful he took me in. My kids all go to private school. My gout only flares up sometimes. Can't complain. Can't complain. What about you? You enjoying yourself here? What's it been, two years now? Three?" He squirmed a bit more and shifted the mushroom beneath his massive stomach, a miraculously levitating mass, that stomach, an entire Soft Rock Café built upon and smothering that delicious mushroom. What a waste.

I'm going to go for a walk.

"Okay, man. Shave your beard when you're out there."

I'm Muslim. It's my religion. My beard is my religion.

"Wait, are you really?"

Well, and Jewish. And Mennonite. And a tree-hugger. And a gay astronaut.

"Oh."

We're a humble people; our people like beards.

"You're too much."

—

I walked in the snow in the park and I looked at the towers through the trees and tried to forget that they were there, that there were people within them doing the oddest of things. I told myself, who am I to judge?

It still felt creepy, all those lights on, how some might have binoculars looking at me. How some might have been tilting there on a balcony ready to do it, all in honor of their cute American puppies recently flung off balconies.

There were sled marks worn in, and at the bottom of hills were bales of hay that looked bombed by children. Each thud would cause a new explosion, and instead of cows to play in the hay there were all manner of birds, blue jays, pigeons, wrens, blackbirds, ducks, geese, and cardinals.

As I walked I thought of my mother.

It was impossible not to. An entire pond completely iced over, a foot of crisp milky-bleached snow seamlessly connected to hills and trees drenched in marshmallow. Whereas the city was a slush-pit of despair and steam and American cream of the crop, the park was a stark reminder of all that used to lie beneath the city. Rock, trees, water, dirt, seeds, bones. And as I walked and gazed upon the nuance of whites, as if before I had never seen these colors, these whites, as if before, all I knew of white was the blank white of a glowing computer page in Word.

As I walked I thought about lamp-white too, with its slightly yellow hue, snow white, which was basically marshmallow, cloud white, which was the same as shower towels with jet stains here and there from overuse, sled-white, which was the color of eggs with little smears of pepper all over the heating mucus—all those albumins, mucoproteins, and globulins slowly became opaque. And sleds were the spatulas scraping again and again and again.

Amidst that gradient of white, as I searched for just one more and always find it, I saw the white of someone's eyes gazing upon all the whites, white reflecting white, one glossier than the other, that, that wet great eye-white, was looking through a glass of fresh water resting on top of a stack of white pages, printed, and their pupils were letters.

And it was then that I'd see a cardinal, red, and as it flew it made candy-cane tubes of power through the air.

It would fly at me with such intensity that I felt as though I were on a windshield sliding like sweat down through the interstate of the chest hair of our entire country, 80 miles per hour, 150 miles per hour, 1,000 miles per hour, yet I'd never hit it. Somehow the cardinal would always know to keep a safe distance, but it felt like an explosion all the same.

All I saw then were, and all I see now are, feathers and blood, eyes fidgeting before me, and the cardinal would hop quickly from white to white to white, from lamps, to clouds, to shower towels, to eggs burning to the white pages burning with water spilled all over them to put the fire out, and the fire was her feathers, that cardinal, the symbol for my mother.

I thought of her divine gesture, and I kept listening for mine, *what about mine?* But I didn't hear anything. I couldn't hear my "Clair de Lune." I tried to hear it in the wind, in the traffic muddled from the trees and the sloshes of tires and the gnashing of teeth in the city's streets and how collectively they compete in a symphony of sorts, but it wasn't at all my symphony.

And then I heard a humming, the same humming that hums and drums beneath me now.

The humming of songs overplayed. The humming of my breath underneath my scarf. The humming of my own pumping blood boiling as I stared at that cardinal. The humming and symphony of static electricity covering my skin from too many layers of clothing I had worn to the park. And in that moment of suffocation, I realized I had made a grave mistake.

I was looking everywhere. I had searched for music *others*

had composed. I had been startled by red birds, beautiful birds, in the snow and had hoped that they could be my moment with all things above and below. I had tried to cry at everything and laugh at everything and not give a shit about anything at all, floating, until I realized I could see everything I needed to see and hear and do and find, rarely or always, from within.

And then, on a day that could have been just like today, I walked out of the park, along Park Avenue, and then through the mahogany door once again.

41

Proceed With Caution

In chalk, on the sidewalk of my writing room, within the blackness of the bright corporate world beneath my feet, in the blood of every park, within repetitive avenues, the words, the words, in the beginning was the Word, *Consistency is the last refuge of the unimaginative.*

Or, *Have the courage to write badly.*

Or, *Close the door*…and open another.

I see myself on my way to the hospital, I am the beanie on my head, every China-spun twist and turn catches the wind of the spring that seems to be on its way, stepping with the sun that seems cracked, egg yolk dripping, in my many lives within Russian dolls, within Russian imperial vodka.

Do I only learn in spring?

Is that my destiny, to be muddled and fuddled for winters upon winters upon winters until another spring of clarity arrives, the sidewalk cracks all around me, and behold the chalky blood drips up, drips down, drips neon-green in the patterns of my now-fading heartbeat, the patterns of stocks, the patterns of microwaves cooking macaroni and cheese for Good Oracula in Astoria, who stripped her name off our front door, because her Polish sister is a drunk, a loser, a macaroni abuser, and trying to find her at 65, homeless and selfish, and as her world turns with that macaroni and cheese in the dark, she hopes no one rings the doorbell below our ding dong names freshly taped on the door of the Book of Life, and she especially hopes it isn't her sister. She hopes for anything but her sister, as she will at some point or she did at some point find me there, here, at my writing desk, a desk that severed my knees, an air conditioner that killed a pit bull, and a day after a day that finally killed an unhealthy relationship.

I had received a call from the police. It was to be a "writing day" for me. I was going to do just that, close the door, and courageously write badly, finally embrace inconsistency, get to writing that story that only I could write, but, alas, my phone clucked and squawked, and as it rang I wondered if the moment would go—that moment when you think you've GOT IT, you'll understand your life, your own story, if you just begin right now. You'll say exactly what you need to and mean to, but I can't have any distractions, laundry, phones, dogs, leaves secretly growing on the wizardly trees trapped by the rooms that make or break apartments.

And the man on the other end asked if I knew someone named Madeline, "Madeline Alli...what's that, ah, Madeline Allison?" He said she was too frantic in front of him, eyes rolling back in her head, to really speak, but oh I could hear her there with him, mumbling as she does, a little bit louder now.

Of course, I said, why?

She was, as I've attempted to explain, something worse off than a mutilated bitter lemon, one of those people in your life that for one reason or another you humor—out of pity, perhaps the abuse of the past coupled with the abuse of her every day, that you've witnessed every single day, so you just let her do it. It's so easy to blame it all on "the abuse," oh, she must have been raped repeatedly by her father, and perhaps she was, or perhaps it was a flick or a tick in the brain that allowed her to see things slightly off, which allures you into her world even as it sickens you, and you allow it to proliferate freely around you, her rocky world of all obligations, battering around, perpetual earthquakes and booty shakes in the dark clubs and leather of her wounded, lonely brain.

Her loneliness shocks you into mesmerized submission, to gallivant and seize the day like no one else would, her over-commitment a frenetic particle swap, or sometimes it strips you of your own moment—NOW I will write, that moment of clarity you had spent all weekend, even years building, waiting, procrastinating, *IT IS HERE!* And *now* you can begin—by a phone call from a policeman who tells you, "Well, she's here in the emergency room, and she called out *your* name, again, and again, and again."

You're drawn to it, that submission, that magnetism, that brokenness, because it reminds you of dead things, gone things, and their memories that seem to echo between the windows, walls, and siding of yourself back and forth until you're deliriously on your way there, to ascertain just what, the hell, the issue is, all for her, and nothing for you.

Questions repeat, *where is she? Where did she go? Is she okay? Why did it have to come to this? Why is this person so bat shit crazy?* And just like that, your moment is gone because you're sucked into someone else's.

And one way or another, the drama of her neurotic call twists and turns like the cheap China-made fabric of your cheap beanie memories; you're not sure where one starts and where one begins. Your life feels interwoven, confused, fused, yet warm.

It's as if your very existence is an update to your photo library, and because this is a new day, with whole new software, your first step out the door is pressing that UPDATE button. And in the process of your walking to the subway to head to the hospital in Manhattan, all your divisions you thought were permanent—these photos were taken on such-and-such day—and another folder the same—these photos were taken on that and that day, but suddenly you look out in front of you and everything you once knew has been combined, copied, duplicated, deleted, renamed, swapped, and everything you've ever felt or saw or knew is now just dumped into one fucking folder and it's beyond overwhelming.

A laugh you had in the Grand Tetons sounds the same as the laugh you laughed with Wayne as the laugh you laughed with your father, your brother, your mother, yourself, alone in your room with your bear lamp glowing your way, you can go your own way, as your balls attempt to follow you, and the scorpion of the moment is lit even brighter, and it stings you right on the lips, and there you are foaming at the mouth, there you are choking on your own lungs, there you are watching birds of the fermented sweet blood of Jesus get hit by cars, exploding as guts in the wind, all we are is guts in the wind.

Your empty bed with Rudolfo is the same pinewood coffin your father was placed into because it was cheaper that way and that's what he asked for on one of the very few days he spoke to you as he died slowly before you. He didn't want anything glossy. He wanted the cheapest. Because he knew that he'd be set on fire and his entire body, his stung lips, his lungs that once coughed and laughed, coughed and laughed, for 65 years would just be set on fire and there'd be no differ-ence between pinewood and the leather of your own skin, and there'd be no difference between this hospital visit right now, this crazy woman, and every other hospital you've ever been to during your entire poofy-puffy-fluffy life, and everything you thought was so completely unacceptable about it, so unaccept-able that you never said anything about it.

Knowing this, that this, that that, that it will be, that it was, that it is one of those few days that rebooted everything and updated, consequently shifting everything I once knew and felt, bringing it all back, rearranging it, and throwing it into a new box I call myself, I hesitated as I walked. Madeline, my "colleague" of three years, half of which were swirled in a soft serve of secret (known around the office) suicide attempts at home with her old friends after she watched *I Love Lucy*, with the other half such pitiful magic, somewhat admirable, that she would enslave herself so dutifully and fully, and so bright this enslavement was that you ignored all the dark side of the swirl and you thought it was all fine eventually, it's just "her," that's just Miss Allison, it all tastes the same, it's all dessert and good for me and I should never stop eating it.

Just get up and get to work.

That's what I do. That's what you do. That's what we all do.

Just get up and get to work.

Get up and go to Park Avenue.

After I got out of the subway, I saw super-condo-tower signs that said "Proceed with Caution," warning me about the elab-orate scaffolding above, and the high winds that have been known to lift up pieces of plywood and sever the heads and limbs of we, the sidewalkers.

With that warning, I knew I was approaching something I

had already approached before, but this time would be different. I'd actually need to decide something this time.

And now I see a finger in the air lift up and scratch the surface of my skin.

Remember? I'm my own beanie now on top of my own head. I'm Chinese.

My body is a warm hat. And time has fused with cotton and hair and oil and past days and future gays.

Let your head lack no oil, especially no boiled foil.

Take a shower in it, ya fuckin' tranny-ass bitch, because ya bessssst not be no snitch.

42

Fart

I am the fart of all art, and on my way to the hospital, on the subway, through the reflection on the subway window I see myself staring at a tall man-not-yet-a-woman wearing a Prada bag, a tiny little thing, that bag. It matched the delicate sprigs of his beard, dyed green, and the thick eyebrows he had painted on so he looked a bit clownish yet draggish yet Middle Eastern, a colorful tranny prophetess of many colors, for her hat was rainbow sparkle sequins.

Her shoes were thick, black leather—tires chopped up. And the way she stood and held onto that pole so delicately, but with anticipation of someone surely about to judge her, with such antibodies already prepared for that judgment, she seemed simultaneously insecure yet vaccinated and ready for anything. She knew herself, and what it meant to fight others as herself, and she knew it was tough, but she's given herself the answer through the needle before. Her eyes wandered, over all of this, over all of us, but present, a colorful little thing, masculine, yet delicate with Prada butterfly wings.

And then I saw before me, a Korean guy with his old-school Korean father, and they seemed ignorant of the fact that the son was beyond stunningly sharp and beautiful in that classic princely sense. He seemed to ignorantly have and to *hoad* all of the family's hopes and dreams, literally the embodiment of the efforts of semen and one basket of eggs of generations previous. And there he sat, one generation, with the older, on a blue subway seat going downtown on the green packed #6 train. I saw his face through the crowds of butts and dicks. Between one covered dick and one covered butt, I wondered how long this man, not so long ago was a child running around with a snotty little nose, green like that #6, infected, but now stood so virulently, aware, buttery-skinned, dark-haired, and he seemed to suck the energy of his father into himself as his father withered before us by the second, suffocating by a crowd of witnesses.

At first I went to the wrong hospital, to NYU Langone. When I left the subway, my scarf and its tassels fluffed in front of me from the subway wind on the steps behind me and seemed to lead the way, which I'd later find out, was astray. The subway wind simply blew where it pleased and it took me with it. With my steps, the blue tassels played the piano on my knees and whimsically guided me to the sunlit hospital along the river. Its purple logo was framed so perfectly in the sunset, and from my angle on the sidewalk, the streetlamp and accompanying pole surrounded the logo, and only *I* could have seen it that way, from that angle, framed, flat, and Downsy, as I stood still waiting for the light to change.

This is it, I thought. She must be here. It's basically the right streets that the cop gave me. Perhaps NYU Langone also means Bellevue? It had to be, because the sun so perfectly lit it up for me. It had to be a sign, because it opened up my mind, you see.

At the hospital entrance, two men in the river-wind were

helping each other light a cigar. Their heads were bowed toward each other and their eyes were squinted and the women next to them seemed proud that the men were proud. That's all they wanted, for their men to be happy and proud, as if it was through man's effort that the baby was born, as if they did anything more than cum into a pussy. But yes, they thought, light those cigars. You're truly men now, now that the women have grown your babies inside them and successfully delivered them onto this planet. Celebrate, dear men, for all that you've completed.

In the lobby there was a clown walking with Jews trying to find someone who was staying there, probably a burn victim. They asked the woman at the front desk surrounded by hundreds of switches and knobs and bed knobs and broomsticks, and I highly doubted she knew what half of them did. The clown and the Jewish teenagers galloped away to surprise their friend with that clown, and it was my turn, another clown apparently, because, "Bellevue is clearly not the same as NYU Langone. Does that sound the same to you, sir!?"

Oh.

"Can ya hear? Are you a clown, too? So many fucking clowns, every damn day..."

Well aren't you a sassy front-desk receptionist, I said. You seem to be under the impression that everything in this world is perfectly organized and efficient, that places and things and people can never be improperly named, no?

Clearly, all those bed knobs and fucking broomsticks got to her head.

"Under the impressha-whaaaaaaaaa? Effishhaaawho!?"

Let's be clear then, lady, you do not know how to use all those buttons, I continued. I know it. If there were a fire, we'd all be dead, and you'd be the one responsible for burning Jews alive, again, but with a clown this time, rubbery Patch Adams. nose dripping all over the purple NYU logo. Is that what you want? Or did you want to just tell me where Bellevue is?

"Sir, you need to leave. It's one block the fucking-fuck down."

OH I'LL BLOCK THE FUCKING-FUCK DOWN, ma'am.

—

When I got to Bellevue, one block the fucking-fuck down from NYU Langone, a man from Barbados was skeptical of my existence, even after I told him that a policeman randomly called and told me to come there. This did not convince him enough.

"What poh-leeece-uh-mon cawled yuh nah mon?"

I don't remember his name.

"Don't you know now he-yer, yuh supposed to always ask the name now mon."

Okay, I didn't know that, Mr. Kind Receptionist Man from Barbados.

"I'm from Juhhhhh maaaayyy kaaaah."

Oh, neat. Jamaica Queens, like the last stop? That's quite a trek.

"NOOOO MY GAWD, from D eeeeyyyeeeee lond."

An even longer trek. Sooooo, the name of the patient is Miss Madeline Majenta Allison.

"Give me one moh-mon sir, go sit down ober dare."

Uhh-huh K.

—

A few moments passed. This was clearly the more ghetto hospital. First, no Jews. No Park Avenue clowns. So, no money. Also, there was a very large number of cops. Instead of a per-snickety button-bitch lady, there were two black cops talking about cornbread and yelling at each other about being surprised by the ingredients,

"Shut yo ass. SHUT. UP. YOU TELLING ME, you put DAT MUCH buttah in yo' fuckin' CORN BRAAAAAAYYYYYII-IID?"

"Mmmmmmmmm hmmmmmmmmmm."

"You fucking CRAY-C. Yo big-ass butter butt gonna blow up even moh. BUT I GUESS DASS WHAT JAMAL WANTS, IDDINIT."

"Ohhhhh *kaaaaaaaaaaaaaaaaaaaaaaaaaaaaaay!!!!!*"

Uproarious laughter. Me sitting there waiting for the island man to give me a fucking sticker to get into the emergency room.

When he finally walked over with my pink sticker that proudly displayed which dirty door to walk through, he insisted on putting it on my jacket himself, like it was a medal from the president, of Jamaica, and I was on the bobsled team.

Oh, thank…um…thank you sir. I can…aaalllrriiiggghhtty.

And when he was done placing the sticker over my heart he made sure to look me right in the eye, breathing all heavy, and sliding his hand about 4.5 times over the sticker *juuuuuust* to make sure it was good and stuck. My penis got a little hard, too, from his grazing my nipple for way too long.

After various dirty doors, depressing waiting areas, depressing shows, with depressing TVs, and depressing ladies waiting next to signs warning you that if you just went to Africa you better be careful and you better PROCEED WITH CAUTION, eventually everyone was wearing black T-shirts with white letters that said "BELLEVUE, NO ONE IS TURNED AWAY," and it all reminded me of my writing room where I never wrote until now.

I got to the right door of the room where I thought I was going to see Miss Allison cracked out of her mind, thinking that Mr. Hah had finally done it—he pushed her over one too many edges and this was the biggest one, the Grand Canyon of edges, the edge of edges, and her sanity tumbled and sloshed to the river as a milky cum shot.

Because I always gave Miss Allison my bread roll that always came with my salad from Nottingham Grill on Park Avenue, I must then be a dear friend to her, worthy of trust, worthy of a scream again and again, "Colin, Colin, Colin, call Colin," and a call from a policeman prompting me to come ascertain just what the hell the issue was.

Well, the issue wasn't with Miss Allison. To be clear, it was she who came running at me, in tears, ranch dressing or something on her lip, melted and dripping with her rouge that had mixed in as white and red swirls on her cheeks.

She must have eaten quickly, as she normally does, but much more frantically this time. Her hair was partly covered in some kind of wetness too, not sure what, but it was disgusting. Her eyes were bloodshot and her clothes were ripped. She looked like a flushable toilet wipe that had gone through the entire NYC sewer system and made it all the way out the other end of the anus of the city and proved that that wipe was indeed flushable but, yet again, indestructible.

She was here, albeit covered in grief, panic, and honest-to-goodness deep, deep pain and horror from some place deep within a person I did not think even possible, another doll face cracked to get to another smaller, even more pitiful one also cracked.

She screamed at me, "Oh Colin!! Thank GAWWD! It's awful, JUST AWFUL!"

She was the Old Faithful geyser, spraying all over me for about 15 minutes every 90 minutes I was there. Something would boil over every 90 minutes deep, deep within her, and the magma of it below would force a release, all over me, just me, her "dear, dear friend, you're a dear friend..."

What was also equally as disgusting and surprising was the state of Mr. Hah, the ISSUE, lying on the gurney, hooked up to all sorts of wires, shaking, eyes half-opened, mumbling something to himself. He, too, was covered in some sort of mucus of the moment.

Her first eruption was like this, and every proceeding eruption was a reiteration of this in some shape or form, a geyser spray of what had recently happened and what she did and why she did it, to gain my approval, and I simply watched the eruption in awe:

"OH GAWWWWD Colin, Colin I'm so glad you're here, I'm I'm I don't know what it's just the Benadryl and the soju, so much soju, bottles, bottles, bottles of them—you know the green ones? You've probably seen them around the office, but I've never seen so many of them, opened, cracked, shattered, dripped out—and Mr. Hah called me...I mean, OH GOD YOU CANNOT MENTION THIS TO ANYONE MY GAWWD YOU CAN'T, PLEASE PLEASE I called you because I didn't know who else to call, and you've always helped me with the paper whenever I don't know which one to use, and I thought I would call you I'm sorry if it's inappropriate but I think you've been here at Heller, Heller, Heller...and, ahah! Hah! long enough to know we're all ONE, BIG, FAMILY you know, and Mr. Hah REALLY needs us and I just can't. I just can't do this alone this time, and you're such a dear friend who always gives me bread, you break bread with me!! Hah! Every single time you get a salad you give ME the bread!!! I went to his hotel and you know how he went on the business trip, well, back to Palm Beach, well, he didn't and he had me cancel everything and rent him a hotel room near here actually I forget the name and I would call him every few hours like usual, but then, but then, but then, but then I just, I JUST didn't get a response! And so I decided it would be best to go down there and MY GAWWWD IT WAS AWFUL THE SIGHT of him if you can believe it, it was even worse than the way he looks right now, and there was kimchi all over his bed covered in vomit, and there were the broken bottles everywhere like I said, but covered in vomit too, and cigarettes, and FUCK—I'm sorry to say that you know I don't like to cuss—BUT FUCK, BUT FUCK I couldn't take the sight of all the pills either and I didn't know what they were and he wasn't responding even when I was shaking him and smacking his face and he just slept there all dead-like and so I saw on a show one time—you know how I like to watch my shows with my friends—but this one was a new one from the 90s about CPR and I remember how you're supposed to pound on the chest eventually if the other CPR doesn't work and even though I know at that point I hadn't done any, PER SE, I did try the mouth-to-mouth and blew and blew and blew and blew and nothing and so I just skipped most of the steps and just when right into the punching of the chest. I ripped open his shirt—one of his many nice shirts, so many nice shirts he has, AS WE KNOW, and I just started beating his chest for about 15 minutes straight and he was foaming at the mouth and at that point one of the prostitutes he was with woke up and ran out the room and pulled the fire alarm I think because she didn't want to get in trouble and she wanted to attract attention away from her and bring it to us, and I wish she hadn't done that, but in the end I was thankful because I didn't know what THE FUCK I was doing. And so I kept hitting him in the chest and screaming 'HAH!!! HAH!!! HAHH!!!! HAH!!! HAHH!!! HAHH!!! HAHH!!!' until finally the foaming was much less foam and more chunks of things and he started gargling and choking, and so I heard that you gotta get the stuff out the mouth and so I did mouth-to-mouth again but instead of blowing I began sucking out the foam and chunks and whatever it was and I would spit it out like sucking the poison out, and screaming, 'Give it to me, blow it all out, Hah, blow it all out, blow it into me, give me the poison, GIVE ME THE POISON!' and I'd suck and spit, suck and spit, and suck and spit until I eventually reached into his throat and helped him gag to throw up some of the pills, which from like I might have said the looks of it was mainly Benadryl and I think Vicodin, and a few bottles of Drano, too, and I think Prozac and his pain medicine that he began taking after he got that pain in his knees after his father passed away and he was on the ground a lot praying, he said, and because that goddamn fucking whore—sorry, I don't mean to cuss—pulled the alarm the firemen came to help me and I was so stupid—STUPID—I should have rung them first but I felt bad because he never ASKED ME TO, per se, and I know, well you know how he gets angry if you do things without him asking and I just thought he wouldn't want us to make such a big fuss you know and but and but at least the whore that pulled the alarm—and when the sprinklers turned on—at least it washed away some of the vomit and pill foam and feces from when Mr. Hah shit himself—and it all kinda soaked into the bed before the firemen actually got there and when the paramedics came they had to pull me away because I was hugging him and holding onto his back, spooning him kinda, and patting him on the back and singing to him that it was 'all gooonnnnaaa be bettteer' I don't know what the fuck I was singing I just made it up, but I just wanted, I just wanted him to know—deep in there if he could hear me or understand me that it was 'all gonnnaaaa be better, all gonnnaaa be better, and you don't have to feel bad or guilt about anything,' and then they brought us here and I didn't know what to do and my phone was dead, but I had memorized your number because all new hires I memorize all their info—Social number, address, bank accounts, all numbers—just in case something like this would happen, which is why I told the policeman to call you because you were the first to come to mind and you always help with me with picking the right paper because you know how I get so confused which paper he likes and all and which envelope goes with which one and which one is the OLD letterhead and which is the NEW letterhead and which of the old is still comparable with the new you know how I am with it and you're always so kind to me, and you're such a dear, dear friend, and you give me bread."

Wow, Miss Allison.

Of course, in this moment I realized this was the moment, the moment I would have to decide something, the moment the signs were pointing toward, and lit up, or maybe this wasn't it just yet. Perhaps it was a training of sorts for the real moment later to come.

I knew I'd have to decide if I was going to go deeper, commit further to this organization, to these people struggling before me, lies or not, it didn't really matter, especially to a man I did not respect whatsoever, who was verbally abusive, who shouldn't be leading anyone, because he only leads them astray, to hate their lives, their bodies, to increased gout, to love money more than men, to worship Park Avenue and all that it could do for you, to its zip line to Palm Beach, so much so that he secretly murdered children so he could keep it all, so much so that he brought others to stab themselves in the eyes with letter openers, so much so that slaves were created, years in the making, battered vomit-eating slaves like Miss Allison, and slaves who thought the world owed them something, a paycheck, without ever having to do anything worthwhile like myself.

He was a hunter who preyed when he prayed. He was a murderer who gave millions to the needy and the Downsy downtrodden. He was the rich son of a family previously in death camps across the world, which in his mind, justified his creation of his own death camp in America, a boutique insurance brokerage firm on beautiful Park Avenue.

Yet before me also, besides Miss Allison the Accountant/Comptroller/HR Specialist/Nutbag being completely covered in bile, soju vomit, Drano-Vicodin-Benadryl (Neapolitan) ice cream, and sparkling sprinkler water, there was not just a hunter, but a man struggling to live, struggling to survive, struggling to simply breathe.

There he was, Mr. Hah. And poor Mr. Hah could hardly breathe, and I knew, all too well, what that was like.

In my mind many times this man had been a villain, *the* villain, my own scapegoat for all *I* had neglected in my own life, like beginning something with I, I, I, remembering something I knew I had purposefully forgotten out of cowardice but was ashamed to admit it and simply begin, a clear symbol and sign and letter of the Devil, perhaps the Devil himself, the embodiment of evil, but now, ever so briefly, he was wired to, wired as something else. Briefly, he became all men to me. He became my father. He became the embodiment of suffocating, of the wounded, of pain, of all fused confusion, of time's untimeliness, of all folders within ourselves, all memories, rebooted, and there before me was just one thing: myself.

It was on the tip of my dick, a wisdom that I knew I was just about to remember, hear, grasp, or see. I heard the beeps and the shrieks from the monitors. In a nearby room a drag queen, clearly on something—and on that something for years, in the cold—moved about on her bed.

The doctor, about half her age, asked her what *her* issue was. It wasn't her long blue nails on her bare feet, or her long purple nails on her fingers, her green accent nails on her middle fingers, her green sunken cheeks, her bleeding black mascara that looked like rain had dripped all afternoon on an unwanted manuscript on my desk, and all words and all my ideas smeared together and simply dripped down the wooden sharp curves and corners of her face. She still smiled, relieved she could share her story with someone—and perhaps that's why she came here, because no one else would truly, truly listen, to a story she knew only she could tell. And my god was she fearless.

With her deep voice, with tears smearing with letters all over her face, her brittle fingers in the air like scarf tassels moving about from a hidden subway wind, she described to the doctor what ailed her, but from her excitement it seemed as though she saw it not as a plague, a disease, or the side effect from years of doing anything, or years of doing nothing, but a gift which needed to be shared by an audience who wasn't just eager to listen, they were paid to listen.

She began, "You see...well, I doubt that...because *I* see...a beautiful landscape, and it's glowing yellow, my friend."

She grabbed the hand of the doctor and her nails dug into his hand like friendly talons of a lost bird, "I see a world, a new world, that isn't cold, but cold is warm and warm is cold, and so all things just are, the way they are and there's not fighting of the sides.…I see home and the people are made of sparkles, and everywhere I look I see sparkles, and it's bright and it's beautiful, but the space between the sparkles is so, so dark, but it's not scary, it's a kind of fluff between, a support system for the sparkles…it's just where the sparkles have to float, you know? Even you, right now, I look at you and your eyes—I know that there's something within you, and I hope to dear gawd within me too, do you see the same when you look at me?—I see such glitter spraying out of your eyeballs, RIGHT NOW, and it's spraying all over the room and it's so pretty and I just wish everyone would know how beautiful you are, just as you are, my dear friend."

The doctor remained professional, "Missssir, so, I think you're hallucinating? Did you take any drugs of any kind before you came here?"

Coming to, "I'm fine now I think. I don't see anything. I'm fine. TOTALLY FINE. I think I'm just going to pee and then go. Good here. WE'RE ALLLLL GOOD."

She pulled out her penis, which was quite enormous—perhaps because it was coming out of a rip in her tight red dress, which made her cock look even larger, coming out of a stretched curtain for a Broadway show—but the doctor went "Oh god!" and she laughed deeply and loudly, "HAH HAH HAH, I GUESS YOU SEE SPARKLES TOO, DON'T YOU DOCTOR!" and then she pissed a cock-sure thick stream of yellow into the little bottle provided, but most of it sprayed on the computer monitor next to her and the intern inputting all the important data of the day.

For a moment, I thought this scene was going to bring a permanent compassion, a deeper compassion, drawn out from seeing those in need, struggle, pain, drag queens on meth, and seeing sparkles within us, and at first it did. It really did.

Mr. Hah struggled to breathe to find his reason for living the same way my father did for that long dreadful year I was with him, the year I attempted to listen, to write down every word, yet capturing so few, so I could hold on to him, so nothing would leave, nothing would change, the same way we all do every single day, eyes moving about, waiting for some kind of lifeline from somewhere, some kind of beep that will allow us to anticipate that next beep, some kind of warning, as if it's owed to us—that next second, as if we can actually keep it—that second previous.

For a moment, I even held Mr. Hah's hand, and he grumbled something to me, and I said, Thank you, for everything, for allowing me to eat these last years, for allowing me to take care of Rudolfo when he was sick too until the day he was shot and that sickness didn't even matter, to take care of his family, their drought and turmoil in Brazil, and for letting me see just how abused Miss Allison really, really is, and while I know I should have left HH&H a long, long, long time ago, probably after that first day, I decided something finally, or at least I felt trained to do so now.

I told him, as he grumbled and garbled, in a sparkling Hollywood moment, eyes rolling back into his head from the Benadryl-Vicodin-Drano-Prozac-soju wimpy-really-when-you-think-about-it suicide cocktail, *I'm no different from you*, I said, even as I gagged from how cheesy it sounded, partly gagging from how true and stinky that cheese really was.

I spent most of my time thinking you are an awful person, I said, and I now know that you really are even more, but in the grand scheme of men and all our scheming, all men combined from when men's time began and when it will end, towers upon towers upon new towers, there's not much difference between what awful things you do and what awful things I do, because whether I know it yet or not, or maybe not even in 1,000 years, but maybe in seven, I'm shitting all over someone the way you've so clearly shat all over so many.

I cannot judge you, not because of wrong or right, not because of what you gave me, not because of my paycheck, not because of loyalty, but because you, like all men, like myself, will die, by your own hand or not, it will come.

Within a universe of sparkles and planets and neutrinos and murderers and loving partners and dead dogs and art in the park that sounds like pigeons that wish they were eagles, what you do or don't do to me or what you do or don't do to others is but a fart in comparison to all things, the good within things, the calm within all things, and all that will continue to sparkle outward and upward—a geyser—from something seemingly so very dark, for so very long. The magma of this life, and its opposite, and its parallel, will rumble, and it is rumbling even now, boiling even.

So Jung (the very first time I uttered his first name, refusing for years to become any more intimate than what was absolutely necessary), I said, should you be successful in your attempt to die, this time or the next, the world will go on, revolve, and revolve, and evolve into something so very beyond your control, so very beyond the pain that you intend to cause or do not intend to cause. You are an inconsequential fart surrounding the shit of life. And so are we. So am I. But life, dear sir, is so much more than the shit we spend so much time avoiding.

Life, your life, my life, the life in all the universe—that tranny in transition on the subway, that drag queen on meth on the gurney were more right than anyone—is a supernova upon a supernova upon a supernova, and each is a piece of glitter erupting outward into space wherever it damn well pleases, even as we sit at desks for hours and get cancer from sea to shining fucking sea. Eventually, we will stand up.

Miss Allison interrupted, even though I was finished, "Colin, I don't think that's nice to say that, what you're saying...I don't think, that's not why I called you, we need to *encourage* him, he's our dear leader, you know, he's our CEO. Riiiiiiiiiigggghhht?"

Not anymore, Miss Allison.

I quit.

Actually, I am not quitting anything; I am simply moving on. And it's probably best that he dies, but what do I know? And to be clear, I really don't say that out of malice, or anger, or bitterness—maybe a while ago, yes, but not now. If that's what he wants, then he should go for it. Running children over with cars might do that to you. Watching their bodies crush under your driver's tires might make you want to do the same painful things to yourself. Pain reciprocates pain. I get it. You know, we should all just go for what we want and move on to that no matter what happens.

And you Miss Allison, I truly hope what you want is therapy, for a very long time. I hope you lock yourself up and hang out with the young and the restless, not the old and the passionless.

You may need shock therapy, possibly a lobotomy. Whatever works until you see more than your missing brass letter, until you realize kindness is more than throwing a free bread roll at someone. We are not dear friends. *He* is not my dear leader. My dear, *you* are fucking crazy. Have a good night.

As I walked away, I heard Miss Allison peeing herself as the monitor flat-lined.

And her lips tingled and shook as bottles of hyphens and lists and lisps in an earthquake.

43

Touch

It's snowing now on the spring sidewalk, on the trees, on foot-steps of snow, snow on top of puddles, puddles evaporating, snowing again, spring upon spring upon spring, seeds raining by the trillions.

I feel a burning in my head. There's a tickle on my ankles, an itch, and one by one I note my observations, each hyphen a tick, a list, sucking on the blood of a clock wand. It burrows into the blackness for nourishment and time takes it for a ride. There's an itch behind my ear, and I hear something that sounds like a propeller, a spigot, a ticket flapping on a bike spoke, a seed of time twirling. I wonder what that burning might be, as it comes and goes, or perhaps it's always there, but only sometimes I notice it, make note of it, attempt to remem-ber it, for the moment, and then it flicks away into a pile of some other snow that someone else steps on, and then once more is covered up with new, the new, the new, the seeds and snow of the new, but I wonder if it also waits for some kind of cue to move on, go forth, or is that what life is really, this in-between cue, a tick sucking on a tic, toc, tic, toc, but instead of those sounds, there's silence because no one wears watches anymore, and because things have so clearly changed, we're tempted once more to say *times will be different* in the future, times were better then, but even then, and even when, it will be, it is, just, like, *this*.

This is it. You will be, you were, you are on a sidewalk of a moment, and you'll feel the gravel-gabble roughness beneath, windswept, snowswept, sunwept, footswept, broomswept, bugswept, iceswept, pissswept, and even after all that, it still retains its necessary roughness. You'll touch it, and it's cold, and you'll wonder how long you've been lying down here covered in your own blood, and you'll be thankful for that wetness because it makes your bed somewhat softer.

You'll be surrounded by all the wrong people at the exact time you didn't plan on anything, and this wasn't a part of your want list, but nonetheless you're lying down next to a dog carcass, gone before you, and you're next. Sirens fly about you in the liquid of the air, prophesying again and again you tell yourself, because then this bloodbath would be worth it—if you just knew the future, you're a sage, you're a prophet, *Colin!*—and they're beautiful, those futures. Their hair is the leafless branches of an odd spring snow, caked once more one last time, and their hair is powerlines cum-covered with ice.

—

Just a moment ago I thought about how a friend down in Brooklyn over whiskey told me she didn't believe in God anymore, and as the candlelight flickered and tickered and flashed its lightning cock at us, I felt nothing except the humming of her words in my ears and the burning as the whiskey slid down my cool throat, and I didn't know what to say to her except, okay.

We talked about space in a bar and we were sad that the

only reason we went to the moon was to compare our vodka-bottle-rocket-cock to Russia's. *That's* America. Winning just so we won't lose.

We hoped that one day we'd forget about dicks—because they'd be forever in our mouths, we, the dick gluttons.

We hoped that one day we'd forget about space in the name of nations and wars in the name of gods, because they'd all be forever in our hearts. Humans. And that next time a massive project to explore the goddamn mysterious particles of the building blocks of the whole goddamn universe is being built in a place called don't-mess-with-Texas we don't fucking build half of it and then give up, lynching our future selves.

We hoped that one day *French* fries would be called *Higgs boson* fries because they taught us 'Murikans a quick lesson, the Fwanch, when they finally found the boson, in being ballsy in the name of that which shall not be named, reminding us that we're still forever seeking so that we can find, and then find some more, always seeking, quoth the pigeon, forever-more.

—

As I lay crying on this sidewalk, it feels like I haven't cum for a week, and my balls are full, and I notice everything. My cheeks are flushed with lust light, and with it I see through time once more, why people do the things that they do, as they're all thrown in a bucket and swished and dished with the best god-damn fried chicken in the Lower East Side.

I cry for Rudolfo, because although I had just walked away from him in bed it seems, or the couch, or the kitchen, I don't remember, I still crave his body to be naked with mine as my blood envelops the both of us. I cry because I want him to drink it with me, to taste the stuff of life, to taste the salty stuff of death, to feel that iron irony, that here we thought he'd go first from that hole drilled in his head, but no, a hole in his back, shot instead, and it would have been years and years for me to follow him, following the rest of my life, all that lies on the sidewalk ahead of me, but I seem to be beating all my plans to the ground, and what's left is a porcelain Mary watching me from a yard of weeds nearby, a hat shattered, and resting on the head of Jesus in a glass box.

And here I thought death would be so loud, but even amidst the screams and the seams of the city, a city that seems to be breaking for me, all is quiet, but nothing is lost.

All of me that falls within the cracks is stopped by the earth somewhere below and there it can hide, and sleep, and creep out and grow whenever it pleases. I'll hear things, like doors opening, as if I were in my room again, next to my bear lamp again, and my god do I hear it roar again! Perhaps I never really left. Perhaps I'll always be there, writing with all my dead friends.

And the bear, its roar is the sound of an open door, and my love Rudolfo walks through, and he had been gone for so long and I thought his plane would explode in midair, that his car would squeal and peel off the road, or that I'd find him once more hiding there, passed out, right next to the commode and surrounded by all that pink.

I thought I'd have to unstick him once more. I thought I'd hear pink and see stink and taste the sounds of tears falling on linoleum, checkers, black and white, as someone above plays with our bodies like carrot pulp from a juicer—that moment when you shove one in, then the other, then the other, and just a few chunks fly out from all that spinning that rips their bodies apart. The carrot pulp will fly through the air and gather some dust too that had been hanging there floating by your eye, and the universe will wonder, will it fall on white?

Will it fall on black?

And my god right now I can hear that bear roar, when once it was oh-so-quiet those many days I wish I had typed and typed, start that first draft, thinking if I just wrote down one, word, if I finally, simply, began, something, anything, then my god I'd be more alive than that picture of my father's grave with an American flag impaled into the earth right above a cross etched in stone.

But here now, I know that bear, that dark, dark bear had been humming within me this whole time, a full-time job, and its light was something far more extraordinary than light, than life, than all things put together, even with a lampshade affixed to its head, the head of all things.

Its voice is a piano. Its voice is leaves crinkled and pictured next to my father's grave. The bear is the sound of blood, and the sound of keys. And its fur is an aimless bottle rolling, as we think we watch it move from one thing to the next, shattering for some, tickling for some, attacking for some, but it's been on this desk right here all alone, affixed, unmoving as we try to get, get, get, and go, go, go, from one corner of the earth to the next on a train that grinds grain in a circle.

The light of the bear is the sound of sleeping, the smell of going, the sound of giving, the sight of dying, the taste of living, the south of northward, the west of eastward, the place right before *got there*, and the spot right in front of *done with*, it's the tongue of my love as it delves into the beginning of my mouth, it's the tip of his dick as it tickles the beginning of my anus, anticipation of anticipations, those moments you know that you're in a moment, and you're actually not dead, and the reason you breathe isn't just to wait for something else.

Waiting for something to change, for another season to come, to come, to cum again all over our faces. For a boss to choke himself on his own feces by grabbing his bedpan full of shit at Bellevue, and pouring it into his own mouth, followed by gagging himself on your beanie you left there on purpose, because you knew he would fist himself in the mouth, shoving that beanie deeper and deeper, punching it down into his own dragon throat—until he actually does and you're not surprised at all because you're a natural-born killer, and the monitor is as flat as an accountant's piss puddling, and it smells like a fucking cardinal that flew into you from the Lord on high to explode, just for you, a mirage of a mirage of an entire garage of divine gestures.

Waiting for your boyfriend to return from a place weirder than Texas and you haven't felt the warmth of his tight anus around your dick as it slides down from the lube of science all the way to the ballsac of your holy breath. For you to finally understand anything really, anything at all, for you to feel as though you've never given one piece of advice to anyone without having to tell yourself afterwards that you know it was all bullshit because who has control of anyone else?

Our minds are such tormented galaxies, and some more than others, and for me to understand what spins in yours and for you to understand what spins in mine, this, this shit, well, that's just light years away, but oh how we try, try, try for years upon years until we have to say goodbye, bye, bye little birdy.

For the door to be opened and for Rudolfo to walk in, completely naked and covered in snow, covered in seeds, covered in blood, and you're there typing in your writing room as you should be and sipping on hot detox tea with chicory root and sunflower, I think, and peppermint, yes! And there are two fucking coconut macaroons on a plate and you know you'd never eat one. You know you just put them there because you like the way they squeeze, the way they burn juicy, and Rudolfo feels the same way on your cock, and you want him, all of him to cum all over your chest, to come into your secret writing room completely this time, to massage you as you type naked, for blood to cover the walls of words and all the galaxies of spinning plates of hopes and dreams and everything in between, forever in between.

But then you taste the coconut.

And it's sweet, and the way its flesh bends on your tongue and teeth and cheek, god how it roars, that bear in your mouth, and its light sprays out your teeth and into the Astorian street, sparkles like trillions of drag queens skipping but understood.

I've been lying and dying here for a millennium it seems, and who am I to even think I can even comprehend that, let alone forever, or forever times two, three, numbers and words, numbers and words, all we try to be sometimes is just numbers and words, time planned and time well spent, pictures taken and pictures displayed, leaves crinkled around a grave and leaves twinkling in the sun with ice cream dripping in our beards of mice and men, and seeds fall and helicopter all around me, and they look like snow, hell it might be snow, I don't know.

I wait for Rudolfo to come grab me. I wait for my blood to stop gushing. For my mind to stop racing. For time to stop ticking, for the tic to stop chewing on the toc, for everyone to just give up trying to live forever, for everyone to stop waiting, so we can finally lie, still, in the fur and glass of everything continuously shattering and forming and rolling and bursting, so we can finally taste the light, smell the burning and the itching, hear the roar of nothing, the silence of everything screaming, and finally touch the beautiful dick of God.

And it was then that I heard my father say that one thing once more, and I remembered the one truth I was never told until he spoke it, until I wrote it, and spent a lifetime forgetting it, only this time I finally decided to really hear it the exact moment too late came early.

44

Pit

Sandy seems quite willing to try anything, especially since the other guests would be here any minute.

Oh yes, we're back to that, the tea party.

We can't very well have everyone dying in the end, can we? Well, I guess we could. I could say that my brother and my mother in the year 2030 took a flight to the moon, but on the way, the moon exploded and so did their ship, and that was that, that was the final cardinal sign from God, a big bang, and true love is killing us off one by one.

I don't want to end that way, though, I love happy endings, I love the idea of all of us popping up in places we least expect, buds after a long winter. You finally see sun shadows from a long, long winter of waiting. You finally feel the urge to stand up and touch that bud and say, finally, I'm here, the beginning, the end, the beginning again. I want all of us to be like that, coming and going, coming and going, withering and coming alive again, yet growing older.

Because of that, that hope, however silly and cyclical it may be, I, like you, crave a resolution, as much as I try to act like I don't. In the darkest of oceans there's light, and really I do want you to be happy as I hope my father is happy, even as a fish eats the remnants of his bones, even as a squirrel stands on top of the leftover particle that he is now, mixed in with the worms and the lady-pug piss, as that squirrel eats a half of an Oreo cookie he found left behind in the park. What else are stories really, but little leftover cookie pieces of how we think our existence here has a purpose, nothing more really, but still delicious, even when partially eaten and stale and being nibbled on by furry creatures in the park, compared to that original Oreo someone somewhere didn't fully appreciate the second it came out of the factory.

As I approach the day of my death, I want to feel a purpose to my death, so that I can completely understand my life. My story, this story only I can tell, and it probably has near 90,000-ish words now, and some stories have been that long, that short, as some lives have included things that are painful, things that don't make any sense, things we wish we understood, and because of that wish, as you rub your own lamp wherever you are, I shall grant you some finality so that you may sleep well thinking, even for a moment, that you are in control, even though it won't get you anywhere when you approach your own end, because then you'll realize it wasn't true, and it must have been the first draft and just a nibble of the whole truth anyway, the second draft, too, and maybe the fifth, and maybe the three-hundred-and-sixty-fifth draft of everything.

And so, Lilly sits there with Sandy and everyone is screaming, and what do you know—poof!—I am back, but not as a barrette.

This time I am butter, yes!

I like that.

I like that I can melt in the way I feel right now, as my blood melts into the earth, as morons watch me die, as you wish I put more effort into making this story perfect, and right, original and well-written, just, for, you. Yes, this train was built just for you.

As I melt I listen to the approaching party to come, and more than words heard, I can smell something, the exhaust from laundry dryers, that fake-happy scent that masks years of socks melted with sweat, that cake-sappy scent that gets us ready for another day because we have told ourselves all dirt is gone and only cleanliness remains, and mixed within this is the exhaust from cars, that sulfur smell of burning oils and boils, and the smell of a McDonald's kitchen, burgers burnt and microwaved, plastic burning, a tattered flag flapping, the smell of rain upon rain upon rain on flag-cloth, faggot-washed and dried, washed and dried, washed and dried in every possible weather condition, and the heaven breath of dogs, pit bulls in particular, saliva, dripping, saliva fermenting, and I wonder why it smells like this at a tea party, but maybe that's just one of the mysteries of the Bronx.

Lilly looks at me with her piercing, all-consuming eyes, and I see rainbows spray forth from them as she giggles at me, poking me with a butter knife and eventually she cuts me in half.

A knock on the door.

The guests are here. Who could it be? Why did they come here? Will they like Sandy's shitty tea? Will they, too, be haunted and slashed by the ghosts of the Bronx returning and returning? Will they, too, be haunted and slashed by me when I'm free? If I could, I would open the door myself.

Lilly leans in and kisses me; she kisses a butter stick, and Sandy screams from across the kitchen, "Lilly, goddamn it, what the fuck are you doing, can't you see the guests have arrived and Daddy is still getting whipped from the demon on the toilet again?"

Lilly laughs again and throws confetti at her mother. With butter on her lips, she whispers to me my father's best and truest of wisdoms, that one thing I didn't want to understand until now, the one thing to always remember when a story only you can tell doesn't go the way you want it to:

"MY SON, SOMETIMES IN LIFE, YOU GOTTA EAT SHIT."

Yes, this is a novel, and you've mostly eaten it, almost done. You've gagged yourself with it, and it was mine. I've decided to call it that at least, a "novel," but no, just to be clear: Those red letters aren't made-up. So maybe rip out the pages with the holy red letters, ball the paper up, and then throw them down the "Memoir" aisle as uninvited spring snowballs, and then throw everything else down the "Fiction" aisle—or just give it all one beautiful exploding star and put it all in "Shit," since aisles don't exist anymore and it's high time we admit it. A man, a real man, actually said those words, verbatim. This same man has since been long burnt with red fire in an oven, his skin, his bones, his eyeballs, his dick, his balls, his hair, his toes, his eyelashes, the purple skin around his neck and his lungs when I saw him last on a table, silent, but deadly.

Your shitty, shitty job. Your shitty, shitty bang-bang bangin' body. And people and those days that seem to treat—just you, all for you—like shit. You gotta eat it all.

This shit, is what I could never seem to remember, and I know now—oh look, an epiphany, is this the resolution? Or

344

is it an arc? A meadowlark?—I know now I didn't want to remember because I wanted to believe this whole world was made entirely for me, that I'm the only one, a chosen one with powerful visions, that God only listens to my prayers, so that I, I, I may advance, and not the billions of other pussies and cocks and pussies that turn into cocks and cocks that turn into pussies that roam this planet. And I do hope we roam more, space whores of the planets and times beyond time beyond.

Think of how many assholes like me pray. Think of how many kind, kind creatures don't. And we all get killed in the end. If that isn't a pile of shit, I don't know what is. And my father, forgive me for how many times I've forgotten. This was your lifetime of wisdom, culminated in the-holy-number-seven words. No matter where you are or what you do or who you love or how long you live or don't, remember: sometimes in life, you gotta eat shit.

You gotta eat the shit of my dying tragically. You gotta eat the shit of your love getting shot in the back after getting shot with cancer in the head. You gotta eat the shit of a man who would have lynched and burned bodies if it meant his insurance agency could grow. You gotta eat the shit of a woman abused and roaming around pissing herself for the brassy approval and wooden love she never, ever received. You gotta eat the shit of knowing your brother and mother will cry and cry when they find out you're dead. You gotta eat the shit of looking at your legs cut in half by a desk for an exceptionally long day, as you die ever-so-slowly next to a bitch. You gotta eat the shit of wishing your life made perfect sense, and you have to chew on the contents of whatever the fucking-fuck it is and what's left for you. And every day you eat the shit of praying to everything you don't know, and this, that badly written stuff, this, the purgatory of the avenue of the park, seems to be your only shitty response. And you gotta eat the shit of knowing deep within that you're exactly where you're supposed to be.

As my heart stops, as my lungs cease to inhale, exhale, inhale, and one final exhale, the butter on the table explodes into a trillion trillion trillion little other explosions, and parallels next to parallels, and there I am, what I am, all of it, all of this, before, now, and ever will be, neutrinos upon neutrinos expelling outwards, and my friends, I can see everything and everyone open the door to the deepest part of my soul and heart and hope and tears and laughter and every big word and every curse word and every gold word and forgotten word and holy red and unread word we use to sum up how much and how little that we are.

As Rudolfo and my father and a mirage of a Google-plex of faces rushes within, the butter explodes all over Lilly's face and the dining room table flips over and Sandy's stupid husband is whipped once more. Lilly smiles as more rainbows shoot out of her eyes, and her face is a vast field of herself, lilies in a valley in the sunlight and each one casts a shadow longer than the tail of a comet, and she whispers two final questions to us all,

The first, "Why does anyone ever worry?"

The second, "Do I make you nervous?"

And then, a resounding om-gong final echo, of everything, "Neither death, nor life, neither angels, nor demons, neither one trillion books published, or no books published, 1,000,000 followers on Twitter, or none, verses mentioned to God every day of your life, or nothing mentioned to God every day of your life, neither green baseball caps of garbage men, nor red baseball caps on Chihuahuas, neither shit-slinging buffoons on repeat, nor diamond-guzzling loons in cement, neither fucked, neither killed, neither lit up in the morning, nor chucked, or spilled, or shattered in mourning, neither living tiny, nor living big, neither so here that you feel far away, nor so now that you never were, neither all the words your father said, nor none of them, stories told, stories forgotten, neither laughing when things die away, nor crying when things are born again, and again, and again, neither sitting down all day, nor finally standing up when for years you knew you should have..."

And it never ends.

And then Lilly stands up and bursts out the door doing flips down the street, and her vagina turns into a dick to a vagina to a dick to a puppy face that withers into a raisin in the sun and then silver drips down her legs and down her head with a basket full of apples and bottles of antique vodka, and she flips and skips all the way from the Bronx to Park Avenue to Astoria to the streets of Thermonuclear, where she shits out the only picture I have left, and everyone there sitting outside spits out their beer in a beautiful in-between of horror and curiosity, and the spit and the bits of bubbles in the air sound like a quiet hymn in a loud pit.

45

Cockflutes in Fairyland

And it sounds like jazz in a new coffee shop out to prove some-thing, yellow flowers, bright stools, all to prove something, and it feels like everyone trying to listen to classical music loudly to drown out the jazz, yet somehow they work together, those conflicting sounds.

And we, we, we we, we the cockflutes in fairyland, we the dead, we the living, we the living dead, we all search for that forest large enough to fit within our living room, roaming, rolling, spiraling freely through you, and all that you think you know, and see, and do, and hear, we hear more! We know your flowers will wilt, and that your life is a patchwork kilt, frolick-ing around the strong hairy legs and bulbous nuts and the long, succulent cock of a woman.

It's funny really, how things can switch on you like that so quickly, the music changes, another teen throws up a pair of old shoes onto a power line connected to your eye, a royal dumpster rests across from you in the sun and it's enchanting as its trash melts into a goo and you admit you want to dip your toes in it like wine in the making, a thousand springs, a thousand winters, a thousand helicopter seeds tickling your left nipple, just the left, and then now, okay, the right?

The tattoo on the neck of a blond man with curls, and the way he quickly looks over at you, he's not famous, but goddamn he should be if even just for you. You'd award him with everything and worship him the way he just looked at you with those galaxy-blue eyes and the light of a thousand splendid suns flies all over your face and each particle flicks to a fly to a kite flicking in the park to a spark in the dark from the wrapping of a nose strip so you won't snore, and from the rip you see that same damn blue again, fiery blue, a text at the best of times, the worst of times, and then a puppy walks by and you want to steal that damn little thing. Switches and color swatches and never-ending watches, and ticks and tocks, but nothing seems to click, until it does.

And what changes when you die?

You spend most of your life trying to flee, wondering what it's like to flee, is perfect love really no love at all? Questions like that. You want to fly away, detach, and then you do, and your reason for existing isn't to detach from everything and everyone, because you just did it, but now it's the exact opposite. You're floating, darting, flying, sighing to have one little glimpse of a touch, but you're too quick. Everything is so quick, when once everything felt like waiting, now it's all going.

Is she Hindu? Is she Muslim? Is she a Hindu-Muslim-American now? It would seem that way from the center of her bindi as she presses her finger into it, and I can see her outfit for today, and it's quite confusing.

Spiraling through Andromeda and back without so much as a goosebump, I have finally become a bindi, Miss Allison's bindi.

She's putting on a full-ass burqa in the mirror, but first she affixes that bindi and smears her lipstick on her cheeks and rubs it in, and she wears the necklace of Hanuman the monkey god, and she puts on the Jewish undergarments with the tassels, and the Mormon undergarments that kinda turn me on, and she puts a Bible in her purse, a little one with the red letters of Jesus. She drapes the large black cloak around all of her symbols and signs and words and help from elsewhere, and she looks in the mirror intently and says to herself, "Our Lady can do this. Our. Lady. Can do. This."

She's screaming it now, "OUR LADY CAN DO THIS!!!!"

Miss Allison never went to therapy like I had suggested that last time I saw her, the day before the day I died, but she took it upon herself to find herself for the very first time and she was not ashamed of looking for it everywhere.

After Mr. Hah died from choking himself on his own shit and compacting it further with my Chinese-made beanie I left there on purpose hoping and praying unceasingly that he would do exactly what he did, and when he did, Miss Allison's God—her only true God, Mr. Hah—had died and never came back to life. His divinity finally left with the urine that slowly poured down her hairy legs and into her high heels that she had put on for the hotel, hoping deep down his emergency at the time was all a ruse to get her there, finally, what all people in all corners of the globe truly want in life more than anything: to get fucked really, really hard.

And when that didn't happen, as we know, one war ends and another begins. As the great new super-tower of Heller, Heller, & Hah lost funding when its dear leader killed himself with feces and a beanie at Bellevue Hospital—to be clear, not NYU Langone, because everyone's welcome at Bellevue—most people at HH&H moved on to other insurance jobs, where they continue, even now, the same struggle of figuring out how exactly they could increase the rate of getting fatter and fatter while their hope and reason for living—beyond functioning as a bank account encased in babbling New Jersey pig lard—dissipated at a parallel rate.

Not Miss Allison, though.

She is on a new mission. To become a prophetess. She renamed herself *Our Lady Guadalupe* and only speaks in third person. Instead of hoping that one day she would become one with the walls with eyes made of polished brass, she now made it her mission to become one with *everyone*, helping them, interrupting their dinners, attempting to fight gangs, cutting bangs, delivering pizzas so that she could give the pizza boy a little break from his dying wage, or so that she could get fucked by a sweaty hungry man during a delivery, which was a fantasy of hers, she told them during a five-course dinner she bought each of them afterwards. Miss Allison is beyond wealthy now.

She was already wealthy, but then when our COMPANY POWERBALL POT actually won, and everyone who wasn't there that day was shit out of luck—including the deadies like Mr. Hah and me and Sandy and most everyone else who refused to partake, Miss Allison got most of it. (Oh and the secretary is dead, too. Got run over by a Google Maps car. And then an ice cream truck. And then a police horse. And like she suspected, no one noticed for months until someone saw her blonde streak permanently blurred across the screen when they mapped their way to a bar called Olive.)

With Miss Allison's family's fortune on top of a lotto fortune, she became a cloaked vigilante. As I roam with her between her eyes on her missions, as she flutters through Times Square with her same H-cubed nervousness—but now amplified even more—most tourists think she is a babbling Muslim terrorist who escaped from a mental hospital, which isn't completely untrue. She did spend some time at a place called Brook Lane, and she drooled and watched children of every religious variety slide down the slopes nearby on snow days. She eventually realized that that's what she had to do. She would become a devotee of everything for everyone. Forget just one person. She would enslave herself to everyone she saw and worship all things, even this very moment.

Her back would pain her from so much running she'd do, and, after years of sitting and sitting in her HR-Accounting-Personal-Assistant rat's nest, her pelvis had tilted, as we all know, forward and the scoliosis and vertebral deterioration had already set in. It doesn't stop her, though. She roams the city like a witch, and her burqa flies behind her like a cape and the more days she devotes herself to everything and everyone her burqa stretches and flutters even more majestically in the wind, covering half a city block from her speed.

And then she falls on her prey, "Oh god, oh god it's a blind man. Oh…um, he looks lost, Our Lady of Guadalupe is gonna help him. Sir. SIIIIIRRRR!!!"

And from that man's great darkness he can't see the great nutty darkness befalling upon him.

By that time he had already walked down the subway stairs, tap-tap-tapping his way down, in unison with Miss Allison's ruby slippers—the real fucking things.

She bequeathed a great fortune—a fart compared to what she still has—to the Smithsonian, upon one condition: She could have the ruby red slippers from *The Wizard of Oz*.

Really, as it was her favorite movie, she'll mumble, "there's no place like_____ there's no place like _____..." She loves to say that over and over again to calm her nerves, and within that blank she inserts what or whom she's about to help, "There's no place like that poor blind man, there's no place like that poor blind man."

The blind man just received a green INSUFFICIENT FARE on his special blind-man MTA-card. I guess blind people get a special MTA card, with their picture on it, that they can't see?

She catches up with him, and the man hears a frantic voice, "Sir, sir, sir, SIR!!! LET GUADALUPE HELP YOU, kaaaaaaaaay?" And she begins speaking to him like he's three. "It. Says. There. Is. NOOOOOOO. Money. DO YOU. HEEEEEEEEEAR?"

This guy is a New Yorker, blind, yes, but goddamn he is a New Yorker. He wears a jumpsuit. He has a beard. He's all sweaty from walking and tapping all damn day. And his Mets hat is dirty and cocked to the right. He has black glasses on, the shitty trendy ones you get on St. Mark's Place in the East Village.

"Of course I can fucking hear you lady, I'm not fucking Helen Keller. Why the fucking fuck does everyone think I'm Helen Keller!?"

Miss Allison, perplexed: "You mean Anne Frank, the Jewish girl that wrote all that silly wonderful stuff in a secret mysterious room, but now everyone reads it now that she's dead?"

"Lady, what, on earth is wrong with you?" They are standing right next to the turnstile still, and everyone is coming and going quicker than usual to avoid the ambiguous duo blocking everyone. He looks angry. She looks scary.

Miss Allison greets that question in the same way she avoids all confrontation, hysterical laughter, and a little pee, or of course a lot of pee if the situation is completely out of her control.

"Is there a cop around, miss?"

"No, oh god no, why? What's wrong?"

"Well, as you said, lady, I got an INSUFFICIENT FARE. I need a cop to help me."

"Oh, let the lady, LET THE LADY! That's why Our Lady of Guadalupe came here, to help you."

"Who? I don't know what the hell you're tawlkin' about, you sure there ain't no cop?"

Miss Allison picks up the cloth of her burqa and envelops him in it and hugs the man, "She is here."

"What the fuuuuuu...you huggin' me? What the fuck you hugginmefoh?"

"OH no, does she make you nervous? Does she make you nervous? OKAY, don't you worry about annnnn, yyyy, thing, you come now. Lady is going to help you."

"Are you sure lady, I'm not sur—"

"Sir, she's never been more sure of anything in her whole life."

They walk arm-in-arm slowly over to the card machine.

"What is all this cloth, you wearing a big ol' jacket? What is all this?"

"It's a burqa."

"Oh, fuck. You gotta be...I gotta get the fuck outta...you Muslim?"

"Well, yes. To be clear, it's kinda a burqa *and* a sari. Guadalupe is a Muslim. Hindu. Jewish. Shaman. Christian. All these crystals, too, see?"

"Uhhhhh...Miss Lady Guadawaterloo, you gonna rip me off? You gonna take my money? I really don't need that right now. I'm having a really fucking bad day. Sorry to cuss. I know you's obviously religious, Jesus Christ is you religious, but, honestly miss, Lady Loo, you sound like a fucking nut job."

Hysterically laughing again, "You-know-some-have-said-I-am!"

Little pee dripping down her legs.

"Uh-huh."

Catching her breath, "So, do you want to put more money on your card, sir?"

"Yes," the man says, and hands her his special blind-man MTA card.

"Oh, priiiitttttty, a picture! Mine doesn't have that."

"Awe, shit, you know, my therapist would be so proud of me right now, Miss Lady, she said I don't trust nobody. Haven't for years, I guess. Especially no damn Muslims, sheeeeit. You know, you gonna make her whole damn day when I tell her. She's not gonna believe it. Damn burqa-wearing crystal lady done help me refill my damn card."

"OH GOOODIE! OH GOOD OH GOOD OH GOOD are you serious, are you serious? ARE YOU REALLY SERIOUS!?"

Miss Allison is truly elated, so much so that she begins to shake and even cry, the first cry she's had had since her mother died. For Mr. Hah there were no tears, just silence and drool and piss. For this man, though, she is truly happy, and tears begin to wash away her rouge beneath her burqa/sari and red paint beads drip down her cheeks and it looks like blood on a sidewalk.

"I tell ya," the man continues, "if this was a few years ago, I woulda done fought you off. I'm serious Miss Lady. I didn't trust nobody. So many mean people out there, taking money from a damn blind man, taking candy from a fuckin' baby, making slaves outtah duh weak, corrupting us all like dat, and it's wrong. I may not see, but I can fucking see dat. I tell ya, if this was a few years ago, I woulda been sittin' here yelling for a cop for hours until an amba-lince come…I'm sorry, I'm sorry for the inconvenience."

Miss Allison presses me, her third eye, into her forehead once more like a reset button, as the sweat slides somewhere else on her face.

"Oh do not be sorry, sir. Sir, SIR, don't you be sorry. It's no inconvenience at all. Even if it was, can Our Lady of Guadalupe tell you something, she would do it anyway."

Her chalky white teeth are shining brightly as she smiles wide beneath the black, "She really would, she would do it…just, for, you."

—

End.

End, end, end. We, oui, we. What, will, oui, end, with?

And my god, I'm so vain.

I actually thought this book was about me.

—

And then the card pops out, and the blind man would never forget it, this crazy, kind lady, this queen of Queens who "shouldn't have," he says, intertwined with the sound of that thin card coming out of a machine he can't see, the sound of a hidden poem written alone in Alaska, the smell of electric coffee in an apartment in Astoria, the never-ending words of an Indian lady in a sari drizzled in moonlight as you fly right by her at the speed of light on a train with innumerable people going somewhere else, the slow letter-by-letter touch of a grand story only I can write, and the bite of a glowing scorpion in the morning, and we, we, we, my friends, we all bear witness in the dark.

It is the spirit that beareth witness.

Because the spirit is the truth.

About the Author

Micah Enloe is an author of nonfiction and fiction, an advertising copywriter, a scriptwriter for feature film, TV comedy, and branded video, as well as a gym goer, world traveler, tree hugger, and Groundlings-trained actor. You may find him working on a TV pilot with friends or daily meditating on the beaches of Los Angeles covered in obnoxious amounts of coconut oil. More at MicahEnloe.com.

YOU MIGHT ALSO LIKE:

American Cream
by Micah Enloe

From the Obscenely Strange Case Files of Dead Things Mikey
by Joel Farrelly

Love, Floppy Disks & Other Stuff the Internet Killed
by Natalie Shields

THOUGHT
CATALOG
Books

THOUGHT CATALOG

IT'S A WEBSITE.

www.thoughtcatalog.com

SOCIAL

facebook.com/thoughtcatalog
twitter.com/thoughtcatalog
tumblr.com/thoughtcatalog
instagram.com/thoughtcatalog

CORPORATE

www.thought.is